KING OF DIAMONDS

Don Strachan

Published by Penthe Publishing, POB 1825, Middletown CA 95461, penthepub@earthlink.net.

Manufactured in Canada
Printed on New Leaf recycled paper
Published April 2004

Strachan, Don
King of diamonds / Don Strachan
p. cm.
ISBN: 0-9632475-7-3
1. Sex—Fiction. 2. Baseball—Fiction. 3. Ecology—Fiction.
4. Biological diversity—Fiction. 5. Frogs—Fiction. 6. New Age—Fiction. 7.
Humorous stories. I. Title

PS3569 . T6766 K56 2004
813' .54—dc21 2003094999

Ten percent of the net profits of *King of Diamonds* go to the Rainforest Action Network, the Natural Resources Defense Council, the Earthjustice Legal Fund, Sea Shepherd and the Fund for Wild Nature. Without these groups we wouldn't have much of a planet left already.

FOR

Kozmick Ladye

and all the Kozmick Ladyes

The author is grateful to the following folks for lines lifted, concepts cribbed, beauty stolen or inspiration absorbed from the bright sunshine of their being: Diana Lonsdale, Shakti Shen, Ryan Drum, Nancy Morris, Janice Aurah, Mark "The Bird" Fidrych, Angela Ms. Tree, Ron Luciano, Kate, Dizzy Dean, Annie Sprinkle, Edith L. Randall, Casey Stengel, Joaninha, Satchel Paige, John Wickett, Julius Hoffman, E.O. Wilson, Red Wilson, Frank Lary, Ron Siegel, Love 22, Muhammad Ali, Joanna Macy, John Seed, Mary Reinholz, Rudy, Prince Charles, Sophia, Richard Jacoby, Orange Charlie, Illona Hanson, Parambodhi, Earl Weaver, Jim Karnstedt, Marnok from the Fifth Dimension, Telos, Ace Backwards, birdbrain brainbeau, Elliot Morgan, Chris Moses, Carole Brenner, More University, Body Electric, Jack Kern, Bob Black, Howard Cosell, Yogi Berra, Helen Donovan, Coco, James Thurber, Moe Berg, X Swami X, Captain Clearlight, Marilyn Mao, Allan Tyrrell, Mordecai the Foul and of course Old Touslehead.

PROLOGUE

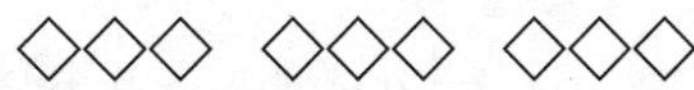

How can anyone say what happens, even if each
of us dips a pen a hundred million times in ink?

—*Rumi*

DUE TO CIRCUMSTANCES beyond our control, our story unfolds in a parallel universe—so far away that the light from ours has never danced across its wobbly edges, yet paradoxically many scientists maintain that it's nearer than your shirt pocket. In some ways it's a peculiar universe, where time travels hand-in-hand with light, streaking through the Void on silver photons; where galaxies sail like frisbees across the ever-widening beach of the vast everywhere forever.

Not that *King of Diamonds* is science fiction. The parallel universe just needs to be explained first. In most respects it's just as ho-hum and Elm Street as our own universe, with gas stations and George Washington dollars and usually nothing scarier than ants at picnics. It does differ from ours in one major respect: there are no baseball playoffs. The two major leagues still consist of eight teams each, with no divisions or divisional champions. Each team plays 154 regular-season games and the two teams with the most wins in their respective leagues meet each other in a best-of-seven playoff called the World Series—somewhat grandiosely, since out of some 190 nations in the parallel world, only one—the United States of America—is represented.

Another difference is that there is no *dh*.

dh, the Designated Hitter, is presently the bane of the American League in our universe. You see, although as schoolboys the best all-around baseball players usually pitch, as they climb the rungs toward the majors the ones who continue on the mound focus on honing their hurling abilities and neglect batting. By the time they arrive at the Big Show, most of them can't hit more than about a hundred and fifty times better than you or me. This happened to even as great a young pitcher as Whizzo Mark Salot IV, and it will continue to happen as long as baseball, like other occupations around the world, continues its alarming trend toward specialization.

In the universe we are familiar with, in 1973 the American League, concerned about dwindling run production (and attendance), instituted the *dh*, allowing a pitcher (not Whizzo, who was not even in that universe at the time) to sit on the bench and meditate on the meanderings of his screwball while some aging slugger could eke out a couple extra seven-figure salary years without suffering the indignity of watching ground balls scoot between his legs in front of 50,000 unforgiving partisans and a national TV audience, none of whom earned seven figures and most of whom were paying their Master Card with their Visa Card and vice-versa.

But the *dh* has its downside, as Foo Foo McGonigle would have known but for an accident of universes: it removes a vital strategic element from the game. If Foo Foo had managed in our universe, he would need not decide whether to remove Whizzo or any of his other starting pitchers in a close game. The pitcher, as Whizzo would have known if he had hurled over here, need not practice the fine art of the sacrifice bunt, whereby he can advance a baserunner from first to second base, from where he may score on a single; or from second to third base, from where he may score on a sacrifice fly or an infield out, while he (the batter) is being thrown out at first base.

For these reasons the National League in our universe has to this day refrained from adopting the *dh*. In the parallel universe of our story, neither league would ever consider such a dumbcluck idea.

Ladies, I can hear you now: Baseball? Forget it. It makes us queasy to read about ground balls: how can you guys stand it? Wouldn't you rather just curl up with a nice soft woman and leave those hard old bats for another time?

Rest assured, dear hearts, that the male characters herein are not just shop-talking jocks with macho minds and roaming hands, but Real Men: big, juicy, tender loving guys less concerned with oversized throbbing hard-ons thrusting into every nooky and cranny than with trying to figure you gals out. The task of the female characters is to show these guys that there is more to love than sex, more to life than throwing and hitting a small round object around an enclosed field.

The Mission Statement for *King of Diamonds* is twofold: 1) to instill into our female readers an appreciation for this sport that they may now view as either just as silly as other sports, or just plain boring if they already enjoy other sports but don't appreciate the drama of Whizzo Mark Salot IV throwing to first base 10 times to hold a runner there; 2) to coax the men back into an arena as unfamiliar to many of them as the national pastime is to the distaff gender: the arena of Love.

And since the laws of Love are universal in all universes, in the arena of Love our parallel universe functions exactly the same as our own.

To fabulize solely about human beings would be the grossest of chauvinisms, given the vast reservoir of biodiversity that creeps, slithers, hops, multiplies by dividing and photosynthesizes across the face of our fair planet. Herpetologists rejoice: to give standing to the teeming throngs of nonhuman forms, the uncounted and often unremembered trillions from tyrannosaurs to trilobites, a member of the genus *Rana* plays a major role in our story.

The game of baseball is nothing if not meditation, American style. Concentration on the diamond must be so complete as to be effortless. The toughest position in baseball is catcher, as Charley Orange can tell you. Buddhists: does Charley qualify as a *roshi*?

Cosmologists, metaphysicians, astronomers and astrologers, philosophers, sages and seers, trippers, open minds and airheads: just what in the hell (and where in the heavens) is a parallel universe anyway? Won't you join us and help us answer the question: Where is we?

FIRST INNING

We're all part of a wonderful, wonderful
dysfunctional family called the human race.
—Cinematographer Conrad L. Hall

So what if we're down 14-0?
We haven't been up to bat yet.
—Charley Orange, age 9

We are the children of the fountain and the lake
Let us awake
Our full-choir shout, as the flutes are ringing out,
Our symphony of full-voiced song
The songs we used to love
in the marshlands up above
—Aristophanes

HARK! THE FIRST SONGSTERS.

It is the Paleozoic Era. Frogs have arrived on Gaia's fair shores. Swamps that have been silent since the first spinning nights ring and echo with burping, croaking, trilling, groaning, bubbling, peeping, piping, creaking, clattering, stuttering, chirping, twanging, bleating, growling, grating, snoring, rattling, chuckling, gurgling, humming, screaming, *jug-o-rum*ing, ringing, dinging, tinkling, barking, booming, crying, buzzing, mooing like cows, quacking like ducks, rat-at-at-at!ing like toy tommyguns—KREK-EK! KREK-EK! QUONK! QUONK! QUONK! PEEP! PEEP! UH-UH UH-UH-UH-ROWR! CUT-CUT-CUT-CUT! W-A-A-H! W-A-A-H! Like the ring of a chisel when a hammer hits it. Like a snore sent by Morse Code. Like a joy buzzer in your hand. Like sleigh bells in the snow. Like a backwards ping-pong game at 78 rpm. C-TUNG! like a loose banjo string. GICK! GICK! GICK! like a metal clicker. NYA-NYA-NYA like a nuthatch trapped inside a tin can. PRR-REEP! PRR-REEP! like running your finger over a comb. CLICK-CLICK! CLICK-CLICK! like knocking two pebbles together. HA'shu HA'shu like cutting wood with a handsaw. DTDTDTDTDTDT like a hundred riveters riveting at once. PU-TUNK! PU-TUNK! like the hammering of a carpenter echoing off the next building. KO-KO-KO-KO-KO-KO-KO-KO-KO like a woodpecker on valium drumming on a hollow barrel. BR-R-R-R-R-U-P! like an alarm clock set by someone who had too many drinks to get up and go to work.

Ain't evolution grand? This sure beats hell out of the old insect fiddle and banjo contest, all of the guys frantically rubbing two sticks together trying to spark a fire in the hearts of their respective paramours. Even insect songs vary in more ways than we have words for, each song copyright that species so the object of the singer's affection doesn't run off with the milk beetle and get labeled a slut or pervert. Listen to those ancient ballads we overhear of a summer's eve: do you long to set back the clock, hunker down in a moonlit meadow and get it on with a grasshopper? Don't be shy: katydid.

As Katy and her inlaws saw away in steady stridulation, our anuran crew types out the prologue to its 150-million-year-long run-on sentence of *amour,* bubbling like Tibetan monks to some Force unknown and unknowable but announced through the rhythmic, body-rocking palpitations of these resonating vocal sacs, bobbing up and down like sewing-machine shuttles, filling the musky evenings with floating sound-bubbles of mystery and allure, pheromones for those galaxy-shaped ears resting behind their bulbous, C-cup eyes. Feel the vibrations in those amphibious throats: how far back lies man's instinct to serenade his lady love?

Call him Schlemiel.

That's what Glory did, the JAP that Charley Orange wasted his time and money on last night.

It was their third date: a record for Charley for the last year or so. He thought he'd found the answer at last: an unhappy married woman. Glory had arrived at the restaurant with her top blouse button undone, revealing a tantalizing taste of what Charley had already determined was major cleavage.

Dinner went well. Glory talked animatedly, her dark, lustrous hair jumping on and off her shoulders like commuter fleas awaiting the downtown dog. She smiled alot; she touched him. Her conversation sparkled, as did her brown eyes as they focused on him. Both hinted at better things to come.

Then, like she had both times previously, as she saw the waiter coming with the check, she ditched for the powder room.

The thought crossed Charley's mind to walk, leaving her to pay the bill and cab it home. But as pissed as he was at women, he was too decent a guy to do that. So he and the tab sat there, not talking to each other, it no doubt feeling insecure wondering who was going to take care of it, the stub wondering who would take it home and file it in his or her "meals and entertainment" drawer for the IRS, and Charley thinking of how he could broach this frustrating aspect of dating etiquette without Glory creating a scene.

Charley sat there drumming his fingers while she continued powdering, excreting, re-applying her makeup, gossiping with fellow powderers, and who knows what all they do in there. He swore she must have been peeking out the door to see if he'd paid yet.

Finally the waiter came over. "We're closing the register, sir. Would it be all right if...?

Charley gave him his credit card. It would be even tougher to collect now.

At last Glory returned. She had removed her bra and undone another button. "Like it?" she asked Charley, leaning toward him and fingering the unfilled buttonhole. She looked luscious, but Charley's resolve was stronger than temptation. With some effort he lifted his gaze from her chest to her eyes.

"Glory," he said, "how do you feel about equality between the sexes?"

"I think it will be wonderful," she said, "when women are paid as much as men for the same job. Do you know how much a woman in management makes for every dollar a man...?"

"Well, how about you, Glory? Your husband's a doctor. You've got all the money you want, don't you?"

"I gave up my self-fulfillment, my dance career, to marry that turd and help put him through med school. Hey come on, we were having a good time. I don't want to talk about him."

◆

"I brought it up because I don't like it that you just assume I'm going to pay the bill. I think men and women should both do things for each other."

"But we do do things for each other. We give you sex. And George is going away and I was going to ask you over for dinner and cook for you."

"Well, I've taken you out three times now and you haven't given me any sex, and now you say you were going to offer me one dinner. Is that even-Steven?"

"You think because you buy me dinner you can screw me? You know what you are, Charley? You're a schlemiel. Just take me home."

Once behind the wheel of his Studebaker Starlight Coupe Charley rolled down his window, but the warm evening air could not thaw the frost in the car. *Why didn't I just leave her there,* he wondered to himself, *let her take a cab and experience the self-fulfillment of paying for it herself?* The answer was that he wanted her to see he really was big-hearted and generous. He was willing to bend 90 percent of the way. Just not 100 percent. "All the time you were in the bathroom," he said, "I was trying to figure out how to approach the subject so it wouldn't turn out this way."

"You're a major-league ballplayer," she said. "You've been in the big leagues for 15 years. You must be making a zillion per."

"Eleven years. And I'm near the bottom of the pay scale: a low six. I'm a second-string catcher. I'm lucky to still be in The Show. I'm 39 years old, my legs are shot and I'm hitting under .200. It's my last year."

"Six figures and you're grinding me over a dinner tab?"

"It's not the money, it's the principle. I'm tired of give, give, give and not getting anything back. Why don't women ask *me* out to dinner? Why don't they think of having sex with me as a gift to *them*?"

"Those are good questions to ask yourself, Charley. Good night." She slammed the door and stalked into her house.

On the seat, where it must have fallen out of her purse to torment Charley, lay her size D bra.

◆ ◆ ◆ ◆

If you have less than sensational talent and want to play in the Bigs, learn to catch. And start learning young. Charley Orange started in his second game in Little League.

His first game, he pitched. Charley acquitted himself well: his team lost 11-7 but Charley allowed only three hits and all the runs were unearned. When Claude Orange heard about it, he gave Charley the worst chewing-out of their father-son career.

"The bottom line is, you can't pitch in the Big Leagues with only four fingers," Charley's father said when he calmed down. Yes, as befitting someone who would play his entire career with the Megaglopoulis Mutants, Charley came into the universe missing both index fingers. Naturally, his friends called him Four Fingers. Four Fingers or No Forefingers, one thing was sure: Someone Up There was playing Genetic Mod with him.

Claude Orange went to see Mr. Saraswata, Charley's manager. "Charley is not a pitcher," he said. "He can't grip the ball as well as someone with five fingers. He can't break it off as well." In another universe, Charley would be classified as breaking-ball challenged.

"Charley is not to pitch for you," Claude Orange continued. "He wants to play in the majors. If he's going to get a ticket to the Big Time, it's as a catcher."

Mr. Saraswata did not relinquish his best pitcher meekly. "I remind you of Mordecai 'Three-Finger' Brown," he argued. "He pitched in the major leagues, did he not? I believe he is in the Hall of Fame."

"Three-Finger Brown was an exception," Claude Orange said. "Charley is a very good ballplayer but he's not exceptional. He's also not Einstein but he's very bright. Play him at catcher."

And so it was that Charley Orange came to don the "tools of ignorance," so-called because, the conventional wisdom goes, no one but an ignoramus would station himself behind home plate and let pitchers fire 90-mph fastballs at him and batters knock foul tips off whatever parts of his anatomy remained uncovered by the tools of ignorance.

Actually the catcher uses more gray matter than anyone else on the field. He calls all the pitches. What's working for the pitcher today?

◆

What can't the batter hit well? What's the score? What's the game situation? What's the count? How does the ball carry today? Do we pitch low and go for ground-outs, or high and go for popups and strikeouts (and maybe give up a couple dingers)? Is the runner on first likely to steal second? Will the second baseman or the shortstop take the throw if he tries? Will the batter be trying to hit through the spot vacated by the fielder who breaks for the bag? Who's on first? What's on second? And so on.

The catcher must also be able to fire bullets to second base to keep runners from stealing. Over the years Charley was ranked with the best-throwing catchers in baseball. As he told Dr. Weisenheimer, sometimes he thought his father's assessment of his mound potential was unnecessarily pessimistic, and that cost him his dream of being a pitcher, a Queen Bee. As a moundsman, his .238 lifetime batting average would have been a plus, not a minus, at contract time.

Of course, Charley didn't throw curve balls to second base, and maybe his father was right that he could never have developed a varied repertoire. And under Claude Orange's early tutelage Charley enjoyed a long if not illustrious big-league career.

In the beginning, Charley Orange and his Megaglopoulis Mutant teammates dismissed Whizzo Mark Salot IV as one of Wellington P. Sweetwater's stunts. In the 17 long years it had taken to build the lowly Mutes into a contender, Sweetwater had kept the turnstiles clicking and the books balanced with his showman's flair.

The son of a Baptist evangelist, Sweetwater entered the working world as a carnival barker. But he found his calling in the nether world of professional poker. To hear Sweetwater say it, poker is the ultimate battle of psychological wits, and those who dwell in its domain see through people like the rest of us can see through Maxwell Veribushi's Research Assistant's see-through blouses (although Sweetwater had never met the woman, he knew how to see through a see-through blouse all right). Nor was shrewd perception of his fellow humans Sweetwater's only attribute. If luck exists in the vast everywheres forevers (and how could it not? Here we all are), then an inordinate portion of it rested inside the corporeal psyche of Wellington P. Sweetwater. He was a legend along the stud circuit (no, not *that* stud circuit—well, actually that one too, but that's another story) for holding a kicker with three of a kind and drawing the fourth. But no mere champion of Five Card Draw, Blind Baseball or Texas Hold'Em could match Sweetwater's ultimate claim to fame: he won the lottery.

Up until that time, despite his successes Sweetwater had been that saddest of all men: a fan whose mother had thrown out his baseball cards as she watched him mature into manhood and shed the trappings of the little boy inside. When Midlife Crisis struck and he longed for an occasional regression back into the innocent dreams of that little boy, he joined a Rotisserie League. But his numerous other pursuits (mostly amorous) came between him and contention—and contentedness.

The $16 million came in the nick of time. He had been attending baseball card collector shows and quickly developed an expensive buying habit: within a year he had spent $50,000 for a collection that was pitiably small but of a quality as rarefied as the air atop Mt. Everest: a Topps Mickey Mantle rookie card, a Leaf 1948 Ted Williams, a 1956 Topps Roberto Clemente and his prize: a 1915 Cracker Jack Ty Cobb. His psychiatrist–Dr. Weisenheimer, who through Sweetwater became the Baseball Shrink–brought him back into reality by suggesting he buy a baseball team. "Hang out," Doc said, "if not mit reals peoples, den at least mit reals ballsplayers." Doc had a therapist's way of removing hurdles from his clients' psyches as unobtrusively as the tooth fairy extracts orificial castoffs from under the pillows of sleeping children. "Why don't I buy the Megaglopoulis Mutants?" Sweetwater asked himself. (In the universe of *King of Diamonds,* $16 million was still the going price for a second-rate ballclub.) Sweetwater sent his general manager, Lance Hickey, out on the long road to building a winner. Meanwhile he drew on all his inherited blarney to keep the seats filled.

Most of his stunts worked. Probably the most successful was bringing up Jellie Mae "Hooters" Buzzsaw, the first (and last) woman

◆

player in major-league history. Amidst disapproving clucks from chivalrous porcines who feared for her life on the field, Jellie Mae batted .234—not good enough for a second-string first baseperson to cut it in the bigs, but higher than some of her detractors. The year Jellie Mae played, the Mutes finished sixth and led the league in attendance, smashing the 58-year-old major-league record for percentage of female spectators.

Sweetwater also instituted Dugout Day, whereby all the kids who were in the stadium before noon on day games could go down into the Mutant cubicle and hobnob with their heroes. To retired stars who needed one more season for higher pensions, he proffered one-year contracts with single at-bat clauses. He signed luminaries from other sports and celebrities from all walks of life to similar single at-bat contracts.

Sweetwater relinquished his private box to winners of free lotteries he held at the turnstiles and sat cheering, discussing strategy and betting pitches with his most knowledgeable customers, the welfare crowd in the centerfield bleachers. He promoted picnics, launched fireworks and roosted at tailgate parties.

Of course, the higher Mutant attendance rose, the lower Sweetwater sank in the eyes of his fellow owners. When a pitch hit Rush Limbaugh in the chest, breaking a rib, they threatened to seize his franchise and boot him out of the game. He canceled his celebrity contracts—only minutes before Dolly Parton was due at the plate.

Charley Orange came from the Old School: he was uncomfortable with Sweetwater's bells-and-whistles approach to a game that required the full concentration of two 25-man squads and their managers in order to be played even passably well. The people who came for skyrockets and sideshows were spectators, not fans. Most of them didn't know a pitchout from a pickoff, and if you asked them what sequence they would throw to Hector Mariachi with runners on second and third with two down and a tie score in the eighth, their eyes would glaze over like Lake Glimmerglass on a windless day.

Charley didn't begrudge their presence: they did chip in part of the low six he would collect this year. He just didn't appreciate them—any more than they appreciated him. His best year he hit .268; the team stats in the sports section showed him at .129 in limited action this year. The dilettantes knew Charley Orange only as a second-string catcher who couldn't hit. Those who noticed his birthday in the scorecard and calculated his age wondered why he was still cluttering up the roster.

"Well, who knows?" Wellington P. Sweetwater had said to him in that agreeable tone he assumed whenever anyone argued with him, as Charley had when he signed a midget to pinch-hit in walk situations, "maybe some of them will turn into fans."

Today Charley was arguing with Sweetwater about his signing Whizzo Mark Salot IV, an 18-year-old kid right out of high school, to a major-league contract. Sweetwater proffered a photo of a beaming teen in a graduation gown, twirling a graduation cap in his hand. Unless his likeness had been massively retouched, the prodigy had thick, wavy hair the color of a phosphorescent persimmon, crystal blue eyes that sparkled like newly minted dimes buying wishes in a Parisian fountain and a face pretty enough to send Michael Jackson running to his plastic surgeon to demand his money back.

"Tonight," Sweetwater said, "Whizzo Mark Salot IV will be dressed in this outfit at his high-school graduation ceremony in Disfunction Junction, Arkansas. Tomorrow he'll be wearing the uniform of the Megaglopoulis Mutants."

"Listen—Sweetwater. If we weren't contenders—well, OK, it's only June and we're not in contention yet. But everyone knows we've got the makeup. We're off to a slow start. And you're bringing up this greenhorn kid with not one professional game under his belt? It looks like a desperation move."

Wellington P. Sweetwater had a mop of hair as dense as a Congressman's head and as white as a salt mine on a snowy day on Blanca Alba, with a moustache to match. He reached up with his lower teeth and pulled a corner of the moustache into his mouth for a chew. "Hm-mm. Desperation, do you think?"

"What else? We might just as well announce that no one among our dozens of minor-league prospects can fill the bill."

◆

"Great!" said Sweetwater, releasing the newly-trimmed ivory hairs and replacing them with a well-chewed cigar. "The other clubs will think so, too."

"Look at the burden you're placing on this kid. I wouldn't want to be in his shoes for anything. I just hope he gets bombed in a couple of blowouts and gets shipped out to Class D Tidewater, with no damage to the team."

"Charley, my boy," began Wellington P. Sweetwater, speaking with that affable paternalism that he affected both when he told the truth and when he told a whopper, "Charley, I know you're not going to believe me when I tell you, but..."

It was his poker training. In another universe, a flamboyant owner named Bill Veeck had a wooden leg with an ashtray built into it. Sweetwater had half the team convinced that he had gone Veeck one better: he had a wooden wanger. He'd had an unfortunate war wound, he had confided to Speedboat Jones, and when his member was dismembered he had a fitted attachment made which he fastened on whenever the situation called for an erection. "Lulu, my main squeeze, swears by it," he told Speedboat. "Fortunately, I'm not a smoker. Well—" he removed his cigar from his mouth and contemplated it—"I don't inhale. Anyway, no ashtrays in my member. Nary an indentation of any kind—nor woodpecker hole nor staple puncture—nay, not so much as a hairline splinter disfigures this lustrous rosewood Roscoe that Lulu spit-polishes each day and lubricates religiously each night."

"Uh huh," Charley said to Speedboat Jones. "Did you see it?"

"Sure, I'm gonna ask him," said Speedboat. "Whaddya think I am, a prong jockey?"

Charley filed Sweetwater's wooden lingam in the Whopper pile, along with his insistence now that Whizzo Mark Salot IV was not just another attendance-boosting stunt. "This kid's high hard one moves faster than snot in a sneeze," Sweetwater told him. "You're going to need a bigger glove and some radar, Charley boy, to track all the zigs and zags in his ball."

"Sure. He'll fill your ballpark once, maybe twice, than it's off to Tidewater and you're out...what did you pay for him, anyway?"

"Charley, lad, he'll fill the park every time he pitches. Wait till you see him. He's got it all: arm, mouth, looks, media pizzazz—and get this: he talks to the ball!"

◆ ◆ ◆ ◆

A frog a-would a-wooing go
Heigh-ho! says Anthony Rowley
—old English folksong

Music, maestro, please! There's *Rana catesbeina* on bass fiddle, *Thump!-a thump-Thump! Acris crepitans crepitans* double-timing on sticks, *Rick!-a-tick-Tick! Rick!-a-tick-Tick!* The songsters join in: *Pseudacris triseriata* on tenor trills, *Hyla chrysoscelis* the coloratura soprano; the whole ensemble sending cadenzas rising and falling across Mosquito Marsh like a looped-tape Om with the hiccups.

It is a warm, moonlit night in the Oligocene Epoch. Had its shores soote been invented yet, the month would be April. Since the beginning of time, or so it seemed to Ngaio the *Rana onca*, that mysterious maiden the moon had been playing hide-and-seek with the batrachian residents of Mosquito Marsh: showing up now in the morning as a hangnail in the sky, next in mid-afternoon as a ball of cheese with a chunk bitten out of it, a week or so later (although frogs, having no offices to go to, no doctor's appointments to keep, no Sunday sermons to drowse through, indeed no deities to name the days after, entertain no concept of a "week") at sunset disguised as a newly-minted quarter and still later as a slot in the piggybank sky with the quarter almost fully deposited in it. And then, just as Ngaio and his fellow choristers have grown to expect this beguiling quick-change artist in the heavens, the following night she is mysteriously absent.

Also since the beginning of time, or so it seemed to Ngaio, he and his songster buddies had squatted on their logs and lilypads and serenaded this peek-a-boo moon.

In fact, as the moon could have told him, Mosquito Marsh had existed for less than 10,000 years, or since her partner the sun sent

◆

the most recent Ice Age off packing to Siberia and melted the glacier that had crept and crawled its way through the surrounding hillsides, dissolving in the valley into the pools of water that millennium upon millennium later, in a characteristic burst of pique, the nonfeathering biped—a newcomer on the scene—would dub Mosquito Marsh.

Ranid legend has it that before the moon took on the task for them, the frogs controlled the tides with the vibrations in their throats, and all that the tides themselves control: the shapes of shorelines, the distribution of rocks and sand and wildlife along them, the best places for frogs to make love and deposit eggs...

But tonight, thought Ngaio, is not to speculate. Tonight is to sing! To tune up *sotto voce*, then to join in the chorus until, everyone aboard, you soared together into glorious, bubbling crescendos that rolled across the marsh like tom-toms (how far back goes the human instinct to drum?), now rising here, now dying there: All together now, We All Live in a Green Dream Machine.

All across Mosquito Marsh lay the fruits of those nocturnal emissions: pollywogs, as googoloid in number as their look-alike descendants, sperm, their top-heavy bodies forming vast black carpets over the bottom, providing fast-food delights for all their fellow denizens of the marsh.

Ngaio puffed out the skin on his throat until he'd blown a bubble bigger than he was and let 'er rip: SKRIEK-EK-EK!

Fifty million years in the future, all the violin teachers in the world turned over in their graves.

Beethoven Ngaio was not, but then neither was Beethoven Ngaio. He struck a resonant chord in Gurgle Gertie, a juicy fellow *Rana onca* in the horsetails with skin as soft and moist as thighs parting in a velvet night. As she kicked off, legs akimbo, Ngaio belched out a fusillade of appreciative notes whose euphonious tones made Gertie's head light, caused the blood to quiver through her cloaca and lubricated her oviduct. She kicked on over to Ngaio's pad, her glabrous gams forming stylish diamonds in her wake. Together they found a tranquil, secluded pond brimming with yummy mosquito larvae and there, while the moon deposited a quarter to watch the PEEP! show, they fucked and fucked and fucked.

That summer Ngaio, *basso profundo extraordinaire,* was eaten by a pterodactyl.[1] He was survived by those of his 36,224 children who hadn't been eaten by each other.[2]

Wellington P. Sweetwater had a standing offer: he would pick up the tab for anyone on the Megaglopoulis Mutants who sought therapy from Dr. Weisenheimer. No, Sweetwater didn't think he had a squad of fruitcakes; he was messianic because Dr. Weisenheimer had changed his life. Sweetwater was vaguely aware that Charley Orange had some sort of muddles with the fair sex; that was enough for him to urge Charley to take up his offer.

What's more, Sweetwater fixed him up. She was the daughter of a visiting friend and she wanted to have some fun.

"I'm not much fun," thought Charley, but he didn't say it aloud. When he saw her photo, he was happy he didn't. "She's young, she's gorgeous," said Sweetwater. "I haven't seen her since she was 7 or 9 or something, but look at those knockers. She sent me this when she graduated college."

"So she's bright, too."

"So what? Show her a good time."

Nervously, Charley called the hotel. Alysse wasn't in; would he leave a message?

Forget it, Charley thought with a sigh. End of the line. She'll never call back. "Charley Orange," he said and left his number. He pulled out a book on one of his favorite subjects: parallel universes.

---

1. Arguing that pterodactyls had been extinct for at least 10 million years before the Oligocene epoch, Veribushi and Pearl hypothesize that Ngaio was actually stepped on by a mastodon

It is generally held that mastodons lived in coniferous forests; however, Veribushi and Pearl posit that conifers grew near Mosquito Marsh at the time and the mastodons journeyed to the marsh during dry spells to drink.

The pterodactyl's response is compelling: "Were you there?"

2. Veribushi and Pearl argue that leopard frogs do not eat their young. Gurgle Gertie's response is compelling:"Were you there?"

◆

If anyone out there thinks astrology and reincarnation are far out, check out parallel universe theory. It's based on the work of Albert Einstein, Max Planck, Neils Bohr, Wolfgang Pauli, Werner Heisenberg—the collective braintrust of Twentieth Century physics.

Ready? First we have to know about black holes. To know about black holes, first we have to know about stars.

We live our lives; stars live theirs. They're born, they grow up, they grow old, they die. When we shuffle off, we shrivel up. Stars expand into "novae": they explode. If a star is hefty enough (a few times larger than the sun), when it explodes its gravitational pull is so strong that its matter can't blast off into space. Instead the star collapses in on itself and creates a "gravitational sink" in space. Once anything enters within a certain distance from the center of the sink—a distance known as the Schwarzchild radius—it's trapped inside forever.

"Weirder than lettuce-and-jelly sandwiches," Charley told the few people he could talk to about such things, "but plausible."

Things are not all that gets trapped in there. So does light. Because light can't escape, the sink is known as a "black hole." Say you are outside a Schwarzchild Radius looking in at someone trapped inside. She drifts toward the center, slowly, then more slowly, more slowly still: it seems like she'll take forever to get there.

Which she will. Or until the end of the universe, anyway.

However, as far as she can tell, the whole billions-of-years-long journey happens in the blink of an eye.

And what is her fate when the universe ends? Where does she go? Well, said Charley's book, these black holes are actually doorways or "wormholes" into parallel universes.

How many of these parallel universes are there? Millions? Trillions? Think big: the number is infinite. And you don't have to wait for the next rocket out to Alpha Centauri to meet one. Every time you look at something in this universe, you create a new one—or a whole passel of them.

As Charley sat contemplating the kazillion or two universes he had birthed just by reading the page, the phone rang. It was Alysse!

“I’m sorry I wasn’t here,” she said. “I just got back from a business meeting, and I’m dying to HAVE SOME FUN! Are you game?”

Wow! She was open to him. She wasn’t a bimbo: she was a businesswoman. Miracle of miracles, she had returned his call! Maybe he had slipped through the bleed into a parallel universe of his dreams, a place where women treated men like human beings instead of shit sandwiches.

“What are you doing tonight, Charley?”

“I’m going to go play like a kid in a parallel universe.”

“Well, that sounds interesting…I think.”

“I’ll tell you all about it tonight. Shall we start with dinner at Ghoti de Jour’s?”

“Yes! I’ll make you a deal. You buy dinner and I’ll provide some *super* entertainment that will really turn you on!”

Turn him on! She wouldn’t be offering the one thing that would do that to a total stranger over the phone, but she was lively and sounded like fun: he was game. And who knows, in the Divine Plan all roads do lead eventually to sex…

Alysse greeted him at the door. After her semi-exposed bosom, the first thing he noticed was her open-mouthed, sparkle-eyed smile. Women smiled at him so seldom, he could fall in love from a smile like that. Her brown eyes teased and invited. Her fragrance enveloped him. And her breasts! Grapefruit-round orbs descending like soft snowy avalanches into her dress, which was stylishly simple, black with a large silver circle in front.

“Hi!” said Charley. “Nice dress. Looks like a big baseball.”

She laughed, a titter like a swallow that had lost its tongue for W’s. Charley wondered, did she actually find him amusing?

“Or two big grapefruits.” The end of her dark red hair curled on her shoulders. “You don’t think it’s cut too low?”

“Yes. Button up or I’m out of here.”

A fuller, deeper laugh this time. She really did like his humor.

Ghoti de Jour’s was one of Megaglopoulis’ most elegant eateries. They each polished off triple-digit cuisine, over which Charley explained parallel universe theory to her. The laughs kept coming, even when he launched into such funnybone-ticklers as superstring theory and eigenstates.

Alysse opened her handbag. “OK, ready for your entertainment?”

“Here?”

“Why not? Here it is.” She placed a small white plastic bottle on the table. “Have you ever heard of Super Power Pond Scum?”

Alysse’s multilevel sales pitch was as long and spit-polished as a banister from here to the eighth layer of the Inferno, where Charley thought she belonged. As entertaining as Fritzi Ritz. As turn-on as Nancy. As much fun as diarrhea in a crowded elevator.

The next morning Charley called Dr. Weisenheimer.

If the measure of brains were books, Dr. Weisenheimer was by Isaac Newton out of Simone de Beauvoir. The shelves covered two walls, floor to 12-foot ceiling. As Charley made his way to the leather easy chair under the window on the third side, he glanced at the titles, looking for a way to connect minds with the man he was about to meet. They were all in German.

“Zit down, Mr. Orange,” came a voice from the vicinity of the desk, behind which were two paintings: “Hunnertwasser unt Georg Grosz. Heights and depths of da human spirit, no?” The leather chair behind the desk rolled sideways, and up from under the desk emerged Dr. Weisenheimer. “Found it,” he said.

German and fat and jolly, he broke all the rules of expectation. At 50-something, he still looked like he combed his salmon hair with a heifer’s tongue. A many-freckled man: where you saw skin of vermillion hue, you saw freckles of cinnamon stain. Not childhood-leftover horse manure-spatter freckles but German freckles, great mahogany clusters the size of German measles. All right, the size of bath bubbles, covering his face, his arms, the top of his head under thinning patches of hair. His attire struck Charley as strange: a black leather shirt cut low both front and back and matching leather shorts.

“Curiously enough, I am not really Cherman,” he told Charley. “My spirit is returning to my Prussian ancestors; dis allows me to be disposing of da guilt. Unt you are Charley Orange. Sit down, Charley. How may I be helping to you?”

“Well—” said Charley, “—it’s about women. They mistreat me. They’re just not nice.”

“Dey can be mean, ungrateful creatures. But you, mein friend, are feeling mistreat.”

“That’s right. You would too if 90 percent of the women you asked out stood you up, and the rest you wish they did.”

“Ninety perzent!”

“Actually, it’s close to 100 percent. That’s when I get someone on the phone to ask her out. They also don’t return my phone calls at a rate of about 100 percent. Dr., I joined a dating service. The women would agree to give me their number and still not return my calls. I thought I might be losing track of reality on this, so for three months I kept a log. In that time I made 155 phone calls to women. I got answering machines and left messages 150 times. Not one return call did I get. Not one.”

“Unt da odder fife?”

“Two no’s, three yesses.”

“Tree yesses, dis is gut!”

“Number one, Rene. Didn’t show up. I finally went to the party by myself. There she was, yukking it up with a circle of guys.”

“Oh my. Vhat did you doing?”

“I went over to confront her. She gave me a big Hi Charley, like everything was hunky-dory. I said I’d been waiting at home for over an hour for her to show up. She said she called me to tell me to meet her there, but I wasn’t home. ‘What did you say on the message?’ I asked. ‘I didn’t leave a message,’ she says. Well, how do I know she called if she didn’t leave a message?”

Dr. Weisenheimer bounced out of his chair. “I am listening, Charley. I am under da desk going to get zometing.”

“Bunny—after several knocks she answers the door in her bathrobe. Clothes are scattered across the floor, starting with shoes

◆

and ending, by the bedroom door, with lingerie and men's briefs. She says, 'Charley! What are you doing here?'

"'I'm here for our date, which is now, at 8:30 tonight.'

"'It's tomorrow night,' she says and closes the door. It wasn't; I wrote it down when we made the date."

"My belly," said Dr. Weisenheimer, "you zee it round like Santa Claus. Like Buddha. My inner child, nefer he is getting enough of da chocolate. Some day he is growing out of it. Meanvhile—still he is feeling very angry. Zeventy extra pounds he is making me carry. Unt sveating too much. I am under da desk hiding da sveets but alvays he is finding dem. But I am talking too much about meinself. Please to go on, Charley."

"Ah—Dr. Weisenheimer, are you sure you're listening to me?"

"Yes, yes, you are telling da mistreatments. I am sorry. Please to go on, Charley."

"Next—Tanya. A couple months after she stood me up I ran into her with a guy she had just married. She said that on the way to my house she had met him at a crosswalk and she knew in that moment he was her dream man, and they've been la-la ever since. No, she didn't apologize.

"And there's more. Sometimes I question whether I've lost touch with reality on this. Dr., the way they treat me—that's not right, is it?"

"Da qvestion is, vhy do you feeling mistreat?"

"I just told you."

"Ja, you vere stooding up. How you are creating dis stooding up? How you are dese vomen approaching?"

"Sometimes they ask *me*."

"Ah-HA! Never accepting a date vhen da voman is asking you. Right?"

"That's how I feel. Right?"

"Wrong. Dat is, right, dat is how you are feeling. Wrong, dat is how da solution to da problem. Listen, Charley. You are hearing of John Bradshaw? John Bradshaw says 90 perzent of us are coming from families mit da emotional dysfunction. You..."

"You say 90 percent? *Where are the other 10 percent?* 30 million sane, healthy Americans can't all be hiding in Walla Walla,

Washington and Kalamazoo. Doctor, you've seen that tee shirt: Meeting of the Adult Children of Functional Families, with one person there? *Where is that one?* Have you ever met him or her?"

"I meet a voman vonce vhat is telling me she is dat von."

"Then you met her mother, right?"

"Vorse dan dat. But dis is my point, precisely. Charley, you are growing up in da forest von of da strongest trees. Now closing da eyes and breadding vhile I say to you: OK?"

Charley closed his eyes. "Charley, you hafe da resilience—it is not unique in da human race—resilience to licking your vounds, retooling unt healing. You must believe dis before I can be helping you. OK?"

"Ding ding," said Dr. Weisenheimer's wristwatch.

"Time," said Dr. Weisenheimer.

"Ah-ha! He's one of the 10 percent."

That's what John Bradshaw would say if he saw Whizzo Mark Salot IV disporting himself through his rookie season.

"Ah-ha! He's the One."

That's what the creator of the Adult Children of Functional Families tee-shirt would say if he saw Whizzo cavorting with the ladies like Dionysus, or Krishna, or Bacchus and his pards, or S/HeIt Hirself—not to be confused with the socio-psychopath God of twelve tiny tribes, handed down through 140 generations—3500 years—and in all the long nights of those 35 centuries allowed but one conjugal visit.

Imagine—just imagine you are Omniscient, Omnipresent and Immortal. You've been around for a few millennia now—and many of your creators, apparently believing immortality is a rubber band in time, stretching equally in both directions, have grandfathered you back to the Go square; nay, Yours, they say, was the Hand that tossed the dice. In all those centuries or aeons, You have been standing on Your Omnipresent corner, watching with Your Omniscient eye all the girls who have ever lived go by. Under Your vigilant eye Helen of Troy

◆

unfolded from a budding blossom into a soft, smiling morsel of yumminess so luscious as to launch—well, thank Yourself she lived before the days of The Bomb and the Moral Majority, or no telling what she would have launched. You peeped in on Cleopatra, sultry enchantress of both the great emperors of her day, disrobing and slipping silently into her bath of milk. Without wearying, you have gazed upon the endless parade of pulchritudinous delights down through the ages—veiled Salomes and sari'd Scheherezades, kimono-clad courtesans, mischievous Eleusinian priestesses in nothing at all, beachball-buttocked pygmy queens, bounteous modern beauties magnified to mythic proportions by the silver screen—all of them with eyes inviting, lips luscious and full, aureolae swelling like jello if jello could swell, lurid labia damp with desire...

And You—You have the whole vast Everywhere Forever to run. Maybe an infinite number of them. Do infinite universes have an infinite number of Gods, or does one S/HeIt reign over all? Until the report is in from the theologians, we must assume You're running the whole shebang—or is it running you? But that's another theological question.

In all Your multi-millenia of All-Seeingness, watching, like some hungry kid with Your giant proboscis pressed to a window, only once have You been privy to the pleasures of procreation. And that with a woman who, from the accounts we have, may have been as much a stranger to the act as Yourself. We can feel only compassion for Your awkward fumbling and poking that must have made her wonder what the fuss was all about, anyway.

And maybe...maybe, poor Yahweh, it didn't happen even once, and You're still a virgin. Maybe this woman, this maid of Galilee, concocted the Whopper of the Millennium to explain a perfectly mortal pregnancy to her husband, and You in Your masculine pride said nothing to deny it. In all the histories of the fruit of whatever union occurred—among the most meticulously detailed ever recorded—not a single description of this singular act was preserved.

(Understandable. Imagine a TV news editor's dilemma. Tonight God and the Virgin Mary are going to conceive Jesus. Dare s/he cover it live? What will the Fundamentalists say? Dare s/he not? Does s/he just park a camera crew outside the bedroom like everyone else (Which bedroom—was it her place or His?), or does s/he violate their connubial privacy and capture the Neilson flag?)

Anyway, imagine you're God; sexually scorned and frustrated. They say our heredity and environment mix to make us who and what we are. If you're God, we don't know much about Your genes, but we do know that you have been subjected to a fate more cruel and crazy-making than that of any mortal man. Is it any wonder, then, that You have grown so bitter and judgmental toward the act of bellywhumping so relentlessly denied You by Your creators that You threaten the Eternal Hotfoot to any who taste its bliss except under the most narrowly circumscribed of circumstances? Shall we judge You for that and be guilty of the same smallness of spirit as Your Holy Wrathfulness?

No, Whizzo Mark Salot IV cavorted not like the celibate God Yahweh (who, if He even masturbated, kept it secret), but rather like His fellow deities in the On-High network.

What was it about Whizzo that caused women to trail behind him like link sausages? Was it his high-school pitching record of 42-1 with 26 shutouts and eight no-hitters, including a perfect game with 23 strikeouts? The shock of wavy red hair and the blue eyes blazing like twin earth-orbs in the endless night?

Ladies, how about his smile? Had Duke Ellington lived to see those teeth, his hands would have itched to play *Take the 'A' Train* on them. If the Cheshire Cat could pick its porcelains, if Signora Mona Lisa had enjoyed the benefits of modern dentistry, if TV evangelists or US presidents could learn to flash their choppers and tell the truth at the same time, all their canines combined could not melt the hearts of everyone who beheld them as could the sparkling ivories of Whizzo Mark Salot IV.

We are warned against the reassuring feeling we get from a smile. Animals, naturalists say, smile to show off their biting prowess. Don't smile at a grizzly bear, they say, should you met one on the outhouse path. (These must be the same naturalists who spent a cool kazillion to verify that this same *ursa horribilis* deposits excreta in its forested habitat.)

◆

But attributing a smile to an ursuline is asinine. Animals don't smile; they grin. A grin is no more a smile than a pucker is a pecker. Humans who bare their teeth usually bring something to their countenance that grizzlies and other grinners don't: their heart. When Whizzo Mark Salot IV smiled (and when didn't he?), his heart seemed to rise right up from his chest and pop out through his mouth.

The heart? Medical scientists (those old oxymorons) scoff. The heart is a machine; it pumps blood. Emotions stem from the hypothalamus. Those of us not trapped in that narrow portion of our body called the cerebral cortex find the seat of our emotions in the area called the abdomen here in the West, the *hara* in the East—just below the navel, cozying up suggestively close, anatomically, to the genitals.

How did the old oxymorons come by this misunderstanding, and why has it persisted so long? Well, if one picture is worth a thousand words, the standard representation of the heart, suggesting also lips, yoni, buns and balls, is not an easy image to supplant.

Indeed Whizzo's smile, a smile that could melt marble and set angels to weeping, engaged equally his mouth, his *hara* and his genitals. A feeling could enter his body through his heart and slide right down into his *cuk-a-loo-loo* or vice-versa, or in through his *hara* and ride up and down his chakras like a yo-yo.

And so while it is true, as one wag said, that if sex were fast food there would be golden arches over Whizzo's head, the larger truth is that the ladies simply adored him. So did the gentlemen, in their fashion. And the kids! Wasn't it the word of gospel spread by the underage underground from Megaglopoulis to Podunk, Iowa, from the redwood forests to the New York island, all over St. Louie and down in New Orleans, from Toontown to Tinseltown to Truth or Consequences, NM—didn't every preadolescent in the land know that Whizzo always carried gumdrops in his pockets to give to kids, bought them ice-cream cones and gathered them up to show them magic tricks?

About Whizzo Mark Salot IV, John Bradshaw and the tee-shirt tycoon would be wrong. Whizzo came from a family that put dysfunction on the map. In fact, he came from a town—Disfunction

Junction, Arkansas—that put dysfunction on the map, albeit misspelled.

Now, it is hardly the place of fiction to deny the emotional beginnings of what makes us who and what we are. But Whizzo somehow broke the mold. Many are those in our urban wastelands who, grown tired of being mugged, beaten, shot at, raped, robbed and treated in other unkindly fashion by those of less fortunate background than themselves, cry out for stiffer punishments—even the Ultimate Punishment. They may read about Whizzo's amorous appetite and want to run him for President.

Still others face the same indignities but somehow keep their hearts open. They believe there is no such thing as a bad boy, and as the twig is bent, so grows the tree, and all that. They are jeered at and labeled "liberals," although the issue is clearly one of the heart. When they learn about Whizzo's upbringing, such as it were, and how it puts the lie to John Bradshaw's whole theory, they may feel betrayed.

Whizzo has no political axe to grind, and just wants everyone, including these gentle souls, to like him.

But then there's Charley Orange. The last person Charley needed in his life was Whizzo Mark Salot IV.

◆

The first inning was scoreless.

Second Inning

Baseball games are like snowflakes
and fingerprints; no two are the same.
—*W.P. Kinsella*

And the rivers shall bring forth frogs abundantly,
which shall go up and come into thine house,
and into thy bedchambers, and upon thy bed...
—*Exodus*

There is a much greater number of miracles, and natural secrets in the frog, than anyone hath ever before thought or discovered.
—Jon Swammadam, *The Book of Nature* (1669)

ACCORDING TO ONE version of time, it was the Holocene Era. Other calendars in faraway places set it at 2500 BC. While certain of the pyramids celebrated their second or even third millennium, that tinpot despot Yahweh was telling the Twelve Tribes He had created the world only 1,504 years ago, in between performing sleight-of-hand tricks for them like parting the Red Sea and hatching a bumper crop of frogs just a few years earlier that got labeled a plague. Here in ancient Egypt, it was nearing the end of the Fourth Dynasty. The four veiled figures making their way across the hot sands paid scant heed to these or any other human reckonings of time, for they had bigger fish to fry.

The quartet was none other than the deities Isis, Hepshupet, Khnum and—the little old wizened one who looked like a frog—Heqt, in the twilight of a distinguished career as a divinity. One of the primal forces who brought life into being, Heqt was a child star, becoming the frog-goddess when she was just a tad entrusted with the token task of embodying *hefnu,* the number 100,000 or an immense number. Serving her post well, she advanced with a splash to the post of Water Goddess. Always a moon deity, Heqt's big moment came when Isis chose her to midwife the birth of her son Horus, the sun. (Hence she and her cohorts today were unaffected by the scorching orb.) She had found her calling: from that day forth, eschewing beauty, she became the deity of birth, fertility and creation. It was a deep and powerful role to play, which sometimes taxed her to exhaustion, but she had the help and cooperation of a number of sister goddesses whose assignments overlapped hers.

◆◆

However, all that was long ago, in her youth, when Froggism and the Frog Look were In, when the true mythological power of the anurans prevailed. Already by the time of her task today, much of her reverence and many of her duties had been usurped by her sisters, including Isis and Hepshupet. This was to be her last hurrah. As Time spun out its shell and fixated into that chambered nautilus called history, the Greeks grew frightened of Heqt: she became Hekate, companion to Persephone, the queen of the Dead, with whom she ruled the Realm of Dark Places. The Greeks did acknowledge her ancient bond with Selene the Moon and, in admiration of her untamed spirit, linked her with Artemis the Huntress and Lady of the Wild Beasts.

Once the Christians got hold of her it was all over: they relegated her to the Resurrection, where she eventually morphed into an egg-laying rabbit.

The Christians also turned their own realm of the dead, called Hades, into a spinoff from Heqt: Heck. Heck was the most horrible afterlife imaginable: eternal flames, escapable only if you promised to have no fun in this life, and kept your promise.

As a being which Maxwell Veribushi and his ilk accredited with only 150 million years' longevity, when in fact she preceded the sun, Heqt cared no more for the humans' projections onto her than the humans cared whom they stepped on or how many children they orphaned when they snatched up one of her friends for dinner.

Anyway, at the time of Heqt's trek with Isis, Hepshupet and her lover Khnum, her ignominious end was still centuries down the pike; there was a dance in the old dame yet. While each of her two sisters outranked Heqt in any pantheon you might want to wormhole into, and Isis got much of the credit due her as a birth goddess (mostly by hanging out with her and bestowing her friendship upon her), when the baby's little eggplant head popped into the light of day, we know who would do the encouraging and guiding. When the placenta needed severing, we know who would bite it off. Neither Isis nor Hepshupet were versed in actually delivering children. Heqt had tried to interest them, but—well, the truth is, they seldom sullied their hands like that any more. They had paid their dues, helping Hathor the cow lift Horus into the sky and fending off snakes and other vermin from gods and humans alike. But now, in their maturity, they left the actual down-and-dirty to others. They called it delegating authority. They called it giving hands-on experience to a new generation. What it was was, simply, goddess nature. Isis especially was a lovely goddess, make no mistake: Heqt was very fond of her. She just couldn't figure how Isis had gotten the birthing reputation. Here she was from the solar system Sirius ABC: why wasn't she the goddess of the alphabet? Or, with the name Is-is, the goddess of Being?

Ah well. Heqt's not to reason why. Besides, she actually preferred performing the sacred act alone.

The foursome arrived at the humble house by the First Cataract of the Nile where tonight Heqt would deliver the next Pharaoh. Horus was bringing him into the world far from the temples and *khoreshes* of Shepseskaf, who claimed to speak for Horus, but who was inhabited by the Dark Forces.

On this night when Heqt was to perform her momentous task, had she any doubts or fears? Nay, none: after all, hadn't handy Khnum already formed the Pharaoh-to-be on his potter's wheel? Things would work out: it was in the cards.

Sending Isis and Hepshupet to boil some water, Heqt entered the trance state from which she performed her art. She saw the New Dynasty that would come to pass because she held the "Mother's Word of Power," the sacred *hakau*, in her trust.

To ooh's! and aah's! and shrieks of ecstasy from the two goddesses and the half-queen in exile, Khentkawes, who bore Ra's progeny, the future historical figure edged his way onstage. No sooner did his tiny toes wriggle through the wormhole than a mighty moan signaled a second head popping out! And a third! This fecundity rap Heqt had was getting out of hand. If she didn't find some way to cool it, before long women would be housing septuplets and birthing into their sixties. She scowled at Khnum, who had kept his potter's secret from her.

Khnum smiled in return. He knew what was needed. When the firstborn, Userkaf came of age, he and his brothers overthrew Shepseskaf and his minions and founded the Fifth Dynasty.

◆◆

A job well-done: blowing on her knuckles, Heqt slipped out the door and through the garden to the First Cataract, where she disrobed to dive into the water.

Some distant cousins of Ngaio's descendants, pouring out their nocturnal emissions at the First Cataract that night, were treated to an astonishing vision: an ungainly human form diving into the water, her useless noodle arms bulking out until they could support the weight of her torso and free her from walking upright; her pallid pink skin, as dull and textureless as a pyramid wall, turning into the gleaming jade and rich lunar landscape of a beautiful young frog as it did. Now, there was a creature to co-habit with. SKRIEK-EK-EK!

"What is so rare as a day in June?" asks the poet.

"A day in February," replies the pragmatist.

Nonetheless, it was one of those rare days in June when a warm, fresh breeze wafts the fragrance of the first massive outbursts of lilac and honeysuckle up the nostrils of amorous youth; when the rustling of apple-green fresh mimosa leaves plays backup to the caterwauling of love-sick mockingbirds; when the chirruping frogs are soaking their sacs in slime, resting up for their evening sonatas in the meadows and marshes; when your team, the Megaglopoulis Mutants, which the oddsmakers have installed as 5-4 favorites over the Lemon Sox to win the pennant, having suffered no major injuries, drug suspensions or other personnel losses, is mired in fifth place, 12 1/2 games behind the Sox.

Charley Orange was telling Bluster Hyman, the radio-TV voice of the Mutants, about Krup the frog. "I caught him at the lake my grandmother lived on when I was nine," he said. "I caught five of them and put them in a terrarium in the basement. I covered the top with glass and left a corner open so they could have air to breathe. The first night four of them escaped into the basement and I never saw them again."

"No kidding," said Bluster, clicking on his tape recorder. "I didn't know you were interested in frogs. Did they die?"

Beneath his few remaining hairs, Bluster's face, as usual, was as animated as granite. He didn't really care about the childhood herpetological misadventures of a second-string catcher, 39 years old and batting .129. Charley had already given the scribes his big story: At the end of the year he was hanging up his cleats. They'd milked it for all of two columns of print: his .238 lifetime batting average, his three years unofficially leading the league in Runners Caught Stealing percentage (he never played enough games to qualify for the title), his dramatic walk with the bases loaded to knock the Louseworts out of the pennant on the last day of his sophomore season, the pop fly he dropped that cost Bobo Burnett a no-hitter (Bluster questioned, unfairly, his quadridigital dexterity), his steadying influence on the young pitchers, his all-around knowledge of baseball. "He always sits next to Foo Foo McGonigle on the bench," Bluster concluded, "and some day he may be as good a manager as McGonigle." Piano Legs Knowland was leaving Tidewater after the season and Charley was thinking of feeling out Wellington P. Sweetwater about the position during the All-Star break.

"Sure they died," Charley said. "There wasn't any water in the basement. It was summer. It wasn't even damp."

"We all die," said Bluster.

"Krup lived," said Charley. "For seven years—Bluster, I can't believe you're taping this. It wouldn't make your high-school newspaper on an off-day. Wouldn't you rather be talking to Foo Foo?"

"It's true, Charley. Foo Foo's better copy than you are, and not just because of the way he talks. He's managing a team that's supposed to be leading the league and they're playing .500 ball."

Just then they heard a commotion, and there by the third-base line Charley saw Sweetwater's latest acquisition. Sticking out of a Mutants uniform—the same uniform, Charley thought ruefully, as he wore—sans the cap, which he was bowing to the players around him, were the reddest red hair and the most shockingly blue eyes he had ever seen.

◆◆

"Hoddy ladies and gentlemen," their owner bellowed, in an Arkansas drawl thicker than Rosie O'Donnell's waist. ""Ah'm here to help y'all win the pennant! Ah'm here! Oh mah God, Ah'm here! A'm here! Ah'm here!"

He tossed his hat into the air and turned a full cartwheel. "Last week Ah pitched mah last hagh-school shutout, and bah this tahme next week Ah'll have me one or two in the Big Tahme! YA-HA!"

"This one must be Foo Foo's grandson," said Bluster. "Will you introduce me?"

"I haven't had the pleasure myself."

Ten seconds later they both had. Whizzo Mark Salot IV spied Bluster's tape recorder, ran over and slid into his feet. "Out!" he cried.

Then he spotted Charley and forgot about Bluster. "Nailed bah Charley Awrnge, the best throw to second in the league. Slap mah hand, hero man." He gave Charley a high-five. "You look just lahke your baseball card. 'Threw out fahve runners in one game, against the Mudhens, that was six years ago August, raght? Hey, we're gonna have us some fun with them Mudhens. Ah got me a pickoff motion..."

"Whizzo Mark Salot IV, this is Bluster Hyman, the voice of the Mutants and the Rolls-Royce of sportscasters."

"Bluster. Shake hands with the Lamborghini of pitchers. What y'all talking about, anyway?"

"Frogs."

"Frogs? Hey, when Ah was about nahne, ten years old me and mah buddy Arol, we caught us a bullfrog in the County Ditch in Disfunction Junction, Arkansas, with its leg was all tahd up with some real thick string lahke rope. We trahd and we trahd but we couldn't undo that knot. Fahnally we took that frog raght across the street into the po-lice station.

"Well sir, old Sergeant Kowalski, he comes over to the counter and says to us, 'What y'all kids doing bringing that frog in here'?

"'We want to report it to the ASPCA!' Ah says. 'This here frog's been mistreated. Looky that rope on his leg.'

"'Y'all can't report that to the ASPCA,' says Sergeant Kowalski.

"'No? Whah not?"

"'The ASPCA,' he says, 'that stands for the American Society of Prevention of Cruelty to Animals.'

"'*For* prevention. We know.'

"'Well, thass not an animal,' says Kowalski. 'Thass a frog. Now get it off'n mah counter.'"

Bluster laughed dutifully. "So then what did you do?"

"We took that frog home to mah daddy, and Ah told mah daddy all that happened, and about how we wanted to file a report with the ASPCA.

"'Well, but y'all can't do that,' says mah daddy.

"'Whah not?' Ah ask him.

''Because thass not an animal,' says mah daddy. "Thass a frog.'

"But then mah stepmama came in and she said it was so an animal, and she and mah daddy argued for a spell, but meantime she got herself the butcher knahfe from the kitchen and she cut the string off'n that frog's leg herself. And Arol and me, we got all the kids in the neighborhood together and took it back to the County Ditch and had us a big ceremony and released it back.

"Good story, kid," said Bluster. "Now tell me: how many games do you think you can win?"

Curve ball; Whizzo swung wildly. "Ever' game they let me pitch. Ah'm the non-parallel of pitchers. Ah'm the cream in your coffee, Ah'm the sweet mango flavor of your tea. Ah can throw a ball over a dahme ever' tahme at 60 feet 6 and give you nahne cents change. When Ah toss mah Sweet Patootie up there, look out Sammy Sosa! Look out Manny Ramirez! Look out A-Rod!"

Way to go, kid, thought Charley. Three minutes in the Bigs and already you've got the three top sluggers in the league gunning for you—and the Mutants. "Ah'll aim it behahnd yo'ear, Sammy, and whahle you're dahving down in the dirt, hit'll roll knee-hagh over the outsahde corner lahke it just fell off'n your dahning room table. Ramirez, Ah can throw Big Peter up at you and have the return throw from Charley Awrnge, the best backup catcher in baseball, back here in mah glove before you get your sweet lumber over that there plate. Mr. Sweetwater, you watch your grandstand: hit may be empty now but when ol' Whizzo starts a game, hit'll be standing-room only in the bleachers."

"Pardon me, gentlemen," Charley said. "I've gotta find Foo Foo."

"Hang with me one second, Charley. Now don't get mah boasting wrong; Ah'm just telling it like it is. But actually Ah'm overwhelmed to be up here. To get to pitch against mah heroes—Sosa, Ramirez, Rodrigues—and to have mah heroes on the field supporting me—Malone, Moseley, Throttlemeyer, Charley Ahrnge. Charley, you remember that game against the Mudhens in Julah about 6-7 years ago, second game of a doubleheader, tah score in the nahnth, heart of the order coming up, and you picked Hasta Luego off'n first base and saved a run?"

"Yeah," said Charley, surprised. "We won in 12."

"That was the first game Ah ever saw," said Whizzo. "We didn't have no TV at all in Disfunction Junction, Arkansas till the year Ah was born and mah daddy was too poor to ever bah us one, but Ah saw that game over to Sammy Lee Ashby's house and her mommy and daddy was at work, and raght after you throwed out Luego, Ah put mah finger in Sammy Lee's panties. Ah thanked you then and Ah thank you now for getting Sammy Lee so excahted that she didn't push me away. That was the first tahme Ah ever did that, too. Hey, that was a day of firsts. You remember what the date of that was, Charley?"

"Nope. Listen, I gotta go find Foo Foo."

Now, baseball is a staid sport, a dignified sport, the National Pastime, where gentleman shortstops throw bullets on hard one-hoppers lest their opponents tire themselves sprinting unnecessarily quickly to first base, where in Japan the two teams bow to each other before the start of a contest, where the players view each other as members of an august body. If there is a congress of frogs, a parliament of whores, a confederation of dunces, then baseball is the senate of sports. The players take their profession seriously. Unlike their fans, they don't appreciate hot dogs.

With no player was this more true than with Charley Orange, who, despite Whizzo's knowledge and appreciation of a highlight of his mediocre career, had been upstaged with Bluster Hyman.

Charley excused himself because he felt unexpected rage at Whizzo for violating baseball's unwritten code of demeanor, especially rookie demeanor. Had he stuck around, he would have heard Whizzo saying he took no personal credit for his talent: it was all given to him by God. All Whizzo needed to get away with his big mouth was the talent to back it up: a tall order.

Anyway, Charley knew he was overreacting. Was it Bluster? Was he feeling his years, smarting at being passed by for new blood? No, Whizzo was a new face in midseason, direct from high school, clearly more newsworthy anytime than Charley's amphibious reminiscences.

What it was, was Whizzo's finger in Sammy Lee Ashby's panties. Whizzo had introduced sex into Charley's universe of discourse—sex, a subject Charley could barely tolerate on his best days, and most certainly not on one of the many days after he had quarreled with yet another member of the distaff gender.

We are about to talk more baseball. Rest assured, members of the fair sex, you who have been ridiculed for thinking a pitcher holds water and a batter makes pancakes; we shall not bore you with too many details of the game. (Charley Orange will do enough of that.) But you do know, we trust, what a *league* is: a group of teams that play each other to determine which is best.

And men, it's time to introduce a term which may leave you a little uncomfortable: *hot stove.* You know, that thing in the kitchen that a woman labors over all day? Not a guy thing, you will agree; not a subject for rough-and-tumble bearded types like yourselves to dwell upon.

Exists there a term, then, more oxymoronic than "Hot Stove League"? But exist it does, and it describes a concept as uniquely American and idiomatically indecipherable from outside the in-crowd as "pork barrel legislation" or "cracker barrel philosophy."

The Hot Stove League season doesn't open until after the American and National Leagues conclude formalities in October. Unlike those august bodies, which employ only 400 each of the most talented ballplayers in Latin America, the Hot Stove League is come-one, come-all: anyone who wants to sit around the old woodstove on a cracker barrel and philosophize on the season or seasons past is welcome.

In the Hot Stove League, Whizzo Mark Salot IV's major-league debut against the Oystercatchers is still a venerable item of conversation.

"In the first inning Whizzo walks the first three batters on 12 pitches," says Bobby Bumpo, a superannuated teenager who buys and sells baseball cards for a living. "Up comes the fearful, the mighty Sam "The Slam" Salazar, who hit 47 round-trippers the year before. Whizzo starts yelling at Salazar. 'Hey Slam, Ah seen you take Lahghtnin' Larrabee downtown a mahle on national TV, so Ah loaded 'em up just to get at you'!"

After the third walk Charley Orange, sitting next to Foo Foo McGonigle on the bench, saw Foo Foo squinch up his bristlecone-pine face and wave the regular catcher, Horst Throttlemeyer, 12 years Charley's junior and batting exactly 200 points higher, to the mound to settle Whizzo down.

"It's all raght," Whizzo told Throttlemeyer. "That ump's doin' a good job. Ah'm just getting his strahke zone down."

"Then Whizzo holds the ball up to his face," says Bobby's best friend Mickey McDoodley, who at age 11 must have heard the story from Bobby because he wasn't in this universe when it happened, "and starts talking to it.

"Then he holds the ball to his ear, like he's listening to it answer back."

"Then he strikes out Sam 'The Slam' and the next two batters on nine pitches," says Bobby, who is not about to relinquish his choicest Hot Stove League lines to any 11-year-old, even if this one is his best friend.

Since everyone in the Hot Stove League knows this story by heart, we may wonder how Bobby and Mickey's audience is holding up under this, their 400th rendition of Whizzo's debut. Well madam, well sir, the audience, consisting solely of Bobby and Mickey, is as excited as if the whiffs are whistling past their very ears.

"Then Whizzo does the same thing in the second and third innings—walks the bases full and then strikes out the side," says Bobby.

During the third third-inning walk, Charley Orange heard Foo Foo McGonigle grunt (Ball 1), clear his throat (Ball 2) and curse his Creator (Ball 3). On Ball 4 Foo Foo heaved his aging body off the bench and hobbled out to the mound to confer with his errant phenom.

"Young fella, you're diggin' yourself into quite a graveyard for us all," Foo Foo said.

"Hit's all raght, Mr. McGonigle. These clowns jist ain't swinging at mah bad pitches," Whizzo told him. "Ah never throwed at nobody didn't chase mah Sweet Patooties up over his ears and Uncle Scrooge down into the dirt. Ah'm jist goin' far as Ah can with these jokers 'fore Ah have to start bitin' off a piece of the plate."

"You got eight teammates standin' around out there with their eyes in their pockets," said Foo Foo. "You come on down the pike with it."

"Then in the fourth inning," says Bobby, "after Whizzo walks the first two batters, he starts waving at the stands. This beautiful blonde lady with a red flower in her hair waves back. After that Whizzo settles down, pitches a 5-hit shutout with 11 walks and 13 strikeouts, and at the end he holds up the baseball and gives it a big soulful kiss like it was Madonna."

The talking heads had a field day: baseball is, as already indicated, a staid sport, and whenever anyone comes along who sticks out of his uniform even an inch, joy bubbleth over in the media.

Whizzo and Foo Foo McGonigle were Bluster Hyman's guests on the postgame TV show. "From high school to the big leagues, Whizzo. Were you nervous?"

"Ah waren't nervous, but they got a lot of hits off'n me once Ah commenced puttin' it over, so maybe Ah was nervous without, y'all know, bein' nervous about it."

"Foo Foo, what do you think of this kid? Are you proud?"

Foo Foo patted Whizzo's backside. "This is a young man coming to us from the sandlots of high school pitching, and so we might expect it of this fellow from Texas got all those strikeouts or that Jewish boy threw all the no-hitters for the Brooklyns before the West Coast ever came to exist. But to step out of that Junction City-whereveryoumaycallit with his riser climbs the steps all those every different whichaways—and this young man is my starting pitcher, mark my words."

"When he was wild early, did you think about taking him out?"

"Well," said Foo Foo, rubbing his Carlsbad Canyon jaw, "my spot man is coming off of throwing two innings of spotless baseball the last night before what with my other fellas needing a night off and a man can't be perfect forever, leastaways when his arm's tired, so with all their muscles due to the plate it would have gone contrary to the odds with my lefty on the mound and with three up on them across we wanted to see what the stuff was the kid was made up out of out there, and there was the time for it."

"Thank you Foo Foo McGonigle," said Bluster. "Whizzo, what do you say to the ball when you talk to it?"

"Different things, Bluster. Today Ah was tellin' it hit's jist a little bitty old ball, and there's a man with a big club up there wantin' to bash it hard as he can, and where and how does it think Ah ought to throw it so's that won't happen to it?"

"And then when you hold the ball up to your ear—it answers you?"

"Does a hound dog at a fahre hahdrant answer Nature's call? You know when they was two on in the eighth and Ah had Hahlemahle at 3-2? Hit told me to throw him Sweet Patootie, and Sweet Patootie struck him out."

"How about your catcher's signals? Does the ball calling pitches cause any problem with the two of you?"

"Nah. Throttlemeyer knows them hitters and he calls a great game. But look at it this way: If you're standin' on the street and a Mack truck's about to run you over, and someone on the sahdewalk yells, 'Jump left!' and you want to jump raght, which way are you going to jump? Raght, raght? As much as Throttlemeyer knows about a batter's weaknesses, as much as Ah know, we ain't in the lahne of fahre."

"Got it, Whizzo. What were you thinking about in the seventh inning when you had two runners on and only one out?"

The cobalt sparkle in Whizzo's eyes revved up a notch. "Well, they was this delaghtful creature sittin' behahnd third base with a flower in her hair, and Ah took another look over at her, and she had the most pleadingest smahle on her face, Ah just knowed Ah couldn't let her down."

"One last question, Whizzo. Do you think the Mutants still have a shot at the flag?"

Media Lesson Number One for ballplayers: Be Humble. All kudos belong to the team. If you have just hit a ninth-inning homer to win the game, pass the laurels to the relief pitcher, who kept the opposition from scoring and allowed you to bat. Praise the great catch by the shortstop that prevented the winning run.

If you have just pitched a shutout, as Whizzo has today, pay homage to your hitters who knocked in the runs that brought you the victory. Yes, you may acknowledge, your screwball was sharp today, but you really won because of the game your catcher called, the diving outfield catch and a bit of Lady Luck.

"No question we'll win," said Whizzo. "Ah'm the nonparallel, Ah'm a credit to mah race, Ah throw lickety-split and them batters can't get their licks, Ah am the way and the laght and the screwball in the dirt. And with mah teammates behahnd me catchin' balls and scorin' runs, the Mutants are gonna take all the marbles."

These foul and loathsome animals are...abhorrent because of their cold bodies, pale color, cartilaginous skeletons, filthy skin, fierce aspect, calculating eye, offensive smell, harsh voice, squalid habitation and terrible venom.

—Linnaeus

Ngaio CLM sat on the bank of the stream admiring himself in the water's reflection. The faint wrinkles from an eddy added a rippling effect to his smooth skin, making him look very old and wise. He liked that, although he was but 60 moons into this lifetime: 35 years by *rib'et!* reckoning.

Ah, what a night he had had last night! *Two* of the fattest-lipped, egg-whitest-torsoed, webbiest-clawed, tendrillist-toed, slime-swimmingest, guttural-burpingest young lovelies—how come all those tadbabies still went for old Papa Ngaio, anyway? Ngaio thought he knew, but he wasn't talking.

One thing it wasn't, though.

It wasn't his tenderness, his open heart, or his particular way of making any of his partners feel safe. No, it was more his...well, his *frogness*. He had a quality about him that was to frog as egg was to nog, jig was to jog, and there was no better way to describe it. "If you gotta ask," he thought, his mouth widening into an ear-to-ear smirk, "you ain't never gonna know."

Suddenly his gloating was shattered by a sound like a tribeful of tom-toms preparing for a frogleg feast.

Jug-o-RUM! Jug-o-RUM!

Ngaio CLM clasped his hands over his ears. This caused him to tumble over into the water, below the surface of which he kept his ears while allowing his big brown eyes to bob up like two Bette Davis balloons. On the Richter scale of fear, he had just experienced the Big One. But then, he reasoned philosophically, if it's time to leave this lifetime—well, what better time to move along to the next station than after last night? (Ngaio, like most frogs, was a Reincarnationist—wouldn't you be if you were an amphibian?— though tadpoles, being vegetarians in their own eating habits and popular fast-food items in those of many of their fellow pond dwellers, lean toward a godless world of Eat and Run.)

Jug-o-RUM! The very mud under Ngaio's feet vibrated with the thunderous sound. Then a shadow crossed the full moon—a flying spadefoot. Attached to it was a frog the size of a muskrat—no, a skunk, a raccoon— sailing over Ngaio's head like a bloated heron, and landing—ker-SPLASH!—within feet of him.

Jug-o-RUM! The message was loud and clear to Ngaio CLM: This is my pond! Jug-o-RUM! I am its king! Jug-o-RUM! Don't mess with me! Jug-o-RUM! Out of my way!

Now, there's only one member of the *Rana* clan crude enough to rhapsodize about Demon Rum, and that's that tropical invader, the bullfrog. It's the original big frog in a small pond, and suddenly it was showing up everywhere, belching out its onomatopoetic *basso profundo* and biting off the heads of any *Rana oncas* who got in its way.

◆ ◆ ◆ ◆

"Hey Charley Awrnge!" Whizzo Mark Salot IV shouted to Charley in the locker room after the victory. "You wanna partake of some vittles and cocktails with me and help me celebrate?"

Charley felt uncomfortable around the kid, but he was impressed with his pitching savvy. He wouldn't mind talking baseball with him.

"Where we gonna go for cocktails, baby-face? You gotta be 21."

"Thass whah Ah invahted you, grampa. Somebody's gotta bah mah drinks for me."

After stopping at the grocery store (he ate breakfast at home), Charley took Whizzo to Let Them Eat Vichyssoise. The menu stumped Whizzo. "Hey, what is this stuff, anyway, Charley? Chahnese?"

"French."

"You order for me. Burger and frahs."

"Is this why you asked me to dinner, kid?"

"Ah told you. Ah hain't 21. Ah need you to buy me drinks."

"You're drinking mineral water."

"Thass sure as shittin'. Me and Ellsworth Spail, we got into some of that moonshahne his daddy used to brew one naght when Ah was 11 and Ah hain't never touched ol' Demon Rum since."

"You threw a good game."

"Yeah, except for Thunderghioch's two-bagger."

"What happened on that? I'd have called for Big Peter, but whatever you threw went straight over the heart of the plate."

"It was Big Peter, all right. Horst called for it too, but Ah got to thinkin' on ol' Bugs Bundy on first mebbe goin' for second and Ah screwed up mah release."

◆◆

"You aren't the first pitcher Bugsy's screwed up. Once in awhile you can catch him leaning. I'll teach you a special counting method for him. We got him with it twice last year."

"You will? You probably don't believe me, Charley Awrnge, but you really are one of mah heroes."

"You're right, I don't."

"Now, whah would Ah put you on about a thing lahke that?"

"To set me up. What do you want from me, Whizzo?"

"Whoa back. Too fast. Listen, Ah lahke lots of second-string catchers. You gahs stay up here in The Show on guts and brains, because y'all know how to call a game better than anyone else. Now yes, Ah want something from you and yes, you are one of mah heroes, and Ah wouldn't want this from you if'n Ah didn't respect you."

"OK kid, you got my ear."

"All raght. Throttlemeyer didn't call no pickoffs with Bundy on first. He called for Uncle Scrooge twahce. Ah think he was lettin' Bundy go because we was two up."

"He might have wanted to make sure you concentrated on Thunderghioch at the plate."

"Look what happened. They shoulda scored. Listen Charley, Ah picked me off 47 runners in hagh school, an all-tahme hagh-school record as far as anyone can determine. Ah can hold a runner on first with the best of them. Now Ah know Ah'm getting a reputation already as a big-mouth rookie, but Ah hain't a badmouth, 'specially about mah own teammates.

"OK, sixth inning, Ah start predicting every pitch Throttlemeyer calls. Ah figure, so can the batter, so Ah have to shake him off. Well, ever' time Ah do, he calls for the same pitch again."

"He doesn't appreciate being shaken off by a hotshot rookie."

"No sir. So how do Ah talk to him and get him to listen to me?"

"You don't. You just earn his respect and don't shake him off for a few games."

"How do Ah earn his respect? Turn 29 tomorrow?"

"You're doing it. Keep pitching like you did today. Just don't shake him off for a few games."

"When am Ah going to get you catching me, Charley?"

"I'll be getting in some playing time after the next series with the Lemon Sox. Horst'll get some rest with the lesser series coming up after that, and I think my bat's starting to warm up, too."

"Well, Ah sure hope—hey Charley, we're in business! —Oops, Ah mean pleasure. Don't turn around, Charley, because if'n you do, your tongue will drop dead raght out of your mouth. Now listen here, Ah'm 18 and you are 39, and these two little fillies are mid-to-upper 20's, raght there in between us. Let me ax you a personal question, Charley, about breast sahze. Is your preference for little bitty teacups where it's fun to tickle the nipples till they stand up and salute the flag, or do you like them big ol' melons you can bury your head in and stick the nipples raght insahde your ears?"

"Breasts?" asked Charley. "Are those those things that make women's chests stick out beneath their clothes? I've been wondering what's under there."

"Reason Ah axed is because Ah lahke them both ways. Ah've kept me so filled up with all sahzes lately, Ah'm happy with anything. So it's your choice."

"Whizzo, it's been so long, I'll settle for cucumbers. Let's just play it by ear."

"Oh no, no, no, we cain't do that. Listen, once we plunk ourselves down alongsahde these two sweethearts, we need to already know who's going for who. Makes a gal feel like you zeroed raght in on her, she's the only one you want."

"What if I don't have much to say to her and I do to the other one?"

"Say? Charley, Charley, we're not thinking dahapers and picket fences here. We're thinking the horizontal macarena, pure and simple."

Hold it! Stop right here! Ladies: Are you listening to these gentlemen (and I use the term loosely) talk? Here *King of Diamonds* has promised you loving, caring male characters and they sound just like all the others, right? They all want just one thing, right? How would they like it if someone talked about their sister that way? Their mother? And how do you feel about this gross reduction of one half of the human race to objects of carnal desire by the other half? Is it the fate of the female to be trapped in shared specieshood with a creature under the total dominion of one small portion of its anatomy with a brainless head and a blind eye?

In defense of Charley Orange and Whizzo Mark Salot IV, someone undoubtedly did talk about their mothers that way, or they wouldn't be here befouling these pages with their pottymouths. What's more, they received no education from these same mothers as to how to revere the opposite sex. From their fathers and their male friends they learned that the only way to feel good with a woman is to be inside her. All they really want is to love and be loved, but they have been taught that the only test of whether a woman loves them is, Will she let them slide their Nebuchadnezzer inside her magic portals? They deduced on their own that love is something that is made during those moments inside her: "making love." They learned to appreciate touch only as a preamble to sex. They learned that a woman who touches them and doesn't let them enter her gates is a tease.

In defense of Charley's and Whizzo's mothers, both of them learned from their mothers that outside of the context of marriage, the carnal desires that constantly tempted and tormented them were planted in their bodies by Satan for the sole purpose of luring them away from their promised afterworld of Hagen Daaz and Chanel #5 forever into His grim barbeque of roasted souls. They learned from their first boyfriends that touching anything male was like pressing a button labeled Fornication, so they stopped touching.

Now here's another fine mess Yahweh has gotten us into! All Whizzo and Charley want is love, yet all they talk about is sex. The women they meet have sexual appetites that could devour armies, yet all they talk about is love. Can we have a translator, please?

The blonde gave Whizzo a big smile as they approached; the redhead looked warily at Charley. "Howdy, ladies!" Whizzo beamed. "Mah name's Whizzo Mark Salot IV and this here's Charley Awrnge from the Megaglopoulis Mutants. Can we buy y'all drinks?"

"I'm Bambi." The blonde's teeth matched Whizzo's. "I'm married."

Whizzo didn't miss a beat. "Do you lahke to fool around?"

"What did you say?"

"Ah didn't say that."

"Well, who did?"

"That was Mr. Twister, Ma'am."

"You're cute, but you're too weird for me."

"Sorry, ma'am." Whizzo bowed. "It's been a pleasure."

Charley, involved in a tentative conversation with…(what was her name? He hadn't even asked her name), half-rose to join him.

"Wait," Bambi called to Whizzo. "You are sort of cute."

"But y'all are married."

"I thought true Southerners only used 'y'all' in the plural sense."

"Well, Ah'm not a true Southerner at all. Ah'm just a pack of lahs."

"Tell me one. Tell me a lie."

"Ah'd love to make love to you."

"That's a lie? Why don't you want to make love to me?"

"Because you're married."

"Maybe I like to fool around."

"Well. Ah'm exhausted jist getting to Maybe."

The redhead didn't look overly friendly to Charley, but there was no one else to talk to. "What's your name?" he asked.

"Melanie. I thought you'd never ask."

"Charley. You could have asked me mine."

"Your friend introduced you, remember?

She still wasn't smiling, but her cleavage was beckoning: it would feel nice to press against that. "Would you like to dance, Melanie?"

"OK. Buy me a drink?"

Another whore, thought Charley. No, not a whore whore, but doing the whore thing all right, trading pleasure for money.

"No."

"*Pobrecito.*" Bambi ran her fingers through Whizzo's hair. "I'm sorry to exhaust you. We better dance and wake you up."

Whizzo sprang to his feet. "Twister says he's wahde awake now."

"Twister…Mr. Twister?"

"Mr. Twister hisself. Mah talking penis."

"A man with a talking penis. Tell me, what does…Mr. Twister talk about?"

◆◆

"Girls, ma'am. All he ever talks about is the ladies. Gets me into a whole mess of trouble sometahmes. Ah'll meet me a lady, and Ah know in mah head she ain't raght for me, but ol' Twister here, he jist jumps bolt upraght and takes off, and Ah got to race to keep up."

Melanie blinked at Charley. "You really won't buy me a drink?"

"Listen to yourself! I'm not your money tree."

"Oh hell. Wait here." She went to the bar, returned with a gin and tonic, took a gulp and led him onto the dance floor. Pushing him back to ease his grip on her, she asked, "Are you really a Mutant?"

Charley released her and held up his quadridigital hand. "In more ways than one."

"Oh! That's weird," she said.

"In two ways." He held up the other hand. She looked away.

Next to Charley and Melanie, pelvic space between Whizzo and Bambi was at a premium. "You think Mr. Twister is getting you in trouble right now?" Bambi asked.

Whizzo smiled. "Ah don't remember thinking none of them dangerous thoughts about you. But Twister also has strange powers. He has the power to steal mah memory raght out of mah brain, cut it off till the morning. But speaking jist for me, Ah'd say Ah don't see any downsahde to you, except for you're married, so Ah dasn't fall in love with you."

"Speaking just for you! I saw Mr. Twister sticking his head out the top of your trousers and saying those very words! I think he's a ventriloquist and you're just his dummy."

"Out mah trouser tops…bah Golly, he's been a-growing, jist lahke ol' Pinocchio's nose! There, you see, Ah must have done told you a lah, jist lahke you axed me to."

"You silly man, you." She kissed him on the cheek. "What does Mr. Twister have to say about me?"

"He says it's too bad you're married."

"Who says I'm married?"

"You said that your own self."

"You believe everything a stranger tells you in a bar?"

"YA-HA! Twister says, let's you and me get out of here.—Hey, but first Ah gotta check in here on mah pal Charley Awrnge. How y'all doin' , lovers?"

"We're hanging in there."

"OK if'n we leave you two to go rahde the rockin' horse together?"

"Hasta luego, hotshot."

"*Arriba! Arribaderci,* lady and gentleman. We'll be expecting y'all at Penis and Vagahna streets come midnaght."

"I still can't believe you wouldn't buy me a drink," Melanie said when they left. "You're not very generous, are you?"

Starting in on me, Charley thought. I've heard this before. "I feel like I'm being used," he said.

"You could at least sleep with me tonight. That is, if you wouldn't feel used."

For a moment Charley's breath stopped, but he kept the excitement out of his voice. "OK." Had his ears deceived him? How long had it been? Two years?

As they drove to her house, Charley explained the Baseball Mind to her. "Ask any kid in New York who were the three Brooklyn baserunners who wound up on third base at the same time and they can tell you," he said.

Melanie reached over and rested her hand on his thigh. Charley flashed back to the dance floor. He could still feel her warm, firm, round melons pressed against him. "It's a classical example," he continued. "This incident happened back in 1926 and occupied maybe five or ten seconds, and it's still a part of baseball lore, known by millions of fans, none of whom ever saw it."

"I don't get it," Melanie said. "Why should anyone care about such a trivial incident that happened before they were born? I don't even know, or care, who won today's game." Charley envisioned her unbuttoning her blouse and him watching those gorgeous globes burst into freedom, knobs first, only to be devoured by his mouth.

Once inside the house, Charley jumped straight into bed. Melanie jumped straight into the bathroom.

Charley lay with his eyes closed, feeling his hammer growing hard just thinking about what was to come. Melanie flicked out the lights and climbed in beside him. Charley calculated where breast level would be, reached over and squeezed. He got only an arm—an arm covered with cloth. His hand explored down—back—forth—"Flannel pyjamas?"

"What do you think you're doing?" The frost spread over those twin pumpkins of his dreams. "I said *sleep.*" She removed his arm and turned away.

Needles shot from somewhere in Charley's stomach, pricking him from head to toe through every pore in his skin. He didn't have to take that. He could get up and go home.—But no, he couldn't face that.

Eventually the pain receded into green bubbles streaming upward from his body. He closed his eyes. Maybe she'd feel different in the morning.

Come 9:30 a.m., Melanie was still feigning sleep. Charley let himself out quietly. He left a cantaloupe from the grocery, softening now to the accompaniment of humming flywings, on her doorstep along with his card. "Not generous, huh?" he thought. "Eat this."

The 1830's: The first covered wagons arrive in the Rockies, carrying fur trappers. Nat Turner and 70 followers go on a rampage, striking fear into the hearts of good Church-going plantation massuhs throughout the South, until Nat is terminated. In the North, white slaves begin digging the Erie Canal. Senator William Marcy coins the phrase, "To the victor goes the spoils."

Following the Indian Removal Act of 1830, President Andrew "Long Knife" Jackson forms the Bureau of Indian Affairs, as part of the War Department. Four thousand dispossessed Cherokees perish along the "Trail of Tears." Meanwhile, back in Massachusetts, anti-Catholics burn the Ursuline convent. Samuel Colt patents the revolver. Henry Clay coins the phrase, "The self-made man."

The American Temperance Union, the first corporations and the Transcendental Club are all founded; Emerson orates on "The American Scholar," even as dinosaur tracks are found in nearby Connecticut Valley. Chloroform is discovered; matches and the telegraph are invented. John Deere designs a steel plow.

The Battle of the Alamo is fought; Texas joins the Union. So do Arkansas and Michigan. Across the pond, Napoleon is exiled and Charles Dickens breaks into print.

In 1836, 29 years before Mark Twain's famous story, Ebeneezer Kowhat's bullfrog wins the first *rib'et!*-sponsored frog-jumping contest, an unheralded event, with a jump of only 8 inches, which it undertakes in order to eat its lone opponent.

The Panic of 1837 shuffles everyone's position on the Monopoly board. E.C. Booz begins bottling whiskey in log cabin-shaped containers. Alexis Charles Henri Clerel de Tocqueville tours the nation and chronicles all of the above and more in *Democracy in America*.

de Tocqueville doesn't mention that it is a rainy decade and in Mosquito Marsh, the frogs rejoice.

Or that Abner Doubleday, inspired by an afternoon in Farmer Phinney's pasture, sits tinkering in his basement workshop, inventing the game of baseball.

Was Doubleday, like so many inventors, unkempt in his surroundings? If so, he might have used a dirty plate for home base, even as youngsters on sandlots sometimes use an old paper plate today. (Baseball, incidentally, is no more played on a sandlot than football on a gridiron or any other cooking utensil. A batted ball will not bounce on sand, and running over sand is like slogging through the 2.64 surface gravity of Jupiter.)

A close look at the language of the game may give us clues to other items Doubleday used for bases. Since only home base is known as the "plate," the other bases, since they are called bases, might have been other items stashed in his basement. For second base, the "keystone sack," maybe Doubleday worked for an architect in his regular life and liberated the *voussoir* for his noble task. For third base, the "hot corner," perhaps an item of Mrs. Doubleday's underwear.

◆◆

What for the ball? Eggs from the henhouse? No, Mrs. Doubleday would never allow that. Would she let him use a roll of her yarn? Like countless other wives and mothers after her, she probably became nervous when *anything* was thrown about the house. For a bat: the treadle on Mrs. D's loom. Mrs. Doubleday is becoming quite perturbed: little can she imagine the future glory that awaits her husband—soon to be her ex-husband if he doesn't get that eggstain off her just-washed underwear RIGHT NOW!

Parallel universes dispel the old notion of a single vast everywhere forever as a closed system. It's true: sometimes things slip through the bleed. In a nearby universe, Doubleday is widely credited with inventing baseball in Cooperstown, New York in 1839—95 years after the appearance of an English woodcut called "base-ball," 41 years after the heroine in Jane Austen's *Northanger Abbey* played baseball as a child, four years after the first publication about the game, and during the time that Doubleday was a West Point cadet and confined to campus. (This is the same universe where most of the inhabitants multiply by dividing, where they label the smallest consumer packages Extra Large, where they invented computers to make life easier and where they wage war to make peace.)

Well folks, it didn't happen that way, in that universe or this: Abner Doubleday did play baseball, but he invented it only in a myth fabricated by a friend who headed a commission—a sort of Warren Commission of its day. Mrs. Doubleday didn't dream it up either, as certain feminist quarters proclaim; nor did the Russians, as *Pravda* once insisted, or the Olmecs in Mexico, who settled their disputes in a most civilized fashion by playing a ball game that more resembled soccer than baseball. Some even hold that, like acupuncture, baseball was a gift to humankind from a parallel universe, because surely human ingenuity could never create anything so miraculous.

This hypothesis makes sense when you look at the rules of the game, which betray a staggering unfamiliarity with what constitutes human athletic prowess.

In what other sport, when the batter succeeds in hitting the ball, will he be out two times in three, whereas if he misses it completely, he will get two more chances?

Where else can a batter hit the ball 400 feet and be charged with a strike if it goes outside the foul pole, whereas if he tops a slow roller 40 feet down the baseline he will likely get a base hit?

What other human endeavor allows a batter to miss three balls entirely, the last of which hits the dirt in front of the plate, and reach first base when the ball bounces past the catcher to the backstop, while the next batter hits the first pitch on the nose and lines into a double play? In what bizarre contest must a starting pitcher go five innings just to be eligible for a win while a reliever can come in with a three-run lead, face one batter and be credited with a save?

In what mad universe can a starting pitcher get two outs in an inning and walk the third batter, while his reliever faces one man, gives up a triple, and the run scored is charged to the starter?

In what perverse strategic arena does the cleanup hitter wind up leading off the second inning 1,016 times as often as hitting a grand slam in the first?

What strange and unimaginable creatures would dream up a game where a batter can hit a home run but be called out if he misses a base during the formality of circling the infield? Their universe must have been created by a triple Virgo.

Like the towers of Ozymandius and the birth of the blues, baseball's origins are buried in the sands of time, although those sands may lay scarce more than a century deep.

If we can't even trace the dawning of the national pastime back less than 200 years, how in the world can we be expected to know Who and/or What S/HeIt is and whether we were created or evolved? Perhaps *we* are the gift from the space siblings to the cockroaches and mosquitoes of the world so they will have a constant food supply, or to the cats so they will have laps to curl up in. Remember, the everywheres forevers are not only queerer than we imagine, they're queerer than we *can* imagine.

◆◆

Charley Orange felt like a Californian who had taken one too many narcissism workshops, but he forced himself for probably the 1,000th time to stand in front of the mirror.

"Look at you, guy," he told himself. Or was it himself telling him? The mirror answered back as fast as he spoke. "You're a major league baseball player—one of the most sexually desirable occupations in the world.

"You make six figures per season. True, this is the last of your big salary years, but you've invested well.

"Your big, strong body exudes the kind of protective feeling women crave." It was so: Charley stood 6 feet 2 inches and his 220-pound body, while having a somewhat rounded appearance, was well-muscled and strained at his untailored tweeds.

"You're young. Only 39. Desirable to any woman over 30. You're irresistibly handsome." Charley's big, beefy face was both round and long and droopy, widest at the bottom: it seemed to be as much chin as all the rest combined. His dark hair was thinning. The smile was gone from his gray eyes. He didn't believe he was irresistibly handsome, but Dr. Weisenheimer told him to keep saying it anyway and one day he would. He didn't see himself as the Phantom of the Opera either, and he didn't hustle the Super-10's that Whizzo and the other guys went for. Could looks be his problem? He didn't think so.

"Your mind is as sharp as a tack." No question there. He was graduated *cum laude* from college, and there are no stupid catchers.

"Your smile is irresistible." Not tonight, guy. 'Not tonight'...Hmm—that's what she said. For probably the 1,000th time he asked himself: What's wrong with this picture?

He didn't have a clue.

But soon, he thought, he might. From inside his lapel he removed a miniature tape recorder and rewound it.

Melody: You just don't turn me on, Charley.

Charley: Why not?

"It's nothing personal. I'm sure a lot of other women would be attracted."

"A lot of women aren't."

Charley clicked off the tape. Would be attracted? he thought. Why not 'are attracted'? I blew it there: should have asked her, 'would be if what'?"

Click! Melody: I think it's because I'm still getting over Rudy. I know it's been two years, but..."

"C'mon, Melody. I can take it."

Click! Was I being masochistic there? But the alternative was to let her off the hook with her little white lie.

Click! "Well...it's something about you that's...needy. I feel your need hovering over me like a mother hen."

"Melody, we all need. I know it's not an In word these days, but the biological fact is that the race can't go on if we don't connect with each other."

"You're in your head, Charley. You're not in your heart."

Click! Damn, that same old cliche'd line. It pissed Charley off. He wasn't in his head *or* his heart. *They* were in *him*. And they both functioned fine, thank you. So did his gonads. At least he hoped they still did.

Click! "And you, Miss Feminine Mystique, are in your heart but not your head. Being human requires both. We need to reach some middle ground, and for that we need each other."

"What can I say, Charley? I think a relationship with you would just be like this all the time." Click! 'What could she say' is right. She really couldn't answer me. Click! "Besides, getting laid is so easy. You can get it anywhere." Click! Rage rushed through him like a flash flood down the banks of the Rio Adrenalino—just as it did when she said it. How can they sit there and say No no no no no, night after night, year after year, and then say getting laid is easy?

Click! "Easy for you to say. You're a woman. You can stand up in Mutant Stadium and say, 'Fuck me!' and you'll have 40,000 takers at your feet. If I did it I'd be arrested."

"If you want sex, why don't you go to a prostitute?"

"I don't really want sex; I want love."

"But I do love you, Charley."

"The only way I'll believe you love me is if you make love with me. That's how the stuff gets into the world—we make it!"

"You're so right, Charley. And you're so wrong! It can be made every which-way, by a dog wagging its tail, or dolphins leaping the waves in tandem, or by two people being friends..."

Click! Another flash flood of rage. Listen to her: she's crassly manipulating the conversation to introduce the single line that I, that all frustrated men, all future molesters and rapists everywhere, have come to dread the most. Still, maybe I should have let her finish...

Click! "I can hear it coming: 'Let's be friends'. Hey, I've got a million friends."

"A friend is a very valuable thing. Not all that many people of opposite sexes can talk with each other about love and sex."

"Is that what you want to do with me? You just said you didn't want a relationship because that's what we would do."

"No, because I'm afraid of your need." Click! Charley rewound and replayed. Nope, that wasn't what she said at all. I let her get that one by me. Whirr...Click! "If you don't like 'need', then how about this? I'm coming from abundance and you're coming from scarcity. I make love to the world and receive love back from it all the time. My fountain is overflowing. You're saving up all your love for one human object, and all the rest, the non-love, is fear...I'm channeling now, sorry if it's too heavy."

"Channeling? Who's talking through you, Norman Vincent Peale? Well listen, I feel better. Good night." Click!

Yeah, she was a New Age airhead, all right.

But Charley didn't feel better. He felt like bread without butter, like Laurel without Hardy, like San Francisco without a flower in its hair.

And he still didn't have a clue.

The second inning was also scoreless.

Third Inning

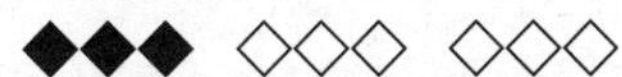

Them foul lines are there to hit the ball on, and those other ballplayers are all out there in the middle.

—*Casey Stengel*

I ain't takin' the trouble
To blow my bubbles away
—*The Jive Bombers*

Q: What do humans say?
A: Rib'et! Rib'et! Rib'et!
—old frog joke

SOMETIMES YOU CAN hear them at the edge of the swamp, peering in toward us in the twilight and making that human-sound: *Rib'et! Rib'et! Rib'et!*

What's it all about? wondered Ngaio XV[14]. He was feeling as blue as an indigo bunting hatched from a robin's egg and fallen into the Danube; as pavonine as a hyacinth with cyanosis trapped between a sapphire and a lapis lazuli under an azure sky; as perse as zaffir made to smalt. Were he not frog but toad, as blue as woad. All spring he had sung his heart out–nightly serenades that would tax a *prima don.* "In fact," he thought immodestly, "if frogs had a Pavarotti, I would be he."

Sure enough, his ariatic ways had won the heart of Greta Galump, the fairest of the fair of *Rana oncas.* "Mirror, mirror in the pool," he moaned; "How can I be such big fool?"

Greta was barely old enough to have lost her tail. But *mama mia,* what a juicy morsel she was! Under his heaving haunches she had shuddered out the longest orgasm Ngaio had ever had the thrill of co-creating: the sun rose and set and rose again, and when her inner trembling finally subsided, more than 48,000 eggs lay strung out in a double layer behind them in the water like the genetic code for the entire population of Noah's ark. But—o saddest day in Ngaio's life—his milt had petered out before she finished ova-lating. He felt humiliated. He felt ashamed.

Ngaio wasn't the only one who was drained—so was his dinnertime ditch. The dry season was rapidly approaching. Soon he would be

setting off on the Great Migration that was planted in his genes by the memories of his ancestors.

Question: Did Ngaio ever wonder how it is that an intangible concept like "memory" can influence a hard-and-fast piece of scientific furniture like a "gene"? Could his .01-gram frog brain question just what mad parallel universe he had hopped into?

Of course, to a Creationist neurologist, "memory" may be tangible while "genes" are no more real than "real" estate, figments of some heathen's imagination.

Little more than a century has passed since the celebrated Scopes Monkey Trial, where the fighting Fredric March disproved once and for all, in a court of law, to the chagrin of Spencer Tracy and all the university-educated miscreants that make up this great nation of ours, such blasphemous evolutionist poppycock as jellyfish come from slime molds, rabbis from rabbits, from the vine came the grape and so on, and that most people are just monkeys with clean shaves and credit cards.

March's victory notwithstanding, controversy stalks our schools like a tiger on hall patrol: Evolutionism vs. Creationism. The trial was a temporary blip: the Evolutionists still have the ear of the Powers That Be. Lately they have been growing careless and spouting off some mighty tall tales. Did you know the dinosaurs are still with us? They build nests in your eave troughs and drop gooshers on you from on high.

That's right: one wave of the Evolutionists' magic wand and the dinosaurs turned into birds. Now, why would a dinosaur go to all the trouble to evolve teeth and then trade them in for a beak that has to scoop sideways just to drink water? It's like some evil witch cast a spell on the entire order of Dinosauria at Hallowe'en and none of them can ever take their costumes off.

Or maybe it was part of the deal where they got wings...

The 4004 BC crowd must get a good laugh out of the Tweeting Dinosaur theory. And rest assured, they are not standing around during this lull in sanity waiting for their children to come home from Sunday School and tell them what they learned from the priest in sex education class. No ma'am, no sir, they are organizing grassroots campaigns and getting themselves elected to school boards, so they can have a say as to just what sort of hogswallow will be used to wash the filthy brains of coming generations (which, because evolution is a shuck, can never evolve into anything cleaner).

And just what sort of hogswallow is that? They think a whole lot of things happened at once: with a wink of God's eye (or six days at most, starting on Jan. 1, 4004 BC), we had us a world, with frogs and cockroaches and *prima donnas* and birds all hopping and running around and singing and chirping at once. Birds can't be reincarnated dinosaurs because there never were any dinosaurs. The dinosaur bones dug up by Evolutionist sympathizers were probably just buried there by God in a Stephen Spielberg mood one Sunday when we all thought He was resting.

Can you, intelligent reader, take either side seriously? Creationism? If God created everything simultaneously, what is the purpose of Time? If He had not yet created days, how could He labor for six of them? Evolutionism? If the *prima donna* is the musical pinnacle of evolutionism, how do we explain the later developments of Barry Manilow and Don Ho?

If one had to cast one's lot with one or the other (and it *is* just like voting, isn't it?—Tweedledum or Tweedledee?), one might be tempted to join the Creationists. Suppose, as they say, God turned out all His creatures as they are. Then they don't need to evolve into new ones. So none of them ever has to go extinct.

Shit, thought Ngaio XV^{14}. Here come those damn *rib'ets!,* with their flashlights. The pond was 16 jumps away, right through the favorite hunting grounds of that batrachopagous Great Horned Owl. Maybe, Ngaio thought, I'll just hop off the other way and start on the Great Migration tonight.

It was not only his ancestors' memories that left Ngaio XV^{14} crunched into a two-dimensional pancake that a passing schoolboy picked up the following morning and sailed back into the swamp like a frisbee: it was Time. Time and the Harley. Time and the six-lane ribbon of death that the *rib'ets!* had laid less than a half-mile away, straight across the path of the Great Migration.

◆◆◆

Gertie Galump knew nothing of Ngaio XV[14]'s fate. She could have cared less if she did. That was it for her: her last attraction to an older frog. What was his problem, anyway? Did he secretly spill his milt on pollywogs? Good Goddess, 10,000 of her children would go unborn! Was this a mortal sin on her part? Or did the eggs have to be fertilized and eaten by Ngaio before she was guilty? Gertie was not up on her herpetheology, but she knew one thing: it was bad survival odds.

Not that Gertie was any paragon of parenthood herself, at least compared with some of her cousins. Whereas her female *Leptodactylus bolivianus* counterpart would spit up mucus and beat it with her legs into a foam nest, sit guard over her eggs until they hatched, and then pump her legs to release attractor chemicals to draw the tads to stick by her, Gertie merely gazed up at the full moon and, calling on some ancient combination of memory and genes, she drew the moon closer and closer to her until…

Whereas her second cousin *Pipa pipa,* the Surinam toad, would somersault forward over and over along a streambed like an underwater ferris wheel, gathering up her eggs into the spongy skin on her back, and carry them around with her until they turned into toadlets and burrowed out, Gertie Galump simply looked back down again. There, to her satisfaction, lay the moon, shattered into shards in the pool. Its silvery squiggliness beckoned to her; when she finished her meditation, she would splash in the liquid glory.

All this while, Gertie Galump failed to notice two ominous forms looming over her in the moonlight.

No, neither one was a horned owl.

Yes, one was a *rib'et!* with a net and a collection jar.

The other one was much larger than that. It did not stand upright like the *rib'et!* and its feet were as long as the creature itself. They were webbed like hers but had no toes. The beast lay still, its huge mouth wide open along the ground—waiting for a frog to hop in? Gertie would hardly make a snack for that monster: its teeth looked like they could bite trees in half.

On its back was a space for a *rib'et!* to sit in.

Yes, it was a bulldozer.

◆ ◆ ◆ ◆

Two hours before Whizzo Mark Salot's second start, against the Wombats, two games ahead of the Mutants in third place, the dressing room door banged open. Enter Whizzo, walking on his hands. He came up shouting: "Hey teamies, Ah hope your lumber is as loose as mah arm, 'cause we gonna knock 'em raght off'n their perch today, gonna do a full gainer on 'em. Ah'm gonna chop me some timber into toothpicks."

How did his "teamies" react to Whizzo? Aren't rookies supposed to be seen and not heard? But Whizzo had tossed a five-hitter, posted a big "W" for them, the first of four in a row before last night's loss to the Wombats in the opener. To the average fan, baseball players are notoriously superstitious, drawing good-luck symbols in the dirt before each at-bat, eating the same meals every day during a winning streak, changing bats every time they get a hit—or make an out...for almost a month throughout his 24-game hitting streak, Moose Hornswoggle wore the same underwear. But who can separate superstition from the ineffable fingers of magic, weaving their web around the mysterious dark corners of life? Could this brash youngster be a divine gift to the team from the gods of baseball, one of those miracles with which diamond lore is rife that brings pennants to lesser clubs and wakes up a talented outfit whose only weakness is not enough youth?

The Mutants didn't have an official team captain. They didn't think they needed one. (Ha!) Unofficially Lightnin' Larrabee, closer extraordinaire, held things together in the clubhouse.

"Kid," said Lightnin', "you pitched us a good game, but you got a way with words can get you in a lot of trouble in this league."

"Mr. Larrabee, sir, with all due respect, sir, Ah harbor no disrespect for them Wombats nor anybody plays on their team. Shit almaghty, these hitters up here in the Bigs are the best in God's green creation, thass a fact. Lots of them Wombats, them gahs is mah heroes. Lots of y'all in this room—Ah growed up with y'all as mah heroes. Ah'm jist tickled pink as mah sweet Natasha's labia lips to be up here. So

hey—somebody tell me about big league love lahfe, anyway. Do Ah have to put barricades on mah door?"

"Hey, who's Natasha?" asked Joe Revige ("Revenge at Second Base").

"Well now, she's a new friend."

"I bet. Did you have a safe sex talk?"

"Safe? Sex? Do them two terms appear in the same language?"

"Hey kid, you ever hear of condoms?"

"Hain't them them rubber suits that snap onto your wiggleworm with an Ouch! and pull out all your pubic hairs Ouch! when you roll them off?"

Ouch! Whizzo will have to pay for his remarks later, eh ladies? ...eh laddies?

"But seriously," Whizzo continued, "Ah'll start usin' condoms when they start makin' them two feet long."

"You'll have to put both feet in one to fill it up."

"No sir, mah arm. Condoms are for protection, raght? Now, for whatever reason, God gave me the greatest left arm in the whole world. Ah done tested it against them Oystercatchers; y'all saw it, they couldn't hit me. Sometahmes Ah think Ah was one of them great lefties from the past— Christy Mathewson, Carl Hubbell, Noodles Hahn, Sandy Koufax—reborn into this body. "

"You ain't Koufax. He's still alive."

"Yeah, but his arm's dead as a doornail since before Ah was born. Hey, Ah got offers from six or 10 clubs. Ah sahgned with the Mutants because Ah knowed in mah heart the Mutants could win the flag. And Ah still know that we can. Mr. Bimbo Terwilliger, sir, Ah been a-watchin' you swingin' jist a tad ahead of them curve balls you so fashionably knock out onto Trombley Avenue and Ah see your timin' comin' closer and closer. You'll be down on it raght soon and go on a tear. Mr. Firpo Fendergrass, sir, Ah seen a hitch in your shoulder jist before your delivery, but hit's only there with a runner on first base and Ah think thass because you ain't confident of holdin' him there, but your left knee, it's gonna be 100 percent in a couple weeks and you won't be worryin' about no balks, and all this will pass. Mr. Charley Awrnge, sir, mah respects. Ah was jist a kid listenin' on the radio eight-nahne years ago when you hit .900 in the clutch. Ah feel that summer heat startin' to loosen up them weary bones and muscles in your body and you'll be gettin' around on that fast one momentarily now and have you a mess of hits and ribbies."

Charley grunted. He did not know what to make of this kid. .900 in the clutch? But Whizzo was right that he hadn't been getting around on the fastball. Everyone knew it; until Whizzo, no one had been impolite enough to mention it. Could they be thinking he was through? Or did they know, like he did, that the reaction time would return when the summer heat stirred his slumbering 39-year-old body? He felt it loosening up already. Now if he could just get some playing time...

Whizzo's observations on Terwilliger and Fendergrass were right on, too. It had taken Charley a month to diagnose Firpo's problem; had Foo Foo seen it yet? Whizzo had been here only five days. The kid's energy and style were loaded pistols ready to go off, but behind that nonstop mouth was a shrewd ballplayer's brain.

"Shit almaghty," Whizzo continued, "this club's ever' bit as fantastic as they all said it was, hit jist ain't started to jell till raght now, and Ah'm the jello, Ah'm the whipped custard in the face of them Oystercatchers, Ah'm the dog that's gonna piss yellow slahme down the legs of them Wombats, Ah'm the strawberries and cream on all you gahs' dessert plates at the World Series winner's banquet, to be held this October in the beautiful rural oasis of Disfunction Junction, Arkansas. YA-HOO!"

"I guess there ain't no shuttin' you up, kid," said Onions Malone, the first-baseman. "I just hope for your sake you keep pitchin' baseballs as good as you do words."

"For *our* sake, son," said Foo Foo McGonigle, who had hobbled out from his office in time to hear most of Whizzo's soliloquy. "It's about a matter of one very important thing here. Now here you've got a youngster–you–he's gonna be walkin' out and POW! POW!—flashes go popgun all over his face and televisionary citizens under every foot flappin' their lips with lotsa dangfool questions. Now, soon's a young fella goes braggin' on hisself gets him sooner or later konked on the noggin in a very very severe place, and then what can I do with him outside he's my starting pitcher? And that's what's getting me an ulcer because it's the Mutants go hurting even though it's your head feels sore. So you say it to the popguns about the Mutants, give the Whizzo Marx routines the soft soap. That's why a young man's got his teammates for, somebody to put his braggin' on them instead."

"You are so raght, Mr. McGonigle, sir. We got us a team to protect here. But don't y'all worry none about me. Ah hain't gonna let nobody get mad at me."

Whizzo sat still for a brief conference with Horst Throttlemeyer, his catcher, reviewing the Wombat lineup. Then he bounded out onto the field.

"Hain't nobody can stop me," he told Bluster Hyman's pre-game show audience; "Ah'm the nonparallel of all parallels. Hey now, ain't the name of the game Capture the Flag, and thass jist what me and the Mutants is gonna do. We got 'em sweatin'. Ah got me three risin' up fastballs–Sweet Patootie, up and in. Big Peter, risin' straight up like a big Peter goes. Choo-Choo Charley, named after Charley Awrnge, up and away. And Ah got mah Uncle Scrooge, makes 'em swing raght through North Carolahna whahle it goes dink! in the dirt."

Bluster pressed his blip button and deleted Big Peter's analogous features. "Whizzo, the front office tells me you sent all the money you got for signing, and all your salary, home to your family. "

"No sir. Ah kept out ten grand for mahself."

"You gave them all the rest?"

"Yes sir, thass raght. Mah stepmama and mah daddy done worked hard ever' day of their lahves raisin' me and mah eight sisters and they hain't never seen no kahnda buckos lahke these. How'd they know their only son had him a gold mahne in his arm?"

Bluster—he of the stone face—was amused. "Well Whizzo, do you think you can manage the rest of the season on $10,000?"

"Oh, Ah reckon they'll give me a raise soon's Ah win 'em a few more ballgames."

"Well, you can never have too much confidence in the big leagues. One more question, Whizzo: Are you going to talk to the ball today?"

"Well sir, that all depends on whether we get us into a situation. It's not lahke we hang out, y'know, me and the baseball. This is strictly a business situation for me and a survahval situation for the ball."

The game proceeded much like any of the other 125,000-plus regular-season contests that have been conducted in a century-plus of major-league baseball, with two exceptions:

In the top of the first inning, after Whizzo had retired Sisi Camarones and worked Denada Mierda to a 1-1 count, he stepped off the mound, doffed his cap and made a sweeping low bow toward Section 12. The girl with the red flower in her hair had returned. She was making her way toward her seat, accompanied by a dark-haired gentleman. Hmm—the same gentleman had sat beside her when he beat the Oystercatchers.

Then, in the top of the seventh inning with the score tied 3-3, Wallersby doubled for the Wombats. Whizzo got two quick strikes on Veracruz Vamanos, then missed with three straight.

Throttlemeyer headed toward the mound.

Foo Foo McGonigle heaved himself off the bench like a slow train going to a funeral and creaked and wobbled out onto the field.

Whizzo was oblivious to them both: he was addressing the baseball.

"Good game, kid," said Throttlemeyer. "Here comes Foo Foo."

"...and remember, little baseball," said Whizzo, "it's your hahde's gonna get bonked raght on outa here, not mahne." Then he held the ball to his ear.

Foo Foo arrived. "Your aim's been takin' you good, son, but now the plate's in this place here and the ball's over there."

"Big Peter!" said Whizzo. "Of course. Hit's callin' for Big Peter. This guy hain't seen Big Peter all day."

"That wing looks like it's all set for the Elysian Fields for today."

"Tuckered, you think? No sir, mah arm hain't tuckered in the slahghtest. Hit don't get tuckered. Ah jist figured after gettin' them two strahkes on Vamanos Ah'd play cat-and-mouse with him, 'specially with first base open. But Big Peter's jist itchin' to blow him away, if'n you'll give him the chance."

By now Buster Hyman, the home plate umpire, was heading toward the mound. You'd never know it by looking at him, but Buster was

◆◆◆

Bluster Hyman's twin brother. While both men were burly, Bluster barely reached 5 1/2 feet tall and Buster stood 6 feet 3. Where all but a few diehard strands of Bluster's hair now clogged his plumbing pipes and lined neighborhood birdnests, Buster's cap was forced to perch on his curly brown moss. Bluster did not waste valuable life energy moving his facial muscles. Buster had a rubbery, made-for-TV face.

"Hey guys," said Buster, "I don't know about you, but I got a hot date after the game. You feel like playing it?"

"Buster, you'll get a hot date one way," said Foo Foo; "if she sprinkles cayenne powder on your family medjools."

"C'mon Foo Foo, change pitchers or go siddown."

Foo Foo squinted up into Whizzo's eyes. "This is the hour, young man," he said. "Either you are my fruitcake or you ain't."

Foo Foo made his slow and weary way back to the bench. Throttlemeyer and Hyman returned behind the plate. Vamanos took a menacing swing and stepped back into the batter's box. Whizzo stretched, reared and fired. Big Peter zoomed toward Vamanos like a roadrunner who has just given Wily Coyote a hotfoot. It shot up from Vamanos' knees to his waist like a UFO that spotted Los Angeles just in time to avoid getting smog in its tachyon drive. Vamanos started his swing. "STRI-HEKE THREE!" bellowed Buster Hyman before Vamanos' bat made it over the plate.

Vamanos protested. "Buster, you call that peetch before ball reaches home plate."

"Any umpire can call a pitch after it crosses the plate," Buster told him. "Only the great ones can call it before. Now go get your glove."

Moose Hornswoggle pinch-hit for Whizzo in the bottom of the seventh and walked. Two outs later, Revenge at Second Base parked a curve ball in the second deck, just inside the foul pole. Lightnin' Larrabee mopped up and the Mutants won, 5-3.

The highs were fivin'. The mojos were workin'. The boomboxes were boomin'. The fans were juicin'. The Mutants were rollin'.

The magic was back.

◆ ◆ ◆ ◆

In a nation deprived of its gods, its heroes, of pride in its ancestry or present patriarchs, two major-league starts, two victories—that and a soupcon of charm—can turn a teen twirler into a Media Sensation. Bluster Hyman took advantage of the All-Star break to take a trip to Disfunction Junction, Arkansas before his fellow talking heads descended *en masse.*

Disfunction Junction was to your typical backwoods Southern burg what your typical backwoods Southern burg is to a modern megalopolis. In 1899, a wary band of post-Puritan neo-Luddites headed by Whizzo's great-grandfather Whizzo Mark Salot I tramped into the Ogamahachihachi Valley and planted their flag. The next year they came to their senses and planted corn, and brewed moonshine, and the rest is non-history. Through much of the twentieth century Disfunction Junction remained the Town that Time Forgot.

One narrow dirt road rambled through it, as a concession to the horse-drawn wagons that brought cigarettes, cocaine colas and other necessities into town and carried vegetables and 190-proof medicinals out to markets over the hill. Once off that road, as far as Disfunction Junction was concerned the wheel had not yet been invented. What use would it be? There wasn't a level surface, straight line, square corner or symmetrical shape in the entire town. Between corrugated tin shacks where rain danced on the rooftops like Gregory Hines tapping out Morse Code messages to the ghost of Isadora Duncan meandered foot trails wobbily cobbled into the low spots along Turkey Foot Creek (which crossed them 12 times), snaked through by tree roots in front of Abe Judson's restaurant/post office, but mostly just compacted dirt, with more twists than a ballerina caught in a pretzel machine and more ups and downs than Donald R. Duncan's name in a yo-yo contest, navigable to strangers (who rarely showed up in Disfunction Junction anyhow) only by following the plops of manure–horse, chicken, cow, hog, dog—deposited by the various creatures who shared the trails with humans.

Local ethnographers do not credit the venerable Salot and his cronies with derisive intent in naming their town: they were simply agin' the Progress that made *fin de seicle* America so...well, so

functional. When the powerful Tennessee Valley Authority wanted to electrify them in the early 1950's, they held out for 20 years. Possibly some sympathetic minion at the even mightier Ma Bell parked them in a lost file in the computer, for not until 1970 were telephones even offered. Information circulated quickly enough sans high-tension wires, polluting newspapers and harsh, demanding buzzes in people's ears, via feet—mostly bare feet.

Clocks? The clock on the belltower had stopped in 1914 or thereabouts and no one ever volunteered to climb up and re-start it. Few were the pocket watches in town. Time was measured by comings and goings—the schoolchildren in the morning and afternoon, Georgia Beveamis carrying her bread and pies to Hiram's grocery and general store at noon, Levi Hennessy's horse hauling water he'd scooped from the river, a bucket on each side of her belly.

Although great-grandfather Salot married Eliza Jonquil, the daughter of his pioneer cohort Elihu M. Jonquil, he apparently was not overly fond of her: his fellow founders convicted him of lashing her to death some seven years after the birth of Whizzo II, when he caught her packing to leave Disfunction Junction with a traveling mountebank.

Whizzo I was sentenced to make reparations of 160 acres of prime cropland to Elihu M. Jonquil.

Whizzo II, the only child, was raised by his father until his 18th birthday, when the elder man mysteriously disappeared. Whizzo I was no kinder a father than a husband. Uncharitable sources in town still maintain Whizzo II was responsible for the disappearance.

Whizzo II was best known for building Disfunction Junction's only bomb shelter—to protect his family not, he said, from the Russkies but from "thim crazy button-down Yanks and Jewdads in Warshington and the Pintagon who'd jist as soon blow up they own ciz'zens as wipe they ass wif they fav'it hoe's silk sheets."

But Whizzo's grandpa didn't buy into the ultimate repository of people's fears in those days, the flying saucers.

"Hain't no alien bein's could be any worst'n humans," he snorted. "Hain't nobody comin' dahn from any dinin' room table in the sky and say, 'Take me to yo' leadah'. Know wha? 'Cause we hain't *got* no leadahs."

(Whizzo II's words were prophetic. "The most powerful earthling," the aliens telebubbled their leader, "is a bristlecone pine tree in what is called the Sierra Nevada region of North America. It hasn't moved or spoken in over 5,000 years, yet everything it wants is brought to it by natural forces and other creatures. When the linguo-bubble finally learned its language, it would not engage; instead it referred us to the most powerful humanoid of the moment, a man named Izen-Howr. He speaks a dialect of the language called English that the linguo-bubble cannot decipher."

The alien leader decided that the world of Izen-Howr was not worth adding to his intergalactic empire, and the cosmic Tupperware party ran away with the spoon.)

Father-killer or no, in other respects Whizzo's grandfather was a consummate family man. He married Abigail Jonquil, Eliza's step-niece, and they begat six children—five girls, four of whom Whizzo II also impregnated, and Whizzo III, his only heir. When Whizzo II passed on prematurely, also under uncertain circumstances, he bequeathed to Whizzo III his corrugated-tin shack, his 2 1/2-acre vegetable plot, his Holstein cow and his proclivity for poking his pecker wherever he could whenever he could.

Not to lay too heavy a stigma on Whizzo's male ancestors: they were merely following the customs and mores of their time and place. And they knew no other way to find their way to the place God in His infinite largesse had created them to find: Tenderness Junction, which is found not on a map of Arkansas but an anatomical chart, especially a female anatomical chart. Imagine starting on your life's journey toward Tenderness Junction and winding up in Disfunction Junction instead. In a later, more enlightened time, the unconscious irony of the name the founders had given the town would turn back on them. With one exception, every last mother's son there, and every daughter too, became dysfunctional.

The women? Surely Eliza Jonquil Salot knew she was risking her life running off with a mountebank. And surely she was not so naive as to think she might find happiness with a man in his profession—

was she? How many beatings had she endured before he came along to tempt her with honey lies, how helpless, how victimized and desperate did she feel?

And Abigail Jonquil Salot: did she feign ignorance that her grandchildren were her step-children as well? This fact is certain about her husband's death: it occurred the very night he caught a cold and she mixed him an herbal potion—a secret recipe handed down through the generations by the Jonquil women, an inordinate number of whom had worn the widow's weeds at a tender age.

In 1970 the Powers That Be installed a military base over in Pochahatwawa Valley next door, and all hell broke loose: within a year everyone had electric lights and telephones. Hair dryers and TV sets followed right behind, and 98 percent of the high-school girls became pregnant. Many of the younger folks, upon learning that there was a world out there, went off to see it and never came back. It was only a matter of time, and not much of it, before the golden arches of Progress were to undo all that Disfunction Junction's forefathers stood for.

Whizzo III was blessed with nine children by his wife, Evangeline, a sickly lass who was also reputed to be his half-sister. Delivering Whizzo IV, the youngest, was her last act on earth. Whizzo and his eight sisters were raised by his half-sister half-aunt Willadean, who came to live with the family when Evangeline died. And if she also shared the connubial bed with his father, who are we to condemn her, she who also tendered the cornucopia, the maternal nurturance so vital to a young boy if he is to grow up into a healthy, emotionally functional man who loves, reveres and worships women?

Bluster talked with Whizzo IV's former coach, with his boss at the swimming pool where he worked the previous summer as a lifeguard, and with an endless string of high-school girls working on their tans there who loaded him down with notes and gifts for their departed heartthrob. He got the final chapter in the story from Whizzo himself upon his return. "Mah daddy grew potatoes and corn and, later, what we called catnip on that 2 1/2 acres. He treated me and mah sisters good except for when he took to drinkin'. But Ah put an end to him drinkin' the day Ah turned 11 years old.

"'Willadean', Ah said, 'can Ah bake mah own cake for mah birthday'?"

"'Whah, sure you can, Whizzo,' she said. She had plenty to occupah herself with trahing to keep a half-dozen teenage girls away from the soldiers at the base and all the males in town past the age of puberty, 'specially mah daddy.

"Now mah daddy, remember, he was dirt-poor and committed to provahdin' for a family of nahne. He hadn't never thought of trahing his number one cash crop hisself. Well, Ah laced that cake with an ounce of shake Ah had pilfered from the harvest. Daddy, he was chocaholic, and he had hisself three pieces.

"An hour later, when that catnip hit his stomach, hit was lahke a flower blossom opening. He didn't say a word; he jist went out into the back yard, sat down on a stump and laughed all naght.

"The next mornin' Ah told him what Ah had done. He gave me a crack on the behahnd, but it waren't very hard. And mah daddy never drank liquor again."

His name was Maxwell Veribushi but he had nary a hair on his face.

As much as this concerned Maxwell, it concerned him less than the equally nonpilose condition of his pubic area.

These concerned him less in Biology class than in Physical Education, where changing into his gym clothes at the start of the period and showering at the end were mandatory. It was not mandatory to do anything physical, and Maxwell usually sat in a corner reading a book or thinking thoughts. He liked to spend every waking moment either reading or thinking about baseball or biology, but other thoughts often crept in— thoughts such as, Was he normal? Would he have to go through life with an atrophied pecker? Changing clothes in the locker room, watching his classmates strut around with their proud new fur-lined, king-sized blunderbusses, while he stood facing his locker as much as possible to hide his miniscule accessory,

hoping no one would decide to aim some ribaldry his way, Maxwell would speculate on rare diseases that he might have, on whether hair implants or stretching machines existed for such a condition, on whether he should raise his daily dosage of Vitamin E.

Maxwell Veribushi was 16 years old, the same age Albert Einstein was when he first envisioned $e=mc^2$. These feelings of inadequacy had gone on long enough! The other guys were amazed when he first showed up at school on his lime-green Harley. Had they thought about it, they might have precognosed the raving Banshee that would be unleashed once Maxwell grew some hair on his…chest.

Maxwell was not in Physical Education this morning; he was in his favorite class, Biology. And there, sitting in front of him, on a plate much like those on which his mother served dinner, was a most unappetizing, formaldehyde-drenched, overly dead frog.

Maxwell, who made few distinctions between culinary sensations at this period of his life, was not offended by the plate or by the stench. No, but he was in shock over the heinous events that had delivered this creature belly-up to his table.

Poor Maxwell, whose only civilized vice (other than baseball) was his dream member the Harley, had only last month made wallpaper out of the husband, however briefly, of this very *Rana onca* that lay unmoving on its platter like a sponge with its life squeezed out of it, and the father of 38,000 of her 48,000 offspring. O tragic irony, that fortunately escaped Maxwell altogether since he had dismissed the slight blip he had felt in his front wheel as a stone on the road.

Yet some will claim that the scene which follows—indeed, Maxwell's entire illustrious ensuing career—was an unconscious reaction to the herpeticide that in his secret heart of hearts he knew he had committed. The possibility that information was communicated deep down, at the level where Maxwell and the frog and the Harley were all connected to the rest of the vast everywheres forevers, cannot be denied; however, all Maxwell thought at the time was that he had bumped a stone.

Unbeknownst to Maxwell when he ran over Ngaio XV[14], but as plain as the pug nose on her face to Ladye Hannah Aura, he had just doomed himself to an extra turn on the Wheel. In the doctrine of

Reincarnation, when you die, unless you have lived an exemplary life you must be born again, until your soul has leaped all of life's hurdles and attained purification (nirvana). It's heaven and hell, Eastern style, only less real estate is involved: hell is right here on earth. The West has the hereafter; the East the herebefore. Hey, Hebrew isn't written backwards for nothing. The Wheel is a metaphor for life: the object of existence is to get off the Wheel, to pass through these illusory lives to the true Reality beyond. Yes, the purpose of life is to escape life. It may sound like chop-logic to you, but to Reincarnationists it's a paradox, the highest form of truth.

Through all these miserable lifetimes it must endure, the soul is burning off *karma* to attain purification. If you are in an abusive relationship, that's your *karma,* or retribution for the way you treated your spouse in the herebefore. If you don't learn how to make it work this time around, or how to avoid being sucked back into it, guess what—you get another lifetime to try again. Stuck in a concentration camp? Paraplegic? Warts on your behind? Shame on you—and better luck next time.

Reincarnation does have its up side too. You don't need expensive funerals; you don't have cemeteries cluttering up prime Zone C lots. You just burn the body; the soul has already found a new one.

Now, Ladye Hannah Aura belonged to a Fundamentalist sect of Reincarnationism called the Doctrine of Eternal Return. Eternal Returnists believe that after you die you must return as every fly you ever swatted, every ant you ever skooshed, every mosquito, every spider, every animal you ever roared over on the highway with your Harley, whether you knew it or not.

Orthodox Reincarnationists find the Doctrine of Eternal Return too insufferable to live, die and live with, but Ladye Hannah Aura is uplifted by it. "My dears," she says, "just wait till you're a frog! I remember well my life as a *Pipa pseudohymenochirus*: how could I ever forget that?" She chuckles slyly. "One night as the stars shone down like spermdrops into the swamp, my ears filled with the most celestial music I'd ever heard. I was drawn toward it as if it were a dunghill covered with flies. It turned out to be the lustiest hunk of swollen-chested, heavy-haunched frog I'd ever seen. And those eyes!— He wore the family jewels right there on his forehead. He hopped onto my back, hooked on his cloaca and began rolling me over and over in the water, eggs gushing out of me like lava, for over four hours! But four hours was hardly a slap and tickle in some of my anuran lifetimes. One night my *Atelopus oxyrhyncus* lover and I went cloaca-to-oviduct for six months straight—until he keeled over dead, poor chap. But no sympathy needed: What a large percentage of his brief lifetime was devoted to lovemaking! What a way to go!"

The Doctrine of Eternal Return makes more sense than orthodox Reincarnationism in that it doesn't require some celestial factory churning out new souls to explain the sudden exponential rise in human population. It could be that a lot of souls have just finished serving out their sentences as flies and mosquitoes.

It also provides a guilt-free explanation of Veribushi's Biodiversity Theorem #1: The population of other organisms decreases proportionately to the increase in humans.

Whatever you may think of the Doctrine of Eternal Return or Reincarnationism of any other stripe, in its own small way it helps reunite our badly fragmented culture by putting the Creationists and the Evolutionists back in the same bed. They both think it's poppycock.

Young Maxwell Veribushi already knew more about frogs than probably any high-school biology teacher in the country. And in Maxwell's varied readings he had come across a curious notion: that all creatures, salamanders and snail-darters, frogs and bank presidents, little acorns and mighty oafs, are created equal.

"The perfumed flowers are our sisters; the deer, the horse, the great eagle, these are our brothers," quoth Chief Sealth.

"The earth does not belong to man; man belongs to the earth.

"Man does not weave the web of life; he is merely a strand in it.

"If all the beasts were gone, men would die from a great loneliness of spirit."

Maxwell had come to recognize his humanness as only the most recent stage of his existence, and to cherish his animal past: his mammalian period, his invertebrate phase, his oxygen-starved fishhood heaving itself onto the crushing gravity of the pre-Cambrian shore. He celebrated being part of the rainforest, the temperate forest, the marshes and mountains, the sea, the very air he breathed...He was even the rocks and soil and minerals. After all, didn't every atom in his body exist 4 billion years ago when the earth formed? Fifteen billion years ago when the vast everywhere forever squeezed itself into a pea and then threw up all over Creation?

His entire techno-culture's approach to nature, Maxwell realized, was anthropocentric. "One tree, one vote," he read. "Hmm—What about mosquitoes?" he thought. "What about ants—does each ant count, or is the whole hive a single organism without skin? What about bacteria? They make the human vote, even at 6 billion, about as meaningless as it is in human votes."

Maxwell came from a Quaker family. When he was 11, he stood up during Witness and said it: "I think animals and plants are all just as good as humans." There had been a few smiles, but then it was accepted as an article of faith, at least for Maxwell.

Now Maxwell sprang up off his Biology stool. "Who killed this frog?" he shouted.

His classmates tittered. Mr. Malarkey, the teacher, walked over to Maxwell.

"What did you...?"

"Nobody has a right to kill this frog. It's murder!"

"Maxwell, for heaven's sake, stop..."

"How would you like it if someone came into your house with a net and carried you away like you were a nubile virgin and they were an Aztec priest?"

"That's just what might happen to you, young man, if you don't calm down," said Mr. Malarkey. This was distressing. Maxwell was his star pupil, but he must maintain order. Please Maxwell, snap out of it.

"And then they laid you out on some table and these huge giants came in with scissors and gouged out your guts?"

"That's *enough* Mr. Veribushi, please dissociate yourself from our batrachocidal presence and adjourn yourself to the principal's office. You may see me after school."

And so it was that Maxwell Veribushi, the world's greatest herpetologist, failed in his first encounter with a frog.

It was subsequently entered into agreement between Mr. Malarkey and Maxwell's father, Mr. Veribushi, that Veribushi *pere et fils* would not mention the incident to animal rights groups and in return Maxwell could dissect beanbag frogs.

Not being able to tell the inside of a frog's asshole from its elbow did not in the slightest affect Maxwell Veribushi's subsequent career. He founded the separate discipline of exo-salientology, the study of the outsides of frogs.

At Dr. Weisenheimer's suggestion, Charley Orange attended a singles drop-in evening. "Da vomen dere, dey are looking for da man. Everyvhere looking for da man, but dere not hiding it." The Dr. told him to "be asking alvays for everyting you are vanting."

Charley looked around with disappointment: only three women, two of whom were in their sixties. The group energy level was low.

"Let's get acquainted by saying our name and what brought us here tonight," said the facilitator, a plump, middle-aged woman whose saccharine voice gave Charley the willies.

Boldly, he went first. "I'm Charley, and I'm looking for someone who will go to a sex party with me."

"Anyone, Charley?"

"A woman."

"Thank you. Do you see anyone here you'd like to ask?"

The third woman looked like her dog had just died, but her features were rather attractive. Besides, at the party he would be sharing his seed with other women. It was her or no one: this was his chance. "I don't know your name," he said to her.

"Adrian."

"Adrian, will you go to a sex party with me?"

"No."

Adrian went next. "My darling little girl is gone forever!" She burst into tears.

Charley sat in silent bravado, like someone who has passed gas at an inauguration. He wasn't going to be intimidated by the situation. He had simply asked for what he wanted. He felt good about it.

Everyone there had major problems. Charley hadn't come to share heavy feelings. That was what Dr. Weisenheimer was for. Bored and impatient, he remembered a letter he had to write. At intermission he made his escape.

Dear DD-38, he wrote,

Your ad said you liked tall, handsome, generous men in their 30's and would answer all letters that included a donation for a photo of you.

I'm 6'2", 39 but young for my age: still playing sports competitively for a living (at the top level; earning six figures).

I'm a large (225 pounds, no fat) but gentle and soft-spoken guy. Not your jock stereotype: I have a college degree and the kind of mind that can size up a complex situation in a split second. This I attribute partly to genetics and partly to my training and occupation, which have taught me how to empty my mind and let all stimuli in.

I like the sexual orientation of your ad: none of those virginal games that all the women I know are always playing. I hope you'll appreciate my sexual directness in return. Basically, I'm flexible and easygoing when it comes to sex, though if I go more than three weeks without getting laid, I feel like I'm on the rag. I think that men are electric and women are magnetic, and that we need to fuck regularly to keep balanced electromagnetically. What do you think?

What I'm really trying to say is: LET'S FUCK!

But wait, I mean let's just meet first and see if we like each other.

Or hell, just show up at my door some night in a fur coat and nothing else; that will be all right too.

But what if someone's here, you ask? Unlikely: my loves are all from other places, other times. Yes, it's been a lot longer than three weeks.

◆◆◆

Jeez, let's be practical. I work evenings. Maybe you can come see me play and we can get together afterwards. Or maybe you don't like sports?

Ooh, this is so romantic—you're the only one I'm writing to tonight. I was going to answer several ads, but I didn't know I'd get so involved, and now it's 2 a.m. What is it about you that inspires me so? So call or write, because it was meant to be.

Seriously now,

Charles the Red (a pseudonym; I'm too well-known). (No, I don't have red hair.)

P.S. I'm not sending money for a photo because I don't get off on them: the only purpose of a photo would be to show me you're not fat, fifty and ugly and if you were, you wouldn't be selling photos, would you? So I trust that you look fine.

Charley had found the ad from "38-DD" in the back of a men's magazine. Did he really expect a reply without sending money? Well, he wasn't sure. He wanted nothing to do with any woman who was just looking for a meal ticket: if she didn't reply, she wasn't for him anyway. It was a sort of litmus test: if she did answer, he could be interested.

Would the fact that he was a ballplayer and earning good money impress her? Should he even mention the six figures? Well, she wanted someone generous. He could be generous if someone were generous in return. But he did not want to be viewed as someone's sugar daddy. Did his P.S. make that clear in a gentle way or might she not get it?

No matter: it was 2 a.m. The letter would have to go as is. He addressed and stamped an envelope, walked outside to the mailbox and dropped it in.

◆ ◆ ◆ ◆

Gussied up by dramatists and choreographers, promoted by kingmakers and opinion shapers and eulogized by mythmakers, sports are in reality remnants of ancient survival skills. He who could throw a stone and konk a rabbit fed his kids; he who missed became extinct. In football the star is the quarterback: he throws the passes. In basketball the playmaker is the guard who dribbles the ball down the floor, then passes to initiate a sequence toward the basket. In baseball, the best thrower is the pitcher: he's the King of the Mountain. These athletes devote their lives to keeping their vehicles in perfect pitch and putting their maximum of being-ness into each delivery of the ball. But ultimately it's up to Nature's machine: the same arm that could konk the most rabbits with stones can also put the baseball where its owner wants it, and not two inches to the right where the batter will knock it downtown. Pitching, they say, is 80 percent of the game. Why did the 1947 New York Giants bash 221 home runs and finish fifth? Poor pitching.

Starting pitchers hurl only every fifth game, and usually not all nine innings then. Relievers may toil less than 100 innings all year. At an average of 15 pitches per inning, when Dennis Eckersley labored 58 innings in 1989, his paycheck came out to almost $2,000 per pitch.

Pitchers' arms are treated like visiting royalty. They are soaked, whirlpooled, iced, heated, effleuraged and petrissaged. Yet they are not insured by Lloyds of London, because Lloyds knows a major-league appendage is a black hole that you throw money into. Hurlers' arms ship out to sea regularly and wash up like old Portuguese fishing balls on the shorelines of careers.

Back in the days when our grandparents walked 20 miles to school every day, rain or shine, starters with arms of steel would take to the mound 50, 60 times a year, usually for the distance, even in extra-inning contests. 400 innings was hardly a full-time season for Hoss Radbourne, who started 20 straight games and toiled 679 innings for the Providence Grays in 1884. In August 1903, Joe McGinnity won three complete-game doubleheaders for the New York Giants. That was standard protocol for Satchel Paige, the Negro League legend who due to a particular concurrence of skin color and spacetime became the American League Rookie of the Year in 1948 at the age of somewhere between 42 and 142, depending on which yarns old Satch was spinning that day. One year Satch hurled 153 games.

Modern times have seen the rise of the relief pitcher, the shift from a four-man to a five-man starting rotation, and an epidemic of torn rotator cuffs, bone-chipped elbows and other forms of blown-out arms.

What's happening? Are pitchers devolving before our very eyes, deteriorating from rabbit assassins with bulls-eye limbs to fragile epigoni, the souls of hunters living in glass houses and unable to throw stones?

Or has the game of baseball just evolved? In the old days, hitters strode to the plate to hit. If the ball was in reach, they went for it. Pitchers adapted to this aggression by developing more pinpoint control and aiming the ball at various corners of the strike zone. Hitters responded by going deep into the count, becoming more selective, waiting for a mistake pitch that edged too far over the plate and maybe getting ahead in the count, forcing the pitcher to come in down the pike. Thus the modern moundsman throws more pitches to each batter and tires before the game is through.

Another evolutionary strategy taken by hurlers is developing a full repertoire of pitches while still in high school or college, before their arms have matured. Breaking balls involve sudden high-speed torquing of the radius and ulna bones, tough even on adult arms. This makes a young pitcher tougher to hit but turns his tendons into oatmeal at an age when hitters are still reaching their prime.

"Every now and then comes along a mound magician who breaks all the rules," Bluster Hyman's voice droned across the late afternoon Megaglopolitan airwaves. "He's an agent of evolution but he'll be called a throwback. Nolan Ryan, who tossed his seventh no-hitter with a broken back at age 44, was a throwback. So too is Whizzo Mark Salot IV, southpaw extraordinaire and confidante of baseballs. At the precocious age of 16 years the kid from Disfunction Junction, Arkansas had already perfected his Sweet Patootie, Big Peter, Choo Choo Charley and Uncle Scrooge. Yet he has never had a sore arm in his life."

Exiting the ballpark, Warren shook his head. "He's only 18 now, Bluster," he said to his boombox. "He'll probably be back in the minors before he's old enough to get served."

His companion smiled and said nothing.

"In the universe of baseball," Bluster continued, "nobody ever wins them all. The 1906 Chicago Cubs had the best season of any team in history, 116-36. They still lost nearly one contest in four, not to mention the World Series. No starting pitcher has ever won all his games. In fact, no starting pitcher has made it through a full season undefeated. Johnny Allen almost did it with the Cleveland Indians in 1937, losing only on the last day of the season.

"Whizzo Mark Salot IV, as brilliant as he is at the art of twirling, is no exception. Yet even in dropping today's 2-0 heartbreaker to the Blue Hen Chickens, he looks to be one of those rarities who just doesn't get shelled. Yes, he lost, but he pitched a game he can be proud of. The loss drops the Mutants 14 1/2 games off the pace with..."

Warren choked off Bluster's airwave supply. "Three major-league starts under his belt, Bluster. You talk like he's been up for three years." His companion remained silent, hiding her disagreement with him.

In the clubhouse, Whizzo was his usual ebullient self. "Hey gahs, Ah don't want no one to get down on hisself for not making any ribbies today," he announced as he buttoned up a brand-new Hawaiian shirt with green flowers on it. "Bullet Bill throwed the fahnest game Ah have seen to date in mah brief but meteoric career. Ah'm a pitcher and Ah know when Ah'm throwin' raght, hain't no one can hit me. And Bullet Bill was throwin' raght." He donned powder-blue slacks and an off-white Armani jacket with the tags still on it. "Those bats be hummin' tomorrow. Hain't gonna see us two games in a row lahke that."

"You're right, kid," said Lightnin' Larrabee. "You take losing well. Just don't do too much of it, OK?"

"Ah'll lose me a few, but they gonna have to throw lahke that to beat me. And even then Ah'll win me some of them, on account of Ah can throw that good too."

"The kid threw a good one for us," said Firpo Fendergrass. "Hey guys, what can we do for him?"

"We can throw him!"

"Throw him in the shower!"

New duds and all, Whizzo was baptized in team spirit, complete with soap in his eyes.

He came up talking. "Ah made me two mistakes. Got away with the first one, Tequila singled but dahd at second. Caballeros' rainbow, Ah come in too hagh on him. Boy, did y'all see him turn on it?"

That was where the kid struck a resonant chord with Charley Orange. Winning is supposed to be the be-all and end-all of pro sports, but it just isn't so. Japanese athletes honor their opponents for bringing out the best in them. They each know they *are* the other: the two are one, wed into a unity of purpose. "Into a separate universe within a universe," thought Charley; "a multiplicity of universes, a googol of everywheres forevers—more than that, an infinity of them."

"Evolution?" thundered a round, tonsiled tunnel surrounded by a sargasso sea of Neptunian hair.

"Evolution?" Professor Maxwell Veribushi drew himself upright to his full five-foot four-inch stature.

"Evolution?" he bellowed once again. "Consider the Black Widow spider, a creature that injects enough venom through her microscopic chelicerae to fell a horse and spins a web strong enough to snare a small bird. Is the lesson of the Black Widow that if a little is good, more is better? If so, is human greed just Evolution at work: if five million is more than you can ever spend, ten million is better? No: for all the overkill that goes into the Black Widow's makeup, it seems to be less successful in either numbers or range than the common grass spider, with neither venom nor web to match.

"Evolution? Consider the Rufous-crowned motmot. Where other birds' tails end, the motmot's central tailfeather extends a full inch beyond, so needle-slender that you can't usually see it, then at the end it bursts into a broom. Is the motmot born with this broom? No, it plucks out the Gaia-given webbing from its tail feathers and makes the broom itself. And I am not speaking of just the male doing this to attract the female.

"Nor, if I may wind down a side road for a moment, is it vice-versa, thank Gaia. Do you ever wonder why human male-female relationships are the mess they are?"

The soft buzzing in the lecture hall became a titter. Professor Veribushi was off on one of the asides, usually sexually-oriented, that made him the most popular lecturer on whatever campus he was attached to. It also made his *curriculum vitae,* despite his outstanding professional stature, read like the lyrics to a game of Academic Musical Chairs.

"We costumed simians do it all backwards from the git-go. In Nature, the guys are stylin' and the ladies pick and choose. We keep trying to do it the other way around. OK, a little survey here. Ladies first: you're walking across campus, now ask yourselves: What percentage of the guys you see are you turned on to? Between zero and 5 percent, right? Now guys, it's your turn. How many of those little foxes just bake your potatoes? More like 30 to 70 percent, yeah? So guys, why do we keep ramming our heads against the wall? Hey, if we want to see double-digit drops in feelings of rejection, in feeling sad, getting mad—how about this, if we want to end sexual abuse and rape—I ask you: who should be chasing whom?

"But I digress. This is about the Rufous-crowned motmot." The class sighed and returned to buzz mode. "Why does the motmot take the perfectly good tail that Gaia gave it and make a broom out of the bottom? Does it need it to sweep out its nest? If so, wouldn't the tail have evolved into a broom on its own, as surely as the Montgomery Ward catalog evolved into junk mail?

"Evolution? Consider how a certain other species mutilates itself, whacking off tonsils, adenoids and appendices, binding feet, stretching lips and ears, inflating breasts, deflating bellies and buttocks, lopping off foreskins and clitorises. If all these are required corrections, hasn't Evolution jumped the tracks somewhere and hurtled off amok into some post-nuclear Frankensteinian laboratory, churning out useless appendages and misshapen anatomical parts willy-nilly? *Que pasa,* Evolution?"

This was the infamous lecture that had gotten Maxwell canned from Ghioch U., his first teaching post. It seemed ideal to deliver at

Oral-Anal Roberts U., where he had mischievously applied after his monograph on "Archetypal Cultural Preservation and Cross-Cultural Correlations for Ethnoanuropharmacology of Amazonian Ranids" became a smash hit in the batrachian community.

But Maxwell had a fatal habit of playing gadfly to people who thought their schooling was over, especially when those people assigned him freshman lecture classes. And unfortunately, one of those freshmen (actually a freshwoman) had submitted a tape recording of his "Evolution?" lecture to the Chairman of the Biology and Creationism Department.

Chairman Lewis limped down the hallway. He had a bad case of Scholar's Hunch, which allowed dandruff to pile up in great billows on the shoulders of his seersucker suit. He had been let off his leash in the library especially for this occasion.

Even the stacks were not what they used to be, he thought. Now they were full of computers, and so much of the information was on microfiche, not in books. *Fiche,* what the deuce was fiche? It—well, it didn't smell *musty.* He *liked* the smell of musty, and after many long years his seersuckers had attained a perfect, slightly mildewy fragrance, not unlike the fine blend of cherry tobacco his father used to smoke.

Approaching the room, he abruptly ceased limping. Walking correctly was too painful to do all the time, but he didn't want anyone to see the limp, so he walked normally when anyone was in view, or when he was likely to encounter someone.

Ouch! He was not feeling well-disposed toward this upstart Veribushi, hair all over him like some kind of hedgehog. Why would a grown man study frogs, anyway? Weren't they the second plague brought upon the Egyptians? Didn't three evil spirits appear in the form of frogs in Revelations?

And what had that sweet young co-ed whispered into his ear? Ah, if he were 50 years younger again. Oh yes—clitorises. The upstart had talked about clitorises. Pussies, weren't they? Only worse than pussies. Something that goes on inside of pussies. Well, pussies had not been his calling, thank you Jesus for that. He had seen many a man's life dashed upon the rocks by pussies, like so many bubbles of foam. Surely Dr. Veribushi understood that. (Oh, Chairman Lewis knew well the temptation, having dashed off some bubbles of foam himself, under the aegis of his right hand, but that was long ago, and now the rocks were as dry as a Saharan martini.) But a young man who would utter such a word in public—could anyone say anything for sure about such a person?

Thank goodness the Old Man would be there. Chairman Lewis didn't relish the prospect of dealing with such a flagrant, unpredictable type as this Veribushi. Entering the room, he breathed a sigh of relief to see that Dean Martin was already there—no, not *the* Dean Martin. Jeremiah Martin, the octogenarian head of Faculty Affairs, was a reflective, grandfatherly sort whose feathers remained unruffled through the stormiest of conflicts. Even Maxwell Veribushi, who was pouring coffee, almost liked him.

"Ah, Chairman Lewis," said Maxwell. "One cube or two?" He was beaming like a new father.

"Three." Chairman Lewis cleared his throat. "Professor Veribushi, the University is...ah, greatly disturbed by your reference, in a co-educational class, to a certain part of the...uh, female anatomy."

As he sat, Maxwell cracked his knuckles. "And which part might that be?"

"Don't be coy, Dr. Veribushi."

"I would not, should not, could not be coy with you, sir. It's just that since I consider all parts of the female anatomy equally worthy of ringing praises to the cathedral rafters, I am unable to discern which of them the University deems too vile and evil for public mention."

"Did you or did you not, in your freshman lecture this morning, utter the word—Dr. Veribushi, the word 'cliTORises'?" The Chairman accented the second syllable, as if the word were dePLORable, peJORative, abHORRent, imMORal, abNORmal.

An image of his Research Assistant passed fleetingly through Maxwell's mind, and he could not stifle a chuckle. "I assure you I never said 'cliTORises' in my life," he said.

A smile broke across Chairman Lewis' pallid face, the kind of snaggle-toothed smile that might broaden a crocodile's countenance in the moment before its jaw guillotines in on some daydreaming

waterfowl. He fished into his shirt pocket and removed a cassette tape. "Shall I play this for you?"

"'CLITorises'," said Maxwell. "The word is 'CLITorises'. Accent on the 'CLIT'." Good Gaia, had the man never heard the word before?

The venerable Dean Martin took over. "Dr. Veribushi, we also have a copy of your last semester's final examination. 'Do slime molds have the same rights as humans?' 'Under what circumstances may destroying a bulldozer be justified?' 'True or False, and why: Man's rise was his fall.' The University finds these questions both irresponsible and imprudent."

Like a fly to a cowpie, like a cosmonaut stepping over the Schwarzchild radius and spinning through the wormhole into the universe next door, the Dean was zeroing in on the truth: "imprudent" missed the mark by but one letter. Maxwell's style—enhanced by his elfin-size—was most often labeled "impudent."

Ah, if the kindly old dean but knew of Dr. Veribushi's final exam at Ghioch U: he had simply taken his class to a nearby pond and given them magic mushrooms.

Not that the knowledge would have made Maxwell's employment situation here any more past tense than it already was. Maxwell said CLIToris, the Chairman said cliTORis and then called the whole thing off.

"I wish you luck, young man," said Dean Martin, offering his hand. "You know, here at Oral-Anal, we spell it 'e-v-i-l-u-t-i-o-n'."

"Thank you, sir," said Maxwell. "I'm afraid I don't believe in the concept of evil. I guess I'm not cut out for Christianity."

"Neither am I, Veribushi. Of course I take Jesus Christ for my personal Savior, but when I see what the Church does in His name...Well, anyway, I guess you and this University are at opposite ends of the hourglass looking at the same phenomenon in the funnel."

"The black hole into the universe next door," said Maxwell. "Where Time runs backwards."

"That is what your idea of God is?" asked the Dean.

"No, that's not my God," said Maxwell. "That's my cosmology. I call my god S/HeIt to honor both sexes and the fact that God is beyond gender, but I pay my reverence to the Goddess."

"Dr. Veribushi, you really should give up teaching, you know."
"I think I'm off to find my Yoniverse," said Maxwell.

The Mutants lost the opener of their road trip to the Woodpeckers, 5-2. After his last evening out with Whizzo Mark Salot IV in Megaglopoulis, Charley Orange wondered why he had allowed Wonder Boy to drag him to a singles juice bar on the road. "Hey, these are hagh-quality ladies we'll be meetin'," Whizzo told him. "No alcoholics."

Whizzo needed less than 10 seconds to scope out the room and zero in on two unescorted beauties seated near the back. He performed his schtick and gave Charley some good P.R. as before. Ginger, maybe 20 and maybe really blonde, seemed duly impressed. Lorene, probably not 30, probably not a real redhead, did not. "Thanks guys," she said, "but we're married."

"To each other?" Whizzo asked.

Ginger laughed. "Actually, we'll both be on the loose before long."

"Ginger! What did you tell them that for?"

"Listen," said Charley, "if you're feeling married around me, that's OK, I'll leave."

"No, you stay there," said Ginger. "Lorene's just feeling a little shy."

"Hey, thass great, Ginger," said Whizzo. "Charley's shah too. Y'all are going to lahke one another."

Mostly by keeping his mouth shut and letting Whizzo do all the talking (not a hard thing to do in Whizzo's presence), Charley Orange wound up with a date.

He actually did like Lorene. She *was* shy, and soft-spoken, and seemed sad rather than mad. He could empathize with that, all right. As Whizzo and Ginger got up to go make the beast with two backs, Lorene announced to Charley, without any solicitation on his part, that she was confused at this time in her life and was being celibate.

Nonetheless, she invited him to a party. And she offered to drive.

◆◆◆

Inside the mansion, nary a wall nor floor was visible. They were covered with artifacts from around the world which the host had accumulated—not from his travels but from local antique shops, museums, garage sales and thrift stores. The ceilings were the most interesting of all, covered with various chandeliers, animal skins and occasional articles of furniture fastened upside-down onto them. The ballroom was lurid red.

The owner, Lorene told Charley, one Jude the Lewd, collected these artifacts compulsively: "sort of a lowbrow William Randolph Hearst."

Jude rented rooms in his velvet Wonderland for a song, sometimes on a work-exchange program, to exotic people who were down on their luck, "mostly porn actresses, who he chases around until they get tired of it and move out," said Lorene. "Sometimes he rents out the house as a porn movie locale. I was in one here last year."

Something inside Charley felt like it was getting a mixed message, but it couldn't transmit that thought to his consciousness because the only way into his consciousness was through his brain, which was in turmoil. *Why is she telling me all this? Why did she undo her top two buttons at the door? Is she really unavailable? Am I supposed to come charging in on my silver steed and sweep her past her fears? Quarter to one; wonder when she'll be ready to leave.*

"Lorene!"

"Oh, hi Dale."

"Come with me, honey, somebody wants to see you."

They went off, leaving Charley surrounded by twirling dancers, their bodies sending diadems of light reflecting off the rotating gels overhead. Snatches of conversation, shouted over the music, drifted through his ears: cut-ups of chop-logic.

"There's no free lunch."

"But life *is* a free lunch."

"I'm not superstitious, but I'd never piss on a fire."

"Yeah. I never make love during a thunderstorm."

"Show us your tits, Candy."

"How can they wage a war on drugs? I can't even drive on drugs!"

"Make love, not war on drugs."

“My guru says drugs give you holes in your aura.”

“That makes me holier than thou.”

“You’ve got a cold, too?”

“Yeah, well, what comes around, goes around.”

“SHOW US YOUR TITS, CANDY.”

“If we didn’t have fingerprints, the FBI would have to invent them.”

“Last Friday Mercury went retrograde and every fluid in my car is leaking.”

“Since I went on the Pond Scum, the wax in my ears has cleared up.”

Charley studied a couple in black: he could not tell which was man, which was woman, or...A smoky haze filled the room: Charley recognized the skunky odor of marijuana. He headed toward the bar, figuring to encounter and recapture the lost Lorene. Lorene was nowhere in sight. Neither was Dale. Charley checked out the kitchen, the patio, the pool.

At poolside he overheard two guys talking. “If a man talks dirty to a woman, it’s sexual harrassment,” one said. “If a woman talks dirty to a man, it’s $3.99 a minute.”

“Yeah, said the other. “Madonna masturbates on the screen and makes millions. Pee Wee Herman masturbates in the movie theater and gets busted.”

Here was a conversation Charley could relate to. “Women,” he said. “They think sex is sexist. Since when did their wells become monuments?”

A woman with her back to them heard him and turned. “Men. If they’re not in heat, they’re in trouble.”

“Hey, I know you’d rather have a headache than a good time.”

“Who are you, creepo, some kind of Republican or something?”

“No,” said Charley. “Republicans don’t pay taxes. I don’t pay women.”

“A real oinker, aren’t you? Ever hear of feminism?”

“‘Feminist’ is masculine. ‘Feminine’ is feminine.”

“Oh yeah? Reverse the penile code, I say. Bring back the matriarchy.”

"Sure. It's as different from the patriarchy as Coke is from Pepsi." Charley started singing:

There's a stone in her bowl
For the want of a bone in her hole.

"That's disgusting. It's all you guys think about. Don't shoot till you see the whites of their thighs."

"Just remember. Men make war because women don't make love."

"Well, remember this, Mr. Dinosaurus Assholus. Cock sucks." She flipped him the bird and stalked off.

Charley headed back inside. Lorene wasn't in a room filled with gynecology examination tables, or in the Blue Room, or Alice's tunnel or the main drawing room.

He entered another room with walls covered with great maps to everywhere, from all times of history. Maps of the solar system, the galaxy, the universe. Maps to buried treasure, maps to infinity, maps of the human mind.

This was Jude the Lewd's master bedroom. Even the bedspread was a map. A map of what? Charley Orange could not tell you, for at that moment he had a dissociative experience. There upon that map of someplace unknown, spread-eagled under the pinioning legs of some lecherous stallion, lay Lorene.

She was just beginning to moan when Charley opened the door. The sound was as mesmerizing as the scene was distasteful: Charley felt compelled to stand and watch.

Each time the stallion thrust, he arched his back a little more. Charley's jaw dropped.

The stallion had breasts. Round, soft breasts with aureolae the size and shape of silver dollars and the color of earthworms, enclosing nipples that jutted out like raspberry popsickles. All of that registered in Charley's brain before the rage hit.

He threw his glass onto the floor, shattering it, watching the shards flash rainbows as they fell through the light. "Hello, Lorene."

"What...? Charley! Meet Sharleen. She's my husband."

"You...said you were..." Charley's brain was saying, "Let's get out of here," but he was somewhere outside his body and didn't know how to make his legs work.

"A misunderstanding. That's all it was, a misunderstanding! Can you believe it?" She laughed and nuzzled Sharleen.

Coordination returned and Charley bolted for the bathroom. Behind the locked door, amid the gargoyles and pinwheels hung on the gauzy walls, he tried to focus on where he could go. He had left his wallet in his car; he was sans cash or credit cards. It was too late to call anyone on the team. OK, he would find a phone and call a cab, and the cabbie wouldn't ask for money until he got to Charley's car.

Good. He had a game plan. He opened the door and started a telephone search. Shit, there was Lorene.

"Charley, where are you going?"

"I don't know."

"Let me take you."

"You don't want to drive me and I don't want you to."

"Charley, there's nothing to be upset about. That's my sweetie I was with."

"Just leave me alone!"

Sharleen appeared from the map room. "Charley's upset," Lorene told her.

"Upset? She's my wife, Charley. What do you have to be upset about? I should be upset with you."

"Let me out of here!" Charley yelled. "None of you people make any sense." He ran out of the mansion and down the long, winding road toward the lights of the city.

It took Charley Orange two hours to find the juice bar and his rental car and return to the hotel. He roomed next door to Whizzo. Undoubtedly Foo Foo McGonigle and Wellington P. Sweetwater were

giving him a gentle hint to keep an eye on their high-spirited prodigy, but they knew better than to ask him.

When Charley arrived at his room, there was a Do Not Disturb sign on the door. Underneath was a note: "C: She wanted to do it in your room. Mahne's open. —W."

Fuck you, Pisso. Charley unlocked the door and strode in. "Ooooh! Aahhh!," he heard. "Oh baby, suck me good."

A porn flick was playing on the VCR. Silhouetted in the moonlight, in perfect, synchronized imitation, were Whizzo and Ginger. Did the sound effects come from the movie or from them?

Charley turned on the lights and clicked off a close-up of a pair of flesh-ridged lips—from which portion of the female anatomy he couldn't tell. "Sorry kids, I'm tired and I want my bed and besides I WASN'T ASKED."

"OK Charley, hold on jist a second. We're almost there."

"NOW!" He grabbed Whizzo by the hips and pulled, causing Whizzo to turn over just as he spurted, spilling semen all over Charley's bed.

"Aw, he's upset, darlin'. Hey Charley, what would you do in mah situation? Ah mean, Ginger starts to thinking about what it would be lahke to be with you—you know, she *lahkes* you—only she doesn't really want to *be* with you, jist sort of, you know, fantasahze it. So she says, 'Let's do it in his bed', and Ah says, 'Well now, Charley's a funny gah, he maght not lahke that,' didn't Ah say that, Ginger? And she says, 'Cain't you jist see the look on his face when he comes in?' and we laughed..."

"Whizzo," Charley said, slowly and deliberately, "I deserve better than this. And you do, too."

"Ah do?"

"You do," said Charley. "You deserve someone who won't get you into these situations."

Whizzo laughed. "Yeah, thass a good one, Charley. You got me there."

Ginger was up and putting on her clothes. "Charley," she said, "I'll bet you don't get yourself into these situations."

"That's right."

"Did you ever think that maybe you ought to? I have another friend who would probably like to meet you, but you're pretty grouchy."

"Forget it. It won't go anywhere."

Whizzo led Ginger toward the door. "Sorry about the *coitus interruptus,* honeydew. C'mon next door and we can finish what we started. Charley's really a cool gah, but he jist don't lahke the ladies."

"Oh no," Charley heard her say from down the hall. "He loves the ladies deeply. He's just one of the wounded."

"Thankya, darlin'. You're raght, as always."

Many baseball aficionados claim the double play is the most aesthetically pleasing maneuver in the game, but the relay from left field to try to prevent a run from scoring is arguably even more picturesque than Revenge at Second Base taking the feed from Bimbo Terwilliger, pivoting as he crosses the bag and firing the ball to Onions Malone at first, even as he leaps to prevent the hurtling body of the baserunner from crashing into his legs to take him out of the play. For the relay, left fielder, shortstop, third baseman, catcher and pitcher all line up at intervals along the left field line. As the shortstop receives the throw from left field, the third baseman shouts an instruction to him: Third! Home! Second! No Throw! (Don't risk throwing the ball away if no one's threatening to advance.) The most common version of the relay is also the most exciting: shortstop relays home to catcher, who straddles home plate. Ball and runner arrive as close together as noon and 12 o'clock. Is he out or safe? The pitcher backs up the catcher—and, if the pitcher is Whizzo Mark Salot IV, he coaches the umpire.

"Out!" yelled Whizzo, his arm shooting out like a snake striking, his finger pointing *a la* Uncle Sam luring innocent boys to war, his entire body consumed by a dramatic flourish in the time-honored tradition of umpires everywhere from the majors down to Tee Ball and diaper leagues.

As close together in time to Whizzo's call as the light changing and the guy behind you getting horny, Buster Hyman spread out his hands in the signal that always reminded him of the time he had massaged two prostitutes simultaneously. "Safe!"

"Oh no!" cried Bluster Hyman in the media booth. "Another blown call against the Mutants! I can tell you this, ladies and gentlemen: no team, no matter how good it is, can beat the pack if the men in blue don't want it to. This call..."

Sportscasters are supposed to maintain neutrality. Bluster's partisanship, which seeped up to the edges under the best of circumstances, often spilled over when brother Buster officiated. He and Buster both played in the Big Show—Bluster on the fringes, up and down for three seasons, while Buster was a 10-year man and two-time All-Star. Umpires do not win popularity contests, but everyone liked Buster—everyone, that is, but his rival sibling. Family ties notwithstanding, he was the mellowest umpire on the circuit.

But even Buster demanded the one demand of all umpires from the majors to the diapers: Don't show me up.

Buster glared at Whizzo. Whizzo looked back with pleading eyes.

Buster removed his mask and handed it to Whizzo. "Put it on."

As Whizzo donned the mask, a ripple of laughter came from the stands.

"I ought to throw you out," said Buster, removing his chest protector.

"Buster, you are looking great. Listen to them fans yukkin' it up. And on national TV, too. And me," Whizzo said, strapping on the chest protector. "Ah'm lookin' lahke a choo-choo fulla doo-doo. And in front of Foo Foo, too. Only Ah got me one question: how do we get ourselves out of this? You gonna pitch?"

"That's your worry, bigmouth. You're the umpire."

"Ah got it!" Whizzo twisted around and whirled himself into a finger-arm-body ballet even more grandiloquent than when he called out the runner. "You are outahere!" he shouted at Buster. "You been makin' too many bad calls."

The ripple of laughter rose to a roar. Whizzo handed Buster back his gear and helped him into it.

"That's it, Whizzo. You broke the code. You're done for this game."

"Buster, Ah jist now let you back in the game. If'n you don't let me back too, you're gonna look lahke fudge from the toilet."

Buster considered for a moment. "You're back," he said, bowing magnanimously. "But not because I curry favor with the fans, which as you know I never do, but because I like you. Now clam up and pitch."

Whizzo returned to the mound and held the baseball to his ear. Whatever the ball said made him giggle and point his finger at Buster. He said something back to the ball, shaking his head and giggling again, all the while looking at Buster. Buster watched the charade impassively, a serene smile on his face.

Finally Whizzo delivered. Choo-Choo Charley came right down the pike toward Hector La Cuenta, batting for the visiting Lemon Sox, hopping every whichway like a plateful of Mexican jumping beans as it sliced and diced the plate into Picasso pieces.

"Ball one!' bellowed Buster Hyman.

Charley Orange blinked: What? He turned his head. "Buster...?"

"Turn around, Orang-utan, or it'll be Ball 2 before he throws. La Cuenta, you've got a free ride."

"Uh—Buster—how many free rides do you figure it'll take before you're even?"

"Ten. Twenty. A hundred. But I'm only calling one. The official penalty for showing up an umpire. It doesn't bother me personally as you know, but I have my colleagues to protect. And you sit right there, Orang-utan. Let Wonder Balls figure it out for himself. And please dear God, let him raise one word of protest."

The next four pitches completed possibly the most perfectly executed sequence Charley had ever been privileged to witness. The first was Choo-Choo Charley again, high and hard. It looked like it might bounce off La Cuenta's left shoulder, but at the last instant it ducked sideways just into the strike zone.

"Ball two!" roared Buster.

Next came Big Peter, low-riding the black like a hobo under a cattle car, knee-high along the outside corner.

"Ball three!"

The next one floated in right over the plate. La Cuenta unleashed a swing that started dust devils spinning in center field. The ball dove down like a Peregrine falcon. La Cuenta and the ball fell into the dirt as close together in time as the Big Bang and Let There Be Light.

Buster Hyman's hand started up to signal Ball Four.

"Buster," said Charley. "If you call that a ball, you'll lose your job. And maybe your life: we *are* the home team."

"Thank you, Charley. *Strike one!* La Cuenta, why in hell did you swing?"

"O-oooh, that peetch! It look so sweet! I theenk I can take that peetch downstown. Free pass *gracias amigo,* but Sox need mucho Boom!"

On Whizzo's final delivery the ball came to a halt and hovered like a hummingbird not an inch from La Cuenta's eye. As he hit the dirt it detoured left and down, nibbling off the back centimeter of the plate.

"Ball four!" bellowed Buster. "And if he throws that again, I'll go out there and issue a beanball warning."

Whizzo was wisely—and uncharacteristically—silent. He struck out Buenos Tardes Chihuahua to retire the side. Seventh-inning stretch; Mutants 1, Lemon Sox 1.

The rookie Developed Smith was off the bench swinging bats and doughnuts, ready to hit for Whizzo, due up second. "How's the bungee, young man?" asked Foo Foo McGonigle.

"Hit's a-snappin' and a-poppin', Skip. Ah can feel them muscles in mah arm, jist rollin' out when mah Sweet Patooties leave mah hand."

"In a tie score, namely ones, my catcher gets on I go with my bench. If not, we keep bettin' your Sweet Patootie we do."

Charley grounded to short.

Whizzo had twice gone down swinging on Hector Tortilla's curveball. Here came—surprise! Another curve. He watched it break a foot off the plate. "Strike one!" shouted Buster Hyman.

Whizzo was as silent as a giraffe with laryngitis. The second pitch was a clone of the first. "Strike two!"

Whizzo turned to Buster Hyman. "Buster! Ah jist figured it out. Ah'm sorry for all them hahjinks on the mound. Ah didn't mean to show you up."

"Too late, funny guy. Now turn around. You're showing me up."

"OK amigo," Whizzo shouted out to Tortilla on the hill. "Chuck it in here. Ah gotta show Buster here how we play ball in the Ozarks."

As Tortilla's pitch sailed in somewhat closer to the plate than third base, Whizzo leaned over on tiptoe, stretched out his arms and golfed at it. A cue ball squirted off the end of his bat and floated like a butterfly over Bienvenidos Buenaventura's head at third, landing on the line and waddling off like a lost mallard into foul territory. Rejuvenated, it bounded into the corner like a hare, caromed off the wall past the left fielder Hector Borracho and rolled to a stop in precisely the spot Borracho had just vacated. Finally Buenos Tardes Chihuahua arrived from center to retrieve the ball and fire it in.

What was that excited roar shaking the very foundations of Mutant Stadium? Had all of Gaia's starving children been fed? All of her endangered frogs been saved? Had world peace been declared? No, it was more visceral than that: Whizzo Mark Salot IV had just steamed across the plate standing with an inside-the-park home run.

The tally stood up: Mutes 2, Sox 1. "Seems like all he has to do is throw his glove on the mound and we're licked," Sox manager Macarena Gonzales Gonzales Ponce de Leon grumbled to the media.

Whizzo wasn't in the locker room following the game. After an hour Bluster Hyman came across a vast circle of kids under the stands. In the center was the Big Kid himself, his red hair still dripping wet, signing autographs and spinning tales of the Bigs to a rapt audience. Bluster tried in vain to get a microphone to him, but Whizzo just shouted and laughed from behind his 20-wide youngsterhood moat.

Out of the blue a manta ray breaches; above it glides a Magnificent frigate-bird, silhouetted against the kind of tumbling white cumulus

cloud that Yahweh Himself might choose upon which to rest His celestial posterior.

Looking up from the ancient rowboat into which he and Sage are hauling anaconda-length ribbons of kelp, breaking them off only when the various marine lifeforms clinging to them become too numerous to remove, Maxwell Veribushi *namaste's*. The waves swallow the manta; the frigate-bird soars off into the sunset.

After a scant 48 years on the planet, Maxwell had achieved enough for two lifetimes: renown among the frogfolk of the world, five failed university posts, two failed marriages, and…uh, his Research Assistant. And Sage, the love of his life, the apple of his eye, the cuddlebug of his arms' delight, the Veribushi mind, soul and passion, preserved in her wispy little eight-year-old body. Sage. Sage is wise. Sage smells good. And Sage is Very Bushy! Her mother liked the name, too. Despite Sage's intellectual inheritance (or, Maxwell thought ruefully, because of it), she had racked up an impressive academic failure record of her own.

Pulling up anchor, Sage gazed toward the shore. Those big birds were there again, swooping and diving through the sky like jet planes piloted by butterflies.

"The Peregrine falcons are teaching their babies how to hunt," Maxwell told her. "See those little birds, swooping and twittering across the swale, just as happy as medium-sized girls who get to eat kelpburgers tonight?"

"Daddy, am I medium-sized now?"

"I just promoted you. Every time I call you 'little girl' you get to call me…what?"

"Uncle Foolsday!"

"All right, little girl."

"All right, Uncle Foolsday."

'Nuff said. It's the kind of conversation you must be part of to appreciate. Back to the Peregrine falcons. "Now, those little birds are swallows," said Maxwell. "They're the swiftest, loop-de-loopiest little birds in the sky, the hardest of all to catch, but the Peregrines don't even look at the other birds. And the swallows—do they go and hide? No, they only want to play: tirra lee, tirra lai, through the tree, through the sky. Now watch..."

Maxwell's decision a few years ago to buy this island, chuck it all and return to the ancient ways, bringing along Sage to love, father and educate, was the best move he had ever made. He discovered what he always knew: he was a master teacher. And Sage was quick to absorb, discover, intuit, as long as no schools existed within 100 miles to interfere with the process.

Off on the swale, the Peregrines, eschewing the slower birds as Maxwell had said, performed a *danse macabre* with the swooping swallows, precognosing their precise location six swoops and 14 seconds into the future and then diving until falcon and swallow vectors intersected in a Blood Wedding of hunter and prey.

Of course, no man is an island, and Maxwell knew Sage needed some socializing. (He also had to placate her mother, a successful ballerina, still performing but aging, soon to give up the second great love of her life. The first—Sage—she agreed to let live with her father because she knew it was best for Sage.)

So every summer Maxwell and Sage packed off the island to experience the hellfires of civilization. First they spent a month in Megaglopoulis, where Sage visited mom and Maxwell visited the laboratory of sorts that he maintained, kept operating year-round by his indefatigable Research Assistant. S/HeIt knows what experiments she would have concocted this year by the time he arrived. Still, the very thought of her stirred feelings in his inner thighs that he thought had congealed into pudding after eight months away or had been consumed by the Turkey vultures of Time.

Megaglopoulis also allowed Maxwell to indulge briefly in his single civilized vice: baseball. For not the first time this season, he wondered how the Mutes were doing.

The other three months of their travels were Sage's favorite times. Maxwell focused all his rebellious energy, so foreign to the hallowed halls of academe, onto the deepest concern in his heart: the frogs. Behold the Jugalog Frog & Toad on the Road Show. Sage ran tech (three light switches), played bit parts and introduced Professor Harebrain (easy for Maxwell to play), Congressperson Rufus T. Green,

◆◆◆

Bobo the Buddhist Batrachian, Captain Clearlight, and finally the interdimensional entity Babar.

Today was still springtime. Maxwell and Sage walked the path through the woods toward home, carrying the kelp in buckets. Once home, they tore the leaves and hung them to dry on the maze of clotheslines Maxwell had strung. They could get $6 per pound for kelp, which worked out to at least $1.49 per hour, plus all the unpolluted, ocean-fresh kelp they could eat.

"Look, daddy!" said Sage. "The ants caught a bee and they're killing it."

"Good eye, Sage. That bee is actually a yellowjacket wasp. See his yellow jacket? And ants can't catch them unless they're ready to die. The ants just clean up for us." Maxwell, usually immersed in the primeval dramas unfolding around him, found his mind returning to the letter that had arrived in his mailbox on the Mainland last week: an invitation to speak at the American Anurology Association's annual meeting in Megaglopoulis.

When he first read it, a strange feeling gripped him from his neck down past his stomach, as if a python were being cracked like a bullwhip around the insides of his torso. In that instant, he knew he was going.

He had something to say to his colleagues.

The third inning was scoreless.

FOURTH INNING

Love is the most important thing in
the world, but baseball is pretty good too.
—Greg, age 8

How could anyone ever tell you
That you're anything less than beautiful?
—Libby Roderick

ANLOIE TURNS HER ancient pink Plymouth Fury station wagon down Earnshaw Boulevard.

She hopes the police won't notice her defective taillight.

On her dashboard:

She has a shank of wool form-fit and glued to it.

She has the wool covered with doily lace.

She has a sachet of dried lavender and jasmine.

She has a bundle of sage smudge-sticks, given to her by a bag lady whom she bought a cup of coffee.

She has a flock of bright blue jay feathers that she has collected on walks in various forests.

She has two sketches given to her by a drunken sidewalk artist who claimed he was the Last of the Mescalero Apache Warriors.

She has a smooth jade stone that a friend sent her from Bora Bora.

She has brightly-colored stones gathered from a streamside walk.

She has seashells from the seashore.

She has a small metal pipe.

She has a "wish box" containing many of the above items, plus paper stars and hearts, confetti, glitter, crystals, Christmas tinsel and an amulet with the number '7' on it. On the lid is a decal adorned with two angels.

She has a 'Love Animals, Don't Eat Them' bumpersticker stuck onto her glove box.

She has a cord extending from her cigarette lighter to an air ionizer wedged in between the seats.

She has a garden in her ashtray: a chamomile plant, a bonzai cactus, a mossy white flower she found by a roadside.

At 47th St. she turns left. A truck driver honks and waves at her. She smiles back.

Dangling from her rear-view mirror:

She has three beaded necklaces that she has strung for sale or for trade.

She has a leather necklace with an ankh hanging from it that she has traded for one of hers.

She has a purple-blue-and-green rollerblade lace.

She has a string of dental floss.

At a red light at 12th Avenue the driver next to her catches her attention and makes a silent obscene proposal. She laughs and rolls her eyes.

On her head:

She has her hat.

On her hat:

She has more feather—from a pet duck that died.

She has a garland of dried roses given to her by an admirer.

She has a butterfly brooch.

She has a pin shaped like a heart with wings on its sides.

She has a pin that says HUGGERS ARE HEALERS.

At 7th Avenue, as she turns right her car backfires. Pedestrians look up and, seeing its vintage pinkness and her laughing face, applaud and shout. The Fury bows and does an encore.

In her back seat (pulled down to accommodate it all):

She has two summer dresses, draped over the other items so as not to wrinkle.

She has a valise packed with the rest of her summer wardrobe: six bikinis, three pairs of cutoff jeans, a few halter tops, pink and purple socks, undies, two bras (one C-cup, one B—she never can decide), some gauzy blouses, various scarves and shawls and a small dark bagful of items we shall not mention here, designed to disguise her Affliction.

She has boxes and bags full of food: fresh organic peaches and apricots and politically correct grapes; potatoes and carrots, onions, dulse, sunflower seeds, rice cakes, organic rice, millet and barley, a small bag of gum drops (she couldn't resist) and at least a pound of blue-green algae (she sells that too, multilevel—oops, make that network marketing).

She has a Walkman.

She has a box of WHAMMO frisbees.

Near Broadway, a cop pulls her over. She stuffs the small metal pipe under her halter. "Your left brake light is out," says the cop, but when she smiles he doesn't cite her.

On the seat beside her:

She has a handmade cloth rucksack containing all the items it usually contains. Space prevents listing them here.

She has a Guatemalan handbag containing all the items it usually contains. Space prevents listing them here.

She has an Evian bottle filled with water and blue-green algae, which she swills from time to time.

She has a ziplock bag full of "sea moons," yummy little balls of quick-energy nutrition for which only she knows the recipe.

She has a Polaroid of her with Warren, dancing under magenta-lit palms.

As she pulls into the stadium parking lot at Broadway and Trombley, she tears the Polaroid in two.

She has, as always, a bright red hibiscus flower in her hair.

"I tell you zometing about da voman," said Dr. Weisenheimer, washing down a chocolate bar with a cup of apple cider. "Vhat she is laying onto da man. Da voman is saying da man be leading around by our dicks. Ha! She is going only mit da man who most is stirring da feeling in her sex. Now, if she be intelligence, she is needing da man's brain for be getting totally turn on; if she be spiritual, needing da man's spirit; unt if she be voman of emotion (unt zome of dem be), needing too da man's heart, but alvays she is vanting most da von ting: his sex. Or, to being grammatic…"— and Dr. Weisenheimer, ever since his arrival from the old country, strove always to be grammatic—"his sexualty."

Dr. Weisenheimer caught himself just as he was about to go on. "But dis you are already knowing, mein friend. How can I be helping to you today?"

"Well Dr.," said Charley Orange, "I've been looking at the few dates I've had in the past year, and these women were just in it for the free food. Why couldn't I have been born female? They flash those furry credit cards and they can get anything they want. I mean, what a mentality! They expect gifts. Like tribute. And what do they offer in return? They don't even like sex."

"No? Da sex dey are not liking?"

"Either they don't like it or I'm the ugliest guy on the planet. That's how I feel: like I'm a frog. Whenever I think about women, I wind up feeling like this, since they do seem to like sex with other guys. At least they have it with them."

"Yes, mein friend, I know how you are feeling. I am never raping anybody. I am growing up batter by rageaholic mudder and den my angry lovers are calling me Oppressor. Ha! No vonder I am feeling abuse. I am *being* abuse. I too am feeling like number one ugly person in da vorld. But den I am looking myself in da mirror unt saying, No, I am not da frog. Not da movie star, but not eidder da Quasimodo."

Like a paronychia forming around a toenail, like a pearl around a grain of oysterous sand, a bead of sweat appeared from nowhere on Dr. Weisenheimer's forehead. Charley watched in fascination as it came into being where a moment before was nothing, as if from a parallel universe.

"So vhat is being go on? Zometime I am tinking dere is zometings terrible wrong mit me. But vhat? I am not seeing anytings. So I am asking my voman friends. Alvays I am hafing many intimate voman friends. Day are all telling me how I have attraction and lots of da voman are lofing to getting deir hands onto me. Not da vons telling me, of course, dey are not *personally* feeling dis vay. Dey are not vanting to risk losing our—how you say it, da friendship."

"Uh, Dr.," said Charley, "your life is interesting but Mr. Sweetwater is not paying you $120 an hour for me to listen to *your* problems."

"No no, of course not Charley, I just be sharing mit you mine own experience for da building rapport, unt also for testing how are you reacting to it. So do ve be hafing about money da issue?"

"No, only about time."

"All right, is gut. Zo zometimes I am feeling ja, ugly unt udder times figuring da voman to being cruel unt crazy. Vhy dey be so pushing avay love? So I am deciding, vhy not to do zometing about it? You tink I be still talking about myself. But nein."

The bead of sweat on Dr. Weisenheimer's brow stood poised to trigger an avalanche down his cheek. It had gathered weight and grown plump toward the bottom, like a pear—or, thought Charley, a dangling, pendulous breast. Two things held it in place: a gathering surface tension and a tenuous balance on a slight ridge on Dr. Weisenheimer's glabella.

"Charley, you are not hermit. Not misogynist. You are deeply vounded person. Not to being overly dramatic: in dis country is everyvon vounded person. Makes ting of da past da terapeutic diagnosis. Zo, you see? Already ve are coming long vays. Tell me, vhat her name is?"

"My current obsession? Lorene—but I'm not obsessed by being in love with her. I'm obsessed with rage toward her."

"Nein, nein, you mudder name. Alvays it is da mudder. Da fadder. Da siblings. Maybe da mean aunt or fondling grandmama. It is writting in da *Agamemnon:* da sins of da parents upon da children are visiting."

Charley's father, he told Dr. Weisenheimer, was a good man who held onto his job as a construction engineer—he helped build the neighborhood Charley grew up in—all his life despite some severe bouts with the bottle. If it ever crossed his mind that he was alcoholic, he did not share the thought with Charley. Only after his cirrhotic liver carried him off when Charley was 20 did Charley's mother dare mention it aloud.

"He was supportive of my major-league ambitions, but, realistically assessing my chances, he insisted that I finish college before signing any contracts. I majored in philosophy, with a minor in parallel universes."

"Ah, philosophy," nodded Dr. Weisenheimer. "No vonder da unhappiness. Unt you mudder?"

◆◆◆ ◆

Charley's mother was a woman of violent mood swings. One minute she would sweep him in her arms and waltz him around the house; the next, she would beat him uncontrollably for giggling at the dinner table.

Charley fared better with her than did Mr. Orange, with whom she never waltzed. She never spoke ill of him while he was alive, but she didn't smile at his jokes either. Charley thought she resented both her husband and her children for depriving her of a career in art, although her only completed work—a woman being swallowed by a fish next to a man tied to a tree and covered with spiders—which hung in the dining room, showed more resentment than promise to Charley.

"So yes," Charley concluded, "my family was dysfunctional, in the current idiom, although an inexact idiom it is: in the eyes of the outside world, we were just another normal, stable family in a normal, stable neighborhood."

As Dr. Weisenheimer took a swallow of apple cider, the motion dislodged the drop of sweat. Swoosh! Down came the rain and washed the cider out. Dr. Weisenheimer's hanky was on it in a flash. "In ze province of ze heart vere being commit heinous crimes, scarring beyond all imagination: your little child psyche vas shooting full of holes, your heart vas beating until behind a vall of terror retreating." Charley felt sweat on his own face. Dr. Weisenheimer's graphic descriptions were triggering flashes of memories not buried but long suppressed.

"You see Charley, alvays it is da family. Mein mudder, she vas beating me mit da belt, unt mein fadder mit da fists. Zometimes all over my body is cover mit da blacks and blues marks. But I am deciding how can I heal dis vound of mine? Unt I am finding out. I can be lofing parent to meinself dat I never have. I learn vhat you are saying in dis country, it is never too late to be hafing happy childhood."

"You think I should be my own mother and father?"

"Mom unt dad. Your little boy is starfing for love, Charley."

"My what? I don't have any kids."

"Closing your eyes unt breadding. OK. Putting your hand on your heart. Do you feeling him beat in dere?"

Charley breathed. Slowly the eensie weensie spider of his nightmares crawled up the spout again.

"Practicing dat until ve are meeting again. Also starting to draw complete picture of your ideal voman, so you are not to passing her by vhen you are meeting her."

"Ding ding," said Dr. Weisenheimer's watch.

"Time," said Dr. Weisenheimer.

Friends, if you want to know baseball, you have to knuckle down and hit the books. Nothing is trivial in the diamond-shaped universe: fans have grasped the Deep Ecological principle that everything is of equal importance. King Kong Keller's lifetime slugging percentage is no more or less noteworthy than the dying of the frogs. The Day the Music Died shares equal billing with The Year the Bums Left Brooklyn.

Billy Beanball is 11. Already he knows as much about baseball as Maxwell Veribushi knows about frogs. He has skipped his Pokemon chat room to be today's contestant on Bluster Hyman's Diamond Quiz.

Bluster: OK Billy, you know the rules. Answer seven questions and win season box-seat tickets behind home plate. Ready?

Billy: Ready.

Bluster: Abner Doubleday didn't invent baseball; Robert Ripley did. Believe these or not. First question: Of more than 40,000 men who have played in the major leagues since 1900, what is unusual about the very first name in the alphabetical listings in the Official Encyclopedia of Baseball?

Billy: It belongs to Henry Aaron, the player who leads all others in baseballs' most prestigious offensive record: home runs.

Bluster; Right. Two: What two significant feats did Babe Ruth accomplish on his final day in the majors?

Billy: He hit three home runs for only the second time in his career, including the first one ever hit right out of Forbes Field in Pittsburgh.

Bluster: Right again. Three: Exactly one player was active that day when the Babe arced his last rainbow and the day Henry Aaron hit his first. Who?

Billy: Phil Cavarretta.

Bluster: Good. Four: Until 1991, no team since 1914 had vaulted from last place to first in a single season. That year, which two of them met in the World Series?

Billy: The Minnesota Twins beat the Atlanta Braves.

Bluster: Kee-rect. Five: What is Ripleyesque about the only National League player ever to hit two grand slams in a game?

Billy: He was a pitcher: Tony Cloninger of the Atlanta Braves in 1966.

Bluster: Six: Who was traded for himself?

Billy: Harry Chiti.

Bluster: That's right. Last question: Who were the only two players whose last names are palindromes who appeared in the same game?

Billy: What's a palindrome?

Bluster: Oh no, busted out. As in baseball, the only probable is the improbable. Too bad Billy, but here's your consolation prize: two box seat tickets along the third-base line for tomorrow's game, with Whizzo Mark Salot IV on the mound.

If parallel universes did not exist, the CIA would have to invent them. The cost would be, literally, astronomical. But if the CIA were to stick its head in the sand and ignore reality, as some have wished it would, we could wake up tomorrow surrounded by alien spacetime without ever knowing it. We may anyway, as the latest notion to come sailing like a paper airplane out the windows of the ivory towers says the parallel universes are as flat as pancakes and stacked atop each other like an infinite pile of dollar bills. (They may even be used as currency by gaseous beings of megaversal heft.) Old Touslehead showed that in a saddle-shaped universe, parallel lines do meet. So too, in a megasaddle-shaped megaverse, if they're all stacked together like dollar bills, must parallel universes.

Thank S/HeIt that parallel universes do exist and we don't have to deal with yet another CIA snafu. In some of these universes (probably dreamed up by the CIA), Mighty Casey upholds American values by dialing long distance. In some (probably dreamed up by daffy southpaws), baserunners circle the bases backwards.

In still others (dreamed up by authors with no better things to write about), Whizzo Mark Salot IV lost his fourth game, evening his record at 2-2, and went on to become just another ballplayer, a so-so hurler with a mediocre record.

Not so in our parallel universe. Whizzo won, 3-1.

Before she knew what she was doing, Anloie bolted over the railing from Section 12 onto the field. In her enthusiasm, her hibiscus blossom fell from her hair.

Propelled gracefully by Cupid's wings even despite her Affliction, her feet swept her into the path of Whizzo Mark Salot IV, on whose lips she planted a full-mouthed, passionate, juicy kiss.

A young boy, inspired by Anloie's daring, rushed after her toward Whizzo. "Great game, Whizzo."

"Thanks, gah. What's your name?"

"Billy Beanball."

"Well, shake there, Elmer. Listen, Ah wonder if'n you would do me a great big favor."

"Sure, Whizzo! What?"

"The lady dropped her flower. Would you be so kahnd as to go get it for her?"

Photo ops: Billy runs to the hibiscus. CLICK!

Whizzo grabs Anloie's hand and they circle the bases together, backwards. CLICK!

Just past second base, Billy Beanball joins them. CLICK!

All three slide into home together. CLICK!

◆◆◆ ◆

Wiping their breakfast off their ties and moustaches, the distinguished members of the American Anuran Association filed into the hall. Unlike most academic disciplines, Anurology boasts a healthy percentage of superannuated Nature Boys and Girls, delightful lifelong frogaholics who, ever since they discovered those fabled creatures at age five or so, spend every free waking moment out in the swamps playing with them.

Unfortunately, none of these types would be caught dead at an AAA meeting. This left that organization securely in the hands of these icons of respectability, who preferred the odors of ether bottles and machine coffee to the redolence of swamp sediment, the petty politics of tenure and titles to the post-anthropocentric democracy of one lifeform, one vote. To them, amphibians were but means to their all-too-human ends.

"I hear Veribushi's keynoting. Wonder what he has in store for us?"

"Poor fellow. Best in the field, but..."

"Poor, nothing. Have you ever met that Research Assistant of his?"

"Is his talk listed? Oh yes, here it is...'Acknowledgment of Recent Declines in Selected Ranid Populations, Examination of Post-Industrial Environmental and Possible Atmospheric Origins and Consequent Ethnopharmacological, Mythopoetic and Other Reductions in Homo Sapient Interfaces'."

"Excellent title. I'd heard he's been living out there on some island, blowing out his brains with drugs and sex."

"Ah—gentlemen," said the microphone, "...and, ah, yes, gentlewomen—or is it ladies?" the chairperson fumbled with the etiquette of equality. "At Dr. Veribushi's request, I am introducing him as—ah, Captain Clearlight."

Underneath the applause that acknowledged his past accomplishments, an undercover of apprehension spread through the room. Across the stage to the podium strode Maxwell Veribushi, wearing a tie-dye shirt, red-white-and-blue bell bottoms and granny glasses with pink heart-shaped lenses. From behind the far wing he wheeled out a gong large enough to announce dinner in downtown Singapore, and a mallet, which he placed on the dais.

"THE FROGS ARE DYING!" he screamed.

Then he picked up the mallet and hammered the gong with a swing that Horst Throttlemeyer would be proud of. GON-N-N-N-N-N-N-N-G!!!

"You and I, my sisters and brothers, are observing and recording the most terrible passage in our planet's 4.3-billion year history.

"All across the fair face of Gaia, her frogs are dying.

"You and I, my sisters and brothers, bear witness to the Eco-Holocaust, and its first and most tragic victims to date: the amphibians.

No one knows why.
Not you, not I.
No one knows why.
Will they all die?

Maxwell was not saying anything his learned ex-colleagues didn't already know. More than a decade ago these same scientists had begun comparing notes at meetings and realizing that across the globe, the frogs, the toads, the newts and salamanders were checking off the planet faster than aristocrats flying to their Swiss banks during a revolution. Even while the billion-beat boogie of biodiversity was being Lombardo-ized into a funeral march by the pied pipers of Progress and sham shamanics of fast breeders and Frankenflora and fauna, Gaia's most ancient terrestrial vertebrates were being flattened into tiddlywinks under the tractor treads of technology faster than a blink of S/HeIt's eye.

"THE FROGS ARE DYING!" Maxwell shouted again. "Will you mourn with me?" G-O-N-N-N-N-N-N-N-N-G!

"Australia. *Rheobatracus silus,* a dutiful parent that swallowed its eggs and brooded and hatched them in its own stomach. 1973, discovered, 1980, extinct." G-O-N-N-N-N-N-N-N-N-G!

"India. *Rana temporalis,* soon to pay the ultimate sacrifice on the altar of human biology study. How many of you, my dear ex-colleagues, dissected *R. temporalis* specimens in your training, or requisitioned them for your students?" G-O-N-N-N-N-N-N-N-N-G!

"U.S.A. *Rana pipians*—Las Vegas Valley subspecies. It evolved in the harsh mountain climate of the Southwest and Mexico and survived ice ages and aeons of dry desertification. But it was no match for the concrete jungles where *Homo unsapiens* likes to live, or the poisons on the killing fields of his agribusiness. Undiscovered until 1992, after it had already passed through that dark doorway to oblivion." G-O-N-N-N-N-N-N-N-G!

"U.S.A., right here in Megaglopoulis. *Rana onca,* the Relict leopard frog, born 150,000,000 B.C., returned to the vortex from whence it came during our lifetimes, 34 years ago when they filled in Mosquito Marsh to accommodate a most trivial human pursuit." G-O-N-N-N-N-N-N-N-G!

"Costa Rica: We all know the tragedy of *Bufo periglenes,* the beautiful golden toad, gone the way of the morning's mayflies in the heat of the noonday sun." G-O-N-N-N-N-N-N-N-N-G!

"Brazil: Eight of 13 species at the Reserva Atlantica, swept under the carpet of human encroachment like so many motes of Eternity's dust." G-O-N-N-N-N-N-N-N-N-G! G-O-N-N-N-N-N-N-N-N-G! G-O-N-N-N-N-N-N-N-N-G! G-O-N-N-N-N-N-N-N-N-G! G-O-N-N-N-N-N-N-N-G! G-O-N-N-N-N-N-N-N-N-G! G-O-N-N-N-N-N-N-N-G! G-O-N-N-N-N-N-N-N-N-G!

By now the gong had put everyone in an altered state, but Maxwell elegized on, tolling it for species after species extirpated or eradicated from the planet or parts of it. Some still survived, but in numbers too small to create viable genetic pools. These he referred to as "zombies: the walking dead."

Fortunately, before his last dismissal at O-A U., Maxwell had secured a research project that paid him enough to live on, investigating pretty much whatever he wanted to. It wasn't that his learned ex-colleagues disapproved of his message; *au contraire,* he was preaching to the choir. But his ex-colleagues mourned less the passing of the amphibia than that of their once-brilliant cohort's gray matter.

It wasn't really the Sixties schtick, though that might have been enough by itself. It wasn't the—what was it, some cartoon character he had named himself after? It wasn't even the ear-piercing echoes of that most unmusical instrument, still GONGONGONGONGONGing in their heads. All these were given as reasons to *tsk tsk* and shake their heads at the mention of his name.

But when you get to the bottom of it, what it was, was plain old-fashioned jealousy over his Research Assistant.

Carefully so as not to dislodge her hibiscus, Anloie tossed her long aureate locks back out of her face where the afternoon breeze had deposited them and looked around the hotel suite that Whizzo Mark Salot IV called home. For a teenaged bachelor, Whizzo was surprisingly neat. It took at least a half-hour after the maid departed for the decor to revert to Early American Rumple. Today, alas, was the maid's day off.

Not a pot not to call a kettle black, Anloie asked, "Why don't you live in a house?"

"Houses are for families. Ah jist left me a big family back home and Ah miss 'em all. Ah'd get lonesome if'n Ah couldn't step raght out into good company."

Oh-oh. Whizzo's words plunked a resonant chord in her heart. "Wasn't that little boy just so cute today, bringing me my flower?"

"Billy Beanball. He wrote out his name and number for me. Didn't that feel good, sugar dumplin', the three of us slahding into home plate together?...Jist like a family." Whizzo gulped. He had never felt quite that feeling before, even with his own family. "You know darlin', Ah do believe this conversation is making me a trahfle dizzy."

Anloie turned on the twinkle machine in her bedazzling blue eyes. "Whizzo, I do believe it's making you a trifle scared." Not a pot not to call a kettle black.

"Scared? Yeah, thass the word Ah was looking for. But don't you worry none. Ah can overcome it. Sweetcakes, would you marry me?"

A guffaw leaped from Anloie's throat before she knew it, like a Chinese frying fish leaping from the flying pan into the file. "Not likely! But I've known you for three hours and I haven't ruled it out yet."

"Well, thank heaven for that. So listen, Ah should ax your daddy for your hand. Where was he today?"

"Same place he's been for the last ten years. In his grave."

"Oh! Ah'm sorry. But…then who is the gentleman Ah see escorting you to the games?"

"His name is Warren. Someone I have had a very special relationship with."

"Ah see. And what maght that relationship have been?"

"He was…well, he's gone back home now, but actually he still is my frisbee coach."

"Your frisbee coach! You are a frisbee pro? Are you on a team?"

"I'm a frisbee champion. I hold the world record for throwing a frisbee out over the ocean and catching it behind my back the most consecutive times."

Whizzo was impressed. Excited, even. "No kidding. You are that good?"

Had he known of her Affliction, and how she had flung her way to the top despite it, he would have been even more excited. But some things, Anloie felt, are better kept secret.

"I am that good. You can look it up in the Guinness Book of Records. My ambition is to throw a frisbee out over the ocean, turn three cartwheels in the sand and then catch the frisbee behind my back."

"You are somethin' else! Ah want to be there to see you do that. So…this Warren coaches you. Now, am Ah mistaken or did you speak about your relationship with him in the past tense?"

"Well, I did…and I'm not sure. I mean, we've broken up before."

The hautboy playing "I Got You Babe" in Whizzo's heart hit an off-key note. "Ah don't believe we're still talking coaches and frisbees here."

"No…we were lovers on and off for four years. He has some scary ideas about some things that are important to me."

"Lahke what?"

"Just...things." About her Affliction, for one thing, and she certainly wasn't going to tell Whizzo about that. Warren was the only man she had ever confided in, and that was only after knowing him for six months. And that hadn't turned out so well now, had it, Anloie? Nonetheless, Warren was the one whom she had let plant his flag in her untouched turf, her purpling cherry pop, her pulchritudinous seas incarnadine. "But still, things happen. We've gotten back together before. I have to recognize the bond there."

"Ah guess..." said Whizzo.

What, was he agreeing? "But I also have to recognize our bond. Listen, this psychic lady told me that in 12 to 15 months I would meet a red-headed man in a uniform. It would be in a crowded public place and very noisy. She said this man would be the main person in my life for many, many years. All I could picture was a downtown cop, you know, or maybe a fireman at a rescue, with the neighborhood looking on. So I forgot about it. Then in June I saw you pitch your first game, and watching you I felt some strange excitement, but I didn't remember her words until just before game time today, and June was exactly 14 months since I saw her."

Whizzo couldn't believe his ears. "Well, let me tell you somethin', sweet darlin', it was haghly cosmic for me too." Looking into those bewitching eyes made him light-headed all over again: he felt he was falling into them. "The naght before mah first game Ah dreamed Ah was nervous and Ah came to a field of hahbiscuits and they calmed me raght down. And then when the game started and Ah got to the mound Ah was so nervous mah knees was knockin', and Ah looked over and saw that hahbiscuit bloomin' in your lovely hair, and hit jist smoothed me raght out insahde. And Ah said to mahself, who is that lovely Goddess who cast such a miraculous spell on me?"

Anloie giggled. "Is that when you decided to propose to me?"

Whizzo had been stroking her hair; he moved to her neck. "Well, Ah don't raghtly recollect since Ah had a lot on mah mahnd at the tahme. But—ah, listen sugarpah, Ah knowed you were the one for me even before you told me about your frisbee accomplishments. Do you suppose we could consummate our impending nuptials tonaght?"

He was serious. Anloie went numb with fear. Her memory flooded with all the nights she had spent crying herself to sleep. "No. Whizzo, I'm afraid I don't meet your ideal of what a woman is supposed to be."

As a toiler whose livelihood depends on chucking up baseballs to batters at varying speeds to keep them off-balance, and as a stud whose success rate with the ladies hovered right around the 100 percent mark, Whizzo Mark Salot IV had an excellent sense of timing. Yes, his proposition came quickly, but it followed by a decent interval his proposal. And it fit Anloie's responses tonight—and her initiations. Her recalcitrance more than surprised him; it downright mystified him. "What in the world is this prahme example of spectacular womanhood talking about?" was his first thought. "OK, she can be coy," was his second; "Ah don't mahnd telling her she's more gorgeous than the Grand Canyon, if'n that's what she wants to hear." But surprise and mystification were mild responses compared with the shock he felt at his own reply.

The time has come, most patient reader, to consider Anloie's Affliction, which may be addressed most gracefully by comparing certain extruding features of her anatomy to two of the planet's most well-known promontories, Mt. Kilimanjaro and Mt. Fujiyama. Between these two peaks is a difference in height of almost 2,000 meters. And one of Anloie's breasts (the left or the right? It depends on whether you're in Anloie's body or looking at it. We'll simply call it Bosom A), Bosom A, was to her other breast, Bosom B, as Mt. Kilimanjaro is to Mt. Fujiyama. The two protuberances did not differ from each other by 2,000 meters, of course, but were one to compare their sizes to the sizes of the mountains (a cruel measure, for Anloie was already scarred enough by self-inflicted comparisons of her mammarian attributes to each other), the proportions were equal. Their respective circumferences were no more than a half-dozen centimeters apart, and even their volumes varied by less than half a baseball. But set on her slender chest, they unquestionably were one large and one small.

As a little girl she had been very pretty, and even before the boys discovered the girls she received lots of attention. Then, like a police raid on the wrong house that forever changes the lives of the maimed survivors, puberty struck.

In one breast only.

Poor Anloie! She tried strapping Bosom A down, but she didn't want to suppress Bosom B's growth if—no, *when* it started. She tried wearing loose sweaters, but the way Bosom A flopped around under them, the boys must have thought she was packing a gerbil. Bosom A was just too out there, and finally she donned a standard brassiere and stuffed the B-cup (the Bosom B cup, not a B-cup at all but a C-cup like its companion) with socks and underwear.

Bosom B did eventually sprout, but it was a tit too little too late, and it never did catch up to Bosom A. She knew in her mind that the final answer to the equation A-B=x (only about a cup size) did not reduce her to freakdom. Her ob/gyn told her, and she told herself, that her Affliction was nothing more than a relatively pronounced version of a common cosmetic disorder which, when and if the male-dominated medical profession got around to it, would undoubtedly be dubbed Asymmetrical Mammarian Syndrome. Nonetheless, the feeling of being unibreasted had never left Anloie's heart. It turned her into an unwilling prude in high school, afraid to tease the boys into running their hands across her chest, and kept her a virgin until she met Warren four years ago.

And Whizzo—Whizzo suffered from an Affliction of his own. Unlike Anloie, he had never shared it with anyone. Men and women have different ways of handling such things, and Whizzo's way, which was to parade an endless train of lovers into and out of his bed, had always worked well—until now. Here was a situation he had not dealt with before: a woman he was in love with. How would she feel if between every time they made love he ran off to balance himself out with someone with little teacups that fit into A-cups?

There was only one way to find out: spill the beans. He blurted out his shocking reply (shocking to him, anyway). "Mah ahdeal woman. You're as absolutely raght about not matching up as mah bread-and-butter arm is left, love punkin'. Hain't nobody ever will meet mah ahdeal. Y'see, Ah got me this unnatural hankering—Ah mean, it hain't really unnatural, but what's dratted about it is, hit keeps changin'. One moment Ah love to be playin' with great big pillow boobies. But no sooner Ah'm with a woman what's got 'em, Ah'm done with her and cravin' me some itty bitty titties. So Ah figured out what mah ahdeal woman is: she has one massive ol' juicy cantaloupe and one little ol' tangerine."

Now, there are women who, upon hearing their appeal reduced to what they view as no more than two jellyfish-textured lumps of adipose tissue that erupt unseemingly out of their chests like twin aliens, would return an appropriate feminist retort and bid Whizzo adieu, slamming the door as they exited. Indeed that response fleetingly crossed Anloie's mind, but...like some webbed creature in the black lagoon of her subterranean side (as in the subterranean side of even the most militant of feminists) lurked the Cinderella notion that there exists for each of us somewhere in the wide world a sole soulmate—the single person whom S/HeIt placed here for us to fall in love and happy-ever-after with. How could that creature not be stirred from its benthic depths by Whizzo's confession? —But no, Anloie, this is entirely too much! Dared she believe her ears? "What? What did you say?" was all she could say.

"Ah'm sorry, ma'am, but hit's true. Ah don't want to lah to you or keep any secrets from you. And honeybiscuits, it looks to me lahke your breasts must be round, luscious cantaloupes. Ah swear to you Ah'd love them maghtily tonaght, bein's as how mah last lady love had sweet little tangerines. Ah know this maght not sound very good, but Ah'm afraid tomorrow Ah'd want me someone with tangerines or teacups. But Ah really want to be with you. And Ah don't mean jist for tonaght. Maybe every other tahme, and Ah'd have me tangerines and teacups in between. But you'd be mah one and only cantaloupes."

More subterranean stirrings; this time Anloie's Feminist Godmother appeared. "Whizzo! You just want to make love to my tits, not me."

"Ah want to make love to you, buttercakes. To your heart. But you've got those big luscious...tits as you call them sittin' raght there on top of it."

This time her Godmother gave him the full feminist special—even as the web-footed creature surfaced.

"Ah deserve that. Truly Ah do. Ah'm sorry, ma'am. Ah call it mah Affliction."

The fangs sank quickly into Feminist Godmother's throat. Webbed feet dragged her silently back into the murk. Anloie and Whizzo: they were bonded, bonded by Affliction. Well, why not? It was a common enough cement in affairs of the heart, and as good a reason as any to fall in love. "Whizzo...you're serious. You really would like it better if I were two sizes?"

Whizzo hung his head. "Yes ma'am. But Ah'm in love with you. There, Ah hain't never said that to nobody before. Maybe Ah wouldn't be lahke that with you." His wandering fingers started to undo her top halter button.

Startled, she pulled his hand away. "No way. You're putting me on." This was going way too fast. How could she possibly let him in on her secret after knowing him only three hours?

Well, as we know, love is a highly unpredictable thing. A Many-Splendored Thing. A Hurting Thing. A Golden Ring. Love is the Answer. Love is Never Having to Say You're Sorry. Love is Strange. Yes, Mickey and Sylvia had that much figured out back in the Fifties: they knew Love is Strange. And strangely enough, even as Anloie clutched her hand to Whizzo's to pry his fingers away from her second button, a joy buzzer buzzed between her legs, sending zingers zinging all over her body—especially at the two rapidly ripening raspberries respectively swelling in her special custom-made bra against C-cup A and B-cup B. Her mind's eye caught a fleeting glimpse of a godmother being dragged through a swamp. No, Anloie, she told herself. No one but Warren has ever seen your Affliction.

As Whizzo's fingertips dusted across the respective foothills and acclivities of Kilimanjaro and Fujiyama, Anloie pondered once again Warren's solution to her Affliction. In a word, it was silicone. Yes, she was considering it. Factory-sealed jellybags had to be better than this feeling of being half a woman. But why did he want them *both* enhanced? Yes, Bosom B was an underachiever, but wasn't Bosom A

bounteous enough already? Of course, Warren liked to sleep on three pillows...

Behold the brassiere, the envy of all mankind, its gaping twin mouths ever filled with those creamy concoctions from the Fleshfields of Delight.

—Well, not always ever. Does a bra cry like a baby or suffer like a man when it is separated, as Anloie's was about to be, from its succulent symbiotic companions and made to spend the night in the clothes hamper? Are the socks and blouses and other hampermates titillated by its tales of tits? In the case of this particular special custom-made bra, does one cup one-up the other? Ah, if brassieres could talk, the tales they could tell.

Hm. We are in a parallel universe here. This is a novel. Already it's populated with cogitating frogs, allegedly eloquent baseballs—even a prattling penis. Bra, we are all ears.

No, no, we dare not go there. Give bras a voice and next thing you know we'll have talking tables, loquacious loquats, catechisms from colanders, sermons in stones, stick soliloquys, burbling beancans, teaspoons with tales to tell—our story will drown in a cacophony of blithering artifacts. It could even get demoted to a parallel universe where the best sellers include such swill as *Jack and the Beans Talk, Say Onara, Mutter Courage* and *Lady Chatter's Sly Lover*—all written, in a worst-case universe, by George Orwell in Gnus Speak.

"Surprise!"

It was not Whizzo but Anloie who, her fear transformed into pure, powerful goddess energy, undid and removed her upper undergarment, which fortunately could not express its outrage. She tossed it unceremoniously into the rumple on the floor, and before it could flash "Rumplestiltskin" in sign language, the halter landed unceremoniously on top of it.

The bra was fit to be hooked—and remember, it had already been hooked all day. That wanton slut! Not only had she deprived it of skin contact, but down on the floor it couldn't see, and covered with the halter it couldn't even hear. Smell? Everyone knows brassieres don't have noses. (Strange, actually, considering what rich aromas they exude. You'd think such odoriferousness would serve some pheromonal purpose.)

At last, to a fading echo of feminist screams muting into murky gurgles, Anloie's closet stood bared and skeleton-free.

Think of the wonder with which the first bushmen must have gazed up from the flat plains of the Serengeti and beheld Mt. Kilimanjaro rising in all its three-dimensional glory. How many samurai momentarily relaxed their warrior demeanor to stand in slack-jawed awe at the base of Mt. Fujiyama, plainly vulnerable to some soul-stealing tourist's camera? Now try to imagine seeing both of these legendary landmarks at once, side-by-side. Throw in a cloudforestful of sexual quickening (it's like shortening, only quicker) and you have some idea of the sight that greeted the eyes of Whizzo Mark Salot IV. He gaped in disbelief. He gasped in astonishment. He gushed in rapture. As had Warren upon first beholding so rare a sight, he kissed Kilimanjaro right on its peak of rose-red snow. As Warren had not, he then turned to Fujiyama, repeating the baptism with matching ardor, then gave it a fondling and sucking such as to cause it to gain several meters in altitude.

During the next hour, as Whizzo revered each tender hummock, in turn and in tandem, so equally that one could not feel less loved than the other, Anloie's mind ran along a tortuous path. "Does he really love them as much as he says he does? It's hard to believe. But he did say it *before* he knew...or could he have known? How *could* he have? But if he did, maybe other guys...Oh Anloie, don't even go there. You'll find out how much he means it over time. Yes, later. (What *was* that feeling he was stirring up in dormant Fujiyama?) Right now he really means it. Stop doubting and enjoy. We'll see how long the honeymoon lasts before we go any further. (A lightning bolt of delight zapped Fujiyama and sparkplugged over to Kilimanjaro, temporarily knocking out the power supply to her brain.) —Well, but how long is long enough? A lifetime? A week? A night? (The delight turned squiggly and squiggled down to the place she wasn't going to tonight.) Hmmm—No, no way tonight! Not this week, either! Anloie, what are you *thinking*? Six months. That's how long before you let Warren...Maybe three months with Whizzo...three *months*! He might be traded to Kansas City by then! Omigod girl, you need to think...

But the time for thinking was past. Whizzo had scaled Mts. Kilimanjaro and Fujiyama, not like some macho rappelling team pickaxing into their turf but like a flutter of butterflies, dancing and skipping their merry way and stopping to smell the flowers. His delight and his tender ministrations smoothed the scars on her soul. Tears ran down her face, pausing on her cheekbones to sparkle in Whizzo's eye. He had unlocked the door to which she thought she had the only key.

Someone, or some thing, perhaps in the linen department, left us an account of what followed, but it was in Pillow Talk or whatever, and ultimately lost in the laundry, or whatever. (Assuredly it was not the special custom-made bra, which lay fuming as the panties joined the pile and upstaged it with a lurid account of the day spent crease-to-mouth with Anloie's *labia majorae*, complete with periodic trickles of milk and honey.) But no matter: we know how lovers do carry on. Whizzo and Anloie looked eye to eye, laughed and cried, knighted and coquetted, flaunted and flirted, joked and jousted, winked and whispered, pinched and parried, teased and tormented, sang and sobbed, shared and shouted, cooed and contemplated, talked and touched, hemmed and hawed, teed and heed, Tweedledummed and Tweedledeed, stroked and straddled, fucked and fornicated, came and cuddled.

Mickey Mouse had barely cuckooed 10:30 p.m. but Charley Orange was fast asleep when Whizzo Mark Salot IV pounded on his door.

"Charley! Charley! Hurry up and open up!"

"I'm asleep."

"Sleep! You don't need no sleep. Jist listen to what she told me, you ain't gonna believe this..."

Charley opened the door in his PJ's, glowering.

"Great polka-dots, Charley. Mah favorite..."

"I said I was sleeping, Whizzo. Can't you let a man sleep?"

"Not on this naght of naghts, Charley. Listen, Ah gotta tell you what she said to me."

"I guess the bottom line, Whizzo, is this. You scored tonight. I didn't score tonight. Or last night, or the night before. I do not want to hear about your score."

"But Charley, she waren't mah score. Ah mean, it was a real connection, somethin' lahke Ah never felt before. Ah mean, Ah looked into her ahes and Ah lahke to fall into everywhere forever, y'know, some kahnda endless space that's beyond tahme. Ah mean, she did more than jist launch mah torpedo. Charley, Ah discovered what it is to feel awe and reverence in the presence of a woman."

"Mm-hm. That's nice," said Charley. "So why are you here and not moving into the higher realms that lie within her loins?"

"We did that, but—well, then she started to feelin' guilty about this bozo kahnd of gah she's been seein'. She's havin' a tad of trouble lettin' him go, but it never can work out betwixt them on account of they don't have the same values, you get what Ah mean?"

"Well now, what values might those be, Whizzo?"

"Whah yessir Charley, Ah'll tell you—but no, not now, Ah didn't wake you out of your beauty rest jist to carry on about Anloie. Anloie—hain't that a purty name?"

"What's it mean?"

"Mean? Don't mean nothin', Ah reckon. Jist sounds lahke music. C'mon, git you some clothes on, we got us an appointment at midnight with Ladye Hannah Aura."

"Who?"

"She's a world-renowned psahchic lady that Ah met. She channels some entity from Galactic Overdrahve or somewhere Out There. And this entity is gonna tell me what's in the cards for Anloie and me."

"Why don't you take Anloie instead of me? I'm sure she'd be more interested than I am."

"C'mon, Charlie. Ah want to surprahse her with the results."

◆◆◆ ◆

Shinolaland...Shinolaland...Shinolaland...Surrounded by a vast sea of stationary automobiles, the sign blinked on and off like a lighthouse to those adrift in the Davy Jones' Lockers of compulsive consumption, Morse Coding its silent siren call to lure them to the neon gardens within.

Urban sophisticates, jaded cosmopolites that we are, it's hard for us to appreciate the awe and wonderment that stirred in Whizzo Mark Salot IV when he found himself suddenly surrounded by dazzling lights and signs taller than magnolia trees proclaiming names he had seen on TV all his life but never live and in person: Macy's. Bullock's. Toys-R-Us. Jack-in-the-Box. Price Club. Victoria's Secret. K-Mart. Ralph's. The Wherehouse. Wal-Mart. It was like growing up and discovering that the tooth fairy does exist, and you're inside the magic toadstool where she lives.

Whizzo reacted like any high-spirited lad might: he burst into song.

What's goin' on what's goin' on? Radio Shack!
Supermarkets are for people; Petco is for pets.
At Pier 1: get in touch with your senses.
Dr. Pepper! It makes the world taste better.

By a fountain gushing emerald and magenta spumes into the air loitered a gaggle of junior high school girls, giggling, smoking cigarettes and ogling boys. As they glanced over to check out the source of the rich tenor voice, one caught Whizzo's eye. He waved and winked back, feeling a pang of regret for his deprived childhood: there were no Shinolalands, no fountain nymphets in Disfunction Junction, Arkansas.

A mall to make Disneyland blush its cartoon cheeks and hang its injection-molded head in shame, Shinolaland came complete with soulful saxophonists, born-again Bible bangers, spraycan Seurats wearing facemasks to shield their naso-thoraxic passages from the toxic fumes they spattered all over their clientele and admirers, chainsaw jugglers, parkbench comedians, origami artists and—outnumbering all of them together— panhandlers.

As decidedly as Whizzo was delighted by seeing the icons of his childhood in the flesh, even more deeply was he dismayed at the plight of those listless beings who came to him repeating the same two-word mantra over and over: Spare change? Spare change? Spare change? Beverly Hills Disfunction Junction was not, but no one down home went hungry or homeless.

Whizzo's response was appalling to many; indeed some would have him arrested for Contributing to Vagrancy, and if there were no such statute, "Make one up!" Charley Orange had a tender heart, and oftimes crossed a mendicant's outstretched palm with silver. But even Charley raised an eyebrow when Whizzo rounded up the entire raggedy crew and led them into Arriverderci's for dinner on him. One old codger had only one eye, with just a web of flesh stretched across the hollow socket where the other had been. "Lost it in the war," he said, touching his finger to the dark Carlsbad Cavern that caused his fellow human beings to avert their glances from his face. "Thank you, father," Whizzo said to him. "Here, go get it checked." He pressed a crisp new hundred into the septuagenarian's hand.

The graybeard was too speechless to even thank Whizzo. He just stopped in his tracks and stared at the bill.

"Whizzo, you're crazy," said Charley.

"Now look at, Charley. It cost me less than Ah'll be earnin' bah next year for throwin' one pitch. And that old gah's a veteran, he lost that ahe defendin' you and me in the war, and he'll remember this naght for the rest of his lahfe."

"Yeah...well, but look at him. No one will even take a C-note from him."

"Ah didn't think of that," said Whizzo. He walked over to the cashier and changed another hundred into five twenties, which he offered to the ancient for the hundred. But the old man, who had never seen Ben Franklin's face on a bill before, didn't want to give it up. "Well, what the hay," said Whizzo. "Here, take these too."

"Say, who are you anyway, Masked Man?" asked one of Whizzo's beneficiaries. "Haven't I seen you somewhere?"

"If you seen the TV or the newspapers you seen me. Ah'm Whizzo Mark Salot IV, the one and only. Ah'm the pitcher that never runs

empty, the answer to the Megaglopoulis Mutants' prayers. And this here is Charley Awrnge, the man who hit .900 in the clutch for a whole year once. Hey, are we all gonna win us a pennant this year?"

In the ensuing ruckus, everyone in the restaurant clamored for Whizzo's autograph—everyone except most of his guests, who were too busy with their unexpected banquet to join the fray.

As Whizzo and Charley stepped outside, a middle-aged woman with frizzy purple hair wearing a clown costume zipped by them on a skateboard, handing Charley a flyer as she zipped, then disappeared into a crowd of applauding feral teens.

The flyer was entitled either "Re-making the Beds of Our Minds" or "The Story That Won't Go Away." Both titles were given equal prominence at the top in letters of equal size but violently clashing typestyles. Sandwiched around them were various headlines, doodles, blown-up newsprint words and scribbled slogans. Charley began reading the text:

Greetings and blessings on your own pains/pioneerings, my dears, and in these awesome times of the unmaskings in the All-of-a-Sudden Zone in the stacked deck of The Cosmos, please *read this with an open mind and/or heart, OK?*

*The NU CLEAR VISION DIVISION of GALAXY CENTRAL CASTING DEPARTMENT and MOTHER EARTH RENTAL ASSOCIATION features phenomenal help during COSMIC WATERGATES, beyond bandaids over the abyss, An ancient cadence and resurrection of knowledge updated to the beat of Spiritual Drummers, Players, Dancers and/or Singers' orchestration for a planetary nation, knowing we're not experiencing an alien infiltration, but, rather, an intra-terrestrial and/or extra-galactic reunion of T*H*E U*N*I*V*E*R*S*A*L F*E*D*E*R*A*T*I*O*N.*

"Get a load of this," said Charley, skipping down to the middle and reading aloud to Whizzo:

...That, having been in many incarnations, with this level of believing, in the beginning the First Big Bang was when Mom and/or Dad Nature-Time (The Cosmos)/Higher Power/The Force/Great Spirit/Superconsciousness/Universal Mind/Mother-Father of Creation and/or all the Holy Names of God/dess had the Idea of Creation, at which "time" everyone and everything was chosen for destiny roles...

Charley shook his head. "She must have been off her thorazine when she wrote this."

"Read on," said Whizzo.

"If you understand this, Whizzo, I'm worried about you." Charley continued:

...in between life experiences our Soul goes before the Big Board to pick/choose a few more details. With it all being cumulative, somehow, it's all coming together/being synchronized to bring a world based on knowledge and compassion. As such, everyone will be a Majority of One; life will be the really real Real Estate; and war will be abolished, which will lower the cost of money, among releasing other horrors...

"I'm telling you, Whizzo. It's the government's fault. They used to take care of people like this, and now there aren't enough beds."

"Look at the bottom," said Whizzo. "Who's it sahgned bah?"

"Ladye Hannah Aura! *That* brain-damaged grandmother on wheels is your friend?"

"Yep. Met her yesterday outsahde the ballpark. She was dancin' through the crowd, blowin' bubbles."

"That's who you got me out of bed to see? You're going to pay her money to tell your fortune?"

"Hit ain't lahke tellin' fortunes, Charley. Hit's more lahke ways to look at ourselves. Not lahke psahchology, where everybody's all messed up, lahke some kahnda O-riginal Sin or somethin'."

"Whizzo, you're attracted to this Anna Lee, right? Why don't you just pursue her like you would any other woman, without asking some ganglia-mangled clown on a skateboard whether she's right for you?"

◆◆◆ ◆

"Not Anna Lee; Anloie. And she's serious material, Charley. Ah say she's mah soul-mate. But Ah don't want to go makin' me any mistakes when the stakes are lahke that."

"Well, it ought to be entertaining, anyway," said Charley, just as the skateboard shot out again from the crowd, headed full-tilt toward them.

"Oh, Ah fahnd Ladye Hannah Aura haghly entertaining," said Whizzo. Ladye Hannah Aura tilted the board up and stopped on a dime at their feet. She was short and stocky, with gray hair under the dye and a pug nose that reminded Charley of Butch Peebles, his best friend in the second grade. Underneath her clown pancake, he saw that her face was crinkled like old leather. But it was her eyes that riveted him: clear, brown and laughing, they fixed on his and bore into him like—the image came to him of the worms that would bore into his eyeballs when life left his body.

"Greetings, magical children, from realms beyond," she said. "Of course I'm entertaining. It's the only way to stir the sleeping souls into receiving the message of the Nu Clear Vision. Look at all their dear hearts out there, promenading under the fossil-fueled phosphorescence: they know not what they are. Are you aware that our lovely mother Gaia is the dance studio of the galaxy? Surely you've felt the dance of sun and wind. Haven't you seen the dance of light and shadow under the sun, under the moon, under the clouds, all yinning and yanging away and doing the Twist in Time? —And who, may I ask, is this fine physical specimen of young manhood?"

"Ladye, this here's mah friend Charley Awrnge. Baseball player of the haghest order, almost as good as Ah am, but unlucky in love."

"Unlucky? Ah, is there such a thing as luck when it comes to love? Love is like baseball, isn't it? It's a game of skill, is it not?"

"You're raght, Ladye! You're always raght."

"Spare me that burden, Whizzo. But who knows, perhaps we shall have a channeling tonight as well as a card-reading."

◆ ◆ ◆ ◆

People have been looking *for deformed frogs*
and so they're finding *deformed frogs.*
—All Things Considered (NPR)

His name, it is said, was Ngaio XV[14]. He lived in the place of the darting crawdad and the green slime. He dodged the white-feathered egret on his nightly forays betwixt the tall cattails, where he coaxed the moon to spread her trail of hot butter over his green-frosted fen. By day the sunlight twinkled on his pond; by night, glistening in the half-moon's jeweled web, the pond became the starry sky. His days were the clouds in the sky: always changing, never changing.

The Terror rode down from the clouds. Raising his cloaca off that of Gloria Glug, Ngaio watched it capture the sparkle of the sun and the stars and lock them in a box. It milked the perfume from the air. It poured the water and its denizens into vials and sucked out their breath. Ngaio saw rivers of fire and days of ashes and dark. Voices called to him from boxes; clangs of metal replaced the songs of his ancestors.

The Terror rode in on four wheels. Ngaio saw great textureless beasts with the heads of *rib'ets!* drop hails of boulders that buried his children alive. By day the stonemaker sang; the siren by night. Their thunder and trespass would extinguish his clan. With a roar out of hell, the massacre spread to the mighty, lace-topped pillars that held up the sky. Gloria Glug was crushed by a screaming falling tree.

The Terror welled up from the earth. The monsters heaved their death into the peat, into the pond, into the sky. They covered the entire bog with a single flat stone and sealed its rainbows inside dark casks. They planted round balls with fire in them that never died out and shined them at the frightened moon, driving her away. They pitched massive monoliths between Ngaio's eyes and the sky, and blew their smoke into the sun. They erected high hollow trees that were leafless and glowed in the dark. They gazed at shadows inside boxes. They raged in their prisons and longed for the stars.

It was the Twilight of Mosquito Marsh, and everywhere was agony and chaos and ruin. Mountains of molten tar rained down all around

Ngaio, permanently converting the habitation bequeathed him by his ancestors into a conglomerate of asphalt and frogbones. As he was about to give himself over to the ages, Ngaio beheld a vision to add some heebie-jeebies to his resignation—or was it a figment of his tortured imagination? Evolutionists would call it genetic memory; would Creationists call it a miracle or a mirage? Whatever it was, he saw, emerging from one of the few remaining potholes, the most delectable lady frog ever to inspire fantasies of amplexus. Her bulging brown eyes shone like twin harvest moons. Her ears were as round as galaxies. With her long legs, tapering from the firm musculature of her haunches down to ankles as delicate as matchsticks, she kicked off like a Calavaras champion, arcing gracefully through the debris-filled air like a rainbow—yea, had Ngaio been able to read the future of his locale, like a round-tripper.

Was there time for a tryst before dying? While she was still aloft, he leaped toward her. But as she landed, she began growing! Her heavenly features...her ears grew long and convoluted. Her eyes shrank into beady *rib'et!* orbs. Her long nose shriveled as—ah, as so many times, after a hard day's night, had Ngaio's lingam. And her legs, those lovely glistening limbs on which she had just sprang forward like Daylight Savings Time— they atrophied before his very eyes until she could not leap her own length.

As the creature slipped on a gown and took a hobbled, tentative step forward, Ngaio XV[14] landed undetected on one of the shiny black coverings that hid her feet. He wedged himself in between two layers of material and made his bid to escape Armageddon.

"A deck of cards?" Charley asked. "You're going to counsel this guy on the most important decision of his life with 52 little slivers of pasteboard? I get it: you're one of those tarrot readers; you're some kind of witch, aren't you?"

"My dear unrealized fellow traveler," said Ladye Hannah Aura, "I'll tell you a secret. I don't even need the cards. And there are so many of us of the pre-Christian persuasion, we often ask each other, 'Which witch is which?' But fear not, Charley: we work only for the Higher Powers. And the Higher Powers have a word for you: 'tarrot' does not rhyme with 'carrot'. 'Tarot' rhymes with 'pharaoh'."

"Oh-oh," said Charley. "I see pyramids in the wings. And behind them astrology, and the I Ching, and UFO's, and channeling, and multilevel marketing..."

Ladye smiled sweetly at Charley, revealing a missing front tooth. "Did you know," she said, "that between the letters P and I in 'pyramid' is the name of the mother of Jesus spelled backwards?"

Charley looked into those clear, laughing brown eyes. "All right," he said. "I know when I'm licked."

"It's all right," Ladye said. "The teachings of the Ascended Ones, as revealed through the cards, are immune to those who see only the reflections of their own mental mirrors. The widening of your vision is an honored occasion." She bowed.

"Now my dears, let me explain the cards. The Universe appears to be chaotic, but that's only because our brain and our senses are limited. Everything's OK, nothing is happening at random, it's all unfolding just as it was destined to. When you shuffle a deck of cards, there's a connection between the seemingly chance order you create and the unconscious mind of you, the shuffler.

"How old are the cards? I'm glad you asked. They originated in Atlantis. The Ascended Sages there saw the clouds on the horizon and hoped they could save the race from doom with the Secret Wisdom they encoded in the symbols and in the numerology of the interrelationships. The cards disappeared along with the rest of that tragic civilization, but somehow the sacred symbols survived: they were recognized by the Rosicrucians and other ancient orders, and they're in the Bible. They re-appeared as cards in China in 969 A.D., and they've been with us ever since. When dear Alice said, 'You're nothing but a pack of cards!', how little she knew!

"Consider their numerological properties. There's 52 cards in the deck. How many weeks in a year?"

"Forty-eight?" asked Whizzo.

"Fifty-two," said Ladye. "Thirteen cards in each suit. Thirteen weeks in each season."

"Four suits," said Whizzo. "The four seasons."

"You've got it," said Ladye. "Also the four elements, the four directions. And 12 court cards?"

"Twelve months in the year," said Whizzo.

"Twelve signs in the zodiac," said Ladye. "And get this: counting the Joker, 365 spots on the entire deck. How many days in the year?"

"365?" asked Whizzo.

"How about Leap Year?" asked Charley.

"During Leap Year," said Ladye, "we put both the Jokers in the deck. Two colors: red and black. Positive and negative. Yin and yang. Female and male."

"Salt and pepper," said Charley. "Alfa and Romeo. Amos and Andy."

"Count the Ace as One and what is the center number of each suit?" asked Ladye. "Seven. The Seven Wonders of the World, the seven sisters in the Pleiades, the seven planets known when the cards were created—the seven days in the week."

"Is *this* the secret wisdom encoded in the cards?" asked Charley. "Why didn't they just invent a calendar?"

"These are just the clues," said Ladye. "Every day in the year is governed and conditioned by one of the cards. Every card has a ruling planet. The cards reveal the reasons behind your inclinations and impulses, behind your emotional reactions, behind what attracts you and who attracts you. The suit is important, the planet that rules it is vital, the card's position in the spread, the number of spots on it, or, on the court cards, the picture, its relationship to other cards in the sequence..."

"I thought the idea of ruling planets came from astrology," said Charley.

"It does. The cards hold much of the same wisdom as the heavens."

"So tell me this. Just what is the magical, mystical quality of a mother's body that shields the fetus from all the celestial influences until the moment it pops out and then, Wham! Zap! Its destiny is imprinted on it?"

"I don't know, Charley, but as the man said, the universe is queerer than we can imagine. Anyway, one more thing the cards can tell you is how well you're suited—no pun intended—to be with specific other individual souls. So now, Whizzo, my dear, tell me: What is the anniversary of your natal day?"

"Anniversary of...Ladye, Ah hain't never been married."

"But you were delivered onto this planet, right?"

"Yep, that Ah was."

"On what date of the year?"

"Febuary the 12th."

"February 12? You're a King of Diamonds!"

"Thass raght. Have been ever since Ah could throw a baseball."

"We're talking cards here, and the cards encompass a playing field infinitely more vast than the diamonds, courts and gridirons of superannuated children like yourselves, and as long as I'm riding this skateboard I can call you that. Now listen, give ear and perpend whilst the cards unfold the deeper dimensions of your life.

"The King of Diamonds is a most powerful card. Diamonds represent autumn. Their element is water and their ruling planet is Jupiter. Many of the wealthiest people on dear mother Gaia are Diamonds who have not realized their true mission, which is to accumulate spiritual wealth. For what profiteth a wo/man to acquire the whole world, if she/he loseth her/his soul?

"Kings represent the masculine principle. Kings are authoritative; they're in charge. But never by themselves: their number is 13, and between One and Three is Two: the mother, the Queen. Alone, a King can never rule well: he must blend with the Queen's feminine balance."

"So what you are sayin'," said Whizzo, "is that Ah need Anloie. Is that raght?"

"That's not for me to say," said Ladye. "It's in the cards, and we've barely begun to see what they hold for you. Anloie is a whole separate soul to look at. But first, take the number of the King: 13.

One plus Three equals Four. How many Kings in the deck? Four. Four times 13 equals...?"

"Forty-eight?" asked Whizzo.

"Fifty-two. The number of cards in the deck. Four: it can also be Two plus Two, 22, the Master Magician, she or he who can manifest the ideal in reality.

"But going back to 13, ever since the betrayal of Judas the Christians have held the superstition that the number 13 is bad luck. But long before that, in the Hebrew language the words for Love and Unity were both 13's. The Hebrew Liturgy contained 13 rules for interpreting the law, and interpreting the law is what Kings are supposed to do.

"Now I'll tell you about the King of Diamonds: you. In your drive for power, you, Mr. King of Diamonds, may be dishonest and calculating. You may tend to accumulate money and materialistic possessions, simply because that's how power manifests itself in these dreary times. The King of Diamonds is the only one-eyed King, suggesting you may be someone who shows us only one side of yourself. You might be very deceptive, the kind of person who would go to work for IBM just so you can tell Apple what they're up to."

"Thass me, all raght. Ah maght let a batter think Ah'm gonna throw up Big Peter and than fahre in Uncle Scrooge instead."

"That's it exactly. You would do that, even to your own sister."

"Naw, mah sister couldn't make the girl's softball team in the sixth grade. Ah'd lob her up some grapefruits."

"That's the other side of King of Diamonds, Whizzo—the King of Diamonds that I vibe is the real you. February 12 is the *creme de la creme* of Kings of Diamonds: Honest Abe Lincoln was born on February 12, and Charles Darwin and John L. Lewis. Central Casting has placed you in illustrious company."

"Lorne Greene, too," said Whizzo.

"You, Whizzo, are generous, a philanthropist; you see money as a tool and use it with compassion and wisdom. You're humanitarian, you're spiritual, you're creative, you're unorthodox, you're wise. My dear, my dear, dear Whizzo, you have Jupiter in the Uranus line, which makes it possible for you to become one of the most highly evolved entities on the planet. You can be an incorruptible politician, a compassionate businessperson, a caring corporate head."

"He can be every oxymoron in the book," said Charley, "but can he win 20 games?"

"Ah'm real pleased to hear all this here good stuff about mahself, Ladye," said Whizzo, "and Ah don't doubt a word of it, but Ah'm only interested in whether a certain person name of Anloie is the mate that mah hungry soul is longin' for."

"Of course," said Ladye. "I do prattle on, but that's just to give you an idea of how magnificent you are and who you can be. What is the anniversary of this dear child's natal day?"

"She was born on January 11."

"January 11! A Three of Spades!" Ladye's voice grew soft and reverent. "This woman Anloie is a very special match for you, Whizzo. For both of you, it's love at first sight. But this is not the superficial love of body to body, mind to mind or even heart to heart. You both reach out deep into each other's souls. You have walked the shores of Atlantis together; your love was unfulfilled when the cataclysm struck. You belong with her and she with you; the two of you have much to complete, perhaps many lifetimes of work."

Ah, yes," said Charley. "About those many lifetimes. I have another question. If reincarnation is true, the proliferation of returning souls is creating a population explosion that taxes the carrying capacity of the planet. Life may be a vale of tears, but it must be a lot better than whatever is Over There to send the Old Souls back in such droves. Wouldn't you think they would have the sense to see that the party's spilling out the doorways here already and stay home?"

"Just because the souls are old," said Ladye Hannah Aura, "doesn't mean they're smart. Whizzo, despite your confluences, your love will not be an easy one to maintain. How does Anloie spend her time here on Mother/Father Gaia?"

"She's the world champion at throwing a frisbee out over the ocean and catching it behahnd her back the most consecutive tahmes. She's in the Guinness Book of Records."

"This is in harmony. She's an athlete, like yourself."

"She sells some kahnda green slimy pond scum or somethin', too. You sposed to eat it."

"Beneath your seeming similarities, you each walk separate paths. Both of you must always acknowledge that you're separate entities and give each other all the space you need. Your union is the Rainbow Bridge; never forget that each of you are its foundation, both holding it up. But should you enmesh yourselves in each other, the bridge will topple and your love will be disrupted, even destroyed."

The fourth inning was scoreless. Under the centerfield bleachers, Ladye Hannah Aura passed a splif to the founder of W.I.T.C.H.

Fifth Inning

She offered her honor
He honored her offer
And so all night long
He was on her and off her
—Men's restroom wall, Megaglopoulis

Baseball is one of the few orderly things in a very unorderly world. If you get three strikes, not even the best lawyer in the country can get you off.
—Bill Veeck

Both women and wolves have been the target of those who would clean up the wilds as well as the wildish environs of the psyche.
—Clarissa Pinkola Estes

TEN-HUT! A salute to the film industry. In an effort to ease the screenwriter's burden when *King of Diamonds* becomes a B-movie, the author offers the following *de riguer* falling-in-love montage:

UP MUSIC.

SCENE: An amusement park. WHIZZO and ANLOIE have a baseball-throwing contest, Anloie flipping them frisbee-style. Both knock over all the bottles. Each gives the other their prize.

CUT TO: A ward in the children's hospital. Whizzo autographs baseballs; Anloie makes shadow-figures on the wall with the kids.

CUT TO: The beach. WHIZZO and ANLOIE:

1) Frolic in the ocean. WHIZZO picks up ANLOIE to dunk her; she SCREAMS.

2) Walk along the shore, arms around each other, WHIZZO sniffing her hibiscus, as the sun sets.

3) Kiss on the pier in the twilight.

CUT TO: The artificial fireplace in WHIZZO'S hotel room.

SOUND: Moans.

PAN to the mirror above the bed. WHIZZO and ANLOIE are making love.

Ding ding ding ding ding ding ding ding ding ding ding, chimed Whizzo Mark Salot IV's wristwatch, *sotto voce* so as not to disturb his sleep.

With but an hour to live, Sunday morning was growing graybearded. In the suburbs of Megaglopoulis the early birds had long ago gotten the worms and retired from their morning labors to carol the churchgoers. The city itself had spun through space almost 90 degrees since the morning sun had bobbed up like a balloon over the wall of the eastern horizon and scampered above the skyscrapers, beaming its Happy Birthday! Every Day is Your Birthday! rays through any window immodest enough to leave itself undraped.

Celebratory photons swarmed over the sports page of Maxwell Veribushi's newspaper, which showed the Mutants in fourth place, 10 games behind the Lemon Sox. Charley Orange was still hitting only .158, but, unreported in the team stats, he was moving into a line-drive groove. The kid phenom, Whizzo Mark Salot IV, was 7-2, with two big wins against the Lemons and 78 strikeouts in 77 innings.

Blissfully unaware of the energy sweeping toward him from nuclear reactions occurring 93 million miles from his hotel room, the phenom himself was about to begin the first day of the rest of his life.

On this birthday of days, Whizzo awoke with a hard-on.

This was nothing to write home about: Mr. Twister was an early riser. Whizzo could not remember the last time he had wakened before his friend. Whereas often his fingers were wrapped around Mr. Twister, this morning they lay draped on his chest. But Twister was still growing. Something was circumscribing him all right, something non-digital, looping around him like a fat, writhing snake—Her tongue! O sweet slippery lubriciousness of Anloie's goddesshood.

Whizzo opened one eye. Sure enough, there was her mouth, fitted as snugly around Mr. Twister as a safety cap on a bottle of adults-only elixir.

Actually Whizzo deduced it was her mouth, as it was hidden behind her long, blonde tresses, cascading like Niagara down into his loins and tumbling across his thighs like silken waves having their way with a sandy beach.

Anloie looked up and, seeing his peeping eye, laughed at him, before returning to her popsickle. From her crystal-blue eyes, the pixie dust of dazzlement scattered through his bewitched being. He was not ready to discover it yet, but he had a ticket to ride those eyes: he could hop aboard and zoom right through into a parallel universe.

Her nose was the kind that women pay thousands for cheap manmade imitations of, pert and as pointed as a politician's remarks, and no cosmetic surgeon could ever quite capture that final tilt that made it flare delicately toward him when he saw her face to face. Her lips—those very prominences that even now were answering Nature's call—were the color and softness of roseblush, as billowed and happy as a pair of cumulus clouds. She had athletic shoulders, set broad and firm, but soft on top and rounded as bannister knobs. Sometimes, when he was not so pleasantly preoccupied, he wanted to slide down and bump into them. Her well-frisbeed pectoral muscles actually bulged, adding length to Kilimanjaro and Fujiyama, those velvet swellings of womanhood which, when she lay on her back with a pillow under her thighs to receive him, rested respectively on her chest like a lake and a pond swollen from the spring rains, their strawberry islands tilted up like the high beams on her Plymouth Fury. When she stood, one swooped down like an occupied hammock while the other jutted out as round and flavorific as an ice cream cone. Now as she lay on her side, they swung gracefully down toward the sheet like teardrops. Last night Whizzo reverently teased and squeezed Fujiyama (the small) and playfully kissed and sucked on Kilimanjaro (the large). Man and boy, he loved her.

Briefly a cloud peed on the porticos of Whizzo's rapture. Last night Anloie had confided in him Warren's silicone solution to her "Affliction." She was with Whizzo now, but she had renounced neither Warren nor his inflationary ideas.

Warren: what a tard! How could anyone naysay the asymmetry of those deliciously deviant convexities? Actually, the guy should be pitied for wanting the same handful, the same mouthful, right and left, wheresoe'er he turned, over and over again. Poor dude, he simply had no imagination, no taste for variety, no stomach for the rich diversity of feminine possibilities.

But the worst part was, Warren wasn't looking to just bring one luscious booby up to size with the other: he wanted to implant them both! Not content with the voluptuous cornucopia of Kilimanjaro and the delicate elegance of Fujiyama, he craved twin Everests. He didn't want breasts, he wanted basketballs. He went for quantitty, not qualititty.

On with the sightseeing tour, Whizzo rubbernecked past Anloie's pink-brown belly, rounded as a saucer, then drummed along the Mohawk trail of soft brown hairs, inching slowly through them like a kissing bug, stopping to sniff and lick between each savory follicle—

until there, before his eyes, the bus stopped at Tenderness Junction: her salmon-and-purple puckered periwinkle, her sweet folded lotus blossom, the mother galaxy.

Shifting, Anloie pressed her flower to his tongue. He licked it once and then helped himself to breakfast. Mah Gawd, he wondered, can there possibly be any electricity or love juice left in mah body after last naght? As Anloie's pleasure built, she took Twister in hand, and sure enough, that seizure struck where his whole body wound up like Robin Hood's bow about to let fly an arrow, just as the Chinese mushroom on his tongue liquefied and began quivering; and then the Big Bang shot showers of silver light through them both.

"So what would you lahke to do today, love-punkin'?" he asked when the love juices had all been slurped up, after a long coda of hugginess.

"Let's play Swallow the Penis."

"All raght." Whizzo lay on his back and swung his legs over his head in a yoga plow position, but he couldn't quite get Mr. Twister in his mouth. "Looks lahke you win."

"Silly man. I love you, Whizzo. So many ways I love you."

"How many ways do Ah love you? Ah love your breasts, Ah love your arm, Ah love your spirit, and most of all Ah love your heart, jist as big and wahde as the Gulf of Mexico that in all mah years in Arkansas Ah never saw oncet."

"I love your arm, too," said Anloie, "and your willy, and not in that order. I love your silliness and your delight in life."

"M-mm. You got body, heart, spirit. Ah don't know if'n you got any brains or not. Ah hain't got any mahself. So you can have them or not, Ah don't care, and Ah lahkely won't even know. But, to do what you done to mah heart, you gotta have something better than brains: you gotta have some kahnd of genius. And you do. You are a genius at being a woman."

Anloie tickled his chin with her finger. "You're so sweet. You're not just attracted to my body?"

"Ah'm maghty attracted to your body, but Ah'm attracted to the bodies of most of the women Ah meet. Though yours is an especially fahne specimen. But you are good with the kids, and thass a sahgn of a tender heart. Ah'm drawn to your heart, your goodness."

"That's what I love about you, Whizzo. You're just a big, wonderful kid."

"This is as growed-up as Ah'm ever gonna get. Thass whah Ah need me a chahld brahde lahke yourself."

"Whoa down! There you go again!"

"Ah realize last tahme was mebbe too soon, but that was then, apple dumplin'. This is now."

"You can't go proposing to me after two nights together."

"Oh no? Show me where it is written."

"I mean we don't know each other."

"You got you a big heart. You ain't gonna hurt me none. And Ah got me a big heart too. Ah hain't never gonna do nothin' to hurt you."

"We'll see."

"Oh, all raght." Whizzo feigned disappointment.

"And that's not a 'no'."

"No, Ah know. Hit's a 'yes', but you ain't ready to say it yet."

"It's probably not a yes. Just the law of averages, you know. But I wish us luck."

"Ah do too, baby. Hear me, Ah also lahke the way your mahnd works. Someone's got to know when to put on the brakes—Ah guess. Me, Ah know you are the one for me. Ah knowed it the first tahme Ah saw you come into the ballpark."

"Whizzo! All you did was see me! You didn't know me."

"Ah smelled you, buttercakes, Ah swear it. They was 50,000 people in that there stadium, and some maghty powerful odors floatin' around: hot dogs and stale beer and jist plain ol' seventh inning sweat, and you walked into that ballpark and Ah smelled it. Ah said to mahself, 'Thass the one, Whizzo. Thass the one God sent you. Hain't no stoppin' it. Ah saw the psahchic lady and she told me, too."

Anloie giggled. "You're too much, Whizzo. You give me two minutes of wooing and then you propose to me. Can we just sit on it for awhile and see how we get along?"

"Sounds lahke lots of fun to me, sweet potato. Where do Ah sit?" Whizzo rolled onto her and sat up. "Hit's your goodness that attracts me most of all. You are one of the true children of the laght."

"Hey, if I'm a child of light, you're the King of Heavy. Now get off!"

"Yes ma'am, and Ah'm the King of Dahmonds too. And you are the Three of Spades."

"Three of Spades? What does that mean?"

"Nope. Cain't tell you. Ah'm afraid you wouldn't lahke it."

"O-oh." Now Anloie feigned disappointment.

"Hey, little angel. Hit ain't nothin' bad. Ah mean, it's good news."

"It is?"

"Yeah it is. Ah jist don't wanna scare you off with good news, y'hear?"

"Tell me more later, Whizzo. Right now, just make love to me."

So Whizzo, surprising even himself, mounted her once again. Afterward he cajoled, and he pleaded, and he backed off, and he charmed her and disarmed her, and so it was that Anloie's fences, which she had always been able to lower (along with her underwear) at a pace that suited her, were beseiged by the persistence of Whizzo's own particular genius, until by the time the sun had climbed to its apogee and morning had crawled into its grave, she found herself engaged to be married.

KNOCK! KNOCK! KNOCK! KNOCK! KNOCK!

"Oh mah Gawd, Ah forgot. It's Sports Central here to interview me. You wanna be mah baby on national TV?"

"If I can do this." She bit his ear and squeezed his participle dangling.

Under Dr. Weisenheimer's counsel, Charley Orange was building confidence by asking women for their phone numbers if he had a pleasant initial contact. "You don't be hafing to call dem," Dr.

Weisenheimer said. "Just be making da request." Today Charley examined his one-month collection: three numbers. He was feeling uncharacteristically bold, having received two of them without asking in the past week.

He dialed the first number. A child answered.

"Hello, this is Charley Orange. Is your mother there?"

He could hear her in the background: "I'm not here."

"She's..."

"...not here. Got it," said Charley. Click!

Number two. "Hello, Maureen?"

"Yes, who's this?"

"Charley Orange."

"Who?"

"The ballplayer. I met you Tuesday in the bookstore. You said you were a therapist, right?"

"Yes, I am a psychotherapist, and I can only talk a few minutes until my client comes, OH! There she is now, 'bye." Click!

Number three. "Hi Lori? This is Charley Orange, you remember..."

"Oh! Oh! Oh! There's little ants all over the phone!" Click!

Charley stared blankly at the receiver, puzzling over what had happened. He hadn't had a chance to say anything wrong. Maureen and Lori had *volunteered* their numbers. How could he go from being a turn-on to a dud with nothing intervening except time? The more he thought about it, the more confused he felt, until he fell into a light-headed place where he had no sense of what was real. Could this really be happening, or was he trapped inside some sort of hallucination? Did he exist in the same reality as everyone else, or was he a little kid trapped in some parallel universe where love didn't exist, his nose pressed longingly against the wormhole into this one?

Charley lay awake until the wee hours, the nonresponsive trio dancing like sour sugarplums in his head. His obsession, he knew from bitter experience, would last until he met another woman.

◆ ◆ ◆ ◆

Painting the skies crimson, the sun sank through the blanket of haze covering Megaglopoulis, tinting the skyscrapers smog pink. The jaded permanent residents of creep-hour traffic had seen it all: eccentric limousines with bubble tops, Lincoln Continentals plastered stem to stern with gold coins and old shoes, Day-Glo schoolbuses with rock bands on their roofs, Volkswagen bugs painted like snails delivering take-out escargot, Cadillacs buried up to their fishtailpits in restaurant rooftops, the Picklemobile, the Redwood-mobile, the Penismobile (briefly, before it was arrested for entering a tunnel in public)... One-eyed, one-armed beggars had washed smudges and smears into their windshields and thrust upturned palms through their open windows; urban daredevils had played tag between their moving bumpers, drunken frat boys in passing cars had mooned them...it was not easy to get the attention of a Megaglopoulis commuter. However, not a few of them were outright startled at the sight, in their midst, of a lime-green Harley-Davidson motorcycle, the entire heads of both of whose passengers were hidden beneath helmets and behind gas masks. Adding to the extraterrestrial look were pink antennae protruding from each helmet: they were equipped with Walkie-Talkies so the two of them could converse while traveling.

The driver either wore his head upside down or else suffered from hair reversal: it grew out the bottom of his head (the helmet and mask hid the top), and despite its frizziness it reached almost to his navel. The little girl on the back—well, what was he doing with one so young, anyway?

Veribushi *pere et fille* putt-putted along at the speed of melting glass, periodically racing and belching fire like a fierce dragon on a leash. Maxwell was tempted to skip between lanes and zoom past a zillion or two of the heavy metal dinosaurs inching along like red snails in the sunset blocking the way to Sage's mother's house, but he could not endanger the precious 9-year-old life that sat behind him, her arms wrapped as far around his torso as 9-year-old arms could wrap. Nor, if truth be known, could he risk another moving violation, or the authorities would turn his wheels into walnuts and issue him his walking papers.

Maxwell was in a quandary: the same quandary he always found himself in when he came to the city. The very quandary that caused him to flee civilization in the first place. —Well, one of many quandaries.

When he missed a chance to pass an aging monolith leaking a death trail of monoxide haze, Sage, who knew him better than some 9-year-olds know how to tell non-digital time, engaged her Walkie-Talkie. "What's wrong, Daddy?"

"What's wrong is, I'm feeling tempted to go to the baseball game tonight."

"Well, why don't you go?"

"Lots of reasons, medium-size."

"Do you have reasons for wanting to go?"

"Lots of them, too."

"You remember what you taught me about Benjamin Franklin? List all the reasons you want to go and all the reasons you don't want to go, then count them up. The side with the most reasons wins."

"OK. Reasons I want to go. One. I like to immerse myself in baseball's nonjudgmental, hierarchical universe, to forget about frogs and other disturbing issues.

"Two. I like to bet on the strategies and pitches (although I can see the pitches better on TV).

"Three. At night games I like to watch the people in the stands light up cigarettes and calculate the attendance from the number of twinkles I count.

"Four. Today I heard Bluster Hyman interviewing Charley Orange, the second-string catcher for the Mutants. Charley told a frog story. Charley Orange is also a man I admire. In glimmerings on the sports pages over the years—snatches of quotes, mere bytes, really, edited out of context by jam-happy cut-and-paste clowns calling themselves sports editors—I have detected in Charley Orange an intelligence and understanding of the game that transcends anything I can deduce from my armchair. And tonight he's in the starting lineup."

"You don't have an armchair, Daddy. And that's four reasons to go. Now what are your reasons not to go?"

Maxwell pulled over to the curb as an ambulance hurtled past, screaming its irresistible message of terror and panic into the already-jangled collective psyche of Megaglopoulis. Like Xianity, he thought, baseball in and of itself was harmless. Like Xianity, what it had evolved into was against everything he stood for—made it more than politically incorrect, made it a threat to the planet.

"OK medium-size, here goes. One: Smog. At each game, let's say 20,000 cars drive an average of, let's say 20 miles to the ballpark and back. Plus ushers, stadium workers, players, umpires—all that produces maybe 500,000 miles' worth of carbon dioxide per game, or about 250 tons. We'd have to surround every stadium with 3,500 acres of trees to take it all back out of the air.

"Two. Then there's plane travel. Each team logs enough air miles to probably double those carbon dioxide figures.

"Three. Energy. At each night game, let's say 1,000 2-kilowatt lights burn for five hours, which equals 10,000 kilowatts of power. Not counting all the lighting in the parking lots and under the stands. If we were to cancel one season, that would be 77 home games times 16 ballparks in the two leagues equals 1,232 games—let's say 1,000 of them at night. We'd save—wow! 10 million kilowatts! We could shut down 10 Chernobyls.

"Four. Trees. Four hundred major-leaguers each go through, let's say, 50 bats per annum. The demand for baseball bats helped doom the hickory tree to extinction. Now the old hickory is made from ash trees. Then there's newspaper sports pages, printed programs, baseball magazines, baseball books...

"Five. Cattle. The chief artifact of the national pastime, the old horsehide, is now cowhide. Imagine switching from the horse, the ultimte symbol of bestial beauty, to the cow, a Frankensteinian half-creature designed not by S/HeIt but by man. Don't get me started on how cattle have polluted all the streams in the West, destroyed the native grasses..."

"Don't start, Daddy."

"Thank you. Six. Hamburgers. Ground-up, factory-farmed, polluted, polluting cows. What produces more greenhouse warming than all the carbon dioxide in Megaglopoulis?"

"Cow farts. Don't get started, Daddy."

Maxwell swerved to avoid hitting an elderly woman who was walking her dog amidst the stop-and-go. "Thank you. Not to mention hot dogs. Seven. Beer. Thirty-five percent of people who drink alcohol become addicted. Drunk drivers kill let's say two-thirds of our 40,000 annual traffic fatalities. Plus x billion dollars in lost productivity, another x billion in medical care, another..."

"Next reason, Daddy."

"Thank you. Eight. Soft drinks. Sugar is even more addicting than alcohol. True, it's generally considered harmful only to the user, but it did prevail as a murder defense in the infamous Twinkie trial. Extracting and refining it is such hellish work that the U.S. had to import slaves from Africa to do it.

"Nine. Ice cream. Ice cream requires freezers. Freezers gulp energy like pigs gulp slop. More Chernobyls. Nutritionally..."

"Ice cream! Daddy, can we stop and get an ice cream?

"Wait till I'm done. Ten. Television contracts. The networks use baseball to sell all kinds of destructive products, from beer to burgers. Cattle..."

"Daddy!"

"Thank you. Eleven. Conspicuous consumption by unconscious millionaires. The players lavish their money on big homes, fast cars, heated swimming pools, exotic vacations, fur coats for their wives..."

"Twelve. Habitat removal. The owners buy up the last pristine environments in urban settings and build stadiums on them. Did I ever tell you the story of...?"

"Yes, Daddy. Lots of times. There's an ice cream place."

Maxwell pulled up in front of 300 Flavors—All Brands. The cooling tongue-tickles of Cherry Garcia could usually assuage his guilt. Although they had to remove their gas masks to eat, he and Sage continued to talk through the walkie-talkies. "Well," said Sage, "you have four reasons to go to the game and 12 not to go. I'm sorry Benjamin Franklin wasn't nicer to you."

Maxwell sidestepped gingerly to avoid stepping in a freshly-melted puddle of Wavy Gravy. "Benjamin Franklin can go fly a kite," he said. "I'm going."

If you want to play in the big leagues, you have to make appearances at charity events. This is a fact of life metaphorically as well as on the diamond: in all fields of endeavor, the top dogs must be publicly seen lifting their legs and offering golden showers to the fire hydrant of philanthropy. None are exempt: not Presidents, governors, Mafia dons or corporadoes, nor across the dress code chasm to teen dotcom moguls and gangsta rappas.

Most of the Megaglopoulis Mutants, like others in their line of work, attend cheerfully. It feels good to help those less fortunate, and it feels good to be the center of attention. Today a quorum of Mutants was enlivening the annual Old Poker Player's Relief Fund bash. It was Wellington P. Sweetwater's pet project. Charley Orange had to force his cheer. He had met some of Sweetwater's friends, and none of them looked so indigent or feeble that they couldn't take a fellow traveler for a grand or two in an evening. As far as Charley could tell, Sweetwater formed the Old Poker Players' Relief Fund so he and his ex-cronies could make tax-deductible contributions to their future selves.

Then he met Dina. She was lovely, tall with straight blonde hair, blue saucer eyes and a smile as wide as a simile, aimed straight at him. She knew a lot about baseball for a woman, she asked him questions about his career, and her eyes widened and her smile added vowels after every answer. And now she was introducing him, praising him to the crowd with sincere fervor. He walked onstage; she greeted him with a hug and a kiss on the cheek. Was that kiss just a millisecond longer than friendly?

Later, when the music started, Charley spotted her across the room. He strode over, for once feeling confident. "Hello, Dina. Dance?"

Dina's smile was different now: disconnected from her eyes, which gazed through him as if she had never met him. It looked more like she had a banana stuck sideways in her mouth. "No."

If he hadn't been so puzzled and confused as he turned away, he might have thought to ask her whether it was an identical twin sister he had met earlier.

Out of the corner of his eye, he saw another guy approach her. Out of the corner of his ear, he heard the guy say, "Hi, Dina. Dance?" Out of the frying pan into the fire, he heard Dina say, "Yes!"

Charley turned around. There they were, already on the dance floor. He walked up to Dina and stuck his face in her face. "Hello!" he said. "You don't have to like men, but if you'll at least acknowledge our existence, you'll find that the numbers on rape and war go way down."

He left and went home to study a videotape of Hector Tortilla, tomorrow's starter for the Lemon Sox. It was after times such as this that Charley most appreciated the game of baseball: a compact, closed universe confined between two lines that were perpendicular, not parallel, and that did meet, right at home plate, just three feet in front of his station in life, and stretched out a manageable 90 degrees for only as far as the ball could be hit. Babe Ruth had extended this universe to 600 feet, and until they started making the balls out of India rubber, that was as big as it was going to get. It was a tidy, comfortable universe: no house payments, no traffic cops, no IRS, no irascible computers, VCR's, cell phones or other technology unleashed on its consumers 20 years before the bugs are worked out, no battles over insurance claims, no pie-eyed love affairs or bitter divorces: no women. If universes are concentric as well as stacked in piles, then Charley's was about halfway between large and small (and through some strange property of hyperspace/time hooked up to the 15 billion light year model with no visible wormhole or intermediary. But we can't say no strings attached.)

As if in evidence of the Platonic thereom that an ideal worldlet cannot maintain itself in isolation, the universe of the diamond has in certain quarters been invaded by astronomical salaries, autograph fees and season-ending strikes, megacorporate owners and taxpayer-

funded stadia with names like Qualcomm, Tri-Star, Bank One and Dotcom, by astroturf, non-alcoholic drugs, Rotisserie leagues, adult humans bouncing around in 90-degree weather in furry animal suits and other sorry reflections of the respective zeitgeists of these quarters.

Still, the average fan can usually minimize these unsavory elements in his mind. Through the comfort of immersion in statistics, the diamond universe is best pictured as tall columns rising until they disappear into the sky, comprised totally of numbers stacked on top of each other off into the vast everywheres forevers, like the National Debt in dollar bills. (If all the infinite parallel universes are stacked atop each other, then as above, so below, microcosm reflects macrocosm, ontology recapitulates phylogeny and all that.)

Sometimes behind the plate Charley felt like the Black Hole at Galaxy Central, or the Void at the spot where the Big Bang blew, from which all matter had hurled itself out into the vast everywhere forever.

(It seems that the universe itself may be a black hole. If so, why does matter appear to be exploding outward? If it's a black hole, it must be imploding into itself. Does that mean the quasars our telescopes spot Out There are visible segments, not folded away from our sight, of the Big Ex/Implosion? Is Time actually running backward? Do we live in a goldfish bowl of an anti-verse inside the universe we have defined as Out There? If so, don't we have to double the infinite number of parallel universes?)

Inside Charley's universe, all the laws were knowable—and known, by the umpires, and fairly well by the managers and players. Charley, a student of his universe, knew them like the sun knows what time to rise and shine.

The universe outside interfaced in the form of the fans. But that was OK: once the fans entered the ballpark they left the outside outside and became the sound effects for Charley's universe.

With what certainty can we say that the universe outside is not but an ear for the sounds of Charley's expanse? Even as we go to press, stranger things than that are being dreamed up in the ivory towers of our think-tanks and universities to be taught in our classrooms of advanced physics. Which will it be now, infinite parallel universes or the universe-as-ear? If we all can just get our minds around some of the esoteric calculus they're using to prove everything with, we can probably go for both.

In Charley's universe he was more of a struggler than a star, but he had earned respect—something he found lacking in the universe outside. Charley's was a universe without women.

Like a little old lady with tachyon drive nearing the speed of light but never stomping the throttle and reaching it, the game of baseball can be played ever more and more perfectly, but the closer you edge toward perfection, the harder it is to become any more perfect than you are.

One of baseball's charms in Charley's mind was, like the laws of relativity, its endless challenge: absolute perfection in the game is as elusive a goal as is the speed of light to anything larger than a standard-issue photon. The preceding century's 100,000-plus major-league contests produced 14 "perfect" games enshrined by the standards of the Grand Old Game's arbiters, but by the standards of a universe these achievements would not be allowed in the same galaxy as the Hall of Fame. A pitcher hurls a "perfect" game by simply retiring all 27 batters that he faces. With odds of less than one in two that even the best hitter will reach base during any particular plate appearance, Charley could compare setting down 27 men in a row to breaking the sound barrier, but $pg=c^2$? He didn't think Old Tousletop would go for that. In a truly perfect game, 27 batters would go down on 27 total pitches, or—more perfect yet—they would strike out on 81 pitches.

On the personal front, Charley had watched the layers of the onion of imperfection peel away, ever and ever more slowly, until six years ago, when his physical skills skii'd over the mountain peak and began their inevitable gravity-powered slalom down the back slope toward the sunset. Since then his talent had more resembled a double onion, one of those stir-fry Siamese twins jostling for subterranean space while sharing a single stalk. The physical onion, like an anti-planet spinning backwards in Time, sheathed itself in ever more calcifying layers. The second onion was the ever-developing brainpower that kept him in the game, even with a .164 batting average. He expected it to keep him in the game after he retired, in the managerial ranks.

Because Charley's universe would absorb as much of himself as he could possibly give, he could climb totally inside it, pull the wormhole shut behind him and remain whole, unaffected by women, for hours at a time.

In the theory of parallel universes, however, while an electron may qualify as a black hole, a baseball diamond does not qualify as a universe. Now, back in those dark-age days before the advent of all these everywheres forevers (discovered and *ergo* created by Hugh Everett III in 1957), a universe was defined as "the whole body of things and phenomena: the totality of material entities." For example, quasars, being capable of detection by our telescopes, and quarks, being detectable by scanning electron microscopes and a bit of scholarly imagination, are part of our universe. If this were in the old days of physics before $e=mc^2$ and all that, then Mutant Stadium would have met the physical definition of a universe for Charley—almost.

For long periods of time, he could make it his whole body of things and entities, his totality. There was the moment of stepping out onto the diamond—the thousand bright lights glowing in tribute to his achievements and those of his 24 fellow athletes. Every time he emerged from the dugout onto the turf, he felt proud all over again. There were the media, the scattering of early arrivals in the stands—the diehard fans, sometimes friends. Warmup: the delicious sting of the ball smacking into his perpetually-puffed palm through his mitt, the miraculous transition, in nine throws, from aching to shotgun arm. Batting practice: high-school lobs. Usually the one time Charley could swing for the fences. But only one time per 10-swing at-bat: Charley was disciplined, using BP for practicing the hit-and-run, avoiding the double play, moving the runner over.

But nothing built his confidence like hitting one out.

There were the guys in the locker room. And the Big Dream they all dreamed and lived together. They shared a feeling of power—a feeling Charley felt nowhere else in the world. The majors was a universe of men, who answered when he spoke to them, who returned his phone calls, who showed up for appointments with him...in short, who treated him like a human being instead of wiping their feet on his tattered heart.

Because his universe was a universe of all men, it seems natural that he would ask himself the question: Why are men so kind and women so cruel? Away from the ballpark, he felt like he was in a parallel universe looking through the window into the one everyone else inhabited, a universe where he saw love and craved all the love he saw.

Ay, there's the wormhole. There's where the universe outside leaked into Charley's. As Charley knew when he thought about it, there's no such thing as a closed universe. Any time a number of things—even universes —squash up against each other in a stack, osmosis takes place, interactions occur, sparks fly. The guys talked about women. About their exploits and conquests. They all had so many. In that way, they were the worst of all possible people to people Charley's universe. When they started in on who they boffed in Pittsburgh last night, who they would be boffing in Cincinnati tonight and what their physical attributes were, Charley would fall silent and leave the locker room for the field or the hotel.

Ladye Hannah Aura says it's dangerous to think negative thoughts because everything in the vast everywheres forevers is connected and therefore our thoughts create our lives. While generally true, it's also an overstatement, because good things can also happen to people who are mentally unprepared for them. Granted, they happen less frequently, and they tend to appear more miraculous to their beneficiaries. To expect the best opens you up to receive and exchange with other positiveness; to expect disaster casts you off with the misery-loves-company crew manning the Lifeboat's dinghy —on anyone's "sea list" at best. But nobody's perfect: clouds drift briefly across the hearts of the most pollyanic of us, while the Gloomiest Gus, the most fearful and downtrodden heart, has secret hopes and moments that may be tinged with the gold of the sun.

Understandably, Charley Orange could not have foreseen the ensuing events that were about to change his life. The beautiful thing about the subtlety and complexity of those connections across time and space is that, with the possible exception of Ladye Hannah Aura on a good day, no one else could either.

◆ ◆ ◆ ◆

Charley Orange felt an inkling of a change when he saw his name in the starting lineup against the Louseworts. The new feeling stirred again in batting practice when he took his one alotted dinger pitch downtown. He was ready to hit! He felt it growing when he crouched behind the plate for Sleepy Joe Sawchuck's first warmup tosses. It burst into full-blown excitement in the third inning when he left the yard against Don't Blink Dinero with two on, staking the Mutants to a 3-1 lead. In the eighth it all crashed down: a five-run Lousewort rally handed the Mutants a come-from-ahead loss, dropping them back to 14 behind.

But no, Charley, if you can imagine it, good things can happen outside the universe of baseball.

After the game Charley sat in the Extra Innings nursing a cold one and contemplating the Mutants' situation. What he wanted most in the world was to exit a winner. The Mutes had the makeup; what was holding them back?

A fresh clone of the brew he had yet to finish appeared under his nose. "From the gentleman in the corner," said the waiter.

An irony flitted across Charley's mind, like the cloud across the moon in *Un Chien Andalou*. Not only did he have no woman to leave him, no woman to buy a drink for, now he had a strange man buying a drink for him. Was the guy gay?

Come on, he cautioned himself; just a fan.

He looked toward his benefactor: what miniscule round-inchery of face he could discern was centered in the most massive tumbling tumbleweed of hair he had ever seen. It looked like a hedgehog, but it walked toward him bipedally, like a human.

Saying nothing, the hedgehog approached, holding up a baseball and pen. A hopeful expression came onto its face. Looking at that face, Charley thought, was like watching a six-inch TV set.

As Charley took the pen, the hedgehog spoke. "My name's Maxwell Veribushi and I've been a fan of yours ever since your sophomore season, when you hit .900 in the clutch. I left the city seven years ago and haven't kept tabs on your career as closely as I'd like to. But I guess it's gone well if you're still around. You're the only guy still on the team from when I left."

"You're the second person this month to tell me I hit .900 in the clutch that year. It must be true."

"Second-string catchers have always been my heroes," said Maxwell. "Probably some rooting for the underdog in there, but it's mostly because what keeps them in the big leagues is their brains."

"You sound like a true connoisseur of the game, Mr. Veribushi."

"Maxwell. Baseball is my favorite sport—my *only* sport—because it's played with the mind as much as the body. I like to call the game with the catcher. If I can find someone to match my gambling spirit, I bet on each pitch. When you caught tonight, I was betting dimes. I made $3.20 off your calls—the price of your drink. You called a great game, Mr. Orange. You deserve it."

"Charley. Have a seat, Maxwell."

"You honor my inner child, Charley."

"Calling pitches is very hard to do from the stands," said Charley. "I look up and see 50,000 faces and I realize they don't have a clue about what's going down here on the field. They pay all the money and we get all the fame and glory, all the fun."

"Not all of it," said Maxwell. "Game tied 1-1, top of the seventh, one out, runner on first, number two hitter up, a lefty. Will they hit-and-run? Sacrifice? Try a steal? A fast ball is harder to steal on, but easier to hit if you can sit on it. Do you bring in a lefty reliever? Who's fresh in the bullpen?"

Charley jumped in. "How did we pitch to this guy in his previous at-bats? What did he hit, what gave him trouble? Is the pitcher's hummer still hopping? Does he have any surprise pitches he hasn't thrown yet? Does the home plate ump have a high or low strike zone? Wide or narrow? Can we double the batter up? How high is the infield grass? How wet or dry? How fast is the baserunner? How's Revenge at Second Base's sprained thumb? Does the pitcher have a good pickoff motion? How close can he hold the runner?"

Maxwell: First pitch is a fastball, outside corner. Harder to steal on. Don't want to fall behind.

Charley: Maybe it's hit-and-run. And does the fastball rise or sink? A sinker could get two.

Maxwell: Not to break the train of thought at this tense moment, but I have read that a so-called rising fastball does not, cannot rise. It would defy the law of gravity.

Physicists maintain that no matter how much backspin Whizzo Mark Salot IV puts on Sweet Patootie or Big Peter, they will merely sink less than a ball thrown with no spin. Gravity causes a ball hurled at 90 mph to drop three feet in the 56 feet between the pitcher's release point and the back edge of home plate. If a sidearm fastball thrown with backspin tails off no more than six inches, how can an overhand fastball rise more than six inches while it's dropping three feet?

All this did Maxwell relate unto Charley.

"If you would be there," said Charley, "you would throw away your book."

Even the learned physicists acknowledge that there are things they do not understand about the flight of a thrown baseball. They report that this is an area where further study is needed. They hope that our university physics departments will address themselves to it. Some suggest that physics departments should create Ph.D.'s in this area and perhaps corral some bigger funding.

None of this did Maxwell Veribushi, Ph.D., impart to Charley. He disagreed violently with the part about creating more Ph.D.'s.

Instead he asked, "Do you know about the deflection and sagitta of the curve ball? Long before baseball was even a gleam in Abner Doubleday's eye, physicists have been studying the curve ball."

"And you know what?" said Charley. "There ain't a one of them can hit it yet."

"You're right there. But check this out. Back in 1665, when Sir Isaac Newton was just 23, he wrote about trajectories of curves in tennis balls. In 1870 his successors were still arguing that curve balls don't curve: they're illusions.

"I will grant you," Maxwell continued, "that these are the same illustrious scholars who claimed birds couldn't fly. We can question just who are the dinosaurs here.

"Anyway, in 1870, a few people with normal IQ's and common sense set up three poles in a straight line. A curve ball artist named Freddy Goldsmith then broke off a pitch that went left of the first pole, right of the second and back left of the third.

"This was quite a feat," Maxwell explained, "because although the *deflection*, or deviation from a straight line, of a 70-mph curve ball over 60 feet is 14.4 inches, the *sagitta*—the widest part of the bow between the release point and the place it crosses over home plate—is only 3.4 inches."

"I don't know about measurements," said Charley. "In the early 1900's, physicists discovered that when they tried to pin down an electron under a microscope, it behaved a lot like Olive Oyl did when Popeye peeped in on her taking a bath: it became very shy. Whenever it sensed a Cyclopean eye peering down at it from above, it made a *quantum leap:* that is, it was instantaneously somewhere else on the zigzag path of its orbit around its atomic nucleus. If they tried to follow this path so they could predict where it would go, it just sat there as still as the dot on an i."

"Did the good scientists question the limitations of their microscopes?" asked Maxwell. "Did they stop to think that an electron jitterbugging around at the speed of light might zig the sub-microscopic expanse from one side of the atomic nucleus to the other faster than they could measure? Did they ever try to catch a flea that was springing around on a bedsheet? No, they didn't say they didn't know; they labeled the phenomenon the Uncertainty Principle, and now they claim the electron gets from point A to point B via a parallel universe."

"Ah-ha!" said Charley. "A fellow parallel universalist. But the electron does not traverse just any parallel universe. This is an entirely new universe, created presumably by the electron for the sole purpose of getting itself from A to B. In other words, every time an electron takes a quantum leap—which is every time one is looked at—yep, a new universe is born."

"Yep," echoed Maxwell. "Don't you think these are the kind of theories being adopted by the guys who route air flights from Los Angeles to San Francisco through Denver?"

"Think of it, Maxwell: ours may be but one of an infinite number of everywheres forevers. The implications of this are truly mind-warping: it means that all imaginable universes may exist. There may be one just like ours only with no nine-digit zip codes, airport food, looped-tape phone menus or Big Dumb Shorts."

"Sure," said Maxwell. "And the Easter Bunny may be real in another, and still lay eggs. In yet another one, the time *before* Christ's birthday may be referred to in Latin (A.C.—Ante Christus) and the time *after* in English (B.D.—Biblically Declared). I'll stick with the universe we've got. The way I see it, it's made of glue and motion. The glue holds things together; the motion gives them room to breathe."

"All these universes may even be connected to ours via our imaginations," said Charley. "Do you ever think that all those surreal events that unfold in our dreams and our daydreams (every time we take a break from the world Out There) are really glimpses of these other universes—that if we could but free ourselves of our 3-D shackles, we would be Surreal Forever?"

"Things are weird enough right here on Mama Gaia," said Maxwell, "let alone in hyperspace. I wouldn't put it past your universes to be playing with us in their spare space-time."

"Come on, Maxwell, take it one step further. The whole world Out There (that we take our breaks from to indulge in these poly-universal flights of fancy) may be but the stuff of our dreams."

"Past philosophers have been paid good money to propose just that," said Maxwell. "And next to the Buddhists, these guys (the Solopsists) are as nuts and bolts are to a castle of sand. The Buddhists believe the world isn't even here. *Maya,* they call it, which is Buddhist for "illusion." Of course, if the world isn't really here, neither are they, and their conceit vanishes like a make-believe soap bubble popping in the make-believe breeze. Me, I choose to believe that Existence exists. It makes life simpler."

"Well sir, it is a pleasure to find someone who is conversant in such matters, even if you are a skeptic."

"And you a believer. Sometimes I marvel at the mischief the human mind can get itself into. I ask you this, Charley: have you ever seen any Buddhist espousing the gospel of Maya while standing in front of a real make-believe Mack truck? As Descartes said just before he disappeared, I think not.

"Physicists dream up this stuff, then they trot out some moonbeam math that no one can decipher and say, 'This proves it's true'. What's it all about, Alpha? And just what are these guys smoking, anyway? Can the Heaven and Hell of the Creationists be half as cuckoo? These brain addicts are slitting their throats with Occam's Razor. What are we ever going to do with all these universes, anyway?"

"Let's go into real estate," said Charley.

"I will say this for parallel universes. They would provide an alternative explanation for a fascinating phenomenon that I am always drawn to when I'm in the ballpark, which until tonight has not been for seven long years. When I sit in the stands at night, I like to look around and watch cigarettes being lit. When the stadium is full, a lighter or match is always twinkling somewhere, like I imagine the fireflies shone back when Mutant Stadium was Mosquito Marsh.

"Mosquito Marsh?"

"Later. Now, maybe those little controlled burns are like gigantic, visible electrons popping into and out of our universe. Anyway, I use them to disprove the Uncertainty Principle. By estimating the crowd at 50,000 and the percentage of smokers at 50 percent (down from 67 percent 20 years ago when I began performing this calculation), I can count the number of flashes per minute and calculate the number of cigarettes the average smoker consumed in a day: about two packs, which agrees with the statistics. Or conversely, I can count the flashes and assume 1/2 (or 2/3) times two packs a day and estimate the crowd, also pretty accurately. And here I throw off the shackles of uncertainty that Heisenberg tries to drape over my shoulders. I can calculate one, and then the other. Not one *or* the other. Both."

"A toast to the Veribushi Certainty Principle," said Charley. "How close were you tonight?"

"Hm. Would you like to make a small wager—say a drink—on tonight's attendance? Tell you what: you give me two guesses to your one and I'll give you 10-1 odds. You can even go first."

"What will I do with 10 drinks?" asked Charley.

"How about my drink versus an evening you'll never forget?"

"What kind of evening?"

"Never mind; just bet."

"OK," said Charley. "I'll say 51,454."

"I'll say 51,453 and 51,455." Maxwell Veribushi rose. "I'll take a raincheck on the drink. You're in training and I have a date."

Charley's heart winced. Even this hairball look-alike could get a date, and he couldn't?

"It's been a very great pleasure meeting you," Maxwell continued. "One final homage. I've always considered the catcher's throw to second on an attempted steal as the toughest play in baseball. You have to throw the ball twice as far as the pitcher, to a target area maybe only twice as wide and high, with no windup or set, with the batter more than likely swinging at the ball. It takes the pitcher .9 to 1.5 seconds to deliver the ball from his stretch, meaning the runner is halfway there before you get the ball. He'll arrive in another 1.5 seconds, and it takes your throw exactly one second. That leaves a half-second for you to rise and release the ball and the second baseman to apply the tag."

Charley stood and shook hands. "I'm a catcher because my father wouldn't let me pitch. Look: only four fingers."

From beneath their furry precipices, Maxwell's eyes gleamed. "Just like a frog! Frogs have only four fingers per hand, although they do have five toes. The better for foreplay," he chuckled.

The mention of the word kicked up a gloom in Charley that settled all over yesterday's balloons. "I wouldn't know about that," he said.

Now most people, especially male people, upon hearing Charley's remark, would not hear it. Would not Go There. Would not touch it with a 10-foot pole. Especially female people too, except those looking for trouble. But Maxwell Veribushi was the recipient of a very special and unique training. He heard the words. He felt them touch his heart. He Went There.

"Charley, I'm a biology professor of sorts. My specialty is frogs. Would you like to come down and see my lab? It's an off-night tomorrow, yes? I'd like you to meet my Research Assistant. I think the two of you might hit it off."

Normally Charley was genial with fans but deemed it necessary to maintain certain boundaries. Now something deeper in him spoke. "Thanks, Professor. You're on. Tell me about your assistant. What does he do?"

"No, no questions."

"A genuine frog laboratory, and I can't ask questions? You don't cut them up, do you?"

Maxwell Veribushi shuddered audibly. "No, no, of course not. Forgive me for being so mysterious. Listen, I'm an animal fan—born one myself—a one-species-one-vote sort of guy. No harm done, no, never."

"*Manana* then, mein Prof."

"*Hasta luego,* my friend."

To confetti showers, a soldier returns home. The Bates Hotel sells another pizza. An otherwise normal housewife hears the Pillsbury Man. Have we entered a garden of parallel universes? Or is it only national TV? Or is it both?

The guard at the gate into Baroque Heights, the poshest real estate in Megaglopoulis, looked up from his blue-hued pacifier long enough to register a motorcycle racing by, a furball at the helm and a hulking man with a dark visage behind. Did the sight plug in so well to his cathode reality that he blinked an eyelid: not? No, actually he recognized Dr. Veribushi—and, had not the long years at the remote control taken their toll on the 20-20 vision of his youth, he might have identified his passenger as well. For through his 40 seasons in the kiosk, he had been a Mutes fan through bad times and good. Like all baseball cognoscenti, he appreciated Charley Orange for the things beyond his mediocre numbers. He remembered the time Foo Foo McGonigle brought in Charley to pinch-run in a down-one situation so he could save his speedster for after a tie. Charley was slow, but he was smart and solid. He scored the tying run on a short sacrifice fly by faking an excuse-me slide behind the plate and going into the

catcher foot-first, dislodging the ball. He knew the best way into every catcher in the league.

Baroque Heights is one of those up-and-down communities in the suburban foothills north of town: up a hill here, down a flight of stairs there. Through a cubist pastiche of cliffsides and ravines, houses totter precariously on stilts, like circus clowns with windows in their bellies. Maxwell veered off the road onto a long, climbing driveway and spiraled toward the top. They were surrounded by gushing fountains and replicas of classical statues. Perched atop the peak of the hill like Golden Arches on a McBurger, the house came into Charley's view, an oversized castle complete with turrets and Dairy Queen cupolas and flags flapping in the breeze.

"What, no moat?" Charley shouted into Maxwell's ear.

"The modern moat is high-tech and invisible. An organic shield, a force field, a cosmic vibration, a pink bubble surrounding the grounds that turns energy unleashed against anyone within into popcorn. But we slipped by the dragon: he was watching television."

From far below, the night lights of Megaglopoulis winked up at them, each one vying for their attention, like 40 million specatators lighting cigarettes in a vast stadium called The City.

Things sure were more complicated in The City than in The Stadium, Charley thought. All his life he had tried to apply his mind to non-baseball situations with the same rigor that he brought to the game, but things didn't seem to work out. A major non-baseball situation, he sensed, was upon him now.

He gazed upward into the heavens and deposited his psyche in the piggybank moon.

Maxwell tore into a graded area beside the garage where at least 20 cars were already parked, screeched the brakes, revved the engine and cut it.

"I thought we were going to your research laboratory," Charley shouted over its death throes.

"*Veni, vidi, vici.* We are. We did. We're here. Good—they haven't started yet. C'mon around the back way and I'll show you something."

Passing by the driveway, Charley saw a handmade sign pinned to a tree. It read:

WELCOME TO W.I.T.C.H.
Speaking this evening:
CLITOREA PEARL

"Maxwell," he asked. "What's W.I...."

"Sss-h-h!" said Maxwell. "Here, come on inside." He led Charley into a guest cottage and lit a candle. The candle shone as two, for it was placed before a mirror. And another two, and another two...twelve dancing duos of light and shadow. In the glowlight Charley saw an altar: fertility goddesses, dried menses, a dildo with the phallus turning into a tree, divining cards, a haunting fragrance. There were flowers: huge vasesful of them. Jasmine, honeysuckle, magnolias, and from Hawaii, impatiens, frangipani and anthuriums with their lurid sex organs jutting out like famished frog's tongues.

There was the bed. Four-postered, oak. With pink silk sheets tastefully turned down just enough to reveal them, under a lipstick-red comforter. From the top of the bed hung a tapestry depicting two overdeveloped lovers; others adorned the walls and ceiling. Charley sat on the bed: the effect of the candles and mirrors was to make him feel surrounded by himself.

"I made the down payment on this place for Clitorea back when I had some money," Maxwell said. "Now not only does it pay for itself, it makes a handsome profit for everyone concerned. Plus a few shekels I toss in for research."

"Dr. Veribushi," said Charley, "you're telling me you own a whorehouse?"

"Not quite that," said Maxwell. "And not really. I sold back 90 percent of my share to the W.I.T.C.H.es at 90 percent of my cost, plus"— he cleared his throat— "a few privileges."

Just then the evening quiet was shattered by a sound like an ox being gored.

"What's that?" asked Charley, "an ox being...?"

"The conch shell. Time for the meeting. I'll show you the rest later."

As they crossed the porch, Charley saw another sign posted on the front door: W.I.T.C.H. The periods separating each letter were as dark and round and mysterious as the Yoniverse. "Maxwell," he whispered. "Are those acronyms acrimonious?"

Maxwell smiled and waved him in. The spacious living room was wall-to-wall with women—young women, mature women, beautiful women, vivacious women, curvaceous, soft, fleshy women, smiling, giggling, wide-alive women with nary an acrimonious hair apparent on their head. Charley felt tingly. Then he felt light-headed.

Then he felt scared. This madman had tricked him into coming to a congress of hookers.

"Hi Professor Fuzzy Wuzzy!" "More men! Yay!" "F.W., you owe me a kiss!" The world's greatest exo-salientologist basked in what was clearly his element. A sassy-looking redhead with W.I.T.C.H. buttons pinned over the peak of each breast, dangling and swinging like tin tassels, jumped up from her pillow beside them and raised her blouse. "Fuzzy, will you rub your fur on my boo-boos?"

"These are Wymen Itching to Take Charge of Humping," said Maxwell, as his mouth followed his beard into her bosoms.

"No, Fuzzy," she giggled. "We're Wymen Idealizing Tits, Cunts and Hymens."

"No," shouted a lusty-looking blonde from the sofa. "It's 'What In The Cotton-picking Hell (do you think you're doing?)'"

Now the silver-lame'd rafters rang with boisterous acronymous sloganeering. "When In Trouble, Challenge Hubris!" "Wymen's Intuitive Talents Coming Home!" "W.I.T.C.H.E.S! Whores, Tarts, Courtesans, Hookers, Ecdysiasts and Sluts!"

"What about the I?"

"Irenes. Good night Irenes!" That set them cackling like—well, like witches.

"W.I.T.C.H. means many things to many people," said Maxwell. "To the cops, it means organized crime. But W.I.T.C.H. isn't an organization; it's a movement. It's great when these gals are out raising hell in public and the cops come. The head cop says, 'Who's in charge'? and they point their fingers at each other in unison: 'She is'!

Then they point to the cops in unison: 'You are'! Then to whatever spectators have gathered: 'You are'!"

According to the woman introducing Clitorea Pearl, her *curriculum vitae* was rich and varied indeed. She launched her career as a strip contestant with fake ID at age 14, moved on to belly dancing, became a phone sex actress, wrote and posed for skin magazines and limned and starred in three X-rated screen classics. Then one night while faking a celluloid orgasm with a plastic dolphin, she had an epiphany. She left the silver screen to practice first Sensual Massage, then Sensate Therapy. From there she became a sex surrogate, then finally a Sacred Temple Prostitute, serving the needs of the priests and visiting dignitaries at a house of unorthodox worship. Presently she taught a course she had created, a $20,000 primer in Giving and Receiving Sexual Pleasure. For $20,000, how long did the class last? Until you got it.

"...An instrumental figure in restoring the Old Religion, in reviving the Goddess from the grave where she lay buried alive, languishing in torment for centuries...CLITOREA PEARL!"

Amidst screams of delight and much bantering and repartee, Clitorea arose from a sofa, where she had been giggling with a friend, and strode to the raised area by the fireplace that served as a stage, blowing kisses.

To Charley's credit, ladies and wymen, the first thing he noticed about Clitorea was the softness of her infectious grin. To many of your dismay, the second and third items were her breasts, which had surpassed comparison to watermelons when she was 14. Her open-top halter exposed a solid double-handful of each, and she shook one of them playfully at a nearby sister. Tall, medium-large of frame and no more than 20 pounds over the misogynist idea of ideal weight, she complemented the halter with a plain mauve mini-skirt and leather boots. After her bosom, what people noticed most was her off-blonde, Jack-in-the-box hair. The W.I.T.C.H.es said it was curled by Hecate tossing lightning bolts through it. Her eyes were as deep-set and blue as Miles Davis, under incongruously dark eyebrows arched to points like chevrons; her lips too were anomalous, as small and soft and crushable as magnolia petals.

Charley usually knew within seven-tenths of a second whether he found a woman attractive. But looking at Clitorea—how could that smile and that chest go with that hair and that face? And what about her demeanor? He liked strong women, not victims, but Clitorea Pearl? She just picked up the hammer and the bell rang itself.

Charley didn't know it, but the eyes had already carried the vote.

"Thank you! Thank you everyone!" Clitorea shouted in a throaty baritone like chocolate pudding. "Wow, it's exciting to see so many new faces here tonight. Welcome. Thanks for coming!" She paused and her eyes gazed straight into Charley's, as straight as Patricia Neal's eyes stared into Gort's before she blurted out the magic words: *Vlatu barada nicto.* The line between Clitorea's and Charley's eyes was charged; Gort couldn't have zapped him any harder. "And hey, a big special thank-you to all the men who showed up. WE LOVE MEN! —Don't we, W.I.T.C.H.es? C'mon, let's hear it!" In Charley's altered state, he heard the ensuing cacophony as if from underwater, until someone started a chant: WE LOVE MEN! WE LOVE MEN! WE LOVE MEN!

"Will all the male members please stand up?" asked Clitorea Pearl.

"Mine already has!" shouted Maxwell as he and the other men rose.

Looking around, Charley saw less than a dozen of what he considered to be the fair sex (women were the unfair sex). Then almost a dozen W.I.T.C.H.es were circulating, dressed in silk sarongs. As soft music played, each came to each man in turn. An enchanting forest of grateful eyes fell upon Charley like grace. He glanced at Maxwell; the professor was smiling softly back. "I send you kisses wrapped in soft, scented bubbles," he was murmuring. "Merciful Being! I love you!" and similar sentiments.

Charley begain blowing kisses—self-conscious, mechanical, 'kiss-me-back' kisses at first; but a thunderbolt from the third pair of eyes, deep emerald fractals into the vast everywheres forevers, started melting his body into love.

Suddenly he felt a pang in his chest—no, not at his age a sign of the Big One. But while a chest pang is not always life-threatening, neither is it ever just a pang. Charley was having a heart attack, all right, but not the kind that requires medical attention. He was hearing, from the mouth of Clitorea Pearl, words that had lain as unformed as miltless frog eggs in the bloodpools of his aching heart since a time when he was too small to remember.

"...Men are just as victimized by their social roles as women," Clitorea said. "In fact, it's worse for men because—men, in their particular form of victimization, they don't even know they're victims. They don't *think* anything is wrong! They don't *feel* anything at all! I say this not in anger but in deepest sympathy. The eyes in their heart are closed; ours are open. —Hey, maybe that's why we have bigger nipples than they do. Maybe our nipples are our heart's eyes."

"Right on," Charley whispered as the audience tittered. "Why else would we rather look at their nipples than their eyes?"

"Nipples don't look back," said Maxwell. "She was jest jesting. There's nothing to fear in honest Encounter. There's only to love."

"...Sex is the Way we have chosen, our life path. Sisters, we know our sexuality is too sacred for us to use it merely to titillate or manipulate someone. What is sex, anyway? It is our pathway to discover who—and what—we really are."

"Right on, sister!" cried a couple W.I.T.C.H.es.

"Sex is no more just the techniques we master as adepts in the art than Picasso's brush and palette were his masterpieces. Sex is a *gnosis,* sex is a path of love and wisdom, sex is the mystery that lives in the center of the sacred circle with which we surround and surrender. Sex is holy; sex is the beating pulse of the Goddess."

"Amen!"

"Awomen!"

"We are here not so much to give sexual release as to give and receive tender, loving touching. Touches of soft silk in the night. We are here to receive men's sexuality. To nurture it, encourage it, validate it. We are here to make men whole even as we make ourselves whole. We are Teachers of the Heart. As the heart nurses the senses, so does sexuality nurse spirituality, which embraces it, surrounds it even as we embrace and surround the lovers who enter our domain. We must serve the Goddess with compassion and wisdom."

◆◆◆ ◆◆

Woody Woodpecker had finally stopped drumming in Charley's heart. Now his stomach knotted and sweat broke out over his hands, neck and face. He hated when he started sweating like this. Was there really a woman living in this world who spoke such sentiments, or had he fallen through a wormhole into that parallel universe into which he always dreamed of being reborn?

Clitorea Pearl shifted gears from the sublime to the ridiculous. "I have been charged with solicitation, also known as the crime of asking a guy if he wants to have a good time. Only I didn't even ask him. And ironically, that's why I'm being charged. He being a vice dick, and I confess it: I have taken pleasure from a fantasy of applying a vice to his dick. But no, he's just another victim out there, acting out his victimhood, and as long as I can hold compassion for him, I know I'll be all right.

"On the phone he says he heard I did 'exotic positions'. Hey, I say, if you just want to get your rocks off, sorry wrong number. So he says, Hey, no offense, so what *do* you do? So I say Sorry, the experience I offer is sacred and you're not emotionally prepared for it, and I hang up. (Applause)

"Fifteen minutes later, two very unhappy cases show up at my door saying they want to go 'around the world' with me. These guys have 'VICE' stamped on their foreheads with indelible ink. There I am home alone, so I act tough to cover up that I'm quaking in my boots. 'Who told you sleazeballs where I live'?

"'Mac', says one.

"'Is this a knock-knock joke'? I ask him. 'OK, Mac who'?

"'Mac my computer', he says. 'You're under arrest for soliciting a police officer to commit a lewd and felonious act'.

"I praise him for his flair for drama and invite him to audition for my next movie, *Beaus and Eros*. He tells me with my priors I'm looking at a year minimum, and I can't juggle my jugs at the judge because he can't give me less if he wants to.

"Then he offers me a deal—get this!—a year in the slam or an hour with him and his partner and he'll screw up the bust so I can walk on a technicality.

"'Let's see', I say. 'A year versus an hour. I can save an extra 364 days and 23 hours of my life, right'?

"'Now you're talking', he says.

"'Clitorea', I say to myself, 'how far can you stretch? Here are two guys in desperate need of your skills, and you could do yourself a big favor at the same time.'

"'Well', I tell him, 'first, I can't finish a session in an hour. And second, I don't do multiples. You'll have to come back, on separate nights.'

"'Nice try, dogbreath.' Dogbreath he calls me and he wants to have sex with me? 'It's now or never'.

"'Sorry, I can't do it. You guys are just too scary for me, too angry'.

"Then his partner starts in. Mr. Pancakes and Syrup. He likes my sincerity. He likes my spirit. He's concerned about the mess I'm in. They have orders to bust me. But he wants to help me out. Oh, here's a sweetheart! All I have to do is let them take out their lifetimes of frustration on my body and he won't tell lies about me in court. 'Honey', I say, 'you don't need to blackmail a woman to get sex. You just need to love her'.

"'Hey barfbreath, I was putting you on. What makes you think we want to be with a slut like you?'

"'Because I got a hot body', I say. 'Men want it. But you don't really want to be with me because I don't want to be with you. Don't you know that? You need to find yourselves, guys. You're inside there somewhere'. (Applause)

"So anyway, like Dr. Fuzzy Wuzzy says, W.I.T.C.H. means many things to many people. To these guys, it means Without I'm Touching your Cunt, you Hang. So...I'm joking about the frame-up, but they want to put me away for a year, and I'm scared." A lump bubbled its way up from her throat through the chocolate pudding cadence and right on into her tear ducts, washing over the top and down her cheeks.

A sympathetic wave from that tear surged across the room and slapped Charley Orange in the face. He cleared his throat, tried unsuccessfully to speak and felt the hot water dangerously close to leaking out his own valves.

What had come over him? He felt like he was under a spell. Enchanted. He was discovering his own meaning of W.I.T.C.H.

The applause for Clitorea had not yet died when a voice like music chimed behind Charley: "Excuse me, gorgeous." He turned: there was a delicious blonde in a magician costume, holding out her hat. "Clitorea's trial begins next week and tonight's a fundraiser for her defense."

Clitorea broke off the post-speech congratulations and hobnobs to greet Maxwell. "Fuzzy! Will you take me for a ride on your mega-vibrator?"

"If your colleagues can keep my passenger occupied. Meet my friend Charley Orange. He plays baseball for the Mutants, Clit. Remember, I told you about him."

"...You're the one with the brain cells instead of baseballs between your ears?"

"Did he say that? It was very kind of him."

"I like the way you hold eye contact, Charley."

"My mother taught me to always look a woman dressed like you are in the eyes."

"God bless your poor mother and everyone in her generation. Here, go ahead and have a good look." She removed a breast from its confines and plopped it squarely on Maxwell's head.

"I'm surprised Maxwell didn't tell me more about you," said Charley. "You're quite something."

Clitorea laughed, sending her chevrons skyward. "Oh, he's very protective of me. So tell me, how am I quite something?"

"Ah...well, I wish I could believe women like you exist. Pardon me—I still think I'm dreaming, and I'll wake up surrounded by harpies screaming to nail my *cajones* to the wall."

"Sounds like a tough childhood, Charley. We all had 'em."

"I'm having a tough adulthood. I think women should all talk like you do, and you're the first one I've ever met who does."

"No wonder. Do you always open a conversation with a woman you're attracted to by telling her you're pissed at women?"

"How's that? And who said I'm attracted?"

"'I don't meet any women who talk like you do'. In other words, I'm not like other women; they're all bitches except me. That gives me a lot to live up to. And if I want you to like me, I can't talk like a woman."

"Just not like the other women in my life."

"That's a lot of women, Charley. You must be picking mighty poorly." She turned her attention to Maxwell. "Ride me, daddy."

"It's true," Charley thought, as the magician brought Clitorea the hat. "I've lost all faith in my judgment."

"Look, Booby!" said Clitorea. "Someone promised a G-note!" She read it and screamed. "Charley! You sweet, wonderful man! You haven't lost the faith after all!"

The moment Clitorea Pearl saw Charley Orange's I.O.U., she knew where she would be spending her nights for the foreseeable future (if not in the pokey). Her watermelon breasts pressed into his ribs; her magnolia-blossom lips wafted over his. "Hey—would you like a sensual massage? I give the best in the business. Free to you."

"No, that's all right. You don't have to repay me. I'm not into one-night stands anyway."

"Why not? —Oh, never mind, you give me too much to deal with at one time. Of course I'm not repaying you. You're a big, good-looking guy and I'm turned on to you. And I'm a healer, not a hooker. Didn't you hear my speech? I'll teach you the difference: it's important. I'm doing it because I want to, Charley. I love that you gave the money, but mostly I'm responding to your confidence and faith in the universe to provide for you. And it did. It provided *me*."

At that moment Charley realized that yes, indeed, he was very attracted to Clitorea Pearl. "Dr. Veribushi," he said, "I leave you now. Should I die of joy before I wake, I will to you all my fame and fortune for turning me on to this turn-on woman."

They adjourned to the very guest cottage that Maxwell had shown him. "I have to tell you," he said as they entered, "that you are the sexiest woman I have ever laid eyes on."

"Thank you, sweet man. I love it when you lay your eyes on me. And I love it even more when your eyes meet mine." She gazed into his pupils. As he gazed back, locking into a hypnotic connection, he fell through her eyes into her—into her Self, into the parallel universe of his dreams, into the aweful All, the vast everywheres forevers.

◆ ◆ ◆ ◆

Is sex interesting? Does the Pope shit in the woods?

Sex, the subject of librariesful of books, galleriesful of art and even, as we have seen, an occasional laboratoryful of science; the object of inquisitions and persecutions, of worship and reverence; the star of subliminal advertising, the glory of the morning glory and the power of the sunflower, the Shaper of the lotus-yoni and mighty Priapus, the three-letter word that rhymes with hex—sex, created by evolution to speed up the dance (so say the Evolutionists), used by the Horned One to ensnare human souls (so say the Creationists). Sex: well, the whole idea makes for some mighty lively cocktail conversation in the human arena.

Anloie was different. Sex did not interest her as much as Spirit. (Yes, at this stage in her young life she still thought they were different.) Her deepest emotions were reserved not for men but for trees and dolphins. She was born a Capricorn, but she had Libra rising. Libra is the sign of balance, and Anloie sought to balance her love life with her spiritual life. And there was her physical life to throw into the equation: quite a lot to live up to. Last year she had met that psychic lady, an Old Soul named Ladye Aura…what was it?—who offered to teach her how to channel, and now she had two boyfriends, and one of them wanted to *marry* her! No wonder her body felt funny: she was out of balance.

Unaware that the Sumerians declared Libra the sign of balance because it commences on the autumnal equinox, the day that day and night are equal, or balanced, nonetheless Anloie knew what was right for *her.* She wished she had learned to meditate, like she had been promising herself to do for the last two years.

Anloie's stomach didn't actually ache: it felt strange. What was it? She wasn't dizzy, like she got when she practiced too many cartwheels. Nor was she nauseous, like the time she overdosed on her birth control pills. She didn't have a headache, like she got when Warren made love to her without some sweet talk first: sometimes in the morning he saw, conquered and came while she was still yawning and stretching herself conscious. But something was going on with her body. It felt like...yes, like when she and grandpa used to play Growing Mr. Wiener when she was nine.

Anloie's father left town when she was a second-trimester fetus, having failed to convince her mother of the seriousness of the overpopulation problem. Since her mother never remarried, Anloie spent lots of her childhood at grandma's and grandpa's. Sometimes mom lived there with her; sometimes only Anloie stayed while mom took some time for herself. As child molesters go, grandpa was certainly not the worst: he did it only a few—well, several times, he never entered her, he did love her, and she felt only mild pangs of guilt for enjoying it. Anloie grew up liking men —especially older men—and able to have orgasms, although she still got that feeling in her body when things were going too fast and she felt out of control.

Whizzo. What to do about Whizzo? Warren was decent in bed, and he was getting better. But what was this excitement she felt around Whizzo? Wasn't it just sexual? A little pleasure dome enhancement and she could feel that way with other guys too. But with Whizzo it felt so good on the natch. Should she stay around and play it through, just in case there was more to it?

Anloie had always chosen crazy guys before. Warren wasn't crazy, and she liked that. Liked that alot. Whizzo? Ay-yi-yi, Whizzo! He made Looney Tunes look like Wall Street. And he made her a little crazy too. She didn't like the way she gave up her power when she was around him. She needed to feel stronger. He was such an awesome athlete. —Well, but if she could pull off the three cartwheels, that would give her self-esteem a real boost...

No, Anloie! He's a kid. I mean, the guy was talking instant marriage! That's not healthy. Whizzo—marriage material? The idea gave her the willies.

But that brought to mind Whizzo's willy. No, no, a thousand times no. Mr. Twister did not have a vote in this!

In his profession, Charley Orange was among the top 400 people in the world. In her profession, Clitorea Pearl was probably in the top One. At this depressing moment in world history—the last days of the Kali Yuga, Ladye Hannah Aura called it, when people are at their worst—in these times when the social structure is so topsy-turvy that most priestesses of the sacred temple arts are reduced to profane pursuits and dangerous health habits, Clitorea Pearl was on a mission to restore the divinity of her calling. The more deeply she could move into love with her clients, she knew, the more sacred, the more healing, her art. While two of the W.I.T.C.H.es prepared Charley for his encounter with her, she prepared herself. Insides first. She bathed in scented waters to the aqueous plunks of harp music. She inhaled the holy smoke. She sat in a lotus position, her hand on her lotus, meditating to love sounds recorded live on compact disc. She invoked the divine Annie Sprinkle. She selected her fragrances and apparel. She inhaled once again and began preparing her outsides.

Poignant minor-key refrains played as Charley Orange removed his size 13's and sank his feet into carpeting as white and soft as cotton tufting in the field.

"I'm Shakti and this is Shanti," said the taller of the two saronged *daikinis* who greeted him. "We're here to bathe you and prepare you for Clitorea."

Shakti—long, dark and slender as a Stradivarius, with a river of hair the color of moonlight that brushed as softly as a forbidden breeze across Charley's skin as she approached him—Shakti unbuttoned his shirt. Shanti —smaller, as full-bosomed as two cellos, her angel face framed by hair the hue of a Louisville Slugger, her eyes the color of cornflowers in the summertime meadows of Charley's boyhood, her skin as soft and white as the Rice Dream in the mushy granola of her heart—Shanti slipped the shirt off his shoulders and let it fall. Shakti unbuckled his belt; pulling down his trousers turned into a mock tug-of-war, leaving them collapsed in giggletry. Is this really happening to me? Charley kept asking himself as his hungry eyes feasted on them removing their sarongs. Shanti's boobs burst out of her chest like marching cheerleaders: Oom-pa! Oom-pa! Shakti's expansive violet-brown aureolae gave her breasts one-eyed Happy Faces the diameter of baseballs. They crowned mounds smaller but more flexible than her sister's: as she swayed her torso to and fro, they swung plenty pendulously enough to tick-tock Charley's clock.

Both women sported fashionably-Mohawked yonis. Below Shakti's amber fuzz, swollen pink labia puckered before retreating coyly between her thighs. Shakti's delicate inner lips protruded beyond the outer like anthers on an anthurium blossom.

Now, the spacesuits of the sweet sisters boasted other features equally worthy of adulation—Shakti's nose, for instance, so aquiline that it had starred in a tissue commercial—but let's face it: if you invite a starving man to a feast, he's not going to admire the cutlery. Charley saw breasts and yonis, yonis and breasts, incidentally fastened to elbows, insteps and other assorted body parts.

"May I hug you, Charley?" As Shakti's softness marshmallowed slowly into him, Shanti massaged his shoulders, then melted into him from behind, wrapping her arms around them both. "Charley sandwich!" she burbled and bit his shoulder. Led by his long-suffering lovestick, Charley's entire body went a-quiver as a Cuisinart. He wanted to throw Shakti down and take her, right there in them old cotton fields back home, but he was trapped between two succulent slices of warm woman. Finally he surrendered the controls. "M-mm h-mm!" he purred. "This is one slice of bologna that's just won the lottery."

Things were getting pretty crowded inside his jockey shorts when Shanti removed them. "Shall we bathe?... Oh my! Speak of bologna! Look, Shakti, he's glad to see us already!"

The bathtub was cream-colored, kidney-shaped and, as Shanti described it, "queen-sized." Already drawn, the water was perfumed

with frangipani and topped with more bubbles than beer drawn from a firehose. Built for multiple occupancy, the tub fit three at once comfortably and cozily. Shakti leaned against the back with Charley resting against her, his head turned sideways so that his cheek lay on the swell of a pop-top breast. His legs intertwined with those of Shanti, who faced him, his knees rubbing the gracefully-arced swell from her waist out to her hips. Squeezing bubbles and water from a loofa sponge over his hairy, muscled frame, she dawdled over those places where whatever time spent is always too short.

Long and langourously did Shakti and Shanti scrub and stroke, Shakti all the while playing with Charley's hair and singing softly into his ear. Then at last came the time for Charley to de-tub, get patted dry and receive anointment with oil of lavender. *Namaste*-ing, his geishas ushered Charley through the portal into the temple proper.

A young girl swallows butterflies. A ship goes up in flames. Ants dance in the streets. Behind a Cajun psychic, rainbows and clouds roll by. In the action-packed parallel universe that Bluster Hyman inhabited, things were always hopping. *Builds confidence and reshapes your body. She's working harder, thinking smarter. Buy one, get one half off.*

"OK Billy Beanball," said Bluster, "are you ready for the first question?"

Yes, Billy was ready. He had looked up the word "palindrome" in the dictionary. Peep! Peep! That's all he had to remember.

"Baseball is tough," said Bluster. "No matter how good you are, it's never good enough." Billy, whose knowledge of diamond lore Bluster now showcased weekly, was tough too…tough to stump. But Bluster had a few tricks up his sleeve. "First question, Billy. Who hit 193 rainbows in three seasons and failed to lead the league all three times?"

"Sammy Sosa in 1998, 1999 and 2001 with 66, 63 and 64 Mark McGwire hit 70 and 65 and Barry Bonds busted 73."

"Respectively. Two: The longest perfect game in history—12 innings —and the pitcher lost it."

"Harvey Haddix, Pittsburgh Pirates, 1959. He gave up a run in the 13th."

"Good. Three: Seventh game of the 1986 World Series, Boston Red Sox ahead, two out in the ninth, who let the ball..."

"Bill Buckner let the ball roll between his legs for an error at first base and the New York Mets won. It was the Curse of the Bambino."

Bluster: They're getting harder now. Four: What two Hall of Famers had nearly full seasons batting under .200?

Billy: The Mendoza line. Mike Schmidt, .196 in 1973, and Reggie Jackson, .194 in 1983.

Bluster: Five. Who won 20 games in his first season and lost the Rookie of the Year award?

Billy: Gene Bearden. He was 20-7 for the 1948 Cleveland Indians but Alvin Dark was named the top rookie.

Bluster: Six. Another tough-luck rookie moundsman: he won 22 games in his first season and was released.

Billy: Let me think...Henry Schmidt, Brooklyn, 1903. He never played in the majors again.

Bluster: Excellent. For season tickets now, last question: Name the three pitchers with losing lifetime records whose names are anagrams for each other.

Billy: What's an anagram?

Bluster: Sorry Billy, you're a loser today, but you have won box seats to the next game pitched by your hero and ours, Whizzo Mark Salot IV. Hey Billy, do you think the Mutes are going to be losers this year?

"No way, Bluster! Whizzo's gonna pitch them to the flag. You watch and see!"

"Well fans, let's all have the faith in our team that a 10-year-old boy has."

◆◆◆ ◆◆

The walls of the Temple of Love were painted pale peach and bedecked with peacock feathers. The only furniture was a bed, a massage table and a mound of pillows. As Charley entered, strains from some sublime, ethereal spacetime—music that might accompany the mating of galaxies—floated into his ears, sending his spirit dipsy-doodling through palaces of joy and sorrow that he didn't even know existed. Enter the mistress of the revels, Ms. Clitorea Pearl, her divine form wrapped to the ankles in a diaphanous negligee of Tyrian purple silk. All of Charley's past experience kept shouting, This can't be! It was too much for him: he left his body, watching her unveil her glabrous gems from somewhere in a parallel universe.

Clitorea's eyes strung with his, yanking him back like a balloon on a string. She smiled reassurance and gestured toward the massage table, draped with apricot silk sheets. Charley lay face-down, his head in the cradle. Clitorea *namaste'd.* She lowered her hands ritualistically, attuning to each of Charley's seven energy bodies, before contacting his upper and lower back and starting to rock his everyday earthling vehicle back and forth. The shifting pressure on his softest spot caused it to be soft no longer; no, longer.

Et tu Charley, at last! Was it worth the long years without, to be here now? Maybe almost? Applying the lotion, Clitorea stroked his back and buttocks: long, langourous effleurages that caressed and nurtured him in ways he hadn't felt since he was a baby in his mother's arms. Not that he could remember being a baby—or, for that matter, being held in his mother's arms. But enough of that: he didn't want to waste any of this time being in that place. Clitorea followed no particular sequence; rather she imagined her heart an open vessel through which flowed all the love in the Yoniverse, pouring out wherever her fingertips, her palms, her forearms met Charley's skin. Cooing and purring, she let his body call to her where she was needed.

Charley entered a deep state of relaxation called *samadhi* by practitioners of the sacred arts and *sleep* by those who are never awake enough to know the difference. He did not lose consciousness, but he was not aware that he was conscious, save twice. The first was when Clitorea sucked his big toe. He had no idea that a mere digit could thrill him almost as much as the Big Digit itself. The second was when she whispered into his ear: "When you like, you can turn over."

When he drifted back into presence, her hands were in his abdomen, the heels of her palms rolling in clockwise circles. His stomach felt like a saucer was wobbling on it. "O-ooh, a knot!" she cooed, pressing, gently at first, and gradually increasing pressure. "How's Mr. Charley doing?"

At this moment Charley was not doing well. Memories of other times, when he expected this to happen and it hadn't, flooded his mind. "It's stupid," he told her. "Here I am, getting what I've wanted all my life at last, and I'm so poisoned that I can't enjoy it."

"It's OK. Just let your thoughts fly around and be bats in your belfry, and *keep breathing*. Breathing into my hand now. That's good."

Charley was three years old. He stood by the rocking chair in the living room, the one with the white doilies on the arms. His mother was brushing lint and hair off the chair. She seemed to be in a hurry. Charley watched her lift the doily from one arm, brush the arm and place it back again. The telephone rang. When she left the room to answer it, Charley wanted to help her. He removed the other doily and carefully brushed the arm. When mom returned from the phone, he proudly showed her his work. Seeing the missing doily, she scolded Charley and gave him a spanking.

As Clitorea continued rocking the saucer on Charley's stomach, tears welled in his eyes. "Good, Charley. Stay with it. Pain comes in little physical packages that fit inside of tears. When the packages get crowded and start bumping into each other, you just open the dikes and pour out the tears. It's ecological: the pain gets recycled." Tears, quoth the goddess, are the golden apples of Iduna; the goddess' gift of eternal youth.

Now Charley's body shook and rattled like a laundromat dryer in its death throes, and the rains came, bumping, tumbling torrents of packages like Christmas on the conveyor belt at UPS, scrubbing down the poopdecks of his cheeks with hot, abrasive salt. Then the clouds parted, the sun came out to play and Clitorea Pearl kissed the brine off the marshes of his eyelids.

"Wow! What happened?"

"There was a li'l ghostie trapped in your tummy and you just freed it up to fly off through the bardo to wherever."

"I haven't cried since I was twelve years old."

"You know, our bodies get all stopped up in that stuff. It's like psychic cholesterol. There's lots more in there. Wait till you reach sob level! Did you like it?"

"I...don't know. I still feel a little shaky." Later, Charley and Maxwell Veribushi would concur that this process of weeping was as mysterious as...well, as orgasm.

Orgasm? Yes, oh patient reader, yes patient Charley, Clitorea Pearl finally got down to business. "OK gorgeous man, lie on your back and close your eyes."

From above his head, Clitorea's hands glided down over his sternum all the way to the pelvic bone, rounded under his sides and returned up over his ribs to his neck. In the process first her nipples, then the pillowed underbelly of her golden arches swept down across his face, lodged briefly in his neck, and then retraced their route over his lips, his nose, his Peeping Tom eyes. Hey Charley! This bud's for you! On the next downstroke, he parted his lips as her nipple arrived, letting its round resilience brush against their puckered insides and tempt his teeth. Then, as her pleasure pods migrated back north, Charley opened his mouth yearningly, like a baby bird eager to gulp a full-course dinner. Clitorea lingered just long enough for an *hors d'ouevre.*

Moving beside him, she tickled and scratched his nipples, giving him tat for tit. She glided down to his pubic shrubbery and drew circles in the hair with her fingertips, pulled and tugged at it, then slid those divine phalanges into the crease between his legs and torso. His would-be iron butterfly inched caterpillar-style toward the source of pleasure. A press of her finger beneath his testicles (on his perineum, he learned later), and the caterpillar wrinkled back into its cocoon. Parting his legs, with the backs of her fingernails she stroked up his inner thighs. While Charley's chameleonic Italian sausage perched on the throes of an identity crisis—would it rather be a garden-fresh zucchini or a strand of limp spaghetti?—Clitorea reached his scrotum and gently rested his *huevos* in her palms, lifted them and began rolling them slowly back and forth between her hands. She sang:

Even little children love Mary Ann
Down by the seaside sifting sand.

A salute to Priapus and the organ he oversees: lives anywhere a creature, animal, vegetable or genetically-engineered, that can match half the growing speed of a delighted ding-dong? Still pliable as filo dough and grown heated as a Florida election, already Charley's member had doubled its length and swelled like the wombs it anticipated sowing with pent-up seed.

Clitorea switched from palms to fingertips to scratchtickly nails. The sounds she brought forth from Charley might have created puzzlement or concern in a small child, but to any W.I.T.C.H. worth her Astroglide, they were the music of magic.

Speaking of Astroglide, lube time had arrived. Clitorea squeezed a puddle of it into her palm and warmed it before turning Charley's scrotal area viscous. With another squeezeful she pressed the base of his shaft firmly down into his second chakra with her right hand, while her left stroked up the stalk toward his fireman's hat, spreading gooey warm wetness across his flesh. Each stroke seemed to Charley not as one but four, as each soft, caressing finger wandered with separate mind, tracing its own course, popping over the purpling ridge in its own time.

All the while Clitorea kept up a running conversation, diverting his attention away from the fantasies he habitually associated with sex toward the tingles and gurgles inside him and into undiscovered branches of his pleasure circuitry. "Like this, Charley? Or this?" "Softer?" "Want some more pressure here?" "Even slower, hm-mm?"

His willy was silly putty in her hand. Laying it onto his belly, she pressed and rubbed it back and forth with her palm and heel. Then she swept it down from noon to six o'clock—slowly, but not as slowly as Big Ben— meanwhile gliding her other hand now down his leg, now up and around his torso, just to remind him that this joystick was but part of a greater whole.

◆◆◆ ◆◆

At six o'clock Charley's chimes started tolling. The silly putty, feeling both loved and kneaded, grew as firm as a Louisville Slugger, and before Charley could shout out, "Ah! No! Ah! Yes!," his hour hand bounced up into 3-D. Clitorea wrapped her hand around it, even whilst deftly dragging her pinky across his perineum. That sneaky, slippery little digit sounded the final note of the reveille: where once hung flaccid skin, pimpled over with pubic foliage, inert, self-absorbed, showing no sign of forward march, now proudly stood a full-fledged phallus, an organ of roaring engorgement, a penile power station with qualities most often attributed to serpents and volcanoes, a mighty oak tree whose roots Charley could feel anchored deeply in the delta of his meat.

Clitorea's face lit up like a little girl who has just been given a lollipop. "So big, Charley! So warm and hard, like a diamond between my breasts!" She gazed into his eyes; he stared back helpless as a newborn at this angel, this goddess in human form.

"M-mm. Yes. That's where it wants to be."

"M-mm, but not to stay. Breasts are soft and warm, but hands have more talent." She began Astrogliding up and down the elongated stalk, whose skin drew tight under its lubricious coating. She pressed firmly on the upstroke, each finger corkscrewing its way toward the top before sliding down the firehouse pole. "Follow my hand, my love, follow my fingers. The next time I do that, tell me where it feels best."

"Mm—aah!" said Charley. "There. —No, RIGHT THERE!" Her discriminating digits had moseyed across his mushroomed mountaintop to his frenulum: the spot at the base of his corona where the borders wrapped around but didn't quite meet, like an overfed cleric's collar: that trumpeting bundle of nerve endings in this, the Carnegie Hall of his body.

Once she zeroed in on his honey-button, Clitorea teased and tickled it, drew circles around it, pressed it, scratched it...Charley's thunderstick throbbed and reddened, straining against the chains of its fleshly package. As his scrotal sacs shriveled like last night's party balloons and began ascending to meet their maker, preparing to launch the next generation, Clitorea inexplicably downshifted, returning to stroking his shaft, merely flicking his hot spot at the end of selected strokes.

"Oh! What are you doing? I was ready to come!"

"That's why I changed. You can come if you want. But why not enjoy an hour or two of pleasure first?"

A voice in Charley wondered whether he could handle an hour of this. Or whether he deserved it. Shouldn't he be doing this to her?

"It's easier to give than to receive, Charley. You can't always be the doer. Let me give you this."

"Huh?" But Charley lost the thought: by now Clitorea's frenulum flicking had him once again climbing the precipice. Looking at his face, she saw a Richter 7.6 a-building. "Relax your ass muscles, Charley. Please, I want to do this for you. Take in some more pleasure."

As Charley breathed and relaxed, he indeed opened to more pleasure. Bliss ice-skated along his axons and dendrites, streaking the bright sparkles of its divinity down his legs, through his belly and chest, and finally triple-flipping into a fountain exploding silver fireworks out the top of his head.

"Oh my...goddess," he sighed, his only words for the next hour.

Clitorea Pearl's talented hands had only begun. She wrapped one around the base of Charley's flute while squeezing upward around his glistening gumdrop with the other. Spreading her fingers out until they covered the whole enchilada, she vibrated his perineum with her other palm. Applying another massive dollop of lube, she pulled the skin downward with one hand while corkscrewing up with the other. She placed one hand underneath and one on top and shook them alternately, as if to bend the rod in the middle. Then she glided her hands in opposite directions, one up and one down.

Charley's shrieks melted into moans as he started getting the hang of navigating Bliss' pathways. Applying still more lube, Clitorea rolled her pliant charge between her hands as if she were shaping gnocci, ranging up and down the pipe like a piccolo playing a jazz solo. She squeezed it in one hand while circling its simmering head with the slithery palm of the other. By now Charley's moans had become gurgles, and a smile that he hadn't smiled since leaving the cradle

filled his softened face. Still Clitorea plied her ancient craft, drawing up his flue one hand after the other, pulling his mushroom up and his stem down, knitting her fingers together and sliding them up and down on the shaft like an oil derrick set on a hummingbird timer.

Over and over she coaxed Charley up to the rim of the volcano, then just as he was about to erupt she eased up and reminded him to release his muscles and breathe. Did he ever lay his crimson chalice between her tender bosoms? Did he finally park his car in her garage, slip his dropsy in her snide, glide his glowing jade stalk into her many-petaled lotus, drive the green fuse through the flower, unlock her mysteries with his master key? Or did his sperm spew unfulfilled into the infecund air? We need not invade his and Clitorea's privacy further for such irrelevancies: what matters is that once again Charley wept—wept until he sobbed, shedding tears of grief, tears of joy, tears of gratitude, cleansing his psychic dead-letter box of a lifetime of unclaimed packages.

Baseball is unique among team sports in that it's a game without a clock.

Even chess, say baseball's detractors, has a clock. Baseball, its defenders retort, is slow only to slow minds. A curious argument: sports are not usually promoted for their intellectual appeal. But the diamond's unique blend of cerebellular and cerebral challenges may well be what catapulted it onto its pedestal as the National Pastime (in, say its detractors, a national past time).

Ossified as the sport may be, it demands athletic prowess in several aspects, as well as strategy and concentration. Most athletic contests—basketball, soccer, hockey—are all action; only football rivals baseball in its cycles of inaction punctuated by action, and in football the action is predictable, starting when the center snaps the ball to the quarterback. In baseball, inaction is shattered by a surprise explosion.

Take today's Mutant game, with Whizzo Mark Salot IV dueling the lowly Woodpeckers, of whom Foo Foo McGonigle said, "The reason they're in last place is, their hitters don't get to hit against their pitchers, and vice versa." The Woodpeckers' team ERA over the past month bordered on double digits, but in 7 2/3 innings today the Mutants had managed only one run against their hefty lefty, Gas Can Gustaria.

That was one more run than the Woodpeckers had scored off Whizzo.

That was also one more run than the Woodpeckers had collected hits off Whizzo.

With two gone in the Mutant eighth, Bimbo Terwilliger worked the count to 3-1. But in the broadcast booth, Bluster Hyman's attention was on Whizzo Mark Salot IV, who sat in the dugout engrossed in earnest conversation with a baseball. "Now he's holding it up near his mouth. He's got his hand up, shielding his face and the ball, so I can't read his lips. I think he's whispering a secret to it.

"Now he's holding the ball next to his ear and listening intently. I don't know what they're talking about," Bluster informed the folks at home; "do you suppose it's a prayer to the gods of no-hitters not to lose his shot at fame and glory in the final inning?"

Sportscasters and writers forever talk about no-hitters in terms of fame and glory and immortality, as if they were as rare as a nun with a bad habit. As a rabbit in a habit. A rabbi in a habit. As a nun cohabiting a habit with a rabbi and a rabbit. While it's true that hitless games are less common than, say, guttersnipes, or the common cold, or common-law marriages, scarcely a season passes without three or four hurlers attaining no-hit "immortality." Nolan Ryan tossed seven of them by himself. Johnny Van der Meer chalked up two in a row in 1938. Bobo Holloman no-hit the Philadelphia Athletics in his first big-league outing. Fred Toney and Jim "Hippo" Vaughn once threw them at each other in the same game. Look at the ever-burgeoning roster of no-hit pitchers: how much fame and glory sticks to the names of Ed Head, Weldon Henley, Nixey Callahan? A no-hitter is a Day in the Sun, like a grand slam or a 5-for-5, not an instant ticket to Cooperstown. Immortality may be bestowed in an instant and fade into the October sunset at season's end.

Terwilliger flied out. Laying the baseball gently down on a towel, Whizzo jogged to the mound and started his warmups.

He fanned Nada Pinson looking and disposed of the always-dangerous "Dos Pesos" Dos Passos, pinch-hitting for Gas Can, on a fly to center. Lorenzo ("Hector") Cacavaca had a good at-bat, and despite Whizzo's continuing dialog with the ball, Cacavaca walked on 12 pitches.

While Whizzo toiled and talked his way toward possible ersatz immortality, Anloie, who had stayed home with a tummy-ache, sat in their boudoir. The television was off. So was the CD player, which normally rapped and serenaded her even while she watched Whizzo's road games.

The earphones on her Walkman lay curled up together like two cats on a cool afternoon.

Even the refrigerator, which liked to hum along in harmony with the other appliances, was still.

Anloie was thinking. Thinking deep thoughts.

Two flies tiptoeing along the hibiscus blossom resting on the dresser stopped in their tracks, aware of a silence greater than their six-legged perturbations. The very motes of dust that surfed and slalomed through the eddies of the room and settled on furniture and floor with nano-auricular thuds registered only by the most miniscule and sensitive of tympani, agreed to stay soundlessly afloat until the vibrations from Anloie's cogitations rippled out of the hotel suite and the air could breathe once more.

Suddenly the silence was shattered by a roll of thunder: the Grinches had tied knots in her stomach, and one of them had just broken open.

Charley Orange was thinking, too. He was thinking that Hector Cacavaca on first, who hadn't been lifted for a pinch-runner, was nonetheless a prime suspect to try to steal second base. The situation called for it, and Cacavaca, not an everyday baserunning threat at 35, was wily and still capable of bursts of speed. Pyjamas Rowland, the Woodpeckers' "little ball" manager, would almost surely send him.

Charley, a student of Sabermetrics, didn't believe the steal was sound baseball, but Pyjamas did: the cellar-dwelling Woodpeckers led the league in thefts. The only question was, on which pitch would Cacavaca go? Whizzo's Patooties had lost none of their velocity or hop: Charley started the sequence with fastballs.

Whizzo got the sign and commenced brainstorming with the baseball, all the while eyeing Cacavaca at first.

He's 18 years old, Anloie was thinking. Just out of high school, yikes! Some 18-year-old; that kid is Going Places. Going?— he's already there! He got to you, didn't he, girl? That flaming red hair is to die for, and all those sweet lovely things he says to you. Yeah, he's a cute kid—younger than my baby brother! Hey, I'm too old for that. —For *him,* Anloie, for *him*. And since when are you too old for *anything*?

The flies on the flower, sensing something with that sixth sense that only six-legged creatures have, do-si-doed and allemanded left in crazy circles. The still-suspended dust-motes had no clue to Anloie's state of mind, but, grown weary of holding themselves aloft, welcomed the gravity of the situation and began colonizing the surfaces below them.

And all the while did Anloie's mind and heart ride round and round on the merry-go-round, even as Charley Orange knelt and flashed the pickoff sign.

Whizzo stretched, turned and tossed the ball gently to first base. Cacavaca, who was no more than six feet off the bag, stepped politely back. Now he led off a little further. Whizzo tossed to first again, a little faster; again Cacavaca was back. Then Whizzo faked a snap throw; the ball arrived slowly but Cacavaca went sprawling in the dirt. He got up, dusted himself off, and extended his lead another foot.

"Y'know," Bluster Hyman extemporized on the air, "baseball has its detractors. There are those who claim the game is too slow and boring. Minutes may go by like this with seemingly no action. But while the dilettantes head for the fridge for a beer, true fans can fall

mesmerized into the contest within the contest, which might be likened to two cats staking out territorial boundaries down to the last inch."

Whizzo and Cacavaca proceeded to re-enact their entire ballet. By the seventh throw, Cacavaca had edged his front foot out flush with the green carpet. Whizzo lobbed another one over. Another lob; then he fired a bullet intended to nail Cacavaca, whose dive back beat Onions Malone's tag by a nanosecond. But the throw did persuade him to shave three inches off his lead.

Turf established, Whizzo turned his attention to the plate. Romeo Romero took a final swing with the lead doughnut still on his bat, shook the doughnut off, rubbed some pine tar on the handle, rubbed a little more into his batting glove, adjusted his glove, adjusted his wristband, touched his left bicep, on which was tattooed a woman he called his "Good Luck Goddess," adjusted his forearm band, pulled the protective earflap on his batting helmet down as low as he could get it, adjusted his jockstrap as inconspicuously as he could before 50,000 fans and several million viewers on national TV, took another practice swing, glanced toward his third base coach who was touching himself compulsively and clapping his hands like Michael Dukakis practicing the dirty chicken, placed one foot inside the batter's box, swung a few more times, adjusted his grip, and stepped in.

As Whizzo began his windup, Romero stepped out and repeated his ritual. Finally he stood at the plate wiggling the bat. Whizzo stepped off the mound. Two cats squaring off, pitcher and batter each tried to disrupt the other's timing. "Romero, get in there," said plate umpire Buster Hyman. "We're overdue for a commercial already. Do you want to jeopardize a $200 million contract?"

Finally came Whizzo's first pitch, Sweet Patootie, an inch low and away: Ball 1. Strike 1, another Patootie, on the inside corner. The infielders pranced in their cleats, their attention riveted on Romero, on Cacavaca, on the game situation, shifting like nervous thoroughbreds back and forth on the balls of their feet, reviewing one more time: hard-hit, throw to second; in the grass or off-balance throw, go to first...

Still no "action." Only gathering tension. Only concentration, concentration like a rock must concentrate. A 1-1 count; now, Charley decided, Cacavaca would be going.

Charley Orange held the record for best lifetime percentage among active second-string catchers for throwing out runners stealing. It wasn't one of baseball's million-and-one official recognitions, because in an oversight out of character with the collective mind of the Grand Old Game, the Powers That Be had not yet quantified what constituted a second-stringer. But it was in the Guinness Book of Records, thanks to a phone call by Speedboat Jones, the Mutes' injured fifth starter and team clown. The secret of Charley's success at nailing baserunners was his quick feet, especially for a big man. He could set them for an overhead peg in less time than it takes for cream to say howdy to coffee in a cup.

As Charley sprang to fire to second, suddenly the crack of ash wood meeting stuffed cowhide electrified the ballpark like a rattlesnake in the desert air. In the .3 seconds it took Romero's smash to travel 100 feet into the hole between shortstop and third base, Twinkletoes Willoughby at third sized up where the ball would hop, dove toward the hurtling sphere and speared it with his outstretched glove. The crowd roared: this should be the game—and the glory. In the next 1.4 seconds Twinkletoes rose, planted his right foot, shifted his weight onto it, cocked his arm and rifled the ball with all the might he dared muster without missing his target, toward Revenge at Second Base. He allowed another .7 seconds for the arrival of the ball.

Were Twinkletoes to miscalculate by as much as .01 second, the runner would beat the ball. In the majors, this almost never happens.

This time it happened. "Willoughby picks himself up," Bluster Hyman reported, "snaps the throw to second...*and sails it over Revenge's head!* Here comes Cacavaca to third. Moseley scoops up the errant horsehide in right field and—he bobbles it! Romero heads for second; he's in there without a play as the throw comes to the plate to hold Cacavaca on third. And traffic slows to a halt in Disfunction Junction, Arkansas as the tension mounts at Mutant Stadium. Ninth inning. Two outs. Two on. Mutes up 1-0 behind the rookie sensation Whizzo Mark Salot IV; just one out away from immortality, just one base hit away from losing the game."

◆◆◆ ◆◆

As Anloie bent over to free her duffel bag from a box of frisbees that Whammo, Inc. had given her, along with $500, for an endorsement, her stomach set up punching bags and started sparring with itself: Bam! Biff! Pow! She put a pot of water on the stove to heat. Then she placed her clothes in the duffel bag, followed by the owl feathers Whizzo had given her, then her algae. A light traveler in more ways than one, she didn't take long.

The water boiled; she added some peppermint and ginger for her tummy. As the brew steeped, she looked around to see if she'd missed anything. Her hibiscus flower! At her approach, the flies promenaded away and, again attuned to that premonitive sixth sense, went buzzing off to the toilet to wait for leftovers.

It was time for the last, most dreaded task. Anloie took up notepad and pen.

The heart of the Woodpecker order was coming up: Quince Que Paso, the cleanup hitter Dogface Cirillo and Miguel "Manana" Mirabella. Charley glanced at Foo Foo to get the "four wide ones" wave to set up the force at any base. But Foo Foo was heading toward the mound. Charley followed suit, as did Twinkletoes Willoughby.

"How's the faculties upstairs, son?" Foo Foo asked.

"Airs happen, Skip. Makes the game more excahtin', don't you think?"

"How's the bungee?"

"Ah've faced so few of them hitters today, Ah could go another nahne."

"OK now, this feller, let's walk him down to first base, that's where we can get him at second."

"No Skip, let me at him! Que Paso hain't got his bat around yet on Sweet Patootie or Choo Choo Charley. And Dogface hit the two hardest balls off'n me all day. Ah can kayo Que Paso 1-2-3- Patootie and leave Dogface in the on-deck circle swishin' away at skeeters."

Buster Hyman arrived at the mound.

"Where's the fire, Buster?" asked Foo Foo. "Hey, I'm looking at two down, one up and no hits off my Bungee Boy since Thursday last. You won't be hurrying me if you're me, now are you?"

"You got me all wrong, Foo Foo. I came out to tell you to take your time. Drag out the drama. Stretch the suspense. It's good for the game. Maybe they can squeeze in another commercial; maybe then the umps can get a raise. If you need more time, I'll tell Pork Chop Chefozewski his fly's open and he'll have to leave the field to check it. Now *get it moving!*"

Foo Foo turned to Whizzo and Charley. "OK, man on second; flash four signs. First pitch fourth one's it, second the third, third the second, last the first and so on."

The conference cleared. Charley walked back with Hyman, donned his mask and, for the one-millionth time in his career, dropped into his crouch. The game was for Charley a never-ending cycle of ritualistic acts, each one created anew, adapted to a reshuffled situational landscape. Check Que Paso's stance: he's going with the pitch. Check the dugout: Foo Foo's arms are still, his eyes intent on Whizzo. Check the Woodpecker dugout: Pyjamas Rowland's doing Willie and the Hand Jive to Ocarina Zacaria, the first-base coach, who relays it in double time to Que Paso. Check the infield: Twinkletoes is back, not holding Hector Cacavaca on third. Unguarded, Cacavaca mock-charges down the line, yelling at Whizzo, who is in deep soliloquy with the ball. Set, flash one, two, three, four...

Of the above, Bluster Hyman reported only Whizzo's antics. "Now he's giving the baseball a pep talk—now he holds it to his ear, listening—now Whizzo smiles! He's into the stretch, delivers...*And there goes a liner into the left-center alley, two runs are sure...*HERE COMES BOBALOO BOYNTON! HE LEAPS—CAUGHT IT! MUTES WIN! NO-HITTER!" A mighty roar shook Mutant Stadium, a roar whose eloquence humbled Bluster Hyman into silence. What words could match immortality?

The herbal tea did not live up to its promise. Anloie's stomach hosted noisy putt-putts racing around in circles like the Indy 500. She set aside her notepad, adjourned to the bathroom and, while the two flies, hovering like vultures, winked their thousand ocelli at each other, chucked her cookies. Within moments she felt better.

◆◆◆ ◆◆

Catching a glance at herself in the mirror, she stopped and removed her halter and bra. As always, her lopsidedness jumped out at her. Whizzo was full of *caca* about her breasts. She could acknowledge that each one was within normal range. But obviously they looked like they belonged on two different chests.

She addressed herself aloud. "He was great fun, Anloie, and now it's time to get your life on track. Warren is a good man; you work well in partnership with him, and you'll feel like a new woman after the surgery. The love is coming along; there's real progress there. As that develops the sex will continue to become more fulfilling. And as for his snoring"—she sighed—"well, there's always surgery."

As the flies tapped their funicles impatiently, Anloie's soliloquy changed subjects. "Whizzo doesn't even know what he wants yet, and besides he's got about a jillion flings left; he's too adorable to settle down at 18. You, girl, you certainly don't want to feel good about your breasts just because Whizzo does, now do you? And furthermore, you're not about to marry *anybody* because he likes your tits. It's so crude!"

Suddenly that warm, melting feeling she got when Whizzo told her he loved Fujiyama and Kilimanjaro filled her body like sunshine. As quickly as it came, it was gone. How to hold onto it?

She returned to the duffel bag, unzipped it and removed socks and feathers. Then, gently smiling, she picked up the remote and switched on the tube.

"Whizzo, what were you talking about with the baseball in the dugout between innings?" Bluster Hyman asked.

"Ah was axing it some basic questions," said Whizzo. "You know, about how baseballs think, what motivates them, questions lahke that."

"And what did the baseball tell you?"

"Hit didn't tell me nothin'. Hit's only the game ball talks to me."

"You heard it on Baseball Central. But Whizzo, we all want to know about your new lady love. Did you really pop the question?"

"Ah did. Hit's true, Ah'm a-gittin' hitched. Her name is Anloie and she's a frisbee champion. Ah'm hitchin' mah wagon to a star."

"Is it true that you've known the bride-to-be for less than a week?"

"Ah've known this lady all mah lahfe, in mah dreams. All y'all gahs out there, y'all know what Ah'm talkin' about, raght? A gal y'all can love and cherish forever. When y'all fahnd her, marry her."

"Thanks Whizzo, and congratulations on two fronts."

Anloie made a mad dash for the toilet. When she returned, she took up her notepad once more.

Dear, dear Whizzo,
I felt bum-rushed into accepting your proposal, and now here I am, committed to you in front of millions of people. Whizzo, I feel like a child bride. I don't even know you. But I know one thing: I'm sure not ready to spend the rest of my life with you. Not at this time in my life, anyway. I need a safe harbor, and Warren is stable and there for me, That doesn't mean I'll ever forget you, because I never will.

All my love,
Anloie

She switched off the TV. As she opened the door and walked out, dustmotes scattered in all directions, like starlight on a still pond when a frog jumps in.

The fifth inning was scoreless. Had Maxwell Veribushi been there to perform calculations on lighter twinkles, he would have estimated attendance at 100,000. Park capacity was only 53,476. Tension was running high.

SIXTH INNING

I've never seen a night so long
When time goes crawling by
The moon just went behind a cloud
To hide its face and cry.
—Hank Williams

Almost every act of baseball is a blending of effort and control: too much of either is fatal.
—Thomas Boswell

BANG! BANG! BANG! BANG! BANG! BANG! Out of nowhere come six parallel universes, off on the adventures of their lives. Or is it the same one six times, an everywhere-forever pistol waiting aeons and aeons between shots?

Bang! Bang! Bang! Bang! Bang! Bang! In this cosmic popcorn popper, the more there are, the more there are. Six universes become 36, 36 become 1,296 and so on *ad infinitum,* creating enough spacetime for many of them to sprout life and, in one of them, baseball players who get paid more money than the combined payrolls of several small nations. In that universe, they were on strike again, locked in a death-grip with the club owners, a handful of megacorporations who had ways of persuading their legislators to exempt the Grand Old Game from the laws governing their other businesses. The problem was, revenues were only $16 billion per year with more than 600 people to divvy them up among: less than $3 million apiece.

The answer was simple, and if only the adversaries could hop the next wormhole to Charley Orange's and Whizzo Mark Salot IV's turf, they could find it: split the intake 50-50. Let the owners divide their half any way they see fit and let the players do the same. Both factions can slug it out internally, and meanwhile PLAY BALL!

That's how baseball was run over here. The Megaglopoulis Mutants, with the largest population market and grossest revenues in the majors, received the same bucks as the Milwaukee-sized burgs to operate their stadium and field their team. In the past, tax-deductible contributions of up to $1,000 were allowed, but that gave the big-market teams such an advantage that after eleven straight pennants by two teams in one league, the tax credit was rescinded. Several representatives from those two cities were never seen in the hallowed halls of Congress again.

◆◆◆ ◆◆◆

Here, mere megabucks couldn't buy a winner: it took megabrains too. Acumen. The kind of horse sense that made a good horse trader. Or poker player. Wellington P. Sweetwater could wheel and deal with the best of them. He had a silver tongue that could sweet-talk a backwoods judge into dismissing a speeding ticket (of which he had a gloveboxful): what chance had an 18-year-old kid, seeing Sweetwater wave a contract with the Megaglopoulis Mutants before his eyes, of resisting him?

Sweetwater's general manager was an old poker crony, Rhodes scholar Lance Hickey. Hickey, one of the shrewdest men ever to appear on the baseball scene, had an almost mystical ability to spot scouts who could consistently spot talent. Hickey and Sweetwater also both personally scouted.

Between them they built a farm empire that year after year sprouted them a bumper crop of star prospects. After five or ten years, when a player had just passed his prime, they unloaded him and brought up a replacement who in his first year was often just as good. The Mutes had produced four Rookies of the Year in a row. (Whizzo Mark Salot IV, with a 13-3 record and a no-hitter, seemed destined to become the fifth.)

Sweetwater and Hickey's combined savvy had brought the Mutants five second-place finishes in 10 years, and they had stayed in the running in four of the other five. Over that time they had the best record in baseball. But, as Billy Beanball had just learned, no matter how good you are in the Bigs, it's never good enough. The decade was a torture of close but no cigar, always the bridesmaid never the bride, scale the ladder only to find your nose in the behind of someone ahead of you on the top rung.

Unlikely as it seems, in their 34-year tenure in Mutant Stadium, the Megaglopoulis Mutants had not won a single pennant.

The city was hungry. In any major-league town live hundreds of thousands of souls who, given that "fan" is short for "fanatic," are by no stretch of the imagination "fans," but who come out of the woodwork of their 9-to-5 lives in a tight race, get caught up in pennant fever and become fair-weather fans. It's the talk of the office: the Mutes haven't won in anyone's lifetime, and this year they're making a run from behind for the flag. Of course, they're still 14 games behind, but a 14-game deficit is nothing to overcome for a town with faith. And it's true the Mutes have folded in the stretch four times in 10 years, but this is the team, the dream team. This time it will happen.

For the biggest city in the majors to miss the brass ring for 34 years straight was a civic embarrassment. Citizens of Megaglopoulis traveling to other states would everywhere be asked: When are you guys going to capture the marbles?

The city had grown bigger and tougher than it was 34 years ago, and its dominant emotions were rage and despair. It needed a diversion from its problems. Thank S/HeIt for the Mutants.

The city was hungry.

The fans, the true fans, the diehards who fill the stands year in and year out, first place or last, were hungry. Many of their grandfathers had been kids when last the Mutes—then of another city—had won. Some had heard tales of that halcyon year, the team's exploits embellished until the players became mythological heroes, in the finest oral tradition of sports subculture.

The Mutants were starting to pick up steam. You could feel the difference at the ballpark. The fans poured bucketsful of energy, both positive and negative, into the race, roaring wildly at a good Mutant catch or run scored, groaning collectively at an error or opponent's rally.

The fans were hungry.

The kids of Megaglopoulis were hungry. They might have appeared more excited than hungry. And it's true: kids are easily excited. Whereas adults become excited only when their club is winning, kids are excited by any major-league team. Give them a winner and they'll rock the stadium, chanting and screaming and pouring out their hearts to their heroes.

The kids had not their elders' history of heartbreak, no frustrating saga of playing perpetual second fiddle. But, as any mom can tell you, kids are always hungry.

The team was hungry. Nearly every player had been on more than one contender for the Mutes and tasted the bitter ashes of eleventh-hour defeat. Only one player, Jeff "The Heft" Lawton, had a

Series ring. (In fact, he had several: he held the major-league record among non-Yankee middle relief men for playing in the most Series with the most different teams.) In the locker room, Lawton would shout out brags about his rings, pumping everyone up.

Many good ballclubs stumble along in the middle of the pack until July or August, and then they jell. The great ones can be unbeatable down the stretch, like the 1993 Atlanta Braves; the near greats can be too late out of the blocks, like the 2001 Oakland Athletics.

This team was starting to jell, and it sensed its greatness. Today the focus was on third place, just two games away. Second place—first place—they could wait. One game at a time. But the same thought lurked in the back of everyone's mind. Three times in eight years they had come down to the last series of the season at the head of the pack and lost the flag. Each time they could have taken it, but a break always went the other way: a bad hop, a bad call, a cued nubber that stayed fair down the line. Always the Mutants seemed good enough, but somehow not in alignment with the forces of the universe.

The team was hungry.

Foo Foo McGonigle believed a lot more in hit-and-run on the 1-0 pitch than he did in the forces of the universe. He had been managing the Mutants for 17 years. Foo Foo had inherited a demoralized team that had finished in the cellar for three straight seasons.

Foo Foo's first two teams also finished under .500. But he had been hired by Wellington P. Sweetwater and Lance Hickey for the long run. When they joined forces, they made promises to each other. Sweetwater and Hickey promised Foo Foo the best farm system in the Bigs, and Foo Foo promised them a World Championship within the decade. This was Foo Foo's 17th year and probably his last. Sweetwater had stayed with him despite his failed promise. Why? Three stories circulated: 1) Foo Foo and Wellington P. Sweetwater were lifelong friends; 2) His late-season collapses were with so-so teams that no one expected to contend anyway; and 3) He was good press. Take your pick; all three were true.

Foo Foo McGonigle had lost a lot of sleep in his 17 years as manager of the Megaglopoulis Mutants, especially during those frustrating pennant drives. Sometimes as he lay awake he thought about the Curse of the Bambino: Since the Boston Red Sox sold Babe Ruth to the New York Yankees in 1919, they have not won a single World Series. Sometimes during those sleepless nights Foo Foo wondered whether there was a curse on the Megaglopoulis Mutants.

Foo Foo McGonigle was very hungry.

No one was hungrier than Charley Orange. Charley had toiled for the Mutants for 17 long years: six years in the minors and 11 in Megaglopoulis. Four times he had sniffed the sweet smell of the league championship, only to have, four times, the hounds of defeat come howling at his door.

Charley's batting average for the last two weeks of the season during those pennant drives was .318. In baseball at least, he was a winner. He ached for this one last shot at the World Series to prove it.

And Whizzo Mark Salot IV, *wunderkind exraordinaire,* he of the anthropomorphic baseballs and simian-sobriqueted pitches, of the 13-3 record and three big victories over the Lemon Sox—Whizzo was hungry too. Whizzo, fresh out of high school, had a chance, at the tender age of 18, to lead 24 teammates, a few of them old enough to be his father, to lead a million fans, to lead the largest megalopolitan area in the U.S.A., to the first championship flag within the memory of any of its residents.

The only question was, did Whizzo hunger in the same fashion as his elders on the team and his elders and youngers in the city of Megaglopoulis, or was his hunger of another, more primal nature?

Whizzo Mark Salot IV, having celebrated his no-hitter by performing magic tricks under the bleachers for Billy Beanball and some of his friends, did not return home until late in the evening.

"Hello li'l ducky pah! Your hero's home!"

◆◆◆ ◆◆◆

The note lay on the pillow. Half of the vibes Anloie instilled in it wanted to shout out in the silence: Here I am; read my glyphs. The other half wanted to spare Whizzo his pain and let him bathe in the afterglow of fame and glory as long and possible.

The first half won: Whizzo rushed into the bedroom, picked up the single sheet and read it aloud.

"But…you said he was your frisbee coach!" he sputtered into the empty room. He read the letter over. Then he looked on the coffee table for the owl feathers he had given her. Gone! The letter had numbed him; the missing quills jabbed him in the heart and wrote her name in his blood. He opened her dresser drawer: empty. The bathroom: bereft. He threw himself on the bed, on her side; he could still feel where her warm, round body had pressed against his during last night's frolics. *Never again?* he thought.

There, on the floor, lay the artifact that proved she was not all just a dream: a pair of dew-moistened panties, discarded—oh how joyfully, how longingly he remembered when. Disheveled and shapeless they lay, but in Whizzo's eyes they still surrounded her sweet bubbly cheeks and rolling hairgrown mound. He picked them up and buried his nose in the crotch. Ah yes, the sweet in bittersweet! For a moment she was right there with him. Then he was seized by an unfamiliar feeling, which those of us who have not always felt in control no matter what the situation would recognize as panic. He picked up the phone and called Charley Orange.

"She left me Charley, she run off with that turkey what treats her lahke Ah wouldn't treat a flea-ridden hound."

"Hey, they like guys who mistreat them," said Charley. "At least you had some fun."

"Charley, Ah feel lower'n a curve ball breakin' across a cottonmouth's knees. Ah hain't never goin' to sleep again. Ah'm sposed to pitch Sunday, Ah won't be able to think about them hitters, all's Ah can think about is her."

"Whizzo, you just found out about this 10 minutes ago. You're in shock. Give it some time. Tomorrow's an off-day; let's go to the zoo. Trust me; I know about this."

"No no, Charley, she's the one. Ah'm jist gonna feel worse and worst. Ah won't never be the same ol' Whizzo again."

"OK, now focus with me. No peeking. What color shirt do you have on?"

Whizzo glanced at his sleeve. "Blue."

"Good."

"Ah peeked."

"Top of the Mudhen lineup, who leads off?"

Whizzo's eyes clouded over. No answer.

"Estabien. Good eye, best to set him up high and hard, then curve him low and away."

"Charley, Ah can jist see the look of torment on her face when she wrote, 'That doesn't mean Ah'll ever forget you, because Ah never will'. She don't want to be with him. Charley, he wants to make her into the Frisbionic Woman. Listen, Ah gotta take me a little ponderin' walk. Ah'll call you back."

As Whizzo hung up, Charley felt a premonition. The kid might be a genius on the rubber, but off the field he was still a kid. Young. Volatile. Unpredictable.

Whizzo Mark Salot IV looked at his wristwatch. Fifty-eight minutes. Almost one hour since his life had come crashing down. True to self-fulfilling prophecy, each minute left him feeling progressively worse. But the pondering walk did clear his brain enough to replay a line from Anloie's letter. "Hmmm— 'not at this tahme in mah lahfe'. Well, ginger pah, tomorrow is another day. Now jist where does this Frisbee gah live, anyway? Ah bet he sent her somethin' to tempt her away."

Sure enough, the top item in the wastebasket was an envelope with Warren's return address in a town called Placid Shores.

"Wahde wahde ocean, here Ah come
Here Ah come, here Ah come

Wahde wahde ocean here Ah come
Gonna get back mah baby."

Whizzo did a little tap dance in front of the full-length mirror, tipped an imaginary Fred Astaire tophat and whistled the melody. Gradually he tapped out of the frame, letting the tune fade out.

Then he was out the door and down to the parking lot.

The peacock feathers on the wall stared with great black unseeing eyes at Charley Orange and Clitorea Pearl, sitting nude on the apricot-colored sheets covering Clitorea's bed.

"I'm scared of you," Charley told her. "You know as much about making love as I do about baseball. I feel sexually inadequate around you." The next sentence slipped out before he knew he said it. "Even more so than around other women."

"Great work, Charley! You never would have told me any of that before."

"You're right. You're not supposed to know that. I'm supposed to be in charge—or so I always thought."

"Guess what. Women know when you're scared anyway. It's our department. So Charley—it's OK to be afraid. Fear is just energy that we resist. Let's use that energy. I want to teach you how to make love to me."

"Yes! Yes! Why didn't they offer that course in school?"

"That's a long story, Charley. Don't get me started."

The prospect of another encounter with Clitorea's divine body excited Charley, but what really set the pollywogs wriggling in his ponds was the prospect of receiving training from the Master. —No, the Mistress. —No, the Goddess herself. But another figure also plunked itself down into the familiar parlor of his emotions and, like a stranger at a family reunion, silent as sunshine and ubiquitous as fog, filled the foetid environs with the promise of fresh air. It introduced itself as a desire to repay Clitorea for the sexual favors she had bestowed upon him. He was here with her not only for what she could give him: he wanted to present offerings in return.

Was this love? Under the six billion feelings we lump together under that rubric, it surely qualifies as one.

"I used a lot of techniques on you, Charley, but I think we won't get that far this afternoon. Next time I'll show you Eggs Over Easy, the Titty-Clitty Meditation, the Juicer—a whole repertoire of yummy strokes to tickle a lady's fancy. But they're not necessary for me: I can come just by thinking about it."

"Are you bragging? I never heard of such a thing."

"It's true. Women, and men too, have been told a lot of stuff about what coming looks like, like for instance it takes x minutes to get there, when all a woman needs to do is let go and pay attention and she'll be saying, 'S/HeIt! I can start coming the second he touches me'!"

"So you do need a man."

"Or a woman. For a prolonged, ecstatic come, it raises my energy. And for sure I can't have a three-hour orgasm by myself—at least not yet."

"Three hours!" That was almost as long as a *Pipa pseudohymenochirus*!

"All those nerve endings are just sitting there, waiting for an excuse to fire. We have to override centuries of misinformation to realize what we're capable of; release a lifetime of suppressions that we accept as natural bodily reactions. Like, 'Don't fart in church'. I say, let 'er rip! Fart loud and long in church. Eat beans beforehand and hold Fart-ins. Do you want to hold all that noxious gas inside you just because Simon Says? You can't contain it even if you want to: it finds the drain and leaks out."

"I still can't believe three hours. I've been with women who have multiple orgasms. That means two or three. Maybe even six. But three hours? No way."

"Charley, yesterday you just had a one-hour orgasm yourself."

"Is that what it was?"

"Of course it was! See the misinformation? Listen Charley, a Blam-Kapow semen transfer made by straining and clenching up, then blowing out your rocks to kingdom come, might be enough for stressaholic wage slaves with attention deficits and no time for love or pleasure. But the Mighty O is way too delicious to rush through and get over with before it's begun. Milk it. Nurse it. Hold onto the sweetness. Linger in Love's boudoir until every ganglion in your body hangs as limp and exhausted as a sultan's scimitar after a long night in the harem. Yeah!"

"It's hard to imagine, Clitorea. Does it feel like what I felt yesterday?"

"I can only speak for myself. For me the pleasure starts in my groin and flows down my legs and out my feet—my feet get real hot—and up my chest and out my arms. I feel like a big fat puffy plumbing pipe. All of me starts puffing up like a rising biscuit. Then I get thicker. I feel like mochi. My backside gets heavy, heavy, heavy on the bed, like I have no muscles or bones. All the energy in my body pours out of my cells all over the place. It feels like little silver fishes swimming up my body, then they melt and dissolve into a spray of fine gold dust billowing up."

"Yeah..." said Charley. "I guess I felt some of that..."

"That's just how it begins. It goes on and on, like...OK, imagine honey pouring from a huge container. It cascades out in a long, long flow, and every once in awhile a big *glug* gushes out, but the flow continues. My orgasm is like the honey flow, and every now and then I'll go over the edge, like a big *glug*."

"Mine must be different. Men ejaculate."

"So do women. Now, S/HeIt made it easy to shoot and come at the same time in order to continue the race, but S/HeIt also made it possible to separate coming from shooting to make life more worth living. But that's another lesson, for another time."

First climaxes as long as ballgames, now women who spurt. Charley's mind felt like it was twisted up in a roll of paper towels. "Come on! Women don't ejac..."

"Just for that I'm going to come all over you." She spread a towel on the bed and lay above it so that it covered the space between her legs. "If this towel doesn't reach at least to my ankles, those sheets will be as puddled as last night's condoms. Now listen up, Charley.

What is the question men have racked their brains about for centuries? It's 'What does Woman want?', right? Well, here's the answer—the lost wisdom of the ages—in a nutshell.

"Outside of a minimal amount more about female anatomy than the average man knows, you need remember only two things to give a woman a stir-fry in her body that will keep her onions sizzling all night and day: 1) Keep her relaxed; and 2) Pay attention to what you're doing to her."

"Pay attention? Like, don't smoke a cigarette? This is the lost wisdom of the ages? What am I missing here?"

"It's the hardest part of what I teach. Paying attention is the essence of tantra: being fully present in every moment. How many men actually get down there and look at a yoni when they're touching it? Talk to it? Tell it how beautiful it is? Charley, I want you to describe what's happening down there for me. 'Goddess, your yoni is beautiful! Look how moist it is in the opening. Now your lips are slowly parting, without me ever touching them. And look at your little love button—just peeking out from under its bonnet'. Focus all your attention on my yoni and on your fingers or whatever you're touching it with."

"I get it," said Charley. "It's like baseball."

"Baseball!" Clitorea was growing accustomed to obtuse remarks from Charley, but this one caught her off guard. "No. Baseball is not the name of the game we're playing here."

"Concentration is the name of the game," said Charley. "Baseball is concentration, concentration, concentration."

"I see. OK, you're in the ballpark with that one. The difference is, paying attention is not cerebral. Concentration makes you tense. Don't concentrate; pay attention. Turn your mind off and your senses on."

Clitorea tapped her yoni. "I have to pay attention too, or it doesn't work. When both of us focus entirely on what's happening, I move instantly into that ecstatic, orgasmic state and stay there as long as we maintain the connection. —Why are you frowning?"

"As Yogi Berra once said to Casey Stengel, 'How do you expect me to think and hit at the same time'? I want to know how I can stay

totally focused on you and remember techniques too."

"Here's the best part, Charley: you don't have to remember anything. A lot of my pleasure depends on you really enjoying touching me. Do what feels good to you. I'll always let you know—gently—if I don't like it. But I generally always will. If you pay attention you'll be interested, curious, creative. And I'll be hot to trot! There's a guideline that says if something you do takes me up a notch, repeat it 8 to 15 times, then switch—lengthen the stroke, change the pressure, move up or down—then start over. The idea is to bring me to intermittent peaks with valleys in between. But if you're really tuned in, the moves come naturally and you won't even think about counting."

"I've had women who give me orders. 'Higher'. 'Harder'. 'Softer'. 'More pressure'. I felt like a human dildo."

"There's nicer ways. 'M-mm, that feels good. Can you try just a tad higher? —Oh, yeah!' Or you can ask her. Yes and no questions only; don't make her think. Remember how I asked you? However, if you're both paying enough attention, she won't direct you like that. You probably haven't been very attentive; your mind has been preoccupied. If you're focused and she's not, invite her to relax and follow you, and promise her you'll do it her way if your way doesn't work."

Part of Charley lapped all of this up and part of him felt knocked into next Tuesday by the way it upended everything he believed and practiced about sex. "What about talking?" he asked. "Is it possible to make love like this and still share fantasies?"

"Sex is reality, Charley. How much of your life do you devote just to creating situations with sexual potential? When you finally get to the magic moment, why would you ever want to take yourself anywhere else? You know, I believe this whole fantasy thing is a carryover from Romantic love: always striving for the unattainable, unable to be here now, to embrace the actual ecstasy that love can be. Forget your lame, culturebound fantasies— but talk, yes. Talk of two kinds only. One, fill the air with words of my praise. If you're not afraid to, tell me how much you love me. Two, communicate about the festivities at hand. What's working? Do I like that? Teeter totter, back and forth between body and heart: that carries us into the bliss."

Another analogy from his own line of work popped into Charley's head. "How about using signals to communicate whether you're in one of those peaks or a valley in between?"

"Why signals? Why not words? It's only our cultural disinformation, and often our shame, that keeps us silent. That dirty old virgin English queen did what she could to stomp out pleasure, but the Queen's English undoes all her efforts: our brains want to fuck too. I love hearing how much you love me, how great you feel with me. And I love it when you ask me if what you're doing is working."

"I hear you loud and clear on that, Clitorea. I always feel so insecure wondering whether my touching feels good to a woman. So why don't I just ask her? Eureka! Wow!"

"Convincing your partner to talk can be hard, but once she tries it she'll love using her tongue for more than just one thing. When you're pleasuring her, nothing beats hearing her say, 'Oh! Right there! Oh S/HeIt!' I mean, do sweeter words exist?"

Clitorea's lecture ended; Charley's hands-on work began. With her guidance he lubed her up and found the walnut-sized, walnut-textured area located a diddle-finger's length inside her misnamed her G-spot. ("It's my *sacred* spot! Imagine naming it after a *man,* who "discovered" it after women around the world have been getting off on it for millennia. It's worse than saying Columbus discovered America and all the First People killed by him and his successors weren't really there until he arrived.") Then she guided him to a smaller spot only one fingerjoint's length in, before the back of the bone. And, her enraptured state overriding her decision to postpone techniques, she showed him one. "M-mm. Charley, that feels so good on my clit—let me show you how to make the Battery Connection, OK?"

"Anything you say, my love."

"O-ooh, Charley! OK, we're going to hook up two pleasure spots so that stimulating one stimulates them both at once. Just keep rubbing my joy buzzer and with your other diddlefinger rub one of my nipples in a circle—OH! S/HeIt, that's good! —OK, now let my nipple go and keep doing that on my button…YES! I can still feel it on my nipple. It's coming up from below from your finger that's still on me. OK, now do both again and then raise your hand off my button—not far, just half an inch so the energy is still there—and keep rubbing my nipple. —YAYAYAYA! Does my clitoris ever still feel it! OH-H!"

"Wow!" said Charley. "Your little dewdrop just swelled up so much, it looks like a big raspberry." He eased Diddle and Fiddle—his third and fourth fingers—inside her. The engulfing pink corrugations of her walls rippled like aftershocks, while her entire body vibrated like a V-8 engine on loose mounts. "I can feel you moving in there."

"Contractions…I'm coming…and coming…and coming. Can you just hold your fingers still right where they are?" Clitorea's face was bathed in a smile that would set angels to dancing. "M-mm, I love the pleasure that happens when my yoni contracts. Feels so good."

And so traversed another afternoon in our parallel universe, an entry in Gaia's archival journal, a fleeting chapter in the peacock-walled boudoir nestled within the concrete contours of Megaglopoulis, in the pageant of the lives of Charley Orange and Clitorea Pearl. As Charley's mind and fingers focused on Clitorea's perpendiculars of pleasure, untold gallons of love's sweet honey flowed and glugged, glugged and flowed their way through her body. The towel between her legs grew heavy with nectars whose very existence Charley had not heretofore suspected, whose distance and trajectory as she squirted them out he could only envy. In between glugs she even taught him the Doorbell and Rock Around the Clit. Om sweet Om.

As our lovers lay basking in sweet twilight sleep, a sound penetrated Charley's afterglow: keys jangling, the door opening. "Jello!" yelled Shakti as she crossed the room. "Sorry I'm late. A cop stopped me."

Clitorea snapped awake. "You're pudding me on."

"Witty even in your sleep. Listen, I…" She stopped when she saw Charley. "Oops, sorry…I *am* late, aren't I?"

"Yes, sorry…I ran a little overtime." Clitorea smiled a lover's smile at Charley.

Overtime! Had Charley encephalated adrenaline, it wouldn't have come on any faster. "What am I, your one o'clock? What's going on here?"

"Charley, Shakti and I have a date at 5 o'clock. I'd invite you to join us, but we've been needing some alone time together."

"You're kicking me out?" He raised his voice. "You're done with me and now you're kicking me out?"

Clitorea matched his volume. "You big dummy! We only have to cut it short because it went so much longer than I expected."

Charley wanted to tell her that their love-making session was a major happening, a life-changing event for him. His heart tried to say he felt hurt and diminished that he seemed to be just an item on her schedule. What blurted out instead were angry reactions. Hurled insults. Harsh words. Footstomping and doorslam.

It was one of those summers in Megaglopoulis.

Ever have humans banded together: since the time *Homo erectus* first bumped his head on the roof of the cave, since the time they were baboons following each other's lurid rosy derrieres off the veldts of the Serengeti and up into the trees of Kilimanjaro; nay, since their very salad days as amoebae, scooting around and colliding with each other like mini-Dodge-em cars inside droplets of water. Yea, and even as amoebae divide in order to multiply, so do humans divide themselves at every crossroads: Male vs. female. Black vs. white. Oriental vs. Occidental. Evolutionist vs. Creationist. Mute fan vs. Lemon Sox fan.

(A Creationist would write the preceding paragraph this way: Ever since God created Eve for Adam and told them to go forth and multiply, men have bonded together that their worship of the Almighty might have a synergistic effect. Many have left the fold along the way: Protestants, Episcopals, Lutherans, Presbyterians, Baptists, Pentacostalists, Mormons, Shakers, Quakers, Jehovah's Witnesses etc.)

◆◆◆ ◆◆◆

But we are talking about cities here, and cities are not the most pleasant of places in this particular everywhere forever at this particular spacetime in its unfoldment, which happens to be summertime in full sweat. The heat and the relative humidity were holding a contest, now into its twelfth day, to see which could climb higher into the 90's. Each day both of them stretched to the max, and, yoga adepts that they were, each day they found they could stretch one degree further, and a thousand new sets of nerves in Megaglopoulis would snap, their owners firing off Uzi's at their wives' lovers, or maybe at strangers. The *gendarmerie* was talking curfews and leg-breaking dogs. Speaking of which, it was the Dog Days of August and, according to official records, dogs barked more loudly and later into the night, pooped on more driveways, provided room and board to more fleas and attacked more innocent citizens than at any previous time in Megaglopoulis history. Many blamed it on the ozone layer—which, if anyone still thought it was disappearing, no, it was falling to earth in the streets of Megaglopoulis.

A mighty conflagration took the homes of seventeen families (and the lives of 357 jackrabbits, 24 black-tailed deer, 627 assorted frogs and toads, more insects than there were people in the whole human race, the entire populations of 38 microbes still undiscovered by human scientists, other flora and fauna too numerous to enumerate and the partridge in the Megaglopoulis Zoo's pear tree).

Maxwell Veribushi, while grieving the frogs, saw the city's woes as divine retribution for its rulers' acts. But his Oedipal perspective was not shared by the suffering populace-at-large, who had their own worries and were not *au courant* with the current status of imperiled bacteria.

People drank more. They were out of money, and the only decent way left to make a dollar was by selling sandwiches in the stalled traffic between 4 a.m. and 8 p.m. Parking was illegal everywhere and all the spots were taken anyway. The streets were all one-way the wrong way, and average speed had declined to single digits. The mayor's declaration made it official: You couldn't get there from here. (It was widely held that the Megaglopoulis street layout was designed in one night on a rip-roaring, piss-stinking drunk by the artist M.C. Escher.)

The mail took longer and longer, Versiteller machines gave short change and pay phones and vending machines were in therapy, learning to receive without giving back. Gunshots and car burglar alarms played duets that would make John Cage churn in his urn.

In this vast miasma of misery burned one ray of hope—one psychic fumigant, one light in the dark tunnel of travail that gave Megaglopoulis' beleaguered citizenry a reason to carry on—the Mutants. The Mutes were down, but they were not out.

As surely as the bubonic plague had gripped all the dog owners in the Megaglop (in the dreams of all the non-dog owners), so did Baseball Fever lay its hands on the throat of the gasping city.

And the Mutants would be nowhere without their 18-year-old Romeo with the bungee cord in his left arm: Whizzo Mark Salot IV.

Mercifully, in his innocence, Whizzo—who had never even seen a member of a minority group, let alone been served a knuckle sandwich by one, who thought policemen were people who stopped when your car broke down to call your family and give you a lift to Roy's Quality Service—Whizzo was blissfully unaware of how desperately the remaining tatters of sanity left in the city clung to his teen-aged being like flames cling to wind.

This helps us understand, but it does not excuse, his subsequent actions.

It was midnight, December 31. Scythe in hand, the Old Year stepped to the podium. Scattered among the Lonely Ones were the Days. According to the ancient calendar, there were only 365 x 8 = 2,920 of them left. And one of them would disappear every 24 hours, Charley Orange knew, taking 50 to 100 species of insects, plants and other Creations with them.

"Listen, Charley. Wolf is talking," said the Old Year.

◆◆◆ ◆◆◆

Ragnar the She-Wolf sprang forth. "I dream of the time long back, beyond the Great Snows," she said. "The Lonely Ones preyed on me, but when their hunger was filled, they left me my space in the Creation.

"O-WOOOOOOO!" she howled. "Bring back the Old Ways! Our young ones are born sick and small; many are not born at all. Our hunters die in their prime. Gone is the time when we roamed freely across the land, keeping our fellow creatures fit, winnowing the weak and building the stock, creating impeccability.

"Once we raised our young to be free and wild, to go for the throat with hearts as pure as alabaster. Then the Lonely Ones—the Fearful Ones—shot us down, with our families, in our dens. They put death in our water, laid out poisoned meat for our young to eat, until none of us remained anywhere around them."

"Speak next, Moth," said the Old Year.

"If they weren't asleep as a species," Moth fluttered, "wouldn't their fashions honor us instead of extirpating us? They rip gashes in their clothes and it's the In Thing to wear. But if we nibble just one hole, it's Camphor City."

Meadowlark, sweet musician of the Beings, opened her warbling beak:

KEEP your FEET
OFF the CONCRETE
DON'T have to WORK
exCEPT FOR to EAT.

Drink NECtar in JUNE
with a PETAL SPOON
Hang TIGHT with the MOON
Keep some JUICE IN your PRUNE

Don't GOTta be SMART
Just O-pen YOUR HEART
CAN'T SAVE yourSELVES
All SPACETIMED aPART.

"Hear, Charley! Now Tree is talking," said the Old Year.

"Just as worms crawl, fish swim and birds fly," said Tree, "so do we travel through time, or non-linear space. We weave the wind with song so we can remain one with each other. The Lonely Ones have lost their song; they have lost their oneness.

"We show them lace inflatables and prisms in dew. We sing them lullabies, we shelter them, we feed them and hide them from their enemies.

"And yet, across the world the Lonely Ones ax-murder us into chopsticks and toilet paper. They clog our aqueducts with concrete and DDT. They befoul the air we pump out, scalding our umbrellas with acids, filling them with scars and rents and slowing our escape from body into interdimensional travel through photosynthesis.

"The children I sacrificed to last year's frosts feed the flowers under my wings. When the vast everywheres forevers shrink to a pea, Time will stop. Therefore, we live at every moment, before the Lonely Ones appeared as well as now. Let us draw comfort and hope from the deeds of our ancestors. We are the epigoni; it is up to us to remember and revere the Old Ways.

"I pity the Lonely Ones. When will they join us in the infinite simultaneous worlds of spacetime?"

"All this philosophy and negativity makes me eat too much," said the Door to Nowhere Through Which All Species Come and Go. "You saw me grow as wide as the sea to let the dinosaurs and all their relatives and in-laws pass through me at once. And now the demands placed on me grow even greater."

"On you!" proclaimed the Undiscovered. "What about us? We're far and away the largest classification of life on this planet, and it's like we're being blown through you like flies in the wind."

From beneath them a soft, rumbling voice filled the arena. It was Gaia Itself, Charley knew, Progenitor of them all.

"I will endure," Gaia said. "But I can no longer support all my children. Many of you will perish. Many of the Lonely Ones will perish. It will be many aeons before we dance together again.

"But some of you will continue unfolding. The songs of change are rising through my pipes and through your genes. This is the time

of Metamorphosis. I must shed my skin in order to grow my wings.

"You must strive, as always, to survive. I am, as always, neither a wrathful nor an enabling god/dess."

The Old Year, now the New Year and looking decades younger, came through the crowd and handed Charley a note. It was addressed: Only the Lonely.

Before he could read it, a sudden gust of wind blew open his balcony door. He opened his eyes and sat bolt upright in bed.

I'm a lonely frog
I ain't got a home
—Clarence Henry

When is a coincidence not a coincidence?

When it's a synchronicity, according to the psychologist Carl Jung. A concurrence of events or developments in time may appear to be merely coincidental when in fact unseen underlying forces have joined to make their synchronous appearance inevitable. The rational mind, which focuses on the separateness of material entities, has traditionally dismissed simultaneous related phenomena as "coincidence" and assigned them no meaning. But we now know that everything in the vast everywheres forevers is hitched to everything else.

Howling like a she-wolf in the night, the wind rushed into Charley's bedroom and filled it with the spirits of departed starburst souls: Lou Gehrig and the Babe, Joan of Arc, Galileo, Beethoven, Einstein and Max Planck, Casey Stengel, Satchel Paige and Dizzy Dean. And Josh White, the greatest catcher, maybe the greatest player, ever to put on the cleats. Not allowed to play major-league ball because of certain tribal customs having to do with skin pigment at certain times in certain universes. Charley shook his head.

A voice in the wind seemed to beckon him to come and take part in this night of magick, of All Hallow's Eve. He dressed and stepped outside. Trees bowed and paid the wind-god obeisance. Yesterday's newspapers blew down empty streets as humans, for once conceding superiority to Nature's forces, retreated into their houses. Overhead, as if they had found the escape hatch from some drear parallel universe where Death held them in thrall, the spirits of the bygone lifted their voices in a celestial banshee hymn-howl. O-WOOOOOOOOO!

Enchanted, like he was floating through Time, Charley drifted down the windblown streets, caught in the swirl of the maelstrom and in his own thoughts.

He came to. Where was he? How long had he been wandering? The wind died down and the rain began.

Rain! Blessed rain!

Across the city, pavement by the square mile welcomed the liquid intrusion into its coating of dust, oil, grease, old newspaper, fast food wrap, dogdoo and other litter. The sporadic trees curled their leaves and flung their grateful boughs to the sky, while breaking out the washcloths and scrubbing and spit-polishing every chloroplast until it glistened as green as a red light to a color-blind ambulance driver. The blades of grass on the parched lawns waved in the wind, each vying for a droplet so it could rinse itself down.

We all know how mean and nasty rain can be. But this was a cloudburst of joy, a downpouring of rejoicing and celebration. Silvery dime-shaped drops danced chorus lines across the pavement. From there they chased each other to the curbsides, merged and sailed to the nearest culvert, where they cascaded merrily down like otters into the spooky caverns below. From rooftops, they bombarded stragglers entering doorways below with water balloons. Those drops that managed to fall between tree leaves and grass blades burrowed like eager moles into the hardpack, searching out root tendrils to swallow them up and pass them back up the blades and through the stomata, where the sun could eventually suck them back into the sky so they could jump their free-fall once again. Wheee!

The high spirits were contagious. Cars drove through puddles and splashed mud on each other. Selected traffic lights took a few hours off to enjoy the fresh air, leaving their metal monster charges to fend for themselves. The temperature, hardy soul that it is, treated itself to a cold plunge. People, instead of hurrying indoors at the first

drop, got into the act, pouring out of their apartments into the wet, shouting and laughing like children in the streets. (The children, bless their hearts, were cursing the power company and waiting to get back online.)

As the shower diminished, Charley's feet led him to Mutant Stadium. Tomorrow afternoon kicked off the biggest series of the season to date, against the front-running Lemon Sox. (The Mutants had just climbed into third place, 11 games off the pace.)

Charley flashed back to his final high-school contest: the state championship. Unable to sleep the night before, he walked to the stadium at 2 a.m. to focus on the big game: to scope out the foul lines, the height and moisture content of the grass, the shape of the mound…A mystical feeling came over him in the empty stadium that night, the sort of feeling he could have gotten by mixing chocolate and good Emerald Triangle cannabis (had he not been the only athlete on the team who actually followed the training rules), and the next day it seemed like he knew just what pitch to call, who would hit where, almost without thinking. With two on and two out in the eighth, on a 2-2 count he knew the pitcher would curve him away. He stepped into the ball and belted it over the right-field wall for the game-winner, still one of his biggest hits and greatest thrills.

He used his parking-lot card to let himself into Mutant Stadium. As he stepped onto the field, the silent, cavernous emptiness of the park seemed somehow more intimidating than when it was filled with the roars of 50,000 excited fans. It was ghostlike, like the wind, but without the wind Charley could not hear the fans of yesteryear, or even yesterday.

It felt incongruous, maybe even somewhat of a violation, to be on the field in street shoes and clothes. As he crossed by the left-field foul pole, he noticed the rain damage to the foul lines, which would require re-chalking, and he could feel how hard a ball needed to be hit to reach the seats. Then he jogged toward center. The new moisture made the outfielders' footing a little less secure and would slow the ball down. Bad News Nelson was pitching for the Mutes against Hector Tortilla. Bad News threw more ground balls; it might give him an edge.

The storm had caught the ground crew by surprise: the tarpaulin circled around its coil along the right-field line, while the infield lay like a wanton maiden with its bare hillocks exposed to the sky. But only enough rain fell to tamp it down. With Bad News pitching, it could use a trim. Charley knew that Bump Shivers, the head groundskeeper, had already thought of that. Charley headed toward home plate. He wanted to crouch behind it and feel Bad News' pitches, vibe out whether he'd be sharp, hold a crystal ball to the Sox lineup, see if he could align his receptivity to the forces behind fate and get a read on what would go down during the game.

This is Charley Orange who wants to seize an advantage by "aligning his receptivity to the forces behind fate"? If Ladye Hannah Aura could see him now! He might prefer Newton to Nostradamus; he may park astrology and reincarnation in his mental wastebasket; but in this wayward corner of his psyche, he was as right-brain as a dolphin channeling Edgar Cayce with a crystal pendulum. Old Touslehead said that physically the universe is shaped like a saddle. The question that arises is this: Metaphysically, is the universe an artichoke of spacetime, connected everywhere forever through the rich heart at its center, or is it just an onion—peel it away and what do you have?

While we cannot answer for sure, we have known a great many people who claim that they can tap into tomorrow, especially in California and Las Vegas. The fact that they are rarely in the chips in either location shakes neither their faith nor our conviction that, in this parallel universe at least, goings-on are going on that our minds have not yet learned how to grasp, and that many of these goings-on have to do with connections across space, or time, or spacetime, about which we homos are not yet sapient.

Vapid? New Age? If everything is hitched to everything else, the universe —any universe—may be visualized as a cluttered storage closet. Try to remove the baseball glove that's been in there collecting dust for 20 years and the whole kit and kaboodle comes tumbling down on top of you.

Ponder, if you will, the mysterious set of circumstances that led Charley Orange from his downtown apartment into Mutant Stadium.

Is this synchronicity? Be it so or mere coincidence, things were leading up to an event that was about to turn Charley's life as topsy-turvy as a flapjack on the spatula of a cook who has fried his short-term memory along with the bacon and eggs.

Consider the trillions of events that conspired to even bring him into this universe and place him in that windblown apartment. And if, as the parallel universalists and virtual realists insist, we are living in a cosmic pea soup of interactivity, consider the trillions of events that have conspired to bring you here reading this page. Therein lies a magic whose power inspires the deepest of wonder.

As Charley crossed second base, he heard a sound—a sound like Susie Elder made back in the eleventh grade when she struck a kitchen match on his fly.

Then the moon—the same moon that had woven her Lagrange point tango and trailed her acned face across this particular spot on the mother planet some 16 jillion times plus change since the formation of Mosquito Marsh in Oligocene times—the moon peeped out from the last of the storm clouds and, seeing no celestial dragons to devour her, no tormenting children to tie a string to her and turn her into a balloon, sailed forth like a frigate ship across the sea of the sky.

Again Charley heard the sound, this time like a wagon wheel whose axle needed oiling.

The frigate moon cruised through Scorpio, splashing waves (and particles) of light all over Mutant Stadium. In their wake, Charley saw something silhouetted on home plate.

The sound, too, came from home plate: SKRIEK-EK! SKRIEK-EK! SKRIEK-EK!

The frog sat on the pentagon, not down the pipe but toward the inside corner; not on the black, either, too far into the sweet spot unless the batter was set up for outside.

It was a small, yellowish-green frog with spots. A frog with a scratchy voice. A frog seemingly without a care in the world, but you can't always judge a frog's concerns from its outer facade.

The same feeling that had beckoned Charley out of his bedroom into the wind came over him again. Without hesitation he kneeled down to pick the creature up.

Did the paddock go catapulting forward, zigging and zagging through the infield grass like a crazy-hop grounder cued off a knuckleball by the tip of a .348 hitter's bat? No, it just sat there like a pitcher batting .048 taking a called third strike and let Charley scoop it with one four-fingered hand into the palm of the other, kicking in protest only when Charley enclosed it with the scoop hand to keep it from springing out and falling.

Now, another question we must ask, if we are considering the role of magic in this course of events, is this: How did a frog find its way into Mutant Stadium? Could it have fallen from the sky? In certain universes parallel to this one, rains of frogs have been documented on the planet Earth. But a rain of one frog? Perhaps it slipped from the beak of some passing egret or...but here, in the midst of bustling Megaglopoulis, where all the water has been funneled off the prime avain real estate into closed, narrow pipes that deliver it from there to here in no-nonsense straight lines? What intrepid heron would flap its wings over such unappealing environs? Yet birds have been known to engage in stranger behavior: gorging on fermented berries, for one; hurtling themselves in front of speeding windshields, for another.

Suppose a tipsy egret did drop it. How could it survive a free-fall from a height greater than Mutant Stadium, at least 150 feet? If the frog, legs outstretched, measured six inches long and a human 5 1/2 feet, it would have skydived the human equivalent of nearly one-third of a mile—without a parachute. Now, if it were some wingless insect, S/HeIt would, in compensation for making it so teensy-weensy that it tumbled off things that you or I would not even consider in terms of height—off furniture onto the dog, off moustaches into the soup—S/HeIt would let it float buoyant as a balloon or give it a shell hard enough so its insides would just bounce around like Clitorea Pearl's sweater at the laboratory volleyball game, before it righted itself and lugged its coat-of-armor away.

But no, this was not some wispy table ant or hard, chitinous cockroach but a frog, softer and gooier than silly putty, that could no

more execute a swan dive onto the hard clay surface of the Mutant Stadium playing field than a rich man can pass through the eye of the needle into the kingdom of S/HeIt.

If frogs could talk, Charley would have learned that this one, although no more interested in baseball than in a *cuisse de grenouille* dinner, had lived all its life within hopping distance of Mutant Stadium. And doesn't that make you wonder whether the same magic that called to Charley called to the frog as well? Who else in all that cast of thousands that entered and exited Mutant Stadium to determine and cheer the outcome of the pennant race would have felt such an affinity for it as to take it home and care for it?

The frog's life is most jolly
my lads; he has no care
who shall fill up his cup; for he has
drink enough to spare.
—Theocritus

Charley Orange put the frog in his duffelbag, got in his Starlight Coupe and drove home, chauffeuring Ngaio XV^{14}+34 past wonders of a civilization he never knew existed: grocery stores and tattoo parlors, newspaper and carpet vendors, freeway interchanges, railroad crossings and Ped Xings. A pity that poor Ngaio, trapped inside the duffelbag, saw none of these. But maybe it was for the better, since Ngaio was developing a bad case of travel sickness, aided and abetted by his growing fear that he would run out of air. In panic and rage, he torqued his femurs to the max and sprang like a jack-in-the-box against the side of the bag, konking all .01 grams of his gray matter on Charley's 33-ounce Louisville Slugger. Reluctantly, Ngaio segued to Plan B: rationing his breath.

Charley entered his bathroom and unzipped the duffelbag, figuring to keep the frog in the bathtub until Maxwell Veribushi could tell him how to care for it.

Spikes—glove—bats—sweats—Charley emptied the bag, item by item. The critter was gone! He turned it inside-out and shook it: nothing. Meticulously, he examined each item again. No frog. Oh well—what on earth had possessed him, anyway, bringing home a wild creature? What did he want with a pet, let alone an amphibian? He picked up his Neatsfoot oil and put on his custom four-finger glove to oil it. Yeck! What was that slimy...?

The elusive amphibian had burrowed into the anterior digit of his glove like a Special Prosecutor's nose into a President's dirty underwear. But not for long. Ngaio saw his chance, sprang from the glove and commenced bouncing around the bathroom like a tiddlywink on fen-phen.

Charley dropped to his knees and crawled after it, but Ngaio stayed one spring ahead of him, finally pausing under the sink. As Charley reached, Ngaio leaped again, and simultaneously the telephone rang, causing Charley to raise his head suddenly, banging it on the sharp porcelain. With a howl, he pounced on the frog, zipped it back into the empty duffelbag and headed with it for the phone.

Wham! Z-zzzzip! Ngaio was in total darkness once more. And now another jouncy two-step journey into seasickness, like trying to fork-tongue a fly in a washing machine. Where in the wide world was his mind when he let the *rib'et!* reach down and pick him up without so much as a kick in struggle?

It was blissed out, that's where—basking in reprieve. From what? Then the nightmare flooded back into Ngaio's memory: being lost in a terrifying world where the ground under his feet and as far as he could see was hard and smooth, a flat rock to everywhere forever. Huge beasts shot across it at speeds faster than flies, moving only in straight lines. As one zoomed within inches of him, Ngaio found a grated opening and, in desperation, plunged through it.

Ulp! His free-fall into darkness may not have taken a big chunk out of his day, but it was long enough for the butterflies in his stomach to form a pool to guess just when Sudden Impact would scramble his molecules and he'd be trying on fly suits in a parallel universe with Ladye Hannah Aura.

◆◆◆ ◆◆◆

The butterflies all lost: he splashed down into a deep pool of the darkest, dirtiest, smelliest water he had ever been surrounded by, and Ngaio XV^{14}+34 had bobbed around some mighty foetid acreage in his time. He scuba'd through the sludge for an anuran eternity, until the kick in his legs faded to a *rib'et!*-style shuffle.

Just as Ngaio thought he might be doomed to an eternal Stygian nocturne, lo! Light ahoy! A pinpoint of it, from above, like a star. He swam to the side wall, rested awhile on a metal rung placed conveniently within his reach and started the long ascent up a sheer, slippery wall, a Half-Dome of mud and fecal mire.

By the time he reached the top, the light had faded. Twilight had arrived and he was back in the nightmare realm of planed terrain and hurtling horrors.

Just hopping distance away was a symmetrical mountain that the behemoths couldn't—or at least didn't—climb. If Ngaio could just dodge the monsters across that level, open turf...

Not eight hops had he hipped when suddenly a beast loomed from nowhere, aimed lickety-split in a straight line right at him. He'd better...

Before his brain finished the thought, his legs sprang, and not a nanosecond too soon. —Here came another one! No time for even a reflex jump this time: In an instant, all of Ngaio's XV^{14}+34 lives flashed before his eyes. And then the monster was gone, its round legs having carried its body right over him.

Shaken, he sproinged wobbily to the mountain. It was as textureless and monochromatic as the ground, and its walls were sheer cliffs. But Ngaio found a hole in it that he could squeeze into and hide. Inside was a massive cavern—again, very abstract: vast blocks of one color. No texture. All symmetry. That same smooth, surreal ground. But no monsters. He could still hear their din outside, but here nothing moved. He was emboldened to hop around and explore.

He came to an opening in the cavern, and springing out, he saw a color that warmed his heart: green. It had that same symmetrical endlessness and textural monotony as the rest of this strange monoworld, but to Ngaio, exhausted and hungry, it looked like home.

With the final reserves of his waning strength, he lurched himself down to the shoreline of the green sea. Looking up, he saw that the mountain was not only a hollow cavern: it was open on top! He could see the stars and the newly-minted moon, that lovely lady with whom he and his forbears had been playing hide-and-seek through oh-so-many aeons. His exhausted frog heart filled with gratitude and burst into song: SKRIEK-EK-EK! His well-seasoned soul, which could trace its family tree back 150 million years, entered into a state of divine rapture.

It was thus that the *rib'et!* was able to approach Ngaio XV^{14}+34, reach down and pick him up before Ngaio was even aware of his presence.

By the time Charley got to the phone, his caller had hung up.

It was 30 minutes to game time. Charley Orange had just parked a batting-practice pitch in the left-center bleachers when Foo Foo McGonigle waved him over. Was the Skipper going to start him against Gonzales? Charley had hit Gonzales pretty well over the past two seasons.

"How did you like that one, Skip?"

"What one?" Foo Foo scowled. "Seems like your young feller here, or not here, as the case may be—and is—he's got hisself his own set of holidays, or nights, and some of these which are running right down into the stretch drive. I mean for instance *today's* a holiday—*tonight.*"

"No Whizzo?"

"That's what I said. He showed up missing."

"Oh-oh. I wish I could tell you I know something, Foo Foo. His lady left him and he's taking it hard. I'm worried about him."

"What? We're chasing a flag with a Casanova chasing a skirt? You tell him some things in life are more important in life than other things, and this is one of them. Charley, you seen this arm, this is a young man's arm wakes up in the sunshine these hot August nights.

All this stickiness keeps it loose like he throws nine every day. Tell him I want to see him for a thing or two I'm going to say to that young feller when you see him."

But game time rolled around and still no Whizzo. Charley sat on the bench next to Foo Foo, who growled and grumbled through the contest which the Mutants, demoralized by the absence of their gift from the gods of the sandlots, dropped meekly, 5-1. That put them 11 1/2 behind with only 43 to play. The locker room was a morgue.

When Charley got home there was a message on his machine from Whizzo. "Charley, Charley, where you been lass naght? Charley, Ah'm out here in the middle of God only knows where, and Ah don't raghtly know when Ah'll be back. Tell Foo Foo and all the gahs on the team Ah'm so sorry to let them down, but Ah cain't see but one way out of mah dilemma, and thass what Ah'm doin'."

Charley called Foo Foo. In the morning Foo Foo would have to tell the media. The whole world would know Whizzo was missing.

Weary and worried, Charley Orange climbed into bed after the loss and clicked on the news to see what Bluster Hyman would say about Whizzo. As the picture faded in, there, holding forth on the County Courthouse steps, her Brobdignagian bazooms bursting out of a bikini, was Clitorea Pearl.

"Ms. Pearl," a primly-dressed female reporter asked her, "are you going to defend yourself in the courtroom dressed like that?"

Defend herself? Charley's ears perked up like those of a hound dog who has sniffed a new crotch in the country. Had that crazy whore switched from digging into men's wallets to digging her own grave?

"Are you kidding?" said Clitorea. "They wouldn't let me through the door of the building dressed like this. Hey, this culture is antimammarian and yoniphobic. Wherever you go, the *sine qua non* of our existence, the great poem behind our being—I refer to s-e-x—is taboo. That's why I'm dressed this way. Now watch this." As a boombox beside her belted out a raunchy beat, she fastened garters to her bottoms and pulled on a nylon, swinging her leg and somehow gyrating as she did.

"I'm not taking it off—and I'm not taking it, either. Instead, I'm putting it on—to show how they put us on."

"Aren't you afraid some people might find your approach—ah, too titillating?"

"Maybe sexessive?" Clitorea winked and arched her brow.

"Some people might judge…"

Come on," Charley said aloud. "Give us the W's. Where's the trial? When? Who's the judge?" He considered switching channels. Then he considered calling the station. Then he considered watching Clitorea first.

"Some people? Sounds like a third-person first-person to me. Listen sweetheart—as a woman, don't you have the right to a rich, full sex life? A right to feel your lust? To indulge in your fantasies?" Nylons on, she slinked across the steps, wriggled her callypygean derriere at the camera and stepped into a modest gray business skirt. Charley couldn't believe his eyes: she was performing a reverse striptease as she talked. And Clitorea made getting dressed every bit as erotic as getting undressed. "We're trained to neglect our bodies," she continued between bumps and grinds, "and that fragments our lives. Let's *honor* our bodies. Let's *honor* our sexuality. Let's all get turned on! That'll fill us with joy, and joy is even more contagious than misery. We'll turn this culture around 180 degrees before you can say, 'Honey, did you bring the condoms'?"

Next came a prissy white blouse. She started buttoning from the bottom, lingering as she worked her way up, trailing her fingers over her triple-dippers as the starched linen drew closed, turning them into amorphous boulders. "Ms. Pearl, it's been reported that you head a male-bashing organization. Do you think we could eliminate much of the violence in the world by putting women in charge?"

"We *are* in charge, honey." She wriggled provocatively into a jacket that matched the skirt. "Hey, when men shoot guns it's because they're not shooting semen. And I didn't say that, a recent lover—a male—said it." Charley's jaw dropped open—she acknowledged *him*? And

as a *lover*? A strange tune played in his heart. What was it? Did he like it or not?

Donning black high heels, Clitorea strutted up the stairs and past the pillars to the doorway. "'Men make war when women don't make love'. 'Women don't make love when men make war'. This whole battle of the sexes is nothing but the old 'Which came first, the chicken or the egg' riddle." She came to the *piece de resistance* of her ensemble: a pair of pink-rimmed spectacles. "Why don't we each say the other side is right, and let's all go to bed? Good night. —Hey, is my hair OK?"

They cut to the talking heads. "Well Glenda, Clitorea Pearl proves the old adage that less is more."

Glenda groaned. "More on the trial tomorrow." A radio grew into a complete sound system, then shrank back. Along a red carpet rolling through the mountains marched an elephant band, exclamation marks popping out of their tubas and trombones. Mr. Peanut ran across the lawn and exploded like a bursting star.

Conniving slut, Charley thought as he clicked off; served her right. Why should he care? As he reached for the phone to call Maxwell Veribushi for some advice on the care and feeding of frogs, it rang.

Maxwell must have been prescient; it was he. "I didn't hear about Wunderkind's disappearing act until this evening. I was in court all day."

"Yeah, I just saw Clitorea on TV, but they didn't tell us anything. How did it go?"

"She insisted on a jury trial and selection is still going on. She's already gotten seven women on the jury. So, any clues as to our hero's whereabouts?"

"No. He's so volatile. He was despondent, Maxwell. The whole team's jittery. We played like whipped dogs tonight. I'm really concerned about him. He could do anything. —Hey, I was just going to call you. Can you stop by in the morning? I have a surprise for you."

"Early. Trial starts at 9:30. Charley, it's going to be a pisser. She's awesome and there's a hundred W.I.T.C.H.es in the peanut gallery. And you won't believe this judge. He's as short as I am, but he wears elevator shoes, and he's meaner than a vicar without a bottle. Francis Bejole is his name, but once a Hispanic attorney pronounced it Pijole, and now everyone calls him Peehole—behind his back, of course. Hey, why don't you forget the Mutes for a few hours and come on down and watch?"

Charley felt a clutching in his stomach. Clitorea was so cocky. He didn't want her to imagine he was there nursing any secret longing for her. In fact, he didn't want to see her at all, person to person. But beneath his anger he did believe in her innocence and in what she and W.I.T.C.H. stood for. And all of those enchanting W.I.T.C.H.es would be there...

High above the spinning earth, Sagittarius shoots his arrow through the stars at Mars. It is August on the Planet of the Apes but in the constellation Perseus it's Hallowe'en: a shower of meteors races out of it toward Gaia well-armed for their annual T.P. assault upon her skies. On the shores of far Hawaii, the trade winds mambo in from the sultry seas. In Jamaica mon, da ganja buds grow sticky on da vine. Above Antarctica, ultraviolet rays play billiards with chlorofluorocarbons, smacking into them and scattering chlorine, which then holds a snooker match with the ozone layer, smacking into it and leaving the world behind the 8-ball. A pole away up in the Arctic, in between blinks of the Northern Lights, a few hundred cubic miles of imprisoned water, dried out and bound up in crystalline glue since back before the mastodons trompled down to Mosquito Marsh for cocktail hour, escape their shackles and head for a new life in the islands. In the blistering heat of the Amazon rainforest, biologists on a Rapid Assessment team discover 13 new species of insects only minutes before a developer's bulldozers send them, tails between their legs, scampering through Oblivion's dark door. In mahogany boardrooms around the world, human doing-doings hail this latest step in the Creationist tendency toward miniaturization: Isn't it true that at the same time, in the blistering heat of sub-Saharan Africa, refugees from their hired assassins are playing host to an explosive transformation in the viral world? In the blistering heat of the Asian subcontinent (and indeed on the nonsubcontinent as well), wedlocked humans with family values founded in antiquity fornicate on their futons, hump in their hammocks and breed in their beds, churning out children faster than any sub-, nonsub- or *uber*continent can hope to accommodate them. In government and religious buildings across the Orient, their leaders applaud this environmental spirit: Are not reusing and recycling keys to ecological balance? What can be more important to reuse and recycle than souls?

In the good old U.S. of A., too many things are happening at once to enumerate here, all save one: in the blistering heat of August in Mutant Stadium in Megaglopoulis, the Mutes are down 6-3 in the seventh inning. On the Mutant bench is an empty seat.

In a vast but finite number of parallel universes, that seat was occupied by Whizzo Mark Salot IV, who was resting his arm after pitching a no-hitter. In this one Whizzo was on a mission, the most desperate mission of his 18-year-old life. He aired out his cherry red Corvette convertible to 90 mph. The starry sky rained twinkledust down onto his pineal gland through the sultry summer night; the luminous moon loomed pregnant in the sky, luring him on deeper into the midnight of his soul.

The Country-Western station was playing a 48-hour tribute to Hank Williams. Whizzo turned it up full blast and sang along with full throat to “Lovesick Blues,” “Cold Cold Heart,” “I’m So Lonesome I Could Cry.”

Onward the car sped. “Anloie, Anloie, Anloie,” he shouted during the commercials. “Whah did you run off with a gah you told me was your frisbee coach? Are you jist a little gal who needs her daddy? Whah hell, Ah can be that—leastaways part of the tahme. It’s true you got a 10-year head start on me in this lahfetahme, but Ah’m wahse beyond mah years. You jist be mah mama once in awhahle too, cuz Ah didn’t get me enough of that from mah stepmama, and Ah’ll take sweet lovin’ care of you forever. —Oh, whah didn’t Ah *tell* you all them thangs? Well, thass what Ah have to do when Ah see you.

"Whatever on earth is the gal doin'? Ah know she loves me; Ah can see it in her ahes. Anyone can see it. So whah did she run off to her frisbee coach?"

And so spun Whizzo's mind, around and around in circles, even as his cherry red chariot followed the starlight trail all the way to Placid Shores.

◆ ◆ ◆ ◆

Be kind and tender to the Frog
And do not call him names,
As 'Slimy skin' or 'Polly-wog,'
Or likewise 'Ugly James'.
—Hilaire Belloc

Ngaio XV^{14}+34 sat unmoving on his rock, staring at Charley Orange. "I bet you have visions of sugarplums dancing in your head," Charley said. He went to fetch a cricket. As he returned, the doorbell rang. Cricket in hand, Charley answered the door. There stood a furry forest, full five feet tall.

"O unfrabjous day!" said Maxwell Veribushi. "When they close the book on the history of Megaglopoulis, this untimely abdication will rank in infamy with the day the bulldozers arrived in Mosquito Marsh.

"But so much for bad tidings. Against everyone's advice but mine, Clitorea Pearl is defending herself. I'm predicting a *tour de farce.* Are you going to come watch with me?"

Just then the cricket, which had stealthily wriggled itself free from inside Charley's closed fist, leaped into the protective grotto of Maxwell's whiskers. Inside this proteinaceous thicket it felt safe and secure. "CHIR-R-R-R-UP!" it stridulated.

"Charley, why were you holding a cricket in your hand?" asked Maxwell, although he was not concerned enough about having one in his beard to attempt its removal.

"I was about to feed my frog. Come on in and meet it. You can tell me if I'm treating it well."

Maxwell took one look at Ngaio XV^{14}+34 and, had his beard not dropped with his chin, both it and its insect inhabitant would have been swallowed whole, so wide did his mouth fall open.

"Charley! See those flecks of cinnamon in its irises? Notice there's no longitudinal folds between its dorsolated ridges?...Holy S/HeIt in heaven! This, Charley—this is a *Rana onca!*

"A *Rana* what? Is it rare or something?"

"Rare? It's rarer than a blue moon made of green cheese. Charley, let me tell you a story. Thirty-four years ago the town fathers of Megaglopoulis in their infinite wisdom and venality sold Mosquito Marsh to Wellington P. Sweetwater's predecessor and allowed him to erect Mutant Stadium upon its cattails. Back then us herpetologists were just a bunch of nuts crying in— and for—the wilderness, and those weasels in City Hall were only too happy to auction off whatever species stood in the way of anyone who would line their pockets with a few shekels. Nobody listened to us when we told the world that Mosquito Marsh was the last remaining habitat of *Rana onca* and this project would send it hopping off the way of the dodo, the milkman, Burma Shave and free directory assistance. Charley, this frog isn't rare: it's extinct."

Placid Shores. The coast. Moonlit palm trees hula in the breeze. Waves suck teasingly, longingly at the sands, whispering timeless tales to them with cunning linguistics. Like these waves upon the billowed sea, the moon tosses the frothy clouds. The old Shapeshifter is in rare form up there between the beady stars, metamorphosing from sailboats into elephant footprints, finger-pointing hands, weary seahorses. The latest DNA-mix concoction, between a tyrannosaurus and a feathered cousin. A map of North America with the bottom of Mexico blowing away in a tornado cloud. Frosty the Snowman underscoring a rhetorical point to an unfriendly-looking Casper the

Friendly Ghost. A sledgehammer pounding out letters that spell nothing. And of course the ubiquitous Hey Sue H. Christophilus (or is it the ZigZag man?). And there—omigod yes, it's S/HeIt Hirself, filling the expanse, the beebee-eyed frog-goddess etched onto Hir cheek like a press-on tattoo, spewing light and darkness from her webbed fingertips.

Four a.m. at the beach under a full moon: what better place to throw a frisbee out over the ocean, turn three cartwheels in the sand and then catch the frisbee behind your back? This was exactly where and when Anloie, oblivious to the all-night movies and divine revelations overhead, was practicing just that. Warren thought that learning to trace the peregrinations of the disc by moonlight would heighten her awareness of where it was at all times and to what point it would return, even in sunlight. So intently did she sling the ellipse, spot and project its trajectory, and fling her full weight upside-down onto first one wrist, then the other, that she did not notice the beam of light from the cherry red Corvette convertible as it splayed across her rotating bikini'd form.

Now the clouds begin to curdle, as S/HeIt thickens the plot. Beneath the celestial collage, luminescent dinoflagellates surf the breaking whitecaps, sparkling like silver-plated galaxies in the sea. A pod of dolphins breaks the surface, glowing like streaking circles of platinum fire.

Is love as blind as they say? Whizzo Mark Salot IV saw none of this. He jumped out of the Corvette and sprinted toward Anloie, arriving just as she completed her third cartwheel and sprang up with her hand behind her back. The Whammo was sailing in right on target. Yahoo! This was it! All that was left was to catch the frisbee, and…

"Sugar Pah!" shouted Whizzo, embracing her.

"Whizzo! What are *you*…?" The frisbee konked her square on the noggin, knocking her hibiscus headdress onto the sand. "No! No! No! Get away from me!" She rushed past him, her eyes filled with tears.

Too much of a gentleman ever to desert a lady with moisture in her eyes, especially one he had just driven 28 hours to see, Whizzo

gave pursuit. "Honeybucket—Ma'am—Ah'm very sorry. But you see, Ah'm very deeply in love with you, and..."

"Whizzo, just...leave me alone!" She rushed past him and disappeared into Warren's house.

This was not working out at all like it was supposed to. Just what kind of line was this Frisbeeface feeding her, anyway? Anger flooded over Whizzo as he rushed to the door.

BAM! BAM! BAM! Who's that knocking at my door? Whizzo Mark Salot IV! Open up!

Open it did. Out shot a burly right arm. Squarely on Whizzo's jaw landed a fist, sending him staggering back. "Go home, kid," said Warren. "You're history with her." The door slammed shut.

What a long line is run to make a frog.
—Thomas Browne, *Pseudodoxia Epidemica* (1646)

"I'm thinking of calling it after my great-uncle," Charley Orange told Maxwell Veribushi. "I always liked his name. Ngaio."

"Ngaio? What kind of name for a frog is *that?* Why not something that reflects its status as the last of its kind? How about Ishi?"

"Hmm. I'll think about it. Bluster Hyman's coming over Friday and I want to see his reaction when I introduce them."

Maxwell fixed Charley's eyes in a vice-grip stare. His ruddy irises, rounder than marbles, floated like ancient mariners in the eggwhite moats of his sclerae. "Charley—you can't let the media know this frog exists, or it won't. They'll send the entire species of *Rana onca* sailing off on a Wagnerian shipboard of exploding flashbulbs to sink in a Sargasso sea of segment producers and anchorpersons. I mean, in this culture that devours its human celebrities for *hors d'oeuvres*, our friend here stands about as much chance of surviving the vicissitudes of frog fame as a sperm in a condom does of growing up to be Bill Gates."

"I've got the name," said Charley. "Nevermore."

"Nevermore. I like it. Listen, Charley, my laboratory is, as you know, ah—not set up at the moment to provide batrachian life support. The only place that's safe for Nevermore is here in your house."

"My house?" Charley suffered a sudden attack of Pet Owner's Regret. What if the frog got loose and shuffled off to Buffalo—or worse, to that Great Pond Beyond? Charley didn't want any trumpets tolling Taps into the sunsets of his conscience. "Where's it going to sleep—in my bathtub?"

"No, it'll be down the drain faster than you can say Caribbean amphibian. Hey, aren't you feeling honored to play a role in this transepochal drama?"

"I'm feeling scared."

"Good. What better to inspire you to caretake well your charge? I'll provide technical assistance—starting with a proper terrarium tomorrow night after court. C'mon, let's go. Trial starts in a half hour."

Picking up the frog at home plate seemed innocent enough at the time, eh Charley? Hell, the critter probably would have—well, croaked if you hadn't come along. You brought home your share of frogs as a kid, and—Jeez! None of them ever turned out to be the last one of its kind in the world!

It's a good thing they didn't, considering the number that escaped from their jars and aquaria, only to be discovered weeks or months later in their next incarnation as dried up endoskeletons flaking away in remote corners of the house. Suddenly, like gusts from the Great Winds of Change, the leaden weights of aeons came to rest like mountains on the reluctant shoulders of Charley Orange.

While generals and politicians do not usually peak until late in life, real talent is no respecter of years. At age 5 Mozart composed *The Teachings of don Juan,* Old Touslehead realized that $e=mc^2$ at 16, and Frankie Lymon was 11 when he recorded "Why Do Fools Fall in Love?" At an age when most girls are wishfully asking their mothers to buy them a training bra and S/HeIt to give them something to put

in it, Clitorea Pearl had already acquired all of her divine attributes. Pity such genius in a world of mediocrity! But perhaps the exploits of her youth can aid and abet her as well as imperil her as she takes the stand in what the sex-starved media are billing as the Year's Top Trial. (Clitorea told the cameras it might even be Topless.) Appearing *in pro per* (and adding new dimensions to the term), she called on herself as her only witness and used the court as a bully pulpit, getting major portions of her testimony repeated on the television sets into which so many of her sleeping American sisters were plugged.

It was a courtroom much like any other courtroom. The sergeant-at-arms, managing to look disheveled even in his spiffy new mushroom-gravy uniform, packed a pistol for the use of any distraught principal (or spectator) who might wish to yank it from its holster and blast someone to Kingdom Come. The clerk carried in the dockets and set them on the dais so the judge could save his biceps for wielding his gavel. The court reporter was invisible except for fingers that moved like daddy longlegs; the most populous county in the state was not yet *au courant* with audiotape technology. The jurors sat on plushy seats designed to suspend the fatty tissue of buttocks off their hard metal base for trials of up to 100 days' duration. At stage center loomed the "bench," actually not a bench at all but His Honor's throne, a cushy swivel chair so massive that Michael Jordan would appear to be a child in it. Judge Peehole looked like he needed his bottle. The bench was buttressed in front with the bedpost-like fortifications accorded jurisprudential power.

On the left, in pinstripe suit and moustache, the Assistant D.A., an abrupt, no-nonsense 40ish-looking man with thinning dark hair. On the right, wearing gray suit and pink eyeglasses, Clitorea Pearl, an abrupt, no-nonsense 40ish-looking (but actually 50ish) woman with electric hair spirogyrating out to the nearest aura field.

Charley Orange and Maxwell Veribushi squeezed into the gallery, which was so packed with W.I.T.C.H.es, it was standing-room only—literally, as Judge Peehole had declared that no one without a chair may sit.

Charley's eye was caught by the single artifact that distinguished this courtroom from others. Mounted on the wall behind the bench, between the American flag and a photo of Peehole and the Vice President, was a blowup of an old cartoon from the Megaglopoulis Messenger. It showed a midget in a black mask, labeled "Bejole," hanging a man dressed in prison stripes,labeled "First Offender." "They call me a hanging judge," Clarence Peehole was fond of telling defendants, "but I can't hang anyone who doesn't put his—or her—neck in the noose first."

Peehole also made it clear that spectators were to remain absolutely still, facing the front, with no talking to each other or they would be fined for contempt of court.

"State your full name, please," said the bailiff.

"Clitorea Pearl."

"*What* did you say your first name was?" asked Judge Peehole.

"I didn't, Your Honor. It's Clitorea Pearl."

"Hm? What's your last name?"

"Pearl."

"So your full name is...ah, Clitorea Pearl Pearl?"

"No, just Clitorea Pearl."

"Then your first name is just...ah, Clitorea."

"No. My first name is my first and last name. My last name is my last name only."

"Very well. Let the record show that the defendant's full name is...ah, Clitorea Pearl. Miss Pearl, where is your attorney?"

"It's *Ms.* Pearl, Your Honor. With all due respect, Your Honor, I address you with the sobriquet that the Court prefers, even though I find it dominating and off-putting, and I respectfully request that the Court accord me the same recognition of my preferred prefix. I am in full awareness that such a request may seem impertinent and displeasing, and that I may be gravely risking my case, so you can see how important I consider it to be—Your Honor."

"You may rest assured, *Ms.* Pearl, that the Court does not harbor prejudice against you. But yesterday I urged you to reconsider representing yourself. Where is your attorney?"

"I have reconsidered, Your Honor, and I have concluded that no attorney will be able to say for me what I have to say to this jury and ultimately to the people of Megaglopoulis and of America."

◆◆◆ ◆◆◆

"Ms. Pearl," Bejole cautioned, "this is a courtroom, not a soapbox. If you're planning to capitalize on the publicity from your trial to write a book and promote yourself on television, this Court is going to order you right now not to."

Clitorea silently thanked him; she hadn't thought of a book. She delivered her opening statement, which she had given a title: "A Slut Nixes Sex in Tulsa." "It's a palindrome," she explained. "Because everything we learn about sex is backwards." When she called herself to the stand as her own main witness, the D.A.'s eyes jumped up and down for joy in their venal sockets. The national television commentator shook his head in dismay and disbelief. "She's just opened herself up to cross-examination on her entire past, which we understand has been quite—colorful."

Clitorea started by recounting the events leading to her arrest. "I don't expect you to believe me, because it's the words of two police officers against mine, but I'm here to tell the truth, the whole truth and nothing but the truth, and it's a sad truth but cops do lie. I just ask you to weigh their words against mine and give me the benefit of reasonable doubt."

Charley raised his eyebrows. He had not questioned her story when she told it at the W.I.T.C.H. meeting. Now he wondered how much benefit of the doubt he would give her if he were on the jury.

On cross-examination the D.A. roamed far beyond the areas covered by her testimony, and she further compromised herself by not objecting.

"Miss Pearl, the D.A. said, "your troubles..."

"It's *Ms.* Pearl to you, Roscoe." A wave of titters swept the gallery.

"Your Honor..."

"The witness is instructed to limit her remarks to answering the questions."

"Even if he won't call me by my rightful name, Your Honor?"

"Counsel will address the witness as Ms. Pearl. Now please proceed."

"*Ms.* Pearl, you seem to be traveling a troubled road that runs back a long way beyond this prostitution charge for which you are on trial—back into your distant past. When you were 11, a neighbor reported you to the police for holding out your sweater and letting the boys look in."

"It's worse than that, Roscoe," said Clitorea. "When I..."

"Your Honor," interrupted Roscoe. "If I am to address the witness as 'Ms', then she must address me as 'counsel'. It's only fair." More tittering.

"That is correct," said the judge. "Ms. Witness, will you abide?"

"Sure. Tit for tat," said Clitorea. "When I was nine my uncle gave me a dollar to let him take off all my clothes and stroke my nubile little rear end. Then he took off his pants and spread honey all over his—uh, kook-a-loo-loo, in your honor, Your Honor."

"What do you mean, in my honor?"

"Your Honor, I don't know which words I may and may not use to refer to sexual parts in a court of law. I don't want to show any contempt of court."

"Very well. You may use whichever words you choose, but bear in mind the impression you are making. I am prevented from giving you legal advice, so consider that paternal."

"Thank you, Your Honor. Anyway, then he showed me how to lick my tongue over it. When it started feeling good to him he rewarded me with strokes to my face, to my hair, to my newly budding breasts.

"Now, all this happened because my father got drunk every night and abandoned me emotionally. Here was a man who loved me, at least for a few minutes while I made him feel good."

The shudder that rippled through Charley was the antithesis of the shudders Clitorea had inspired in him a week before. No wonder she was the way she was.

"By the time I was 11, my bustline was the same size as the one my mother had shelled out $5,000 for. I had a budding sex drive to match, and no one to turn to for advice on what to do with it. The boys liked me when I let them look down my sweater. And I was proud of my boobs. Why did Mrs. Armbruster want to punish a little 11-year-old girl with no self-esteem?"

"You're not 11 any more, Ms. Pearl," said the D.A. "At age 11, while your parents both worked full-time jobs to take care of your

needs, did you or did you not begin skipping school and staying home with boys, lying naked on your bed with them?"

"My parents weren't taking care of my needs. I needed attention. They wanted a summer house at the beach, another car..."

"Just answer the questions, Ms. Pearl. One afternoon, did or did not your mother arrive home ill from work and discover you in coital union with an older man while two of his friends looked on, waiting their turn?"

"Older man! He wasn't even 18, or he'd have been guilty of statutory rape, now, wouldn't he, and I'd be legally the victim. Which I wasn't: yes, one thing did lead to another. So my parents pulled me out of public school and enrolled me in St. Mary's, where the good Sisters could keep an eye on me. But they couldn't keep an eye on my father—my poor abused, sex-starved father for whom I am now filled with nothing but love and compassion. He would close the bars every Friday and Saturday night, come home after my mom was asleep, stop off in my room, climb on top of me, wiggle around, breathe stale alcohol into my face while I pretended to be asleep, and pump his drink-diluted semen sometimes into me and sometimes across that general area of my body. I never knew how I felt about it: he made it furtive but maybe he secretly loved me after all?"

Despite himself, Charley was feeling moved, not by her cause, but by her, Clitorea, the woman. There was something in her voice. It was powerful and expressive and she could project it like a foghorn. Even without her zaniness and overdose of life energy she could command center stage whenever she wanted. Yet there were times, and this was one of them, when he could hear a child's cry peal through her voice like a minor theme emerging, out of her control.

"Ah yes, St. Mary's," said the D.A. "At age 13, Rector Sherman deemed your prurient interests an 'irremediable distraction' to the male student body and you were asked to leave, were you not?"

"If by prurient you mean sexual, that was a factor. I had a sex drive like a rabbit crossed with a billygoat. Sometimes I thought I must really be a guy. But I wasn't turned on to girls—at least not until later..."

"And after St. Mary's..."

"Wait, I haven't answered your last question with the whole truth yet. My so-called prurient interests didn't distract the students as much as my burgeoning bazooms distracted the male faculty. By now they were so big, I wondered if I might topple forward whenever the desert wind started blowing the dust and sending the leaves rattling down the streets of Tulsa. Do you know what it's like to be 13 years old and have men who are old enough to be your grandfather following you home at night? Hey, these knockers would have propelled a lesser girl into lifelong hibernation as a spinster librarian or a court reporter." Clitorea looked at the middle-aged mama sitting motionless as a statue except for her perpetual-motion scarlet-tipped anterior extremities. "Nothing personal, dear.

"Anyway, St. Mary's had a drama coach—Mr. Silver, an infidel hired to supplement the overworked nuns who taught the three R's—reading, writing and religion. He talked me into trying out for the play. I had never seen anyone like him, with his trim, dark moustache and laughing blue eyes. The night of dress rehearsal, after everyone else had gone home, he seduced me on the set. He was 34. And I was 14, not 13."

"Everyone had gone but Rector Sherman, who caught you in the act. Why were you still there after you thought everyone else had left?"

"To be seduced, of course. As I said, he was a fox."

"So you quit school and took to the streets."

"Not until the following year. One night when my mom and dad were out, I got this phone call. A real sexy voice told me to take off all my clothes, blindfold myself, leave my door unlocked and climb into bed. The voice was such a turn-on that I couldn't resist. When I heard the outside door slam, a thrill ran through my body. When the bedroom door closed, I almost came. He tied my wrists and ankles to the bed and mounted me. As the action grew more rambunctious, my blindfold slipped down just far enough to get a peek: it was Luke Sherman, the son of the rector of St. Mary's, he of the fire-and-brimstone view that Satan needed to be beaten out of every child. After Luke finished his business, he stole my new necklace and left.

"I was still crying when I heard my parents arrive home. When my father came into the room, I actually cried to him. 'Daddy, daddy, an older boy came and tied me like this and stole my necklace'. I was afraid to tell him who it was; he'd never believe me. But he didn't even care! Instead, he had just enough time before mom finished putting away the groceries for a quickie.

"My heart was broken. I had reached down so deep—deep below all the rapes and molestations, the abuses of all the years, to the place in me that still needed my daddy, and he had betrayed me even then."

Clitorea's voice broke, and so did Charley's heart. All he could hear was the little girl who cried out for help so many years ago.

"And then something happened." Clitorea came out of the distant place from where she was drawing out the memories and looked deeply into the eyes of the jurors, one after the other, connecting with twelve sets of eyes as she continued. "Suddenly I saw this man who had created me as an angel, with wings on his back and a huge, bloody dagger stuck right into his manhood. I saw the intense suffering on his face. My hate had bottomed out, and what I figured out later was that Mr. Silver's genuine love for me had shown me that love did exist in men, and I was redeemed."

Goosebumps covered Charley's body like a bad case of acne. Clitorea should have been a preacher, he thought. But her material was so much richer than the Bible: hers actually happened.

"A touching story, Ms. Pearl," said the D.A. "One question: From your testimony, it seems that you never passed up or were passed up for any sexual opportunity whatever. Yet you promised you would show us how a slut *nixes* sex in Tulsa. How can that be?"

"I left and had it elsewhere. I hitched a ride with the first trucker headed out and slept my way all the way to Megaglopoulis. And in every pair of demented eyes of every lost soul who glanced briefly into mine before they closed as he grunted out his colloidally-suspended polliwogs of posterity, I saw an angel. Even as they used me and sold both me and themselves short, I loved them. I loved them all."

Despite Judge Peehole's insistence on strict quiet in the courtroom, an audible sob escaped from Charley. Fortunately, it had company: the W.I.T.C.H.es were snarkling, blowing noses and sighing audibly. Maxwell Veribushi, his own eyes reaching dewpoint, whispered into Charley's ear: "Why didn't I marry her? Why don't you? —No, why don't we both?"

Bang! Bang! Bang! Judge Peehole's gavel sounded just like the capgun he used to fire when he was six years old.

The sixth inning was scoreless. Munching an ice cream bar, Oprah Winfrey leaned across an empty seat to extol the evils of beef to George Foreman.

Seventh Inning

Let me see, then, what thereat is, and this mystery explore—
Let my heart be still a moment and this mystery explore;—
'Tis the wind and nothing more!

—Edgar Allan Poe

It ain't over till it's over

—The Old Philosopher

My babies all born wid 8 legs on each side
If I don't watch out my legs be deep fried
An' when dem rib'ets! get done treatin' me so bad
Dey drop me in formal-hald-de-hyde

—adapted from Gary Larson

DO FROGS HAVE MORE FUN?

Despite a Mutants win that night, Charley Orange sat vegging out on the ultimate drug, the tube, depressed. Listening to Clitorea Pearl in court, he felt like the ninth place team in an eight-team league. She was a class act and she had been genuinely interested in him. His jealousy had caused him to blow it with her. Yes, he knew it was his wounded little boy, not him, but he still felt ashamed and angry with himself.

He looked at Nevermore, resting on the stone he had placed in its Mason jar, its opaline throat pulsing in a slow-dance beat. When it came to women, Charley had always thought of himself as a frog. If only he knew what a rip-roaring amorous life Nevermore and his forefathers had led, he would have had to change his self-image—or his self. But in his blissless ignorance he felt an uncommon affinity with Nevermore, the last of the *Rana oncas*.

A man lies in a hospital bed with radio signals coming through his head. Other patients push his head into contorted positions, at last tuning in to the ballgame. As they swing him around, he kicks open an ice chest full of brew. Everyone grabs a cold one and enjoys the game. Voiceover: *When you're having a few friends over...*

The beer ads were always the best. Even Ngaio XV^{14}+34, who sat on his stone watching Babewatch with the *rib'et!*, agreed to that: this

one even featured a frog. Ngaio had led a promiscuous life, yes, but only because that was preferable to nonogamy. Ever since he could remember he had been searching for Mrs. Onca, hopping in vain from one pond to the next. And now here he was, trapped inside invisible walls—or maybe they were force fields. He couldn't see anything: all he knew was that whenever he leaped, his head hurt.

The *rib'et!* turned off the likenesses of other *rib'ets!* even more misshapen than he and crossed the room to stare in at Ngaio with big, bulging eyes. Every time he approached, Ngaio figured it was curtains. Oddly, however, he did not feel bitter toward the *rib'et!* for keeping him imprisoned. His life, which had once seemed so miraculous to him, had now become almost too stressful for tears. Most of the acre-feet of eggs his mother had laid were eaten by various swamp denizens while she and other new parents recovered from the epic *in complexa venero* that had fertilized them; he was one of the few fry that had survived egghood without becoming somebody's breakfast. Then he hatched into a tadpole and became one of the few who avoided becoming somebody's lunch. He was one of just a half-dozen siblings who made it into froglethood and hopped out onto land. The other five hopped straight into the mouths of, respectively, a heron, a muskrat, a hedgehog, a garter snake and a fox. He alone escaped all perils and grew into...Ngaio XV^{14} +34! Undisputed king of the gene pool! Ngaio was one in a million, and he knew it. He was a Hot Child in Frog City. SKR-E-E-I-K- EK-EK!

But that was then, and this was now. The world outside Ngaio's glass cage was growing scarier by the day. When he zapped out his tongue, it retrieved items that didn't set well in his stomach: balls of tinfoil, plastic bottlecaps, used condoms...one thing the *rib'ets!* excelled at was making everything inedible. Water visibility range kept steadily dropping, making morsels of real food even harder to spot. His sister-in-law Geraldine had just given birth to 16,000 babies—all boys.

No one knows for sure just how many *Rana oncas* lay down their heads to be lopped off by that meatcleaver of Progress (the antithesis to Evolution) called Mutant Stadium, but 5,000 probably gets you in the ballpark. Plus 40,000 eggs from Gurgle Gertie, 25,000 from her sister Griselda and so on and on gets you 50 kazillion, give or take a kazillion—reduced after attrition to 50,000. Charley Orange tended to think of extinction as a slow withering away of a population until it's reduced down to a solitary individual, a last pterodactyl winging its lonely way through the horizonless Cenozoic swamps, squawking in vain for a mate—even a tennis partner—any kindred spirit with which to share its peculiarly Pterodactylian viewpoint, until finally, after a lifetime spent in the super-angst of longing search, its weary wings fold and it plunges silently into the primordial slime, taking with it the multimillion-year history and consciousness of *Pterodactyloidea pterodactylus*.

But once you get the final population isolated, Ngaio knew, it can be as healthy as his own erections and something can come along—a flush of toxic fertilizer from a factory farm, a passing chlorinated breeze in the stratosphere playing pinball with the electrons on the O^3 atoms, parting the ozone layer like Cecil B. deMille parting the Red Sea, and all of a sudden 50 kazillion baby frogs all have 11 legs and no tongues. And then there were none, only this time the only mystery is who put these *rib'ets!* at the top of the evolutionary heap, anyway? One nice thing about Creationist theory is that it doesn't tout any one species as being better than any of the others (although Creationist believers also have a separate tenet that says their God put them in charge of the other creatures). Ha! Leave it to the *rib'ets!* First they thought their kings were gods. Then they thought *they* were gods. They thought their earth was the center of life. Next they thought *they* were the center of life. What other creature would want to put itself in charge of everything?

It was all so discouraging. Ngaio had grown weary of sneaking around, trying to find living space: all the best ponds were taken by the invader bullfrogs who would rather eat you than sing along. It meant farther travels and longer searches for potential lovers. And that put Ngaio into such a scarcity mentality that he had been jumping on the first cloaca he happened across. Had he been born a few generations earlier and had a choice, he would never have amplexusized onto someone as green as Gretchen. Still, though...Gretchen. Hm-mmm. Things could be worse...

Immersed in his own problems, Charley Orange stared in at the frog's big, bulging eyes, unaware of its meditations, oblivious to the seriousness of its plight. "I'm in my last year on the gravy train," he addressed Nevermore, "playing on a team that's about to sink like a stone with all aboard, a friend is missing and maybe dangerous to himself, and...well, I realize now that I'll never have a woman. I finally had one and I'm so screwed up I made a scene and ran away from her."

Nevermore stared back. Charley's eyes also tended toward big and bulgy. Four bloated eyeballs, two brown and two as gold as topaz, locked in on each other. The eyes, Clitorea Pearl had said in an uncharacteristically trite moment, are the windows of the soul. For several electrifying seconds Charley felt a connection with Nevermore that seemed the equal of the connection he had made with Clitorea Pearl when their eyes had locked. He was sharing tantric communion with a frog! No, there was nothing sexual about it. But it did lift Charley out of his own woes into a place of compassion for Nevermore.

"Little frog," he said aloud, "how can my woes hold a candle to yours? The last of your kind, all alone, trapped in your glass cage inside the house of one of the giants who has eradicated your race." Unexpectedly, tears came to Charley's eyes. "Poor amphibian, I could turn you loose into the wild world outside your jar, but for what? You would hop and sing forlornly for the rest of your days, never again to come across a mama-frog to make love with, to pass on the germ of your progeny."

At the thought of mating, Charley's empathic connection with Nevermore was spent, and his focus returned to himself. "Ah, me neither, though my species is rampant with females. Maybe we're in the same boat after all." Then, suddenly aware that he was carrying on discourse—albeit one way—with an anuran, he closed his mouth, turned out the light and went to bed. He fell asleep wondering—did perhaps Nevermore vibe his feeling of oneness with it; was the frog really there with him for a brief interlude of interspecies bonding?

In his Mason jar, Ngaio $XV^{14}+34$ shuddered. He had just had the scare of his life. *Never look into the eyes of a* rib'et!: you can see straight into your doom.

◆ ◆ ◆ ◆

"Ms. Pearl," the assistant D.A. addressed Clitorea when trial resumed, "I must point out to the jury the glee you derived yesterday out of recounting the sordid details of your career as a teenage slut."

"Mr. D.A., you brought up my so-called 'career' and now you label me a slut with the intention of shaming me and painting me as lewd and disgusting in the eyes of the jury. Now, the word 'slut' is an anagram for 'lust'. And what is lust? Lust is passion, before the Christians got hold of it and turned it into something sinful. If I were a good attorney, I would have objected to your line of questioning the moment you started it. But I'm not a good attorney. I'm the World's Greatest Slut, and I'm proud of it, and I'm using this pulpit to bring back pride in Sluthood to everyone who hears me."

To a woman the audience rose, cheering and clapping. So did Maxwell Veribushi. So did Charley Orange.

Bang! Bang! Peehole's gavel quelled the uprising and law and order was restored. "Ms. Pearl, I have warned you not to turn this proceeding into a circus, and I also warn you that it is not a forum for your blasphemous ideas. Mr. Prosecutor, I think you have more than established what you wish regarding the defendant's past. May we proceed to the charges at hand?"

"Very well, Your Honor. Ms. Pearl, two detectives have both testified under oath that you solicited them to pay you for sexual favors. Did you or did you not..."

"Fuck those two turkeys? No way! I have standards..."

Bang! Bang! Bang! Out of Peehole's gavel a trio of new universes sprang forth. "Ms. Pearl, I erred when I gave you permission to utter whatever words you want. I cannot allow the use of that word in court."

"Turkeys, Your Honor?"

"Don't be coy with me. You know the word I mean."

"Sorry, Your Honor. You mean the ancient Anglo-Saxon word for the most beautiful and healing act on the planet, repression of which has brought us rape, teen pregnancies, AIDS, millions of molested children and flocks of defrocked priests. Thank you for further illuminating my point that our culture is so twisted that while acts of violence and murder are everyday fare here, the act of love is unmentionable in our courts of law. But Your Honor, since that is the very act I'm accused of trying to commit, there must be some way I can refer to it in these proceedings."

"There is, Ms. Pearl. The official term for it is 'penile insertive behavior'."

"'Penile insertive behavior'! Besides being more repugnant lexicographically than any street term I could come up with, that's sexist. May I use 'vaginally receptive behavior' instead?"

"That strikes the Court as equally sexist."

"How about 'vaginal receptive/penile insertive behavior'?"

"How about 'penile insertive/vaginal receptive behavior'?"

"How about I'll take turns?"

"Very well. Use 'penile insertive/vaginal receptive behavior' first."

"Very well, you're the judge."

"Thank you. Mr. Prosecutor, please continue."

Charley sat listening to his tax dollars at work. Peehole and Clitorea were locked into an infinite regress. Like the World Series: two games in one park, three in the other and back to the first for two if necessary. No matter how you juggle it, one side still comes out on top. In the behavioral matter at hand, no neutral solution was possible. Lovers would offer first billing to the opposite sex; the fearful would clutch it to the bosom of their own (figuratively speaking). Where, he asked himself, did he stand today: in love or in fear? His feelings seemed to be locked into an infinite regress of their own.

"Ms. Pearl, I will ask you again whether you solicited the officers to receive money for sexual favors."

"You mean for vaginal receptive/penile insertive...that is, penile insertive/vaginal receptive behavior? Of course not. I turn business away dealing with a much higher level of clientele than those limp—I mean vice dicks."

"Ah, so you admit you're in the business of prostitution?"

"Prostitution? That's illegal! I'm the director of a scientific laboratory at the University."

"You're...what...?"

You didn't check me out? Pretty sloppy research, Roscoe. You'd never get a job in my lab."

"Do you have any proof of that? A paycheck stub? Letterhead with your name on it?"

"Again, I could object. If you think I'm lying, it's up to you to prove it. But there's my employer over there in the second row. You can ask him."

"Oops," Maxwell whispered to Charley. "There goes my job."

Once again anger flooded Charley's body. "She sacrificed you to beat a lousy...what? Thirty days?" he whispered, much too loudly.

Bang-bang-bang-bang-bang-bang-bang-bang-BANG! Peehole's gavel sounded like a shootout at the OK Corral. "Who is that disrupting my courtroom?" Maxwell held up a few hairs from his beard and studied them with eyebrows aloft, as if noticing for the first time that his chin was the only one in the courtroom to sprout such appendages. Charley fell into a deep meditation upon the cracks in his fingernails.

"Very well then, if the disrupter is too cowardly to admit her guilt, I shall be forced to clear all spectators from the courtroom. Now, are you all going to let one guilty person's actions punish everyone, or will someone please tell me who the perpetrator is?"

Charley sprang up. "Thank you, Your Honor, for pressing me to acknowledge my discourteous conduct in your courtroom. I was talking when I was supposed to be quiet, and I am ready for my punishment."

"$100 for contempt of court, and you must leave this room as soon as you pay."

"No, Your Honor," cried out Clitorea. "Don't make him leave. He's a baseball player!"

Maxwell stood up beside Charley. "I talked too, Your Honor. I should pay half the fine."

"One hundred dollars for you as well. And you get out too."

"No!" cried Clitorea. "That's him!"

"The defendant will please stop...That's whom?"

"That's my employer. You can't throw him out!"

Peehole peered down at the furball in blue jeans whom he had been addressing. Well, it did wear glasses. He stared at Maxwell for a long, long time, maybe half a minute, no doubt understanding for the first time why his children had become drug addicts when they had gone off to University. "You are her employer?"

"I am. Or at least I was until this trial. And I promise not to talk any more."

As slowly as a snail cruising down the side of an aquarium with a palsied pseudopod, His Urinary Miatusness nodded his head. "Very well. You may remain. We may need you."

"Thank you, Your Honor. And may my consultant remain also, if he promises to be quiet?"

"Your consultant? The defendant claims this man is a baseball player."

"He is, Your Honor. My current research involves comparing the loft, trajectory and sagitta of batted baseballs to that of rainbows to determine the ideal angle at which a bat should be swung to hit a home..."

"All right, the Court is not interested in your research beyond establishing the veracity of the man's employment with you. Do you, sir, also agree to stop talking for the duration of the proceedings?"

"I do."

"Then pray, let us move on."

When they sat down, Maxwell wrote Charley a note.

C. had my permission. I have $$ enough for myself without the job. It's her own petard she's hoisted herself on. I just won't have the $$ to support her research.

Old pond
Frog jumps in
The sound of water
—Basho

Ngaio XV^{14} +34 sat on his stone in the Mason jar, battling his claustrophobia by reflecting on the nature of his connection with the stars. He was hatched under the sign of the Ram, as were so many *Rana oncas.* "We're an Aries species," he thought. "Yikes, just like the bullfrogs." Ah, but if you are Ngaio XV^{14} +34, do you chart your destiny from the time of your conception, your hatching or your turning into a frog? The metamorphosis was too gradual a process for astrology to apply, and most anuran theologians placed the magic moment at hatching. If so, reasoned Ngaio, that implied some mysterious quality of the protective slime around the egg to shield it from those cosmic vibrations until hatchtime: the same quality imputed to the mother's skin (or aura) in the *rib'ets!* Now, the *rib'ets!* calculated their horoscopes from their birth, but for a frog that's a long time after the egg is laid. In ancient times *rib'ets!* dated their birth at conception, though, and on this point Ngaio agreed with them. It is the male phallus, he chauvinistically assumed, that shields the cosmic vibrations: the astral influence strikes the sperm the moment it spurts out the tip, and the sperm carries the astral influence with it into the egg.

His ruminations were interrupted by the entry of the two *rib'ets!* What was that the larger one carried in his hands? A cooking pot! Big enough to boil his and another hundred pair of frog legs. Oh yes, Ngaio had heard all about the culinary habits of the *rib'ets!* More than a million of his friends and family they shanghaied and shipped in each year from Asia and Australia, just to scarf down their lower limbs. Time's up, Ngaio: this is the final hop.

"Never underestimate the DNA of any critter that got this far," Maxwell Veribushi said to Charley Orange as Charley set the 20-gallon aquarium on his desk top, "with the exception of university administrators, Creationists—children of Hell descended from the Legion of Indecency and the Inquisition—and the inventor of the car burglar alarm."

"This should hold him," said Charley.

"We humans like to think we're leading the ratpack," said Maxwell, "but think about it. When the first fish slung their slimy, wheezing carcasses up onto terra firma 350 million years ago, most of them couldn't hack it. But the frontier spirits thought" —and here he turned to Nevermore and *namaste'd*— "'if we can only figure out how to breathe up here, there's a whole new world for the taking'. Voila! They created the lung."

"And frogs followed," said Charley. "The Navy created frogmen. These guys created menfrogs way back when."

"They invented lungs and what did humans invent? Lung cancer. Frogs also found that when dust got in their eyes on land, air didn't wash it out like water did. So they dreamed up the blink."

"Right on, Professor. I've never seen a fish blink."

"And you never will. Next they discovered the air didn't hold up their water-bloated bodies very well: they couldn't dart to and fro and do the shimmy on a dime like they did down deep. They needed some anti-gravity devices."

"So the frogs grew those long, high-kicking legs," said Charley. "Able to leap over tall grasses with a single bound. It's a bird. It's a plane. It's Superfrog!"

"Sure beats hell out of that crazy two-step shuffle of ours." Maxwell inserted a wedge of cut glass into the tank, dividing it into two areas, one about twice the size of the other. "Of all the megavertebrates from human size up, he continued, "guess which is the slowest? Even a hippopotamus can outrun us. And did you ever listen to a bunch of herpetologists go crashing through the swamps like King Kongs chasing Godzillas, crunching everything in their path?"

"Look at those magnificent legs," said Charley, his eyes falling upon Nevermore. "Eat your heart out, Betty Grable."

Ngaio was prepared to die: his affairs were in order. They flashed before his eyes: Germaine, Griselda, Gretchen...He had no desire to take Jesus Frog for his personal savior, nor did he pine to sail into Valhalla on a burning ship. He had toyed with the idea of a Happy Hunting Ground until he found out it was invented by the *rib'ets!*: he knew who would be hunter and whom huntee.

It is axiomatic that the threat of imminent death can trigger an epiphany. Suddenly the shutters of speciesism that blinded most of the animal kingdom including the *rib'ets!* flew open in Ngaio's perception. He accepted the frogma of karma: that he would have to come back, in some parallel universe or other, as every fly he had ever eaten. Did that mean there were no herbivores in his herebefores?

"Gams," said Maxwell. "Betty Grable had gams. Women today have legs. Like frogs. But returning to ranid antigravity science, the frogs also had to figure out eating on land. Tasty morsels abounded, but these freewheeling morsel creatures, being less encumbered by gravity, could dance rings around the frogs, hop onto their eyelids, kick off for the Flea-Fly playoffs using a frognose for a football, and halftime would be upon that slo-mo amphibian before its mouth opened in attempted retaliation. So the anurans cunningly concentrated a shotload of speed into one area of their body, an area that was as light as a frog's tongue: their tongue. Add some stickum on its surface, fork it like a banderole, unfurl it at the speed of light, and zap!—that taunting six-legged joy diver is suddenly buzzing its wings against the unyielding wall of a salient gizzard. Burp!"

"Wow—the first bullet," said Charley.

"Combined with the first superglue and the first boomerang." To the larger side of the tank Maxwell added a bucketful of sodden dirt, making a huge mudpie that rose as high as the glass wedge, topping it off with a meringue of verdant moss. Were the *rib'ets!* practicing mental torture, Ngaio wondered, or were they just too insensitive to know better than to concoct dessert before his very eyes?

"Then there's the science of cryonics," said Maxwell. "Frogs in Antarctica mastered it long before the first Australopithecus was even a gleam in S/HeIt's eye. When February rolls around and the South Polar days start growing shorter and frost is on the penguin, these guys just hanker down and freeze up. Eight months later they thaw

out, and after a cup of coffee they're ready for some roly poly gammon 'n gimmitch.

"And how about that miracle of Twentieth Century technology, the space suit? Frogs went beyond that early on, too. Out on the parched Australian outback they seal themselves inside membranes that cover their skins. The aborigines have to find them and squeeze them for a drink of water. They'll live underground inside those membranes for up to five years, waiting for rain."

"*Praying* for rain," said Charley. "I wonder what goes through their minds sitting their life away in one spot? I'd go so crazy after all that time without even seeing a woman that I'd jump on the first one I saw when I got out."

"Alas, that is the sad truth about them as well," said Maxwell. "They drop the membrane like a frat boy dropping trou and do the wham-bam, thank-you-ma'am. The tads have to hatch, grow faster than the national debt and get out of the pond while there's still a pond to get out of.

"But the truly ingenious frog first, as any musician will tell you, is the croak. It's the first song sung with no stridulations attached. Nor do they even open their mouth. First they push air out of their lungs into a sac in their throat. Then they flex their throat muscles, forcing the air over their vocal cords back into their lungs."

"No human could ever do that except Louie Armstrong." Charley tried a frog-style croak. "It feels like blowing bubbles out your ears."

Maxwell added water to the small side of the tank, making a pond about half a cubic foot in size. The glass was a hair too short to require wedging, allowing mud to ooze into the water and reduce visibility to zero. However, it also let water ooze into the mud to keep it and its hairpiece well-wetted.

Normally Ngaio preferred to dwell on past wives, not future lives. But two *rib'ets!* honking and hooting at each other and gesturing toward him with a see-through guillotine were not normal circumstances. "Next time you see old Ngaio,", he thought, "he'll be a speck on the wall, waiting for someone to defecate. As a frog," he reasoned, "I have this aversion thing to feces, but maybe flies don't have it so bad after all. Think what accomplished alchemists they are, extracting gold from shit. I'll probably be just as happy crawling over a fresh turd on a suburban lawn as I was crawling over Gretchen's cloaca in the swamp." At the prospect of spending his next 3,247 lifetimes mining for a heart of gold, Ngaio's face broke out in a grin—although, frogs having such wide mouths that they perpetually grin, his grin was not noteworthy. A light sparkled in his coppery eyes—however, since through a frog's eyes, even the pale light of stars reflected in water is magnified into glitter, this particular illumination was nothing to write home about either. His heart leapt—nope, a frog's legs are ever leaping, carrying with them the rest of its body including its heart: again, no big deal. It can be said only that Ngaio's speculations on the beyond, like those of many of us as we prepare to cross the bar, brought joy to his spirit beyond the power of metaphor to express.

And yet, even as Ngaio XV^{14} +34 conjured up a paradise of fresh, steaming poop, his will to live burned even stronger: he turned his legs imperceptibly and coiled, ready for one final spring for freedom should the *rib'et!* open the jar lid.

"However, the basic teaching of the frogs," Maxwell continued, "was what to do with their eggs. The pioneer types just laid them by the pondful, gulped a bunch of them back down and headed south. Well, you can bet what was for breakfast in the marsh for months: Eggs Nevermore. Somewhere along the way, the lady frogs figured out that if they would just hang out at home awhile and pack the guys' lunchbuckets with *pate de fruit fly,* they wouldn't have to churn out so many fry. Not that they didn't love sex, mind you. But these were some mighty long rides in the hay. After 72 hours straight, and the guy hasn't even asked you your name...

"Anyway, they answered the egg question in some ingenious ways. Some papa frogs learned to eat the eggs as soon as the Missus dropped them onto the forest floor, and give them the ultimate wraparound protective shield: themselves. Cyrano de Paddock crouches under Froxanne's window, ukulele in hand. He opens his mouth and out comes—not a song but a baby."

"He sings with his mouth closed anyway," said Charley.

"And he's a lousy ukulele player. My favorite, though, is the Flaming Poison Arrow Frog." Maxwell added a bonsai basking log to the mini-pond. "There. All he needs now is sunglasses and a cell phone. *Dendrobates pumilio* perfected chemical warfare to the point where a single drop of its protective *curare* can kill a human being. An inch long, Mrs. *Pumilio* climbs those huge rainforest trees and drops her eggs one at a time into tank bromeliad puddles. No one would ever think to look for frog eggs up in trees, and if somebody does find one—well, it's only one. Then the problem arises: Tank bromeliad puddles not being cornucopias of animistic activity, what will the tadpole live on when it hatches? Well, it turns out mom has to haul herself back up those skyscraping treetrunks every night and deposit some infertile eggs in each tank. Her tads grow up on a diet of their half-brothers and half-sisters."

"I don't know," said Charley. "Now it's beginning to sound like the human enterprise: all this so-called progress only adds hours to the work week of Mrs. Frog."

"Maybe so," said Maxwell. "Maybe that's why after 50 million years on top of the heap—a dynasty 25 times longer, incidentally, than the current pretender, *H. sapiens*—along came the reptiles, including those early birds, the dinosaurs.

"The reptiles ruled the roost for nearly 200 million years and also tossed a few coins into the Animal Kingdom's fountain of knowledge. They were geniuses at waterproofing. They sealed their eggs with shells so they could lay them on land, and from the fish they adapted scales, which have it all over shingle roofing for keeping the raindrops out—and they're a darn sight prettier, too.

"Yet because the amphibians and reptiles never learned to hide their bodies in shame or write TV commercials or tell each other what to do; because they did not create Monday mornings or taxes or shrinkwrapping, manufacturer's tires, handling charges, telemarketing, Teletubbies or Beanie Babies—because of this, they are ranked below humans on the evolutionary scale.

"Nevermore," said Charley, picking up Ngaio's Mason jar. "Come check out your new home!"

"By whom?" said Maxwell. "By the humans, that's whom."

"I get nervous even opening the top," said Charley. "A well-timed jump and..." He must have read Ngaio's mind.

We could always put the jar in the refrigerator for awhile," said Maxwell. "Nevermore can take the cold for a couple of hours. We'll give him a half-hour and then he should be moving slower than traffic."

It's a good thing Ngaio XV^{14} +34 couldn't understand English, because for all their inventive genius, frogs never developed much of a sense of humor. Having made his peace with S/HeIt, Ngaio watched Charley as he set him down, opened a door and disappeared: a momentary reprieve before being called upon to sing in the celestial chorus.

Ngaio was about to learn a lesson so profound that he would never be able to explain it, not even in his genes to his posterity: *Not all* rib'ets! *are to be feared.* He could never even teach it to his own body: even though he came to learn that Charley and Maxwell sought him no harm, his legs automatically turned into pogo sticks whenever they came near.

The *rib'et!* returned with a net and headed toward the jar. Wait, thought Ngaio, that doesn't look like a spit he's holding—oops, there went the pogo sticks: he jumped and made the un-Bashovian, non-kerplopian sound of skull bashing against glass. The *rib'et!* unscrewed the jar lid—Arrgh! Less than a second after Ngaio's reflexes took him out of escape position!

One *rib'et!* dumped Ngaio into the terrarium while the other flung in a rain of crickets. Ngaio's emotions were askew. He'd blown his chance for freedom. But the *rib'ets!* were not after his life. Not for the moment, at least. And check out these new digs! Still not enough room for a good leg-stretching boing-boing, but hey, direction is all.

"There you are, little frog," said Charley. "Crickets for dinner."

Quoth Nevermore: SKRIEK -EK-EK!

◆◆◆ ◆◆◆ ◆

The news of Whizzo Mark Salot IV's disappearance hit the down-and-out city like a 9-point earthquake. Blind streetcorner prophets warned of imminent cataclysm. People drank still more. Violent television shows sent formerly normal viewers into the parks and malls as vicious ax-murderers, serial killers and Hare Krishna proselytizers. Citizens taking target practice at 60 mph ruled the freeways; surface streets belonged to the gangs and to the beggars who roamed them with outstretched hands.

With two gone in the sixth against the sixth-place Blue Hen Chickens, the demoralized Mutants were down 7-1. Foo Foo McGonigle sent Charley Orange up to bat for Jeff "The Heft" Lawton, the third Mutes hurler of the evening. On a 2-1 count Charley guessed hummer up and in. He stepped into the bucket and drove the ball down the left field line and out, his first rainbow of the season. While tarnish spread over the golden dreams of the team, Charley's average kept shooting up like it was on Viagra: .178. Rounding the bases, some emotion came up for him: this could be his final 360-trot. The applause was disappointingly lukewarm in the lost cause; but then he saw a few hundred loyals standing and cheering. He wanted to doff his cap to them, but no; given the score, that would be hot-dogging.

SEVENTH INNING STRETCH

As galaxies collapse into the black holes at their centers, the black holes, consuming an ever-shrinking universe, collapse toward and into each other, finally merging into one Super-singularity, and then Bang! It's Time.

With a Bang!, Huachinanga lined to Revenge at Second Base, and it was Time: Time for the Seventh-Inning Stretch.

Take me out to the ball game
Take me out to the park

Buy me some peanuts and crackerjacks
I don't care if I never come back
It's root, root, root for the home team
If they don't win it's a shame
For it's one—two—three strikes and you're out at the old ball game.

Imagine a universe whose Valhalla is located in a Norman Rockwell hamlet called Cooperstown, New York. Imagine a sport that has its own official poem—entitled "Casey at the Bat"—and its own official song. Let your mind riffle through the words to that venerable tune and you will know something about the Grand Old Game. If Elm Street wrote lyrics and Wonder Bread could sing...Baseball is root, root, rooted to the past. The year 1927 rests quietly in its grave for everyone but diamond-heads, to whom it's Babe Ruth's 60-rainbow season. Maybe baseball's function is to connect us to simpler, halcyon times.

The games are too long, its critics say. Maybe that's just the result of deepening strategy as the game becomes more and more cerebral. Mabye it's baseball's version of inflation, its resonance with the expanding universe. Ultimately baseball is like Frank Sinatra: an institution whose reasons for endurance are too ineffable to elucidate.

Besides, what's the alternative? Football? As George Will points out, "football combines the worst features of American life: violence and committee meetings." Rugby? Is America ready for athletes who ram their fingers up opponents' anuses, or for cancer groups that use photos of this to promote prostate exams? Boxing? Pass the ear, please. Basketball? Harper's magazine notes that 59 times as many people attend bingo games as hoop encounters.

From the field, Mutant Stadium felt like a mausoleum. Attendance hadn't died altogether, but the fans, like the team, felt dead inside. Noisier crowds could be found at piano recitals. The few cheers that made themselves heard sounded like they came from pallbearers.

The bleacher crowd, like pre-schoolers throwing tantrums, littered the outfield warning track with debris. When Bimbo Terwilliger booted a chopper at short, angry boos and catcalls cascaded down like he had just dropped the pennant.

"It's like they blame us guys who stayed instead of the turkey who split," said Pinky Hollobaugh to Charley on the bench.

"Screw the fans," said Charley. "Focus on the game."

Foo Foo McGonigle let Throttlemeyer rest his knees for the last two innings and Charley Orange finished the game behind Speedboat Jones, whom Foo Foo wanted to assure himself was ready for a game situation after his long stint on the disabled list. Speedboat's status went from question mark to question mark. His location was erratic; Hector "Adios" Amigo bid one adios with two on in the ninth.

"...Tonight there is no joy in Mutesville," a familiar voice intoned into the living rooms and bars of Megaglopoulis. "Final score 10-2. Three straight losses, and that leaves the Mutants 12 1/2 behind with only 31 to go. Me, I'm an optimist. I still think they can finish third. In Las Vegas, the odds against the flag have climbed to 100 to 1. Bluster Hyman; I'm outta here! Sweet dreams."

Outside, the police began shooting anything black that moved, and the Inner City rose up like the erstwhile waves at Mutant Stadium. Rumor had it they were trading a zillion AK-47's for enough pocket-sized nukes to blow the smile off the Man in the Moon's face. Smoke, still hanging in the air after the big fire, mixed with the dense layers of other particulate matter obscuring the sun. The Air Quality Board denied it, but everyone knew the sky was falling. Morale in Megaglopoulis was so low, it was out crawling around under snakes that had been run over by steamrollers.

The jurors filed out of the room to ponder the possibility that Clitorea Pearl had maligned their mores. Judge Peehole felt a calling in his abdomen and declared a recess. As W.I.T.C.H.es filled the hall, cackling and casting their spells upon any passing males, Clitorea made a beeline through them Charley Orange's way. Charley's heart tricked him, dancing like a butterfly, leaping like the *Rana onca* in his terrarium trying to get over the wall. But the bee buzzed right past him and he felt a butterfly flutter by: the flower she sought was Maxwell Veribushi, standing beside him.

"Oh Fuzzy Wuzzy!" She was near tears. "It came out before I knew what I was saying. Are you sure it's all right with you?"

Maxwell took her in his wings. "I told you and I meant it, sweetheart. It's your money. My only concern is that you lost your money."

Standing next to them, Charley could feel the love energy radiating from them. Suddenly an image popped into his mind: he was trapped in a glass bubble, screaming to get out but no one could hear. He let out an involuntary gasp.

"Are you all right, Charley?" asked Maxwell.

"Yeah. Sorry." The bubble was gone, and his thoughts cleared. Maxwell was donating $50,000 a year to Clitorea because he believed in who she was. And Clitorea was throwing it away because she, too, believed in who she was. And what was he doing? Didn't he believe in W.I.T.C.H. and its potential to heal the ills of men and of humanity? Hadn't Clitorea healed his? Well, almost—at least until he stopped her.

"I know, Fuzzy," she was saying, "but I'm not worried. Hey, I've been on the 10 O'clock News all week. Whether I do time or not, when this is over I'll have guys lining up to give me $50,000—Hey, here comes Channel 7 now. I'm gonna tell them I need the bucks and you just watch magic happen!"

If urgency, like Time, could be measured with sand, then Charley was suddenly buried in the dunes. Before he knew he was speaking, the words spilled out of his mouth like lava from a presumably dormant volcano. "I'll give you the money, Clitorea."

"You? Charley?"

"Yes, me." Did she have to be so obtuse? "I want to give you the money."

Clitorea looked at him like a Fundamentalist who had just been told that the Second Coming was the ejaculate from which she had been created. What, was she going to turn him down?

"I think I'd rather ask for it on Channel 7, Charley. Thanks for the offer, but I'm afraid you're acting in a burst of feeling and you would resent it later."

From over his shoulder he could see the cameraman making his way across the hall. "Was I resentful when I gave you the $1,000? No."

"Yes, you certainly were." She turned toward the approaching microphone.

"No. I was resentful later because I didn't think you really cared for me; you only felt obligated to give me my money's worth. How would you feel..."

The talking head began his singsong spiel: "We're speaking with Clitorea Pearl..."

"No you're not, I am," said Charley, planting his ample frame between newsman and news. Viewers of the 10 O'clock News that night were privilege not to Clitorea's plea but to this behind-the-scenes scoop:

CHARLEY: ...How would you feel if you and I were having sex in my bed and another lover showed up and I asked you to leave?

CLITOREA: Charley, I...(she gives him a pained look but holds his eyes. The pain turns to puzzlement, then back to pain as she bursts into tears.) Oh, Charley! You're right! There was thoughtlessness, and probably some anger behind the way I exercised my power over you. Thank you for calling me on it, and for being right about it. I love you. (They embrace.)

NEWSMAN: And as the world turns, it's love, some say, that makes it go round. Until tomorrow night...

At noon, courtesy of Charley Orange, Maxwell Veribushi entered Mutant Stadium, prompted by a rumor he heard from Sage, who heard it from Billy Beanball, who heard it from a friend, who probably heard it from another kid...it was a long shot, but in a matter like this, any possibility was worth looking into. Besides, who knew better about these things than kids?

Around Maxwell's neck was a pair of binoculars. Directly behind home plate, at Section 1, he headed up the ramp to the upper deck. He scanned the city, from the news vendor hawking numbers directly below out past the concrete slabs of stadium parking lots all the way to the downtown skyscrapers. Not an unpaved square meter could he see. Then he traversed the first base side to the right field foul pole and scanned again. Freeways looped over and under each other like a clusterfuck of wriggly concrete snakes. Down the ramp, across right field and up again to the top of the centerfield bleachers, beside the scoreboard, he looked out on a panorama of smokestacks with no Surgeon General's warnings, coal and limestone pyramids with no pharaohs, power lines with no power lunches, and enough railroad tracks that, laid end to end, their parallel lines would meet in a parallel universe.

The view from the left-field quadrant was the outfield wall. Maxwell left the park and switched to Plan B. Mounting his trusty Harley, he cruised up Trombley Avenue parallel to left field. Then he made two right turns and cruised back down the next street out parallel to Trombley, going a block longer, then a block farther out, a block longer, a block farther, a block longer, carving out a wedge of pavement pie equal to one-fourth of the 16-mile square in which the stadium was centered.

The pie was now a mile in radius, and its photosynthetic frosting on this hot day stung Maxwell's eyes like needles and made his throat feel like the Harley's exhaust pipe.

Abruptly the tattoo parlors, X-rated theaters, chartreuse-Mohawked hustlers and jive mamas gave way to tree-lined streets with faded but still semi-affluent dwellings. The lots were spacious; century-old trees slurped up the din and hullabaloo like so much carbon dioxide and spit out quiet and stillness, even as they exhaled oxygen to soothe Maxwell's throat. Glop Heights, as the sign casually proclaimed it, was a welcome oasis from the concrete juggernaut, maniacal horns, screeching brakes, accusatory car alarms and relentless drone of engines that surrounded it.

Rounding a corner, the Harley squealed to a stop to avoid running dead-on into an eight-foot-high wall. Maxwell climbed onto its seat for a peek over. The wall was probably two feet thick and it went on, like the Great Wall of China, in both directions as far as he could see. The terrain beyond, unlike the well-manicured and pedicured lots he had passed, looked like the set for a Tarzan movie, a miniature jungle erupting like a counter-cancer across the very midriff of Megaglopoulis. If Maxwell could live anywhere in the city—and he couldn't—it would be here, at the price of about $200 million more than his entire island.

The question was, could a *frog* live here? Maxwell didn't see any water, but dinosaurs could be lurking in that piece of Lost Continent and who would know it? No anuran cadenzas burbled through the afternoon air and into Maxwell's tympani, but this was August. The Frogaroo Men's Chorus was busy tamping out its cigars, spray-misting its throats and fitting its tails and ties: the wooing season was months into the future, giving the brothers north of the Gulp time to practice up on their trilling harmonies.

Maxwell cruised around all four sides of the wall, which enclosed at least 10 acres, before coming to an ancient, rusted iron gate with several warning signs from Sinbad Security ("Direct Line to Police Emergency," as if they had a monopoly on dialing 911). Could the dwellers within be Mafia? But no, the Mafia is part of the Ecomafia: they would mow their lawns and trim their displaced vegetation.

Maxwell buzzed. BUZZZ!

No reply.

BUZZZ! Again, no reply.

He remembered a grocery store a ways back—not one of the block-long megamarket chains that contract for an independent farmer's fields, then tell her what to grow, then get their oil crony buddies to sell her petroleum-soaked hybrid seeds to grow it with; and not an all-night convenience store, built mostly to advance the growth and expansion of our penal institutions by providing them with endless numbers of small-time desperadoes who hold up six or ten 7-11's before getting caught. Perhaps America's most egalitarian corporate institution, he thought, the all-night quick-stop store makes more poor folk rich than the lottery.

Maxwell's mind was slipping into *that* mode again. How long would he be able to remain in Megaglopoulis?

No, the store Maxwell remembered was one of the last of yet another endangered species, the family-sized independent grocery. The checkout clerk, who looked and sounded just like Walter Brennan, knew who lived behind the wall: "Femily name'sh Loosh. Brothern shree shistesh. Ol'asha hillsh, alluvm, bya shounda dey voishes ona tilephone, 'n weirdern bidbugsh.

"O' lady phonesh ina grocia odors an' lish me inna gate da drapm off whin I buzzh a shirtain way, but she don' lit me inna housh, hazh me leavem by de door. Leaves a She-note ina unvlup 'n I leave shange."

"Ever see any water on the property—like a pond or pool?"

"Niveh shee nuddin' pasht da vinesh groan all ovuh on trillishesh on both shides a de walk. Thet don' mean they ain't inny. Shit, could be a zhungle in there, could be lionsh, tigahsh, iliphantsh. My shishtash o' man, he duzh landschcapin', if I could git him in there, he be shit fer life."

That night Maxwell was back at the Loosh's with a stepladder tied to a rope. He climbed up the ladder and onto the top of the wall, hauled the ladder up and over, and descended into the jungle. Hearing no dogs, he began exploring. Some areas were so densely grown that he would have needed a machete, but others had apparently been landscaped long ago. He almost bumped into the house before he saw it: a great, gray edifice with no light shining out. The ground-floor windows were heavily draped or perhaps boarded from the inside: were they all?

Past the house, the terrain slowly dipped away. Off somewhere in front of him, through a tangle of shrubbery, a ghostly white glow hovered in the moonlight. As he tried to circumvent the thicket first one way and then the other, the glow seemed to follow him. It gave Maxwell an eerie feeling, like he had stumbled into a Beckett play. "It is that ghostly white glow," the thought came to him, "that deprives me of the mercy of no light at all."

Suddenly the earth gave way under his shoe, and then his foot went cold—and wet! He had struck goo! The ghostly white glow became blinking silver slippers: moonlight dancing on water.

The Loosh estate was a veritable swamp.

Splash!

Splash!

And again, splash!

Frogs!

Had this been Calavaras County, Maxwell would have wagered his heart against any of them, so wildly did it leap in its cavity in his chest.

But were they *Rana oncas*? He stepped back uphill and sat to await the dawn, when he could make visual identification.

What a thrill if they were! Decades after Mosquito Marsh was filled in and paved over by the moguls of Mutant Stadium and the final curtain had rung down on *R. onca's* 150-million-year barefoot boogie upon the planet—to think, the creatures might have found refuge in some social misfit's back yard and returned for an encore. As the old philosopher said, it ain't over till it's over.

This swamp looked large enough to support a genetically viable population. And Nevermore would have a home. If Maxwell's hopes proved true, it would be simple enough to sneak back with the frog tomorrow night and effect a family reunion.

Or so Maxwell thought.

Clitorea Pearl's jury was out for three days. Between Whizzo's vanishing act and the W.I.T.C.H. antics, the Megaglopoulis media were in hog heaven.

On the fourth morning, Clarence Bejole barely had time to straighten his toupee before the deliberating dozen returned. "While 'innocent' seems an inappropriate sobriquet to bestow upon one so experienced as the defendant Clitorea Pearl," read the forewoman, "on the charge of soliciting a police officer for the purpose of purveying sex, we find her Not Guilty."

Amid shrieks, screams and laughter, the W.I.T.C.H.es launched balloons, blew kazoos and party favors and passed out chocolates all around: to the media, to other spectators, the jury, the opposition, court officials. Molecules of air that had been loitering on the premises in suspended animation for years sprang back to life and played dodge 'em cars with falling confetti. Peehole gaveled silence and ordered the W.I.T.C.H.es to clean up, but, mindful of the media, he eschewed contempt of court charges.

As cameras flashed, brooms flew and trashbaskets filled, Charley Orange strode across the courtroom toward Clitorea. She ran to him and kissed him. "Charley darling! I won! I won!"

Charley faked a quick hug and return kiss. "Congratulations. Clitorea, Whizzo's been missing for three days. Anloie left him and he's left the team and I'm worried sick about both him and the team."

"Don't fret about Whizzo, Charley. He's a young man who goes after what he wants. And what he wants is Anloie. It's simple: find Anloie and you'll find Whizzo."

"Will you help me?"

"Oh, Charley! Today? No! I'm going to celebrate today." Then the Goddess tapped her gently on the shoulder. "Oh, all right, Charley. You owe me bigtime for this."

Charley gave his keys to one of the W.I.T.C.H.es and drove Clitorea in her car over to Whizzo and Anloie's hotel room.

"Here's the logical question I've been dealing with," said Charley as he drove. "Suppose that of all the infinite parallel universes, in 10 percent of them Whizzo returns and we win the flag. Is 10 percent of infinite infinite? How can it be, if 90 percent of the universes lie outside the bounds? How can it not be, if the actual number in the 10 percent never ends?"

"Charley! I just won my case. I defeated the jackals of the patriarchy. I went through a lot of fear and sadness in the last few weeks, and you want to talk about parallel universes?"

"I'm sorry, Clitorea. I'm just trying to avoid thinking about Whizzo, and I blocked out your triumph too. You were outrageous, and you

were wonderful. Who could vote to convict you? Will you come over here and snuggle beside me?"

"Your queen?"

"Will you snuggle beside me, my goddess?"

"You bet I will, you wonderful man, you."

"Your god?"

"Oh my God!"

Fortunately, Anloie had laid off the maid when she moved in. The wastebasket held other envelopes written to her with Warren's return address in the corner.

"I'll tell you just one more thing about parallel universes," Charley said as they got back into Clitorea's car and headed for the coast. "You can get from one to another through something called *wormholes* in space-time."

"Wormholes." Clitorea Pearl mulled over the concept. An image came of a great yoni twisting between universes, cosmic labia turning ever on the mouth of the vast everywheres forevers. "Wormholes. I like them. I'll take a dozen."

"Take a zillion. They're infinite."

All the labia rotated simultaneously, kissing each other in kaleidoscopic splendor.

"Charley! I'm having an orgasm! YEE-YII-IY!"

At 8 p.m. the cherry-red Corvette abruptly pulled away from Anloie's (and Warren's) house. At 9 p.m. it returned with the following additions: a notepad and pen, a dozen roses and a second-hand guitar.

And a burger, fries and a coke.

Whizzo Mark Salot IV picked up the guitar and started plunking tentatively, singing along to Hank Williams. He hadn't played the box since singing "Happy Birthday" at Emmy Lou Jonquil's party when they were 11. But he was born with music in his bones. That and the most inspired motivation known to Nature had him performing a tolerable rendition of "I'm So Lonesome I Could Cry" by 10:30.

As the music and the legend of Hank Williams seeped deeper into him, he began composing a song of his own: first a few bars, next a hum, then a line of lyric...About midnight, the light from Anloie's (and Warren's) bedroom finally went out. Whizzo emerged from the Corvette and stood beneath the window. Even with it closed he could hear Warren snoring away like a lawnmower. Poor Sweet Petunia! Timber-r-r-!—This tree would fall. He began his serenade:

Sleepless naghts dear, without you
Sleepless naghts and lonely too
Ah feel so alone and blue
Sincet you said that we are through.

A soft light filled the window. It cranked open and Anloie's heavenly face appeared, her luminescent hibiscus-highlighted golden tresses haloed by the bedlamp behind.

"Whizzo, you can't be here," she whispered hoarsely. "Go away or I'll wake Warren."

"No honeypot, please don't do that. Ah'm sort of AWOL from the team, and if someone fahnds me, they'll take me back, real quick-lahke."

"That's just what I want, Whizzo, don't you see? Your being here can only confuse me and hurt you. I love you but you're just...too crazy for me."

"Ah'm crazy for you all raght, but not *too* crazy. Jist c'mon down and talk to me for fahve minutes. Thass all Ah ax."

Anloie glanced at Warren's horizontal form. The decibels continued undiminished. "Two minutes. And then you go."

"Whatever you say, Punkinflower."

The light went out and the door opened. "OK, two minutes, Whizzo. What do you want?"

She wore her angry face, but Whizzo could see right through it to the tears lurking behind. He handed her the roses. "Red as your sweet lips. Fragrant as your sweet lower lips at heaven's gate."

◆◆◆ ◆◆◆ ◆

Those sweet fragrant lips started to smile in acknowledgment, but Anloie took charge before they could part. "I can't take these, Whizzo. What will Warren say?"

Unseen by the starcrossed duo, the bedroom light flashed on.

"Sweet Magnolia Blossom, please stop breakin' mah heart. Ah hain't never had no woman run away from me and Ah hain't never had no woman Ah cared whether she run away or not, before you, darlin'. You tell me you'd rather lay in bed all naght with a man who sounds lahke he's got his silverware caught in the garbage disposal? What is it this gah is for you that Ah hain't?"

"Well, for one thing, it just so happens that Warren is interested in the plight of women with breasts of two different sizes. You know my special custom-made B-and-C- cup brassieres, with padding inside the B-cups? He got his brother-in-law, who is in Undergarments, to make those for me. And that was a cheap shot about his sleep apnea, Whizzo."

"It was, angel. Anger and jealousy was doin' mah speakin' for me. Ah'm sorry."

"And next month Warren is taking me in for reconstructive surgery. I'll be breast-equalized."

Whizzo felt like he had been kicked in the stomach. This was the cruelest blow of all. She was going to destroy her most perfect of all breasts? Warren had zeroed in on the fear and self-loathing that she had grown up with and with Whizzo was so beautifully growing out of. Since the day that he arrived at puberty at age 11, he had been looking for a partner with the loving heart and asymmetrical cleavage of Anloie. Many had he met with one attribute, many with the other, but never before Anloie had he encountered both in one person. She loved *him*; she was *his*.

"No, no, Honeycakes! Your breasts are so perfect the way they are...so soft lahke little jellyfish, with the bottoms rounder than half-moons and little upturns with strawberries on top—and then they change shape when you shift yourself, or when Ah touch them, and then they come so *alahve*..."

"Whizzo!"

"Sorry, jist that they'll lose all that. They're gonna feel lahke baseballs."

"Maybe that's so in Disfunction Junction, Arkansas, Whizzo, but out here in the wide world they can make them soft and keep them responsive. Anyway, the operation is already set. Come September 25, these bosoms will be eight cubic inches larger."

Whizzo's hand shot out instinctively to fondle and protect Mt. Fujiyama. "No, no, sweet little pillow that Ah love…"

"Hey you! Asshole!" Warren shouted from the window. "Get the hell out of here! I've called the cops. Anloie, close the door."

"Sugar pah! You don't love him, you love me. Marry him and you'll make all three of us as miserable as hounds what mistook a porky for a 'coon."

"I didn't say I was marrying him, Whizzo. I'm just not marrying you. I'm at loose ends and confused at this point in my life and I'm not marrying anybody—for awhile, anyway."

Relief flooded over Whizzo like the moonlight flooding over the mountains behind the condo and, in the distance, the eutherian-rimmed sands. She's jist *confused.* She jist needs *tahme.*

"You are too wonderful for words, Sweetpunkin. Ah can understand you bein' confused. Hey, Ah'm confused sometahmes in mah lahfe, too." Whizzo gave a nervous laugh. "Lahke raght now, for one. So you jist take your tahme gittin' yourself unconfused, and when you do, Ah'll still be here for you."

"Whizzo!" Tears gathered in Anloie's eyes. "Listen. I don't want to see you. I don't want to hear from you. Can you hear that? You've got a wonderful life ahead, with any woman you want. Go and have it."

As Anloie closed the door, two headlights shined into Whizzo's eyes.

The seventh inning was scoreless. Matt "the Bat" Moseley hit a towering ball that had Downtown written all over it. The ball hit a hot-air balloon stationed above the field and dropped for a harmless single.

Eighth Inning

When your heart is in your dream
No request is too extreme
—Jiminy Cricket

Creationism cannot be disproved
because it claims to explain everything.
—Charles Darwin, King of Diamonds

It ain't over till the Fat Lady sings.
—Anon.

THE CAR PULLED UP alongside Whizzo Mark Salot IV.

"Get in," said Clitorea Pearl. "Charley, you take Whizzo's keys and drive his car back."

"No, Clitorea, I'll ride back with him. Whizzo and I need to talk."

"No, Whizzo and *I* need to talk."

"You don't understand, Clitorea. This is about the team..."

"*You* don't understand, Charley. This is about love. It's my department." She dropped the keys in his hand and drove off.

Charley stood there like a caboose uncoupled from a train, looking at the keys. He had just traveled all night, above and beyond the call of duty for the team, only to be finessed by a brassy bitch with a commando mentality. And he had let her! With the fate of the team resting on his shoulders, he had tried to stand up for himself, and she had steamrollered right over him.

No, Clitorea, this is about baseball. Sure, baseball was just a piece of the dream—like love. But baseball was a piece where Charley felt comfortable with the rules of combat—where the combat *had* rules—and where he also came out a winner sometimes. Baseball *felt* more real to him. It was played in edifices the size of city blocks, with equipment that was tangible: Bats. Balls. Gloves. Uniforms, cups, cleats, treatment equipment, spectators, the twinkling of cigarettes being lit in the stands...It was part of the economy; it provided people with a living.

The melodrama grew in his mind. The pennant was at stake. He had to talk to Whizzo before the Sighing Pronoun IV returned and further pissed off everyone on the team with some choice morsels of unrepentant braggadocio. Fucking bitch anyway! He jumped into the Corvette and started up, ready to race her down, run her off the road if need be and rescue Whizzo.

◆◆◆ ◆◆◆ ◆◆

Suddenly car lights shone in his eyes from all directions. Wailing sirens raced toward him. For good measure, a helicopter droned overhead.

"FREEZEEEZE!" ordered a voice as amplified as the Wizard of Oz.

Porch lights popped on; neighbors in nightdress peered from their doors. "NOWOW STEPEP OUTOUT OF THE CARAR," bellowed the Wizard, his vocals careening off the suburban walls and falling back on themselves. "KEEPEEP YOUROUR HANDSANDS IN VIEWIEW AT ALLALL TIMESIMES."

Charley got out. 'FACEACE THE CARAR AND PLACEACE YOUROUR HANDSANDS ON THE ROOFOOF." Two cops rushed up. While one held his .38 to Charley's temple, the other frisked and handcuffed him. "OK shithead. Over to car."

More porch lights joined the party. "Jeez!" Charley heard himself say. "What if someone recognizes me?"

"You're lucky we didn't bring along a TV news crew," said one of the cops as he threw Charley in the back seat. "Stalking some tail that's dumped you—I've seen turnips with more *cajones*. You're looking at two to five, pervo. Igor, would you say this wimpdick's hard up?"

"Hey, I'm not the guy!" The worst part of it was, Charley *was* hard up. Everyone on the Megaglopoulis Mutants knew it. He wondered how many of his teammates would hear the news on Good Morning Megaglopoulis and decide he was guilty—at least until Clitorea and Maxwell and Whizzo showed up.

Igor laughed—not exactly the kind of laugh produced by tickling a baby. "Always wrong party. Always innocent." He cracked his knuckles.

"Knock on the door and let her see me. She'll tell you."

"Let *you* see *her,* you mean. Sure. Got ID?"

"My name is Charley Orange. I'm not a stalker. I'm a baseball player."

"Looks like your name is Whizzo Mark Salot IV. At least according to your license plate."

"I'm driving his car."

"Mr. Salot has been missing for more than 72 hours. Tell us everything you know about him. And it better be good."

Charley told them. Being cops, their sports were boxing and football, and they didn't know Charley Orange from Jonathan Apple: his story wasn't good enough. As they drove him off to County Jail, trading tall tales with crackly voices on their radio about who had caught the most "dangerous animals" tonight, Charley brooded about the series opening tomorrow against the Lemon Sox. The Sox were still a dozen up with less than a month remaining in the season. With Whizzo back, and probably getting the start if he wasn't suspended, the game was critical. Throckmeyer's knees were crying for a day off, and Charley was starting to bang the ball. He had to be there.

The cuffs were too tight on his wrists; his thumbs went numb. How long would the damage last?

Silently he cursed Clitorea Pearl.

According to the speedometer Clitorea Pearl's XK-120 was capable of speeds of 140 mph but Maxwell Veribushi, sensitive to her recent legal difficulties, kept the needle hovering barely above the triple-digit line. "This is the wrong way to go about it, son," he said to Whizzo, who sat in the back seat with Clitorea. "You've got to let her go and turn your efforts toward saving Megaglopoulis from a fate worse than second place. This is the most important matter in the city, and even though you may not think so now, it's the most important matter in your life."

"No way, Professor Veribushi—with all due respect. Anloie's the most important matter in mah lahfe."

"Of course she is, at this moment. But you've got to leave her now, Whizzo. Give her some space, and have faith. Isn't that right, Clitorea?"

Clitorea Pearl did not reply. She was thinking.

"Professor Veribushi—Ah can still hear that tahny part of her trapped in there that wants to bust loose and come spend her lahfe with me."

"Whizzo, have you heard about the Hundredth Monkey phenomenon? After a certain number of monkeys in a tribe—say, 100—learn something new, suddenly, as if by magic, every monkey in the whole tribe knows it. Philosophers of the New Age use this phenomenon to predict that their form of consciousness will one day suddenly envelop the world. However, there's a fly in the ointment: while a hundred furless monkeys begin to think peace and love, ten thousand of them get recruited to build bombs. That tiny part you hear is just that: a tiny part."

"So what you are sayin's mah hopes are outnumbered 10,000 to 100? Thass lahke ten to one?"

"A hundred to one, Whizzo. She's left you. Her heart is with him."

"No sir," said Whizzo. "Ah know Anloie's heart. And even you say they's a chancet in a hundred you are wrong."

"Just drive, Maxwell darling," said Clitorea. "Let the goddess handle this."

Maxwell turned on the radio. Click! "...tastes better with 75 percent more beef!" The Fat Lady cleared her throat, preparing to sing. From the back seat, Whizzo sprang forward and changed stations. Click! "...you'll get the lowest price this plan can offer!" Click! "Outrageous! So loaded, you don't eat it, you survive..." Click!

Above the desert outside, gentle Dawn spread her rosy fingers in the East. Clitorea sat watching the approaching sun manicure those crimson fingernails and listening to Whizzo Mark Salot IV. He had the Male Disease, and he had it bad. Time to go to work.

She leaned over Whizzo and kissed him hard on the lips. As her tongue forced itself into his mouth, her hand dropped to his crotch and fondled Mr. Twister, which, despite Whizzo's surprise and puzzlement, exercised its 18-year-old duty to stand up whenever a lady entered the vicinity. Zip! went his fly. Boing! went Mr. Twister, out of confinement. Schlupp! went Clitorea's tongue as her mouth closed over Twister's unfurled glory.

After a few seconds of pleasure and a few more of confusion, Whizzo tugged her head loose. "Ah—Miz Clitorea, Ah surely do appreciate your display of affection, but Ah don't know if'n this is the best tahme for you and me to have a sexual engagement. You hafta understand, me'n Anloie..."

"Whizzo. Answer me a question. Truthfully. How did you like that?"

"Oh, no ma'am. Ah don't want to hurt your feelin's none..."

"Don't worry about my feelings. The truth."

Whizzo stumbled and stuttered. Always he observed the full chivalric code of a Southern gentleman, as much from his kind heart as from his upbringing. He would never lie to a lady—well, except maybe to avoid upsetting her. Hurting her feelings certainly qualified as upsetting her. But she said—but just because she said didn't mean she meant—but still—

"Whizzo? The only thing that will hurt my feelings is a lie. If you did something to me that I didn't like, wouldn't you want me to tell you so you didn't do it again?"

"Ah...Ah guess so, ma'am, yes Ah would. Ah...well, Ah didn't lahke it. Now Twister here, he's got a mahnd of his own, and his whistle tends to always toot along the same track, if'n you get mah drift. But me, Ah actually did not enjoy it no way."

"Why not?"

This was getting easier. There was no hurt in her voice, no accusation. Whizzo started to enjoy the conversation. "Nothin' personal, ma'am, you caught me off guard, Ah suppose. You jist jumped onto me, you was all over me, and hit waren't mah choosin'."

"In fact, you didn't have any choice in the matter at all, did you?"

"No ma'am. Ah mean, you are a very attractive woman, even considerin' how much age difference between us, and if'n Ah waren't in love with Anloie, Ah maght lahke a repeat performance. But not so sudden-lahke lahke that."

The sun popped over the horizon like an underripe beet. As all the frogs in the county faded into silence and sleep, the tentative overture of the avian symphony burst into the Hallelujah Chorus. Clitorea Pearl smiled. She was good at what she did. Even Whizzo Mark Salot IV, a tender 18 years old and as backwards in his male-female dynamics as the hills that he came from, was already halfway to enlightenment. To many women he was just a piece of ass. To her he was a piece of cake.

◆ ◆ ◆ ◆

Classical music filled the ears of Whizzo Mark Salot IV as he entered Wellington P. Sweetwater's palatial stadium-top sanctum. A 180-degree panoramic view of Megaglopoulis greeted his eyes. Nestled cozily between two skyscrapers was a hot tub, blowing caressing bubbles on two immersed bodies: Sweetwater already had a visitor.

"Whizzo my boy! Lulu, meet The Man with the Golden Arm. Glad to see you back, son."

"Ah apologahze if'n Ah'm interrupting, sir. Your secretary said Ah should come raght in." Whizzo's eyes took in the Oriental carpet, the largest TV screen he had ever seen, the fridge, the Barca-lounger, the bar...He spotted Sweetwater's infamous cooler filled with gin. "You press the spigot and it measures out precisely one shot," Bobaloo Boynton had told him. Off to the side was the canopied bed, subject of lore surpassing the water cooler, where curious hot tub partners allegedly cut their teeth on Sweetwater's wooden lingam.

"Are you a yo-yo man?" asked Sweetwater as he and Lulu rose from the tub.

"Ah can rock the cradle with the best of them." Sweetwater laughed as he and Lulu toweled and robed. Lulu's glittery eyes and silicone breasts beckoned to Whizzo, but Sweetwater's backside faced him, depriving Whizzo of a glimpse of his storied member.

"Look in that glass case. It's my electric yo-yo collection." Sweetwater's voice filled with pride. "I've made arrangements to leave it to the Toy Museum when I move on to the next realm. Anyway, sometimes I have some of the boys come up and we turn out the lights and get them all going. It's quite a sight. I'd like to have you join us."

"Ah'd be honored, sir. Gosh o'Golly, Ah never did see an office quahte lahke this one."

“My office is furnished to fulfill my dreams—with one heartbreaking exception.” Sweetwater pointed to two dust-covered shelves above the massage table. “You see those two empty shelves? One is reserved for the league pennant. The other is reserved for the World Series trophy. My maid keeps this room immaculate, but I have ordered her never to dust those shelves until I have something to put on them. That dust you see has been accumulating there for 17 years.”

“Ah owe you mah deepest apologies, Mr. Sweetwater, sir. You are payin’ me a chunk of’ money fit for a king to win you that pennant and Ah done left the team.”

Whizzo, I heard on Sports Central that you’ve already given away 140 percent of your salary this year,” said Lulu, wrapping a towel around all of her attributes except one breast.

“No ma’am, Ah kept about 10 percent of this year’s salary for mahself, and Ah gave away half of next year’s. So actually, if’n Mr. Sweetwater fahnes me Ah cain’t pay it till next year, less’n he takes it out of mah 10 percent, but then Ah’d have to borry it back, so a fahne mahght be too drastic.” Whizzo turned to Sweetwater, who was approaching the cooler with three glasses in his hands. “After all, Ah can bring you the flag. The Series. The whole ball of wax. It’s what Ah’m on the planet for. Ah’m a miracle worker. The psahchic lady told me so.”

Sweetwater pressed the spigot into the first glass precisely twice. “Drink?”

“No thank you sir, Ah’m a teetotaler.”

“Good for you, lad. Keep those athletic skills as long as you can.” He squeezed out a companion double and then, to the closing strains of Shubert’s Serenade, he crossed to the Barcalounger and drew Lulu onto his lap. She ran her long ruby fingernails through his silver locks like blood through snow. “Yes, you do owe me an apology, and I won’t know whether to accept it until after I hear your story. Where were you, lad?”

Like a nightingale before some drowsy emperor, Whizzo poured forth his woebegone tale of love won and lost. When he finished,

◆◆◆ ◆◆◆ ◆◆

Lulu's eyes were red and puffy with tears. Of course, they were red and puffy before he began.

"I remember a time…" said Wellington P. Sweetwater, shaking his head. He and Shubert fell silent; the only sounds were of hot tub bubbling and—bless her heart— Lulu blubbering. Finally Sweetwater returned from his parallel universe.

"I accept your apology, son. You're a lad after my own heart. I'm a romantic myself. I'm not like those other owners. That bully who fires his manager and trades half a dozen players every time his team hits a losing streak. That braying loudmouth on his Save the World kick. That harpy bigot with her potty mouth and smelly dog. And Bud, he'd vote against change if it were diapers they were changing. Rube, he sold off his championship team to buy junk bonds and lost his shirt in the S&L scandal. Poor bastard, hasn't finished above the line since. Jerry proposed some harebrained rule change called the *dh*: a moron, what can I say? Calvin, the ballclub is the only business he has, been in the family 50 years. With the big bucks running the game now he can't stay competitive. The leagues need to compensate the smaller markets to keep them in the running, but whenever I bring it up in meetings those turds change the subject.

"But I digress." Sweetwater cleared his throat. "Your challenge is not with me. I'm easy. But you're going to face some heat from Mr. McGonigle and from your teammates. If I even put in a word for you, they'll view it as front-office interference. They don't tell me who to sign and I don't tell them how to play baseball. Good luck with them. We need you; we can't win it without you. And my son—I offer you my deepest condolences on your dream that didn't come true."

"Oh, Mr. Sweetwater—sir. Mah dreams will come true, jist as sure as yours will and those two empty shelves over there will be occupahed come next month. Ms. Clitorea Pearl has convinced me that Ah need to give Anloie some space, and Ah cain't go forcin' mahself on her and make her decisions for her. So Ah've come up with this ahdea, and Ah cain' t do it without your help. But when you hear it, Ah know you will lahke it. Because it's good for you, sir, and it's good for the Mutants, it's good for mah teammates, and most of all it's good for mahself."

When Whizzo told Sweetwater his idea, the owner's eyes lit up under their bushy canopies like phosphorescent dinoflagellates in bottomless rotund nights.

"I like it," said Wellington P. Sweetwater, pressing the spigot twice again. "You're on, my boy, you're on."

◆ ◆ ◆ ◆

"Your name Anloie?" asked the deliveryman. He held a dozen long-stemmed roses.

"It is."

"Sign here."

The greeting began:

Rosses for my sweat red rose. Tommorow Ah'll win No. 16; were only 11 out. The miracel will come to pass . You were raght as usule Honeybunch when Ah returned Ah felt real bad about leaveing mah teamates. Less'n we win it all Ah will feel unwurthy of your love, do you notise Ah am rispecting your wishes and keping mah distants.

Twenty-two pages later, it concluded:

Im exited, affraid, pacient, prayerfull, compationate tender, blissfull, confussed and FULL OF LOVE! —W.

Had Cygnus the Swan, winging by at astronomical speeds overhead as Maxwell Veribushi made his clandestine way to the Loosh mansion once again, shrunk by about a hundred light years, it would have relished the morsel Maxwell bore in the Mason jar in his right hand: Nevermore, *Rana onca celebre.*

◆◆◆ ◆◆◆ ◆◆

Carrying Nevermore over the wall was too risky: Maxwell might drop the jar. He had brought with him an acetylene torch and a pair of heavy-duty wire clippers, the kind he had carried to snip open cattle fences back in the days when he had roamed the range with Cactus Ed. Sooner or later the Looshes would discover their gate violated—but, unless they inventoried their amphibian stock daily, they'd have a hell of a time figuring out why.

Though silent enough for human ears, Maxwell went not undetected. A killdeer, its slumbers disturbed, cried out as if from a bad dream. Maxwell froze. Then he lit his torch. The hinges were even weaker than he thought: in ten minutes he had burned and snipped his way through.

A mongrel trotting down the street spied the intruder and began calling hysterical attention to him: ARFARFArfArfArf! ARFARFArfArfArf! Why don't you go defend your own property, Maxwell thought, and let the neighbors take care of themselves? The dog was apparently well-known and respected in the hood, and soon the rooftops rang, the poop-filled lawns reverberated with canine braggadocio, a sound which to Maxwell compared with the shrieks of Nevermore's Last-of-the-Big-Band kin, which he intermittently discerned above the uproar melding into jazz riffs with the crickets, as did Don Ho and Ice-T to Beethoven: dogs were devolution at work.

As far as Maxwell could see through the gnarled thicket that lay between him and the house, no lights went on. He waited long and patiently for the din to subside. "C'mon, Nevvy," he said at last, slipping inside and heading toward the pond.

Suddenly all hell broke loose. The entire compound lit up like Las Vegas. As the lights blinked on and off, sirens that had been lying in ambush for years with the patience of ticks began whooping and screaming in a frenzy of excitement. "We GOT you, o-O-oh! We GOT you, o-O-oh! We GOT you, o-O-oh!"

If Maxwell could only get to the pond before he was caught...He sprinted like Michael Johnson would sprint if he had just held up a 7-11 store, until he got a soaker. He stopped and impulsively kissed the Mason jar. "Goodbye Nevermore, and good luck."

Before he could unscrew the lid, a gunshot rang out.

"Come out with your hands up." The voice was so weak and tremulous that Maxwell momentarily debated ignoring it. But only momentarily.

"I'm coming. Don't shoot." Under the half-light of Cygnus and the milky moon, just four days old and hanging upside down in the sky like a ripening papaya, he saw a small, stooped figure wearing what looked like seersucker pyjamas. In these days of semi-automatics at every bedside, the old man brandished an ancient double-barreled shotgun.

He was almost hairless. Nonetheless, dandruff piled up on his hunched-over shoulders like snowdrifts on the Canadian Rockies.

Good Gaia, could this be Chairman Lewis? He must be 99 years old by now.

A very old woman dressed only in her slip ran out the door behind him, followed by another one wearing about 16 sweaters. "Fourth of July! Fourth of July!" shrieked the first as she headed for the gate.

"No Emily, come back inside," said the second, catching the first by her slip and leading her back.

The nonagenarian motioned Maxwell inside, into a large room with a single barebulb light. Maxwell felt like he had entered a museum. The saucers on the floor with milk for cats, or maybe for rats, were worth probably $500 each. The walls were lined with leather-bound books. Tinny music played softly on an old victrola:

Tiny bubbles
in the wine
Make me happy
Make me feel fine

Spread across the room like drapes before a paint job was a carpet of dust so thick and soft and comforting that Maxwell wondered whether Chairman Lewis slept under it.

For Chairman Lewis it was. He sat in a stuffed leather chair aiming the blunderbuss at Maxwell. Even at the ten feet that separated them, the mildew pungence from his pyjamas was unmistakable. The two old women paraded in and stood beside him, one in her slip, one in her sweaters.

"Don't shoot him, Meriwether," said the second, buttoning her top sweater.

"I'll handle this, Sadie. Call the police."

"Police! Police! Bad boy! Bad boy!" shrieked Emily. She cackled and ran out of the room.

"Sinbad Security," said Sadie. "Remember? The police are already coming." Outside, the carnival of sights and sounds continued, while *R. oncas* danced down the main stage and barked games on the midway that only frogs can bark. If Ngaio XV^{14} +34, perched precariously aloft in his panoramic cubicle atop Maxwell's upstretched hand, harkened to the revels of his erstwhile companions, he didn't let on.

"Turn off the alarm, Sadie," said Meriwether Lewis (no, not *the* Meriwether Lewis). Sadie left.

Suddenly he sat bolt upright, peering at Maxwell over the barrel of his shotgun. "Young man. Haven't I seen you somewhere before?"

"I don't believe so, sir," Maxwell lied.

His captor grew livid. "Don't dissemble with me, Professor Veribushi. Yes, I remember. You corrected my pronunciation in front of Dean Martin. 'Clit-*or*-is'. It's in Webster's Dictionary. Looky there." Chairman Lewis' Webster's rested on a stand next to Maxwell. 'Variant pronunciation of *clit*-or-is'." He hissed out the 'clit' like he was spitting out a watermelon seed. "What do you think of that?"

Maxwell read the pronunciation. He couldn't answer. He had a frog in his throat.

Waving his weapon unsteadily, Chairman Lewis picked up an academic publication from his desk. "'With frogs, the sperm comes *after* conception, before the eggs hatch. Is this the beginning of one life, the end of another? If, as the Creationists believe, there is life after death, then it follows that there is also life before birth: herebefores as well as hereafters. This places Creationism where it belongs: in the same boat as reincarnation. In fact, the beginning is the end for nearly all of the eggs: in general only the fittest survive'. Written by Dr. Maxwell Veribushi. Now really, Professor, just what sort of nitwit claptrap is this you're espousing? This hero of yours, Darwin—danged fool went and got himself a frog named after him. Know what that danged frog does?"

Maxwell's voice returned, along with his unfortunate habit of resisting authority—any authority, even the authority of a lethal weapon pointed at him. "He substitutes 'danged' for 'damned' and tells himself it isn't a sin?"

Fortunately Chairman Lewis was too busy answering his own question to hear. "No sooner does the father frog fertilize the eggs than he slurps them up and they hatch into tadpoles and grow into froglets—all in his belly, before he regurgitates them back out."

"Actually, two different Australian frogs do—or did—that," Maxwell compulsively corrected. "*Rheobatrachus vitallinus* and *R. silus*—now extinct. GON-N-N-G! The male *Rhinoderma darwini,* found in Chile if any are left to be found—GON-N-N-G!—broods in its vocal sac and spits the tads out."

"And that," said Chairman Lewis, "is not evilution. What a narrow, manmade concept your evilution is. That's the Great Imagination."

Maxwell's personal survival apparatus finally made an appearance, peering through binoculars for common ground. There it was: go for it. "Yes, the Dream."

"No, young man, it's not a dream. It's Reality."

Reality, thought Maxwell, is relative. A long time had passed since anyone had called him 'young man'. Again his rebel KO'd his survivor. "Reality is a set, Dr. Lewis. That's as in psychological *set.* As in movie *set.* As in mathematical *set.* Evolution works in mysterious ways its wonders to unfold."

"Well sir, if the fittest survive, you're unfit. Because you know what? I'm going to blow your head off." Chairman Lewis half-swung, half-rolled the shotgun until it pointed directly at Maxwell's knees. "What do I have to worry about? I'll probably croak before the trial."

Maxwell fought down panic. "Remember the Bible, sir," he pleaded. "'Thou shalt not kill'."

Chairman Lewis paused and frowned. "Your manhood then. The Bible doesn't say, 'Thou shalt not splatter the family jewels of Satan's

agents all over that wall'." With all his strength, the old man lifted the barrel.

"Don't..." Maxwell closed his eyes and, even though his deity, unlike that of his antagonist, was not the type to beseech for personal favors, he prayed to S/HeIt.

The room became a reverberation chamber for the shotgun's blast.

Charley Orange had an old college buddy who lived in a nearby suburb. Maybe the guy could post bail for him. "When do I get to make my phone call?" he asked.

"After you're booked," said his chauffeur. "We'll be back to make sure you get it." Igor laughed.

All the cells were full—"too much jigaboos, hippie faggots, drug fiends," Igor told Charley. An orderly threw a mattress on the floor for him.

Once he was booked, Charley never saw Igor and friend again. Finally he called to the booking sergeant. "Sir? How do I get to make my phone call?"

The sergeant did not look up from his paperwork. "Pay phone's right there on the wall. Just put your coins in and dial whoever you want."

"I can't. You took all my money."

"Just put your coins in. We don't pay for the call, you do. Just put your coins in and dial whoever you want."

"I have to get out of here," Charley pleaded. "It's very important." The sergeant continued writing.

Somewhere in a parallel universe, the bars dissolved and Charley got to shake the son of a bitch until the coins regurgitated out of his arrogant mouth. Here there was only the wish, and the anxiety and frustration. Wasn't it enough for the Mutes to suffer the trauma of Whizzo Mark Salot IV disappearing?—and now him! He, Charley Orange, who in 17 years in organized baseball had never missed a game or even been late to batting practice. Guilt and Remorse, those twin tweedledum and tweedledee packhorses of grief, gnawed holes in his heart like rats turning Tillamook into Swiss cheese. Due to circumstances beyond his control, he would be responsible for the team temper degenerating from anger/betrayal to fear/insecurity: what could happen next? He understood the story of Job: Why me, S/HeIt?

On the plus side, his athletic exploits would be missed less than Whizzo's. But Throttlemeyer was hurting. Moreover, teamwork is made up as much of intangibles as performance, and Charley's bench role as Foo Foo McGonigle's student and confidante, the quiet assurance that rested in his demeanor, and his patience and clarity as mentor and strategist, made him a vital cog in the Mutant machine.

He could blame only his own desperation for ever getting mixed up with Clitorea Pearl in the first place. How low could he sink, wooing a glorified hooker? Why not a librarian? That was more his style. Or, if he could dream, a nurse...

Rr-r-i-i-n-n-g-g-g! It was the phone on the sergeant's desk. —No, it was the pay phone. —No, wait: it was both of them. They were the same line! As the sergeant began talking, Charley answered the pay phone and launched into a filibuster. "Hello, I'm sorry to interrupt but my name is Charley Orange and I'm being held here without receiving my Constitutional right to make a phone call and it's very important that I post bail and get out so I'm not going to stop talking until someone..."

The voice on the other end chuckled, undoubtedly visualizing the scene unfolding in the jail: Wearily, the sergeant set down the phone, rose, opened the main gate, opened a cell gate, grabbed Charley by his collar and the seat of his pants, tossed him inside the cell, locked the cell gate, locked the main gate, returned to his desk, sat down, picked up the phone and resumed his conversation.

"Dude," said a kid with a pink Mohawk. "What you in for?"

"Being in the wrong place at the wrong time. You?"

"Fishing with an unattended pole. They brought me in Friday a.m. and set bail at $14K. It's a holiday weekend; I can't see a judge before Tuesday the earliest."

Labor Day, thought Charley. Again he was reminded: 8 behind, 24 to go. Even if I got out this minute, I'd have to get Whizzo's car out of impound, drive 200 miles to the airport and catch an immediate flight to Megaglopoulis to make the game on time. Why, oh why didn't I stop her from driving off?

"See that Rasta mon there?" Mohawk gestured toward a black giant with long, matted dreds and Orphan Annie eyes. "He's the badass on the block. Did two in San Quentin for armed robbery."

"What are you here for now?" Charley asked the Rasta.

"I's a homicidical maniac. Don' fall 'sleep 'round me."

Mohawk giggled. "He was riding a bicycle on the sidewalk."

"Mon, don'tze go put oud dat zhit. I god imazhe, keep de imazhe. Don' be puddin' my ashe in eah 'fore I be doin' summun, 'ere? Ish u-mil-i-a-zhun."

"I don't belong here either," Charley blurted out. "I'm not a criminal. If I hadn't let Clitorea Pearl..."

"Hey, none of us done it, dude," Mohawk laughed. "And we was most of us done in by the ladies, the bitches, the whores, cunts, gashes—hey, but ain't they doorways to heaven with trouble wrapped all around them like three-headed dogs? But Clitorea Pearl: Now there's a calling card. Ain't many of them read like that."

The cuckoo in Warren's clock began the countdown with the excitement of a dog greeting its long-lost master: soon it would get to ride out into the light and announce itself eight times before being locked back up behind the face of Time for another hour. Anloie, wearing Warren's white bathrobe and slippers and holding hibiscus in hand, scurried down the stairs to answer the doorbell. Not again, she thought.

A uniformed courier handed her a vase with a dozen long-stemmed roses, a cellophane packet containing a lock of flaming orange hair and a 28-page handwritten *billet-dous.*

Anloie smiled wanly. "Thank you." What to do with all these items? Warren would just not understand. And she—did she want to read 28 more pages of misspelled words? She put the letter in her frisbee pouch to think upon it: maybe, maybe not.

She looked at the velvet crimson folds of the roses. A thought leaped into her mind that made her blush; quickly she banished it. Poor flowers! —they were too lovely to be sacrificial victims in this frenetic game Whizzo was playing. She plucked them from the vase, clipped the stems and placed them in the freezer with the others, chipping away some ice with a knife to close the door. Warren would never look there; he didn't cook and he ate food at room temperature only.

The lock of hair: she held it in her hand and crossed to the wastebasket. Before she tossed it, she brought it to her nose and sniffed its fragrance. "Goodbye, Whizzo," she thought and dropped it in, there to meet its ignominious fate among molding dinners, rancid avocado flesh and other offalous festerings. Warren didn't empty the garbage either, but just to be sure she covered the lock with denuded corn cobs and black potatoes. Phew! She would have to remove the entire quagmire before breakfast.

At the top of the stairs she stopped by the mirror. Last night on the tube she and Warren had watched a documentary about ancient Egypt. If churches were phallic symbols, she thought, removing the bathrobe, then surely pyramids are homages to the breast. Reaching under her negligee, she pushed Fujiyama gently up and in, trying to see what it would look like as a full-fledged pound of flesh. Of course it would be even bigger, and perpetually firm and erect…and so would lovely Kilimanjaro, so perfect as it already was. Well hey, she thought, there must be worse things to get used to than big tits.

As she draped the bathrobe across the chair by the bed, a single strand of red hair clung to its whiteness. Now surely Warren wouldn't notice one lone hair. Would he?

Warren was hypnogogic when she climbed back into bed. "M-mmh. Who was that?" he mumbled.

"Nobody. Go back to sleep." She patted his shoulder. Soon he was making sounds a frog might make, were it of human heft.

◆ ◆ ◆ ◆

Having safely delivered Whizzo Mark Salot IV to Mutant Stadium, Clitorea Pearl sat in her kidney-shaped tub soaking in a frangipani bubble bath, recovering from her journey with a glass of Moet Chandon, treating her yoni to a jacuzzi jet massage and listening to—no, not Mozart, nothing more soothing like Debussy or Deuter—none of these, but her answer machine. The tape was full; no telling how many messages she had lost. Two couples wanting pleasuring instruction, a half-dozen single clients, both sexes, a half-dozen lovers, ditto, all looking forward to sessions ASAP...Clitorea sighed. Things piled up so quickly, being away for even a day. When would feel-good loving catch on in the general population so she could take some time for herself?

The next message brought her to a sit-up position. "Miz Clitorea, this is Whizzo Mark Salot IV. Ah'm sorry to disturb you, but Charley Ahwrnge has not showed up at the ballpark yet. You and Ah saw him together up to Anloie's last naght, so maybe he's still there, or maybe she knows where he is. But if'n Ah follow your advahse, Ah dasn't call up there. Hain't that so? Would you be willin' to make that call? And jist tell Anloie Ah love her. No pressure, raght? Here's the number..."

The next message stirred her to action. "Ah jist thought it over and Ah realize Ah wouldn't be callin' Anloie to talk about our love for each other. So Ah guess hit's all raght if'n Ah call her mahself, soon's Ah get home where it's quahet. Thanks for listenin'. 'Naght."

Clitorea called Whizzo's hotel room immediately. "Yes, it is pressure," she told his machine; "let me call." Then she called Anloie.

"You don't know me," she said. "My name is Clitorea Pearl. I was at your house last night with Charley Orange to get Whizzo Mark Salot IV off your back, and now Charley..."

Anloie's voice was on Third Stage Alert. "Where did you get my number?"

"I got it from Whizzo."

"Oh no! Where did he get it?"

"I don't know."

"Ms. Pearl, that man is pure crazy. What am I supposed to do with all these roses in my freezer? My boyfriend says I should get a restraining order, what do you think? —Though I am sorry Whizzo's in jail. He sent me a 28-page letter. Just listen to this..."

"Jail? Whizzo's not in jail."

"He is! The police just came and hauled him away out of my front yard last night. Unless he's out already. Did you say you were here too?"

"I was. Let me guess. You didn't actually get a good look at Whizzo, but the man they arrested was in his car, right?"

"I saw him all right. He came to my door and I talked to him. It was Whizzo."

Clitorea deferred explanation; she was curious to learn how Anloie felt about Whizzo's incarceration. She switched to the topics women new to each other use to get acquainted so easily. While Charley Orange and his new companions ate their lunch of reconstituted swamp stew washed down with machine-oil coffee, filling the empty spaces between them with stares into the distance punctuated by sports palaver and narrations of fictional sexual conquests, Clitorea told Anloie how to preserve roses with lemon water. Anloie explained how the roses got into the freezer. Clitorea clucked understanding and maternal support. Anloie, whose own mother had been largely missing in action during her formative years, opened her heart and her tear ducts to this soothing telephone presence. Soon she was reading her Whizzo's latest outpouring, all 28 pages of it. Clitorea, whose life was devoted to cultivating such love wherever it sprouted, asked questions that reminded Anloie of why she had loved Whizzo. Of why she still loved him, if she cared to admit it, but she could never live with him: he was just a wild kid, too impulsive, too off-the-wall.

"But please don't let him stay in jail," Anloie implored. "I feel responsible. I know he's a bit crazy, but he isn't a criminal: he's just

in love." The thought of Whizzo as an outlaw caused an inappropriate turnover in her love engine.

More girl talk followed. Clothes. Sizes. Envy of each other's proportions. Meanwhile the County brought Charley Orange a treat for dessert: cowpie brownies.

"Anloie dear, Whizzo's not in jail. It was another player driving his car. When we finish talking, I have to call the ballpark so they can arrange his release."

The news that Whizzo was still at large jump-started Anloie's batteries again. Where was Warren? She wanted to make love.

Bluster Hyman scrutinized the announcement of the media conference again. One sentence stood out: "A surprise will be unveiled regarding the Whizzo Mark Salot IV situation." Had the prodigal son returned to the fold?

Walking under the stands toward the media room, he ran into Wellington P. Sweetwater, with Lulu on one arm and another blonde, who might have been Lulu's sister, on the other. Sweetwater was beaming like a new grandfather. Bluster knew what that meant. "Whizzo's back, isn't he, Wellington?"

"We'll tell you the latest developments in the Salot situation in twenty minutes." Sweetwater's eyes wiggled and danced like a man at a public urinal trying to keep the last three drops from going into his pants.

"Wellington, come on, I'm on your payroll. It's in your financial interest to tell me."

"Not this time, Bluster. This one is for the world. You're gonna love it!" And then Wellington P. Sweetwater and company were gone, leaving only an echo of backroom giggles and a vapor cloud of knockoff perfume.

Burly as he was, Bluster had to exert himself to force his way into the media room. He recognized faces from every city on the circuit, as well as all the big nationals.

Burly as he was, Bluster was not tall, and from his back-row standing-room seat he muttered a curse at his boss for not giving him the story. A buzz went through the room like a bee caught in a spiderweb as the door opened and four figures strode into the room. He could see only the hair on four heads. The first was as white as a new baseball: Wellington P. Sweetwater. The second looked like it had been through too many wash/dry cycles: Foo Foo McGonigle. The third was as red as a flock of cardinals preening in the carnation blossoms along Cherry Street: Whizzo Mark Salot IV. The fourth was graying and looked female. Was that a beanie she was wearing?

As if they represented the masses in baseball Congress and got to tell the Commissioner how many jackrabbits to put into the ball, rather than merely chronicling the deeds and misdeeds of their heroes, the members of the Fourth Estate arose as one and applauded the return of the Lost Savior.

"Ladies and gentlemen," began Wellington P. Sweetwater, "the Megaglopoulis Mutants are pleased to announce that Whizzo Mark Salot IV is back with the team, following some urgent family business that required immediate resolution. Mr. Salot has requested that the particulars remain private and we request that you respect Mr. Salot's tender years and wishes and not pursue the matter with him. In return, he has a story for you that dwarfs anything you can hope to dig up. But first, if you have any questions for Mr. McGonigle or me..."

"Foo Foo, we know how you and the team felt about Whizzo's disappearance. How do you feel about his return?"

"Well, this here what we're in here for, it's a race for the flag, and nobody's getting the flag without they're sending some mighty good horses to the hill. So we been coming at it from behind from the start and then our horse run off what's more—which is the kind of odds you don't want them to be ridin' on your back down the stretch with you, namely 100-1 is what I hear. And at 100-1 it figures that my ballplayers was feeling as how the odds was agin' us. And now this young bungee here is back here from wherever he went don't matter none to me, and any hard feelings between them has been sublimated,

and anybody from the batboy on down, we just want to get some juice back in their prunes and play ball."

"Foo Foo, you're 8 games off the pace with only 24 left. If you win 20 of those, the Lemon Sox still only need to play .500 ball to back in. Can the Mutes still capture the marbles?"

"We're down from a couple teams up from us in the standings, that's natural when you're not in first place. But baseball bein' a crap shoot, and I ain't sayin' my boys ain't as fulla crap as the next team, but you know what I mean. We're in there hittin' and pitchin' and runnin' every day, and the chips are gonna fall. Nothin' ain't over yet. And especially what ain't over yet is them seven games that ain't over with the Lemons."

"How about you, Whizzo? You think you guys can win?"

"Ah don't thank, Ah know. Sir, we have to win. Ah owe it to mah teammates. Ah owe it to the fans of Megaglopoulis, after leavin' 'em hagh and drah lahke Ah did. And most of all Ah owe it to mah brahde-to-be. Ah done told mahself Ah wouldn't marry her until Ah done throwed the Mutants to the pennant. Sincet Ah cain't live without her, mah teammates and Ah, we all jist have to capture that there flag."

Inside Bluster's head wheels took to whirring and, in unconscious sympathy with the weird-looking woman's beanie, spinners took to spinning. It was only last week the Boy of a Thousand Bedrooms had popped the question. And now "pressing family business"? Had Whizzo eloped? Now, there was a story. But what's to be secret about? Especially Whizzo; it wasn't his style to be silent about anything. Besides, where's the bride? Hm, had they broken up? No, Whizzo had just called her his "brahde-to-be." So what the hell was going on? Whizzo's announcement had better be good enough to dwarf whatever he and Sweetwater were hiding, or some of these guys would get investigative. Like Bluster himself, for one.

Questions rang out. "Where is the lucky woman, Whizzo?" "Have you set the date?" "Is that the bride's mother beside you?"

"Our weddin' day is September 25, the fahnal day of the season. Ah figure the race could come down to the wahre, and thass mah day to throw. And no, Anloie's mother has done traded in her human vehicle for a different model. This here is Ladye Hannah Aura. She's the psahchic lady who's helping it to all come about."

Ladye Hannah Aura *namaste'd.* Then she hoisted her water glass as if she were giving a toast. "Greetings magical/mystical children and fellow plyers of the scrivener's trade. I'm Whizzo's minister and consultant on the blessed event. I'm here to announce that September 25..." —from out of her pocket she produced a kazoo, upon which she tootled a fanfare— "...September 25 is the Five Billionth Birthday of the World, also yclept Gaia. On that day Whee! the people will be up for Contact Renewal. When we lost herstory to history, we sacrificed mystery to mastery. The nuptials will orchestrate an ancient cadence and resurrect the epithalameon, updated to the beat of Spiritual Drummers, Players, Dancers and Singers for a planetary nation and extra-galactic reunion of the Universal Federation. So my fellow Coopetitors in the Cosmic/Human Pennant Race, let's all wear our Union Suits on that day so we can graduate from Tranced Humanity to Transhumanity.

"September 25 is presided over by the Queen of Hearts: the ruler of fecundity and fertility. What better day for a planet's birthday or a couple's handfasting? The celestial alignment concurs: The sun is in Libra and the moon is full in Aries. Libra is the sign of balance: come September 25 and all's right on our wondrous mother earthan spaceship. Moon in Aries announces the dawning of the Nu-Clear Vision, the rebirth of the planetary soul. Fellow earthlings, awake!

"For the lovers: Moon in Aries: a time to put feeling above thought, a time for optimistic undertakings of plans that others see as impossible. Sun in Libra: a blessed time; Libra, ruled by Venus, is the sign of marriage. And September 25 Venus is in Scorpio, portending a lifetime of intense sexual fulfillment and commitment to the proposition that love is worth all challenges. Scorpio..."

Bluster Hyman's brow was already too knitted to knit, so he double-stitched it. This was the Big Story that would make everyone forget Whizzo's absence? The five billionth birthday schtick was OK, but where in all this star-fraught mumbo-jumbo were the quotable quotes, the five-second sound bytes? Had this overripe melon on the New

Age vine no clue as to what makes the media go round? "Whizzo!" he and three colleagues interrupted at once. "Where's your bride?"

"She ain't here today. All raght, y'all ready for mah big surprahse? We are going to tahe the knot raght here in Mutant Stadium, on the field, and ever'body in the whole world is invahted—even y'all gahs and gals. Hit'll be on the television and the radio, and we are makin' us a movie and showin' it all over the world. Hit'll be an inspiration to ever'body who ever sees it, that love is the most powerful force in all the Creation."

"Six billion people are invited to this event?" asked an unbelieving photographer.

"Whizzo has bought up all 14,000 unsold seats for that day," said Wellington P. Sweetwater. "He's reserving 2,000 for orphans and for deaf, blind and crippled children."

"The rest are free," said Whizzo; "first come, first served, limit four to a party. Ever'body else, we'd love to have y'all on the TV, on the radio, in the moviehouses—hit's gonna be beamed on satellite all over the world."

Within seconds, all the phone lines to the Mutants box office were jammed, and they stayed jammed until long after all the tickets were gone.

"After we say 'Ah do', we'll hold the reception raght there on the field. Ah'm axing all the great musicians and performers to come help with the festivities: Hank Williams Jr., Madonna, Snoop Dogg, Cameron Diaz, Mahchael Jordan, Mahchael Johnson, Stevie Vah, Busta Rhahmes, Ricky Martin, Li'l Kim, Carmen Electra, Maha, Johnny Depp, M.C. Hammer, Leila Ali, Sean Penn, Britney Spears, Picabo Street, Gwyneth Paltrow, DMX, Drew Barrymore, Moon Unit Zappa, Wayne Gretzky, Jello Biafra, Brad Pitt, Demi Moore, Bruce Willis, the Spahce Girls, Halle Berry, Julia Roberts, Pump Daddy, Jon Bon Jovi, Babyface, Jewel, Jim Carrey, Tracy Chapman, the Beastie Boys, Monica Seles, Monica Lewinsky, kd laing, Howard Stern, Andre Agassi, Jay-Z, Natassja Kinski, Julia Butterfly, Janet Jackson, Sting, Eddie Murphy, Nicole Kidman, Heather Graham, Alec Baldwin, Nicholas Cage, Peta Wilson, Lauryn Hill, Ashley Judd, Naomi Judd, L.L. Cool Jay, Christina Aguilera, Sandra Bullock, Ahce Cube, Elizabeth Hurley, Jennifer Lopez,

Kate Beckinsdale, Heather Locklear, TLC, Ziggy Marley, Antonio Banderas, Googoosh, Marahah Carey, Patricia Arquette, Cuba Gooding Jr., Angelina Jolie, Anna Kournikova, Erykah Bader, Brandy, Leonardo di Caprio, Hugh Grant, Meg Rahan, Kate Moss, Queen Latifah, Missy Elliot, Darryl Cherney, Uma Thurman, Parker Posey, Cindy Crawford, Dr. Dre, Minnie Drahver, Paula Poundstone, Cate Blanchett, Don Johnson, Kevin Spacey, Helen Hunt, Catherine Zeta-Jones, Naomi Campbell, Mahchael J. Fox, Ewan MacGregor, Carrot Top, Lance Bass, Winona Rahder, Mel Gibson, Tahger Woods, Gwen Stefani, Christina Ricci, Hope Davis, Garth Brooks, Reese Witherspoon, Ellen De Generes, Adam Sandler, Claudia Schiffer, Courtney Love, Faith Hill, Claire Forloni, Neve Campbell, Kiefer Sutherland, Jennifer Love Hewett...and thass jist the beginning."

Wellington P. Sweetwater added a guest list of his own that included Dennis Rodman, Prince Charles, Annie Sprinkle, Muhammad Ali, Screamin' Jay Hawkins, Spike Lee, Cher, Michael Douglas, Wolfman Jack, Oprah Winfrey, Tom Hanks, Pamela Anderson, Bob Dylan *et fils,* Michael Jackson (*et fils?*), George Foreman, Bill Gates, Dr. Ruth, Donald Trump, Vanna White, Barry Manilow, Hugh Hefner, Willie Nelson, Dolly Parton, Rush Limbaugh, Taj Mahal and Little Richard. Good golly, Miss Molly was even there too.

As Whizzo continued his litany of still more pop luminaries, Sweetwater sat beaming like a signal from SETI. Next to a loaf of bread, a jug of wine and Lulu, her sister, Pamela Anderson, Dolly Parton, Britney Spears and Li'l Kim beside him swinging in his hot tub, Whizzo's wedding drama was the best thing he could imagine. This was the way it was done. Great baseball wedded to great promotion. Here was a kid after his own heart. Behind the table he surreptitiously tapped out a 3/4 beat on his wooden lingam. How sweet it was!

"Whizzo, when do we get to meet the bride?"

"September 25, and not a day before," said Whizzo. "On account of at the tahme bein' she's off livin' with some other gah, and she says she don't want to never see me again. So what Ah'm sayin' is nobody (cept'n me) can be absolutely sure she will appear until she actually shows up at the stadium on our weddin' day."

◆◆◆ ◆◆◆ ◆◆

If silence were a housecat, it would have lost seven or eight lives, so suddenly, from such a lofty height, did it fall. Bluster Hyman's breath actually stopped. The same thoughts ran through his mind as everyone else's: Big story? This it was, all right. Running it involved a certain amount of cruelty. Christ, the kid was only 18 years old. But the only alternative to running it was not running it. And that was out of the question: everyone else would.

"Whizzo, your—ah, fiancee, she's with another man? And she's not speaking to you?"

"Thass God's own truth. However, Ah intend to keep her informed of our plans, and as soon as y'all tell the world she'll know all about the weddin'. It's better if'n Ah don't speak directly to her at this tahme. She jist has some matters to clear up in her mahnd first."

Again the insides of Bluster's head began agitating like a scene from *Modern Times*. "Your—uh—bride-to-be, Whizzo? She's the one who was with you on that Sports Central interview?"

"Yeah, thass her! Thass Anloie."

"Doesn't she live with this frisbee coach over on the coast?"

"They're both jist lukewarm, Bluster. They deserve more, both of them. Listen—Ah'd lahke to make a personal statement to her raght here and now, if'n y'all don't mahnd. Sweetpea—honeypot. This is your Whizzo talking, your one and only duckie-pah. Now hear me out, darlin'. Ah'm arrangin' the biggest weddin' that ever was, jist for you and me, at the Stadium on September 25, thass the day Ah pitch the Megaglopoulis Mutants to the pennant. Sugarlips, Ah'm holdin' the love space for you. Ah'm invahtin' ever'body in the whole world to come be part of our love. Ah don't have tahme to tell you who all is comin' to sing and entertain and perform, but it's in the invitation Ah'm sendin' you."

Wellington P. Sweetwater was on his cell phone. "Wait, Whizzo," he said. "I've just received permission from the mayor and the Megaglopoulis city council to install 17,000 temporary bleachers and a 40-foot video screen in Parking Lot C. The Mutants ballclub will hire a fleet of buses to drive our fans from public lots beyond ours. With standing room in Lot C, we can accommodate another 47,000 people at the World's Largest Tailgate Party in the Mutant Stadium parking lot."

"And capacity in the ballpark, Mr. Sweetwater, is...?"

"Yeah! Y'all come!" Whizzo shouted into his microphone. "What a day it's gonna be! The Mutes take the marbles and Ah hold the grand-daddiest weddin' in the history of the universe, which is as it should be for the fahnest lady with the loveliest smahle and the sweetest, gentlest heart on the face of the good earth. Hit's absolutely historical."

"Whizzo," said Bluster Hyman, "I hate to shit in anyone's Easter basket, but..."

"C'mon y'all, cain't y'all jist see it? When mah sugarpah walks into that box seat, and when she walks down the ahsle from it and into mah waitin' arms, people will start weepin' tears of joy everywhere in the whole world. Our love will burst back into bloom lahke a beautiful rose and ever'body who sees us, their hearts will melt. Thank of the love bubble that will rahse up out of this ballpark and float over all of Creation. This is the gift Ah want to give to the fans, and to all the people ever'where who live with doubt or fear in their hearts."

Megaglopoulis Airport was not Clitorea Pearl's idea of a good time. And after spending 85 minutes negotiating the 17 miles there from her house, she had a few choice words to deliver to the dude who coined the phrase "rush" hour. Brakes on, brakes off. Hostile Chevy in the left lane. Stuck on the offramp when she was trying to go straight. Another 15 minutes up and down monoxide-filled parking garage aisles. Ah, must be the last spot in the house, only a short commuter's flight distance from the terminal. The shuttle was late. The shuttle was full. A 15-minute hike to Charley Orange's arriving flight gate. Bumped by suitcases, harrassed by solicitors, deafened by planes blasting off, nearly run over by maniacal trams, yelled at by a cop to use the crosswalk. Clitorea felt slickness where her arms rubbed her torso: not the type of bodily fluid she preferred to manufacture.

The arrival gate looked like a scene from a Cecil B. De Mille movie. You'd think it was Whizbang IV himself arriving, not just Charley Orange. Well, Charley Orange was all right in her book. He was on his way to becoming a fine fuck, and for a guy he was pretty bright, despite all his baloney about parallel universes. Clitorea, who before her chest had erupted and drawn all attention away from her other attributes was considered the smartest girl in the fifth grade, wasn't even sure about relativity. $E=mc^2$, OK fine, but how do you feed the numbers into the formula? Are they in metric or—how do you call it, American? What is e measured in: Watts? Joules? Calories? Horsepower? She preferred her own, simpler equation: e = ♀ + ♂.

An unsupervised toddler crashed full-speed into her legs. "Norman!" shouted his father. He reached to grab him, swinging his duffel bag off his shoulder and nailing her in the back. Oof! What was he packing, anvils? She prepared a remark, then smiled and accepted: she was on a mission of love. For whom else would she subject herself to the teeming *hoi polloi*? She also felt some responsibility for her role in Charley's misadventure. Poor Charley! She wanted to smother him with Mother love.

At last, coming out the tunnel, there he was. He looked like balsamic vinegar at a Wesson Oil party. He hadn't slept. He hadn't shaved. A worry line dug a Grand Canyon into his third eye.

When they kissed he wasn't present. What, was he pissed? Clitorea didn't like that: lighten up, Charley. You can choose love or fear, but love is the only choice for me. She told him what she endured to meet him, how badly she felt for him, how much she wanted to hold him, about the long drive home from Anloie's and the methods she had to resort to to get Whizzo Mark Salot IV to wake up…

"You had to do *what*?" Charley exploded.

"It's what I do, Charley," she replied testily. "Don't fall into your wounded act and go giving me shit about it. I brought him back."

"Yes, it's…what you do…" Charley fought to understand, but the Clydesdales of Suffering Past kicked out the still-wet bricks from the foundation of joy he was laying. The old heartache washed over him, spreading across his neural landscape like a sewage spill, clogging up the last rivulets through which the gurgling liquids of love could flow. He felt it as a circle of pain spinning around and around inside him, sparking parabolic boosts of energy that raised the pain level with each spin. His mind, following the process, was a spiral galaxy of holographic stars and planets, a hundred billion signals beaming out, "I don't understand!" Meanwhile his gizzard was tying itself up into full hitches. He ached for Her hand there; instinctively he substituted his own. The gasworks fired up.

Next came rage, like surf in a storm. She had exchanged fluids with him, made him feel special to a woman like he had never felt before, and..."I'm just another guy in your endless series of projects, aren't I? Part of your harem of glorified johns."

"That's right," said Clitorea. "Diminish yourself. Here, take the car. I'll catch a cab."

"No, I will. And fuck you!" He stormed off and hailed a taxi. What was love anyway but a Hyde in Jekyll clothing, rose petals that fell as you did onto a bed of thorns? It was a set of social conventions, an illusion, a bubble that pops after procreation. "Shove love!" he bellowed to the driver. "Mutant Stadium."

Shot lodged in the rafters and dust drifted down, dancing in the dim light like the ivory-clad moon danced outside on the waters of *R. onca*, as it settled as slowly and softly as snow onto Maxwell's Veribushiness.

Sadie hastened in from the kitchen, where she was quartering an olive for Meriwether, as Maxwell opened his eyes. "Dear, dear, what a racket," she clucked. "Are you all right? Look, he's fallen asleep. While we're waiting for the police, would you be so kind as to change a couple of light bulbs for us? This is the last one working in the house. None of us can do it except Meriwether, and he likes it as it is, says this bulb is going to outlast him, and that's all he cares about."

In the hours that it took for Megaglopoulis' finest to arrive, Maxwell also repaired two leaky faucets, re-wired a defective toaster and put shelves in a kitchen cupboard. He learned from Sadie that the Lewises Three had inherited the property from their father, who had gained it in a lesser-known sidebar to the Teapot Dome Scandal. They figured to set up a land trust to be administered by the County when they crossed the divide, but that was an unpleasant subject to dwell upon and they hadn't yet gotten around to it.

The County. The same County that built Mutant Stadium. Maxwell glanced at Nevermore, still sitting in his pellucid rotunda on Chairman Lewis' desk. Maybe he wouldn't turn him loose after all.

"Now you see this closet door?" asked Sadie. "The hinge is loose. Here's a screwdriver right here." She handed him a putty knife. "Are you cold, Mr. Veribushi? I'm going to get another sweater."

Maxwell was making slow but steady progress with the putty knife when the front door flew open and six wild banshees burst in with pistols drawn.

"FREEZE!"

Whizzo Mark Salot IV took plenty of heat in the clubhouse but he was of course reinstated, because, as he so succinctly put it, "We cain't win the flag without me. With me, we have to win."

"*Have* to?" exploded Lightnin' Larrabee. "We're 8 out with 24 left. If we're hot and they're not, we still have a prayer. Even if you're as great as you think you are, no one player…"

"That hain't what Ah'm sayin', Mr. Laghtnin'. We have to win because if'n we don't, Ah dasn't ax Anloie to marry me, and that will be the heartbreak of mah lahfe."

Foo Foo McGonigle fined Whizzo $5,000—a slap on the wrist, which Wellington P. Sweetwater deferred until next year—and handed him the ball to open against the Lemon Sox.

A bull wearing a red cape trots through an empty stadium, lord of all he surveys. Purple explosions; things wiggle and dance, enlarge and shrink. Metal monsters munch on new Cadillacs. *And gingko and garlic to vitalize and electrify your body, all for only $12 a month.* "Nine and one-half innings played," Bluster Hyman's voice announced over televisions in darkened bars and living rooms throughout the Megaglopoulitan area. "Nine and one-half exhausting, sweat-soaked at-bats and in-fields in the sweltering, muggy late-summer heat," his voice boomed into gridlocked cars throughout the city and suburbs. "Whizzo Mark Salot's usual pinpoint control has been an inch off and a dollar short this afternoon. He has held a thousand conversations with the baseball, a few of them so lengthy and animated that home plate umpire Rufus Wooster has intervened. Zapote Cheramoya is off-form for the Lemon Sox too, but with both teams' bullpens depleted, the starters are still in the game. And after 9 1/2 uniform-drenching innings at Mutant stadium both teams are back to Square One: it's Mutes 4, Sox 4. The line: Sox 4 runs, 10 hits, 6 walks, 7 strikeouts. That's the most free passes Whizzo has issued since his debut. Mutes 4, 7 and 3, also with 7 K's. The Lemons got to Whizzo early but he's settled down, allowing just one run, three hits and two walks since the fourth. The Mutes are playing long ball against Cheramoya, with two blasts from the rookie substitute Developed Smith and a solo shot by Charley Orange, his second in two weeks, to tie it in the sixth."

Charley figured Whizzo's erratic start was some sort of reflection of what he was going through in his head. The kid keeps telling Anloie he's leaving everything up to her because Clitorea Pearl said he shouldn't pressure her, then he lays his life on the line to her. No pressure there.

Whizzo, slated to lead off the tenth, approached Foo Foo McGonigle on the bench. "Skipper, sir, mah arm thrahves on hot weather, and hit's jist beginning to hit hit's strahde..."

"I know, I know," said Foo Foo. "All right, you stay right where you are and git yourself up to the plate. And git yourself on base on account of no one can pitch all day and night even if you want to before the hot melts all the icewater in your veins."

"Breaking ball low and away for Ball One," came Bluster Hyman's voice, catching up on the action after the commercials. "Whizzo is

batting for himself. What a much-needed rest he's giving the Mutant bullpen!

"Whizzo is batting .260 with two rainbows on the year: the first rookie southpaw Mutes hurler to go yard twice since 1937. He digs in as Cheramoya winds—delivers—and it's a line drive over Quesadilla's outstretched glove at short! The Wonder Boy delivers again! And the Whizzo Mark Salot IV Marching and Chowder Society sounds off in force: just listen to this stadium rock. That brings Bobaloo Boynton to the plate in a bunt situation. Beinvenidos Buenaventura and Poo Poo Perez are in at the corners.

"Boynton squares around and takes a strike on the inside corner. Bobaloo tops the circuit in sacrifice bunts by a right-handed leadoff batter with one strike on him, partly because Whizzo reaches base so often. But does Foo Foo McGonigle want to risk Whizzo sliding in this situation? Cheramoya into the stretch: *hit-and-run!* Boynton knocks a liner cleanly behind Whizzo into right! Whizzo, running with the pitch, should make third in time to send out for a Bug Light, sponsor of...*He hits the dirt!* For whatever reason, Whizzo Mark Salot IV has just executed a 20-foot slide into third base. Now he's jumping up and down on the bag with his hands in the air and shouting. Let's see if I can read his lips...looks like 'Hot dang, that felt good. Haven't had a chance to slahde in a whahle'.

"Listen to that crowd roar! That's Boynton's 48th opposite-field single this year, a new Mutant record for right-handers, and now Rufus Wooster halts play to hand the ball to the batboy to hold for Boynton. With Whizzo the winning run on third and no one out, the Lemon Sox are hanging on by a thread. They move the infield in, hoping to cut off the run at the plate. The situation calls for a pinch runner, but Whizzo is still in the game."

Revenge at Second Base stepped to the plate. Bobaloo Boynton stole second uncontested as Cheramoya, unconcerned with his run, worked from a windup.

Revige struck out. The crowd groaned.

Onions Malone stepped in. The crowd roared.

Malone struck out. What looked like a sure victory was slipping from the Mutants' grasp. It was up to the cleanup hitter, Matt "The Bat" Moseley.

"Moseley 4 for 11 lifetime with two gone and a runner on in game situations. Cheramoya winds," said Bluster Hyman, "and...*there goes Whizzo!* Cheramoya cuts short his kick, Moseley steps back from the box, Cajones is out to take the pitch, ball and runner arrive closer together than politician and payoff—*Whizzo's hand is on the plate! SAFE!*"

The ballpark exploded like a string of exuberant firecrackers that had been deprived of matches for too long. Grown men cried. In the broadcast booth, goosebumps ran down Bluster Hyman's body like frozen waterfalls. "Whizzo Mark Salot IV, the flame-throwing Bumpkin from Disfunction Junction, has just found yet another way to beat the front-running Lemon Sox. He steals home in the tenth inning! The first-ever theft of home by a Mutes pitcher in extra innings! Mutes win 5-4. Whizzo is now 15-4 and the Megaglopoulis Mutants refuse to be counted out of this race."

The Mutants swarmed out of the dugout like a hive of bees welcoming home a floozy queen after a three-day night on the town, surrounding Whizzo in a vortex of male bonding energy and hoisting him onto their shoulders. He was back in their good graces.

The police phalanx with their braided arms were treated as little sisters in a game of Red Rover, Red Rover by the army of fans surging onto the field to surround their heroes as they bore aloft their prize toward the dugout. The fans, too, forgave and forgot.

In the streets of Megaglopoulis, above the background din of internal combustion, car burglar alarms, howling dogs, boombox rap, wailing sirens and streetcorner prophets, car horns blared, announcing the momentous event to each other in peals of pushbutton joy.

Seven down; 23 to go. Pennant Fever was once again the reigning affliction in Megaglopoulis.

◆ ◆ ◆ ◆

A frog poses a more daunting scientific challenge than a star.
—Martin Rees

Maxwell Veribushi froze.

"Drop your weapon."

Very carefully, as if he were holding a scorpion by its tail, Maxwell extended the putty knife and laid it on the carpet.

"Did you see my sweater?" As Sadie entered the room, her eyes swept past the sextet of Megaglopoulis' finest to the open door. "Emily's loose!"

"Police, ma'am," said the cop in charge, as if in their badges and blue uniforms they might be mistaken for cub scouts.

"Really?" asked Maxwell. "What's new with Sting?"

"Is this the intruder, ma'am?"

"Well, yes, but he's such a nice young man."

Still another uniform entered, with Emily in tow. "Police! Police!" she shrieked. "Bad boy! Bad boy!"

"There's a corpse in the next room," said Emily's captor.

"What!" said Sadie. She hurried into the study. "Meriwether! Wake up! Someone's dead in here."

Yet another cop was in the study, shining his flashlight into Meriwether Lewis' undiluted, unseeing pupils. "He won't be waking up just yet, ma'am," he said. "He's the dead one." He took out his radio and sent a message to someone in the universal police language of Crackle.

"Put your hands behind your back," said the head cop to Maxwell. He was all of 25 and his voice sounded like, with training, it could hit high C. "There's a body in there and a gate off its hinges outside. You have the right to remain silent and anything you say may be held against you."

"*Rib'et! Rib'et!*" said Maxwell.

"Don't you worry, ma'am," the cop told Sadie as he handcuffed Maxwell. "His life of crime is over."

The homicide solved, the investigation adjourned to the study, where Meriwether Lewis still sat, his body half-slid out of his chair, his head and shoulders thrown back by the recoil of the shotgun. A fine layer of dust had settled on him, and motes of it pirouetted and plie'd through the musty air like galaxies unfolding their starry, spiral skirts and intertwining.

The devil, they say, exists only in the minds of those who believe he exists. (Just think of the ramifications of that for parallel universes.) If so, then Satan may be considered a romance of the imagination. In life, no one ever accused Meriwether Lewis of having too much imagination. In death, what Maxwell was to call a photograph of his imagination appeared on his face: his jaw was slack, his nose-hairs (the hair on his head having long ago scattered to the four winds) stood up like military recruits, and his eyes—his eyes, so wide and fearful did they shine, you could look into them and see the Horned One coming to carry him off.

Kines, wahinis
Okolehao
Aloha mahalo
Kealakahu...

Sadie walked over to the victrola and took Don Ho's needle away from him.

"Thought you could plant the gun on him and we'd fall for that?" the head cop squeaked, shaking his head back and forth. "Tch tch tch. You guys get dumber every day." His radio crackled assent.

"Don't be obtuse," said Maxwell. "I didn't shoot him. He tried to shoot me!"

"You mean you broke in and when he tried to defend himself, you shot him and put the weapon in his hands."

"He must have had a heart attack. Holy S/HeIt, did you guys get your badges from Crackerjack boxes? If I shot him, where's the bullet wound?"

A check of the mortal remains of Chairman Meriwether Lewis failed to yield any holes that were not filled with hair, wax or false teeth. Nor were there any bumps or contusions to suggest that Maxwell had clubbed him with the butt end of the shotgun. "The charge is reduced to breaking and entering," sighed Squeaky. "Sergeant, call the station."

◆◆◆ ◆◆◆ ◆◆

Crackles snapped and popped, shattering words into shards of letters that only police "Humpty Dumpty" decoders could put back together again. "OK fuzzball, let's go get you a haircut."

"Wait!" cried Sadie. "Who's going to finish my door?"

"Not him. You just told us he broke in."

"But he's the repairman! Of course he did! We never answer the door; it's not safe. How else could he get in?"

Squeaky paused and mulled that one over. When he spoke, his voice raised an octave. "I can't hold him unless you're willing to press charges."

"Oh good. Dear sir, will you be so kind as to finish the door? Afterward there's a bat in the attic."

"Lieutenant, sir?" said one of the cops to Squeaky, holding up Nevermore. "Look at what he has trapped in this bottle. We can charge him with cruelty to an animal."

"You dummy," said Squeaky. "That's not an animal. It's a frog."

"Thanks for the reprieve," said Maxwell to Sadie when they left. "Why did you do it?"

"Aren't you the repairman?" asked Sadie. "Oh dear, did you murder my brother?"

"No no no no no! I came here on...well, personal business." Dare he tell her? He needed time to think. "Wrong house, I...I'll just shoo the bat and be on my way."

"I see. My mind gets a little mixed up when I don't keep warm enough. As for Meriwether, his time was near anyway. Bad plumbing. It runs in the family; I have it too. Doctor says I could go tomorrow." For the first time, Maxwell took a good look at her. Under all those sweaters, she weighed no more than 80 pounds.

"It may be a sin to say it," Sadie continued, "but Meriwether wasn't the kindest of brothers anyhow. Now I can turn up the heat. Now I can order two-ply toilet paper. Hee-hee-hee." She grew pensive. "But it is a shame anyway. He had his good side too. When he found out about the frogs in the pond, he fought the City to keep from filling it in. They said it bred rats and mosquitoes. That's nonsense. The rats breed in the basement. Why didn't the City ask him to clean the basement?"

Maxwell could have done a double-take, had he taken anything in the first place. He could have choked on his drink or even fallen off his chair, had Sadie offered him either. In light of his good breeding and her twin *faux pas,* all that can be said is that he was startled. "Chair...ah, Mr. Lewis wanted to keep the frogs?"

"Oh yes. He said they were God's creatures. And I said, 'But aren't all of God's creatures God's creatures?' Well, what happened was that once long ago he had a row with a faculty member at Oral-Anal Roberts University, where he taught—a wretched, disagreeable person from what I surmise. He believed the Divine Creation was the undertaking of some English gentleman named Darvon or something; isn't that the most preposterous idea you've ever heard?

"Anyhow, the very next night a frog showed up in the kitchen, eating the catfood of all things. Well! Two frog incidents in two days. Meriwether saw it as a sign from above. He re-read the plague of frogs in Exodus and he concluded that God had chosen the frogs to be His agents. Probably they were venerated On High. Meriwether felt like he had a lifetime of judgment against them to undo.

"He studied frogs, quite compulsively, for at least a year. Turned out everybody thought those frogs in our back yard were extinct. He felt very protective of them, kept them a secret, installed the alarm system..."

The tragedy, thought Maxwell, even as the excitement spread through his body, was that he and Meriwether Lewis had held very close to a shared vision. Lewis thought the frogs had arrived here only six thousand-plus-change years ago and Maxwell dated them back 150 million years, but aside from that minor quibble about their birthday, the Chairman shared Maxwell's fervor to save them. Alas for Lewis, he could focus only on his and Maxwell's differences. As Maxwell gazed upon the coming of Satan in those frozen eyes, he acknowledged that he had been something of a little devil himself back in his days of academe. But that was a healthy response to the kind of oppressive systems practiced by such folks as Chairman Lewis. The proof? He, Maxwell Veribushi, was alive and as happy as a

beachball while Chairman Lewis, bless his constricted hide, had just heard the Fat Lady sing and departed on an off-key note.

Maxwell was looking at his greatest professional coup yet: rediscovery of a species that had supposedly gone the way of the dodo, free information calls, the dollar haircut and Burma Shave. Ten years ago he would have brought in a team of graduate students to take a census of the pond. Then he would write a monograph and receive accolades from exo-salientologists the globe around.

But nowadays he wanted none of it. He knew who the real hero was. He told Sadie the saga of Nevermore: how he had somehow survived hopping through a mile of inner-city Megaglopoulis (a feat not too many humans could guarantee pulling off)...well, the particulars must have embodied dramas that could never be known. He concluded with the events leading to his (Maxwell's) trespass onto the Lewis property. He suggested that the Nature Conservancy might afford the frogs better protection than a land trust administered by the very County that so unceremoniously sacrificed them to the gods of boyhood pastimes. Might she consider donating the land to the Conservancy instead?

"Why, that's a splendid idea!" said Sadie. "Only... Meriwether always handled those matters. I have no idea how to..."

"I'll take care of everything," said Maxwell, heading out the door toward the swamp to at last free poor Nevermore. "You can just sign the papers when I bring them. And maybe we can replace that gate with something more solid so nobody else can break in. And no more of the frogs will break out."

"And so Emily won't break...EMILY! Oh dear! Mr. Veribushi, can you...?"

The deliveryman smiled lewdly. "This seems to be the best time of day for this stop," he said, nodding toward the stairs, down from which Warren's snores tumbled like bolts of thunder being tossed by Thor's wife as she cleaned out the closet.

Anloie sighed. Once again did she trim stems to fit roses in the freezer. The fridge needed defrosting *now,* but what to do with its extra botanical contents? One more lock of hair did she deposit under last night's leftovers. One more epic letter did she start to toss, then file in her frisbee case for surreptitious later perusal.

When Warren arose, yesterday's red hair, still lingering on Anloie's bathrobe, hit him right between the eyes, but his mind's eye was still beaming in from a parallel universe. He saw it not—at least in any way that registered. And it wasn't until he opened the refrigerator and the freezer door fell off that he saw the roses.

He was not happy with Anloie's explanation. In his unhappiness he removed the roses and broke what remained of the stems over his knee, first with a growl and then with a yelp of pain as the thorns found virgin flesh to sacrifice to the gods of serration. That drew the unpleasantries to a close, as Anloie washed and bandaged him, cooed and cajoled him. For the nonce, Warren felt loved once more.

In the eighth inning the pot began to stir at Mutant Stadium. But it was nothing like the ninth inning, when all Heqt broke loose.

Ninth Inning

The nearer your destination
The more you're slip-slidin' away
—Paul Simon

You can fill your cup
It won't run dry
—Sophia

It ain't over till I say it's over.
—Buster Hyman

The long, hot days rolled by like calendar collages in an old movie. The Megaglopoulis Mutants were hot; the Lemon Sox were not. But it's easier to pass through the eye of a needle than to gain seven games in three weeks.

The night of September 24, the world, in its final slumber before the momentous milestone it was about to reach, heaved itself over in bed one more time, pulling all the covers off gentle Dawn, who, grumbling, finally sat up, scratched her backside and rose, raking her scarlet fingernails once again over the topless towers of Megaglopoulis.

The Northern Hemisphere had officially turned off its alarm clock three days ago and was sleeping more than half the day away. The media had announced Autumn's arrival, but Autumn's plane was still circling the runway, waiting for the mercury to come down and land first.

As Dawn's crimson phalanges slowly cat-burgled their way down the tower walls and into the streets and backyards of the city, a light mist arose, bathing the skyscrapers in an almost angelic hue. The miasma of smog that normally hung from the rafters was absent today; so too the gridlock of snarling commuters. Today was Sunday. Saturday night had hung over but moved on: the clubs, the parties, the concert halls, the bars, the ballpark—all were as quiet as a graveyardful of ex-Quakers. Soon the ringing of churchbells would break the silence, but the real religion was right here, right now: that great troubled behemoth Megaglopoulis was, if only for the moment, serene. In this quiescent moment, landlord could lie down with tenant, employer with employee, policeman with jaywalker, husband with wife. Om Shanti Megaglopoulis.

◆◆◆ ◆◆◆ ◆◆◆

Sunday, September 25: the earth's five billionth birthday. Four billion, nine hundred ninety-nine million, nine hundred ninety-nine thousand nine hundred ninety-nine times had fair Gaia pirouetted in her celestial space, waltzing around her solar dancemate, weaving astral rings in her wake like a cosmic slinky on an ancient redwood tree. Four billion, nine hundred ninety-nine million, nine hundred ninety-nine thousand nine hundred ninety-nine times 365 1/4, plus 364 times more had she whirled like a dervish, spun herself dizzy like a child on a barstool, treating all aboard to a dazzling daze of nights and days. Fortunately for her passengers, she was one of those indefatigable ladies who never want to leave the ballroom floor or slow the beat. Don't challenge her to a marathon dance; your legs will rot and fall off your body to feed the worms of her soils, and still will she whirl.

By galactic reckoning Gaia was as yet in the bloom of youth, with the sun's blush still radiant on her hills and seas. After all, she had turned 4.8 billion before she gave birth to the mammals and her first gray hare appeared. In places her skin had lost its luster, but, she told herself, her rivers mostly still ran. Her forests still pushed up new round-ringed oxygen factories—though, she had to admit, more and more of them were Just One Thing, violating her First Law of Diversity. Her great waters, lazy behemoths that they were, still pursued their lackluster attempts to heave themselves out of bed—and soon they might succeed, she thought, if the icecaps at her nether edges kept melting. If Ladye Hannah Aura and Maxwell Veribushi noticed a little clouding in her aura these days, the first traces of a pallor on her delicate skin, it went undetected by most in the virus-colonies that busied themselves creating pockmarks on her fragile skin.

North of her midriff, the long, hot summer rounded the stretch in a lather, still a nose ahead of the challenger, Autumn: Megaglopoulis was as hot and humid as a drop-the-soap game in a steambath.

The Mutants had gone 19-4 in September while the Lemon Sox played only .500 ball. The standings:

Mutants 94-59

Lemon Sox   94-59

To play: one game, season finale, Mutants vs. Lemon Sox.

Showdown.

You knew it would come down to this, didn't you, fans? Dead heat. Last game of the season. Last book of the novel. Would that our lives were as tidily constructed as novels, and that we could manage to pull all of our affairs together at some point in our life, and not have to spend time on our deathbed dictating memos, canceling utilities services, clearing with estranged family members and wondering to whom to bequeath the antique Latvian andirons to minimize friction.

The preceding thoughts were brought to you by Sadie Lewis, who will not be attending today's game because of a previous commitment: she is about to step into that great parallel universe beyond, created by a God named, of all things, Oral-Anal Roberts.

A novel dares not expire before getting all of its frogs back into the pond; for a human soul to do less would surely put it either in eternal flames, as Meriwether Lewis held, or back on the wheel of karma, as that strange little man joked who killed Meriwether—or was it Meriwether who killed *him?*—But no, wasn't he just here trying to buy a frog farm? Or was he selling? Sadie shook her head. Her mind didn't work that well any more, and she had tidied up her own life 40 years ago. "My only concern," she told Emily, who was making faces at herself in the mirror, "is whether that Furribaldi what's-his-name fellow can keep you from running out the door in your slip and into traffic.

"Can't catch me! Can't catch me!" said Emily.

"Well, dear, he'll just have to. I'm tired of doing it...very tired. May I have another sweater?"

Saturday night, as the world tossed and turned, Ladye Hannah Aura burned the candle at both ends. First came long hours poring over forgotten volumes of lore. Then she dragged out the pentagrams,

eyes of newt, Caucasian chalk circles and other accoutrements, and the incantations —there, that took care of the first task. Then she was overdue at consulting those cards. Long did she hobnob with kings and queens, consort with knaves and the faceless minions. She rapped with spades, joined clubs and tried on diamonds for size, but she could never break hearts. (Yes, there it was: it was, as they say, in the cards.) By this time, Dawn's rosy pedicure had turned as yellow as jaundice: it was time to call her bookie. She greased her skateboard wheels; at last, some shuteye: she was due early at the ballpark.

September 25: On this morning of mornings in his life, Whizzo Mark Salot IV arose at 8 a.m. In the bathroom, he held his precious lone photo of Anloie's face up to the mirror next to his. "Good mornin' Angel Pah, welcome to your weddin' day! *Our* weddin' day! Ah jist gotta go out 'n pitch them fellers to the flag, and then we can be together forever and ever. Ah cain't wait to see you sittin' there on your throne, with all the ahes of the world on us when we step into Eternity together. Mah darlin'. Mah darlin' darlin' darlin'. Ah love you so deep, lahke a flower loves rain, lahke a dark thought loves laght." He brought the likeness to his lips and touched it tenderly to them, growing briefly passionate before tearing it away.

On his way out he took out the panties she had left there and sniffed deeply. Yes, a few bewitching molecules of her champagne still tickled his nose.

At Mom's Home Plates, he ate his usual pregame breakfast of six fried eggs, a half-pound of bacon, a half-pound of grits, three slices of toast with ketchup and three with jelly, washed down with a quart of orange juice. As he autographed napkins for the kids at a nearby table, he shouted out: "Hey, ever'body in here's invahted to the ballpark tonaght. C'mon down and see Whizzo Mark Salot IV pitch them Mutants to the pennant, and then marry the sweetheart of mah lahfe!"

If Whizzo felt any apprehension about pitching the game of the year against the toughest-hitting team in the majors, a team whose nose he had rubbed in doodoo all season, a team that had vowed to fry his potatoes in scalding oil, it didn't show in his jaunty swagger, his banter with whomever he encountered.

If he felt even the faintest concern about the iffiness of his upcoming nuptials, or if he fell subject to any of the standard wedding-day jitters that have left so many an erstwhile bride or groom standing alone, humiliated and broken-hearted at the altar, not a wispy cirrus cloud of it crossed the beaming sunshine of his demeanor, nor did so much as a telltale tremor tiptoe across the high-wire of his braggadocio voice.

He slipped into his cherry-red Corvette and drove to Megaglopoulis Hospital, wearing his Mutants cap. As a nurse escorted him to the Children's Ward, she stopped to greet an elderly charge in a wheelchair. "Do you know who this man is?" she asked him, nodding at Whizzo.

The old man peered through snot-colored eyes. "Nolan Ryan! All my life I been wanting to meet you."

"Yassuh!" said Whizzo. "Today we're gonna win us a pennant."

As he entered the Children's Ward, he shouted out, "OK, how many hits do y'all want me to give up today?"

A kid at the far end removed his oxygen tube long enough to bellow back: "Twenty-five!"

"Twenty-fahve! If'n Ah give up 25 hits, you win but Ah lose. So y'all lose too. We all lose. The Mutes lose the pennant."

An emaciated kid with freckles and glasses giggled. How about 2.5?" he asked.

"Two point fahve. Lessee, thass three hits, but one thass really an out but the umpahre blows the call at first. But Ah cain't control how many mistakes that umpahre's gonna make today, only how many hits Ah'll give up to them knock-kneed, sawed-off, hammered-down, pigeon-toed, dilapidated, evaporated, good-for-nothin' lemon-toed Lemon Soxers."

"Six hits!" cried out another kid.

"Six! Thass alot. OK, six it is. But no runs!"

◆ ◆ ◆ ◆

Being a scientist, Maxwell Veribushi wouldn't have believed today was Gaia's five billionth birthday even if he had received an invitation to a surprise party for her. Scientists shared a collective conventional wisdom that she was barely 4.3 billion years old. But women have their ways of deceiving us about their age. Besides, what stock can we put in the calculations of a species that can't even celebrate the millennium on the right year?

Brushing gentle Dawn's ubiquitous fingernails off his tablecloth along with the crumbs from his breakfast, Maxwell set his laptop atop it and began composing: To Whom It May Concern...

Swift as a brown fox coming to the aid of its country did his furry fingers fly across the keyboard: the time was growing short. Finishing, he folded the letter into his pocket, jumped on his Harley and *vroom-vroomed* his way over to the Lewis mansion.

His idea of donating the land to the Nature Conservancy had been conceived in haste. On thinking it over, he didn't really trust them any more than the County. Once Sadie Lewis passed on and the pond was in their hands, they would invite his ex-colleagues in to swarm all over it. It might even become an eco-tourist attraction.

He had a better plan for the property. Would Sadie go along? Why not? He had been kind to her and changed her light bulbs. Besides, who else did she know?

Dawn's gently prying digits found Billy Beanball as he had fallen asleep the night before, curled up with his radio still blaring, his 33-inch, 32-ounce Louisville Slugger in his hand and his A-Rod glove, with a baseball in the pocket, on the pillow beside him. His eyes popped open like two one-eyed jacks-in-the-boxes. The earth's five billionth birthday promised also to be the greatest day of his young life. His friend and hero Whizzo Mark Salot IV would pitch the

Megaglopoulis Mutants to the pennant. And Whizzo had sent him a ticket! True, the ticket was for the bleachers. But it wasn't like Whizzo had insulted him or anything: he would be sitting with some of Whizzo's other friends. Billy understood that the orphans and the deaf and blind kids came first. In fact, he loved Whizzo for it.

It would be fun to sit with all the celebrities—maybe even next to Jewel, and protect her from a foul ball by catching it. Ah well, *c'est la vie.* Billy already had a dozen big-league baseballs, courtesy of Whizzo and his teammates. But they weren't the same as catching one that a player had actually hit in a game. He got out the neatsfoot oil and worked his glove, oblivious to the unlikelihood of snagging a ball in centerfield, 420 feet from home plate.

Billy arrived at Mutant Stadium at 4:30 p.m., an hour before the turnstiles opened. Already there was a line.

At noon, as clocks all over the city did vegetable impersonations and pointed their fingers at the sun, Bluster Hyman rang Foo Foo McGonigle's doorbell. Foo Foo answered in his pyjamas, demanding to know the time.

"Twelve o'clock. Our 12 o'clock interview, remember?"

"No. What do you think I know that you think you don't think you know? Who's gonna win?"

"That's a good place to start, Foo Foo. Who's going to win?"

"Ha! This is a no-brainer, you see, because anyone's got a brain, that brain knows they don't know. Every game is unique, and this one is no different than any other. Whatever happens is going to happen, regardless of what happens. Where we're playin' today, or any other day for that matter up here in the Bigs, give or take a few, any team can beat any team any time, but only sometimes, half the time to be exact, if you calculate the figures. It's a no-win, no-lose situation. So yes, if you're gonna be politically correct, we win, but to be in it mathematically, who knows?"

"I guess the big question is Throttlemeyer. Will he be able to play?"

"That feller's got a dinger on his finger, which it might as well be harm in the arm, his ball's a slow boat to China to second, which I guess still beats the jello in his elbow like that Venezuela kid come down with ruined his career. I can't even pinch-hit him on account of his finger sticks out like a sore thumb."

"Oh-oh, bad news for Mutants fans. Foo Foo, how will it affect the Mutant strategy, not having Throttlemeyer's bat in there?"

Well, that's half my one-two punch divided into one, but one may be as much as two with the kid on the mound talks to the baseball, but then I got my seasoned veteran in his place and he knows how to work the kid and he can carry the hot bat when it counts and everybody knows it's his last game including him in his life unless we get a bop or two from him and some of my other fellers can hit too, and we wind up not winding up until after the Series, which is where wouldn't you want to go before you hang up your cup?"

"What you're saying, Foo Foo, is that you think Charley Orange will be highly motivated out there today?" Bluster regretted the question as soon as he asked it: he had just broken an unwritten rule. Foo Foo McGonigle did not like being asked what he meant.

"Listen to me," Foo Foo barked. "I'm saying what I'm saying. Everybody's motivated unless they're not motivated, in case of which they're not motivated and they wouldn't be here, or out there at all, now, wouldn't they?"

At the same time as Bluster Hyman rang Foo Foo McGonigle's doorbell, Clitorea Pearl lifted her succulent orbs off the silken sheets of the king-sized (not *her* term!) bed where she had spent the night doing click clack front and back with Shakti, Shanti and a client who had ordered the five-figure Saturday Night Special.

As Clitorea tiptoed into the crack between a.m. and p.m., Shanti stirred.

"Shanti," Clitorea whispered. "Can we trade cars today?"

"My sunbleached Corvette for your shiny new XK-120? Sure, but why?"

"Yours is a convertible. And I'll treat you to an Earl Scheib."

"Deal!"

For a mere mortal, Earl Scheib was closed Sundays and required 72 hours' advance notice. But a goddess does not wait—especially a goddess with an Earl Scheib franchise owner for a client.

Five billionth birthday? So fair and foul a day Charley Orange had not seen. It was the best of days; it was the worst of days. Now was the winter of his discontent made glorious summer by this sun of Megaglopoulis; now was it reversed. He felt for Throttlemeyer, whose damaged digit would bench him for the most important game of his career. He rejoiced that he, Charley, would therefore be catching. If the Mutes lost and this was his swan song, he would exit from behind the plate, not collecting splinters on the bench. He vowed that the team would not miss Throttlemeyer's thump. Lately Charley was banging the ball like Ngaio XV^{14} +34 and his ancestors banging their way through the female ranids of Time. He had upped his anemic average to .199. He vowed also not to bow out of the bigtime under the Mendoza line. Who, he asked himself, was more motivated than he? With a victory he would crown his career with a pennant. If the Mutes won the World Series: baseball's most coveted memento, the Series ring.

One game to decide the pennant! The excitement of that was a new feeling.—No, actually it was the same tingly agitation that coursed through his body before any game, only amped up. An unqualified good feeling that agitation was not—some seasoned veterans regularly hurled their $100 Chateaubriands before games—but he knew he would miss it.

So was that what kept the bluebirds of happiness from nesting in the eaves troughs of his heart? Retirement? Beneath the buzz, the gaping crocodile of the Void opened its maw: Never married, never divorced, today Charley knew what splitting up felt like: it felt like this. What to do: what to substitute for the adrenaline rush of all-out competition?

But no, he would not slide into a winter of discontent touring the celebrity golf circuit or hawking Mr. Coffee or BVD's on the tube. Wellington P. Sweetwater had already offered him the managing job at Tidewater. He'd be out of the Bigs, maybe for good, but still in the comforting, nonfemale universe of baseball.

OK, so that's what was gnawing at him like a gnome gnashing at his gnu steak: the Clitorea Pearl fiasco. For a few weeks the hope that he might be able to actually relate to the fair sex—more accurately, to live with himself, to channel his obsessions into self-discovery—had buoyed him above the cesspool of his lifelong despair. But a single incident (well, two, but one woman) and his mind took a high-dive right back into the doo-doo: Ker-plop!

This time, he tried something different. He pulled out the Four Wisdoms that someone had given him: was it Dr. Weisenheimer or Clitorea Pearl? Or maybe that weird woman with the skateboard?

1) It's all my doing
2) It's OK by me
3) What is the gut feeling?
4) Why?

So how was Clitorea talking him out of his keys his doing? She ordered him, like a cop—like his mother. Yes, so what, Dr. Weisenheimer? *Da mudder is ordering, ve are doing. Later, da vife, da girl friend, da voman at da bank is ordering, ve are doing.* Yes, there was a little boy inside Charley that he could love. And if he could love him, so could someone else. He just had to defy the order once and the spell would be broken. He had the chance with Clitorea; he blew it; he would get it right next time.

"It's OK by me?" She had given Whizzo a blow job. So what? So she belonged to Charley? No. So he was in love with her? No: his pain was just obsessive. So it was his social conditioning? Yes, but not all. Judgment? Some trace cultural cling-ons, but he honestly believed in her work. Territoriality? He knew it was her work, but he hadn't been confronted directly with it before. Maybe a little. A pinch of this, a soupcon of that. Any trigger he could think of had merit: had its own universe, in fact, where it reigned as Truth Supreme. Fear of her ways with men? Bingo. He did feel ready to try out his new self with another woman, but maybe someone less formidable than Clitorea Pearl.

Hey, this was working! But 3) and 4) could wait: time to go play ball.

"PeaNU-UTS! POPcorn! Cr-r-r-r-rackjacktatachips!" He climbs up and down the aisle steps, his basket strapped onto his shoulders, a small man with a weathered face, toothless from consuming too many of his wares. "PeaNU-UTS! POPcorn! Cr-r-r-r-rackjacktatachips!"

Scents of hot dogs, stale beer, the newly-mown lawn that glistens lime-green under the skyborne banks of light, sharing sod with nary a single yellow dot of dandelion. The ripple of the pennons mounted on the bleacher wall, unfurling west, toward left field: there could be a few rainbows tonight. The retired numbers of former Mutant heroes painted inside baseballs along Hall of Fame Pavilion in right field, looking over the newest crop of hopefuls, invoking hallowed days of bygone glory. The neon orange glow of the last 3,000 still-unoccupied seats exchanging indelicate banter about whose buttocks will soon be wriggling into their confines.

And one seat—in the celebrity-packed Section 12 behind the Mutants dugout—one seat with a white bridal arch placed over it, a trellis bedecked in roses pink, peach and blood-red. This seat, itself covered with white pillows, would exchange no ribaldries today, for it had been chosen to receive no ordinary buttocks but the dainty derriere of a bride. It was indeed an honor for the seat, and the pillows leered at each other uncertainly. So far, no dainty derriere in sight.

The rich, ripe KONK! of ash wood meeting cowhide as ageless Pookie Pendergrass, at 82 still the best fungo hitter in baseball, lofts

◆◆◆ ◆◆◆ ◆◆◆

one lunar shot after another from along the left-field line onto the right-field warning track. First baseman Onions Malone plays third, third baseman Twinkletoes Butler plays center, star closer Lightnin' Larrabee goes yard in the batting cage while his mound colleagues conduct windsprint races along the left-field track as, one after another, Mutants in Gothic-lettered uniforms as starched and white as the downtown Athletic Club take nine swings and lay one down against coach Scratch Skaggs' 50-mph fastball.

Charley Orange emerged from the Megaglopoulis Mutants' dugout and looked skyward. Overhead, in the hollow light preceding sunset, S/HeIt, having gorged Hirself on a celestial feast, littered herringbone clouds across the sky. And there, smack in the middle of S/HeIt's debris platter, midway between home plate and the centerfield fence and no higher than 300 feet above the field, floated an object that caused Charley to shake his head and speculate to the batboy on possible ties between their boss, Wellington P. Sweetwater, and P.T. Barnum: a hot-air balloon. It was tethered to the tops of four section poles at the four corners of Mutant Stadium—if indeed an oval-shaped ballpark can be said to have corners. Ladye Hannah Aura was later to claim they marked the four directions.

As Charley stepped onto the field he was met by Wellington P. Sweetwater himself, with Lulu on his arm. Lulu was dressed knockers-up for the occasion: great mounds of the finest cleavage money could buy spilled over the neckline of her dress. Although if that was her neckline, Charley thought, I'm wearing jockstraps on my feet.

For a guy who usually wore work jeans to the ballpark so he could relate better with his clients, Sweetwater was spiffed up, too: he even carried a blazer for the hoped-for postgame pennant award ceremony. His eyes showed a little of that same clouding that dimmed fair Gaia's visage. "Smile, young man!" he boomed at Charley, waving his free arm toward the balloon. "You're on Candid Camera!"

"Congratulations, Sweetwater, this is the very essence of egregiousness. How many TV cameras have you sold the rights to to hang up there in the sky?"

Wellington P. Sweetwater beamed. "Yeah, and how many paparazzi going telephoto here, telephoto there, here a zoom there a zoom everywhere a zoom zoom, capturing for the millions Kevin Costner taking notes for his next movie, Sisqo dressed in a pennant-shaped thong, Chyna holding Don King in a headlock?"

"I'll say a prayer for your taste buds. Why didn't you hire the Fuji Blimp?"

Foo Foo McGonigle was less concerned with aesthetics and more with nuts and bolts. "If you ask me he's reaching the heights of a new low. But what I need to know is where is that low in relation to how high is the popup ceiling? They might be gonna have to pop it up some more."

Matt "The Bat" Moseley steps into the batting-practice cage. All activity in the park ceases. KONK! KONK! KONK! Eight of nine balls rocket into the seats; the ninth caroms off the right-center wall. If Pete Gray, the one-armed outfielder, were here, he could count on his fingers the number of batters the average fan can look at and distinguish superiority over the others. A hurdy-gurdy man can see it in Moseley—can see, beyond the whipfast wrists, the laser vision, the fluid ripple of muscles through his body in his swing, his fierce concentration. Moseley epitomizes the adage that baseball is concentration, concentration, concentration. When people stop what they are doing to watch him swing, it is to watch the ultimate in singularity of purpose.

Lest any underprivileged patrons be denied the official version of the game, ghetto blasters in every section are tuned to Bluster Hyman's play-by-play to flesh out the action and comment on the strategy, to pay homage to the numbers, to preserve with the ears where the eyes lose their memory: to saturate the senses with this historic moment in the hallowed annals of the National Pastime .

In Section 11, parallel with third base, sit Whizzo Mark Salot IV's guests the orphans. Even if for this night only, someone has painted life into their irisless, pupilless eyes. On the outside seats of each row are orphans laughing, shouting and dancing, doing what end-orphans do: making people happy.

Every time Whizzo would strike out a batter tonight, he would wave to Section 11.

In Section 10, parallel with first base, sit Whizzo's guests the deaf children. They have no ghetto blasters, but some of them will take turns announcing the play-by-play in Hand Jive. Probably a classroom assignment.

Let us pray that none of them spontaneously remit and unplug the wax in the old auricular canals tonight, for if the monumental blasts of sound waves to emanate from the packed 53,746-capacity Mutant Stadium and the 47,000-strong parking-lot tailgate party were the first emissaries to greet a pair of ears after a lifetime of peace and quiet, the tympani of those ears would surely steal back into the silent world like Dracula skipping the sunrise.

Every time Whizzo would end an inning tonight, he would salute Section 10.

In Section 1, directly behind home plate—the best seats in the house—sit Whizzo's guests the blind children. "They never get the best seats anywhere," Whizzo told the media. "Hit's lahke, they cain't see, so whah waste good visuals on them? Well, they can hear, cain't they? Sittin' behahnd home plate they can hear the umpahre call balls and strahkes, they can hear mah Sweet Patooties pop into Charlie Awrnge's glove—they git so's they can see that ball in their mahnd's ahes."

Every time Whizzo would retire a batter tonight, he would call the pitch to Section 1: "Choo Choo Charley, jammed him insahde."

"PeaNU-UTS! POPcorn! Cr-r-r-r-rackjacktatachips!" "ICE-cold coke!" "HOT dogs!" "Heeyy, ICE cream!" Above the din of the growing crowd, vendors bark their smorgasbord of *haute cuisine* designed by the nutritionists in preadolescent heaven.

Twenty minutes to game time. Above the stadium walls a thousand thousand-watt bulbs flick on, like eyes of flies lighting grounders and flies. Outside, a 60-foot high can of beer bursts into bloom on the upper-deck wall by Parking Lot C. Forty-seven thousand throats cheer as one, and many fill with that very substance: the video projections are up and running. Inside Lot C, tailgates drop like lingerie at a W.I.T.C.H. and Warlock party. Poptops pop and beer overflows like warlocks losing ejaculatory control. Hot dogs and opposing players are skewered like the warlocks by the impregnated W.I.T.C.H.es. An ancient black man with a sax and a tin cup and ear plays a unique blend of "Take Me Out to the Ball Game" and the theme song from "The Sopranos." Scalpers hawk their last remaining wares. The turnstiles are clogged with lines of ticket holders receiving unsocial security checks.

Inside the park, the aisles are alive with spectators streaming to their seats. Cigarette lighters twinkle like parallel universe-hopping tiddlywinks. Atop the centerfield bleachers, the P.A. system clears its throat, sending bronchial irregularities echoing through Mutantland. Triclops, the three-eyed Happy Face, the Mutant mascot, bounds onto the home dugout and leads a cheer, accompanied by foxhunt music on the P.A.: Doo-do-da-DOOP-da Do! "CHARGE!" Doo-do-da - DOOP-da-Do! "CHARGE!"

On the sideline mounds near the outfield foul lines, the starting pitchers—for the Lemon Sox Hector "Lave sus Manos" Guadalajara, a known spitballer with 23 wins, 18 hit batsmen and wild eyes that don't focus; for the Mutants Whizzo Mark Salot IV, confidante to baseballs, would-be bridegroom and at 19-4 a shoo-in for Rookie of the Year—toe their respective rubbers and lob their initial warmup tosses to the bullpen catchers.

As Whizzo received the ball back from Bubba Osmond, he looked toward Sections 11, 10 and 1 and, to soprano-pitched cheers, doffed his cap. He glanced at Section 12, behind the Mutant dugout. Prince Charles and Rush Limbaugh were already seated, sharing political observations and a bag of peanuts. Madonna, wearing a saran-wrap dress, waved toward Whizzo. Dennis Rodman opened his shirt to show Martha Stewart his new nipple ring. Bill Clinton was there without Hillary, wearing a padlock on his fly. Dolly Parton stood on her chair blowing kisses to the stands. Clinton held her shoulders from behind so she wouldn't topple forward. Beside them, as if Section 1 had lost a tooth in a brawl, was a gaping hole: HER seat.

"'Course'n the game hasn't even started yet," Whizzo told himself. He scorched one into Bubba Osmond's mitt. "Hey, take it easy," said Osmond, shaking his hand. "You just started. Warm up the noodle first."

◆ ◆ ◆ ◆

A box of cereal gains weight before our eyes. As a mother catches a basketball, cartoon bluebirds land on her shoulder and a white goose strolls through her garden. Lightning strikes a haunted house, a purple flamingo speaks fluent English to a puzzled housecat, a woman with carrots growing out of her face is replaced by a being from a parallel universe.

Cut to Bluster Hyman. Having not yet received his stats package, he was winging it: "Today one team will pocket the pennant, grab the glory. They'll win the Oscar of the national pastime, be the Rolls-Royce of teams. They'll hear the wild cheering of their fans in the streets, ride beneath the downtown skyscrapers waving from open convertibles as the confetti falls about them like rainbow-colored snow—which is the only kind of snow we'll see around here until the mercury drops about 60 degrees. Anyway, one team will represent the league in the grandest adventure in baseball: the World Series.

"The other team will see all its struggles, all the adrenaline it has churned out all year, all the nagging injuries and bone-weariness it has gritted its teeth and played through—all turn to putty and fade into memory. The players will sit in the dressing room with their collective heads hung between their knees, not believing they could come this far and lose the prize. Many will weep outright. They will analyze what went wrong—the little factors, chance factors perhaps, a checked swing, a gust of breeze that held up a fly ball, or, as so often happens, a bad call—that spelled the difference between victory and defeat, between glory and ignominious oblivion.

"Talk about baseball being a game of inches. There is no way to calibrate a measurement of the difference in quality between these two teams in this pennant chase of chases, a chase that has recalled the valiant performance of the 1951 New York Giants and the "Shot Heard 'Round the World": a team which was 13 1/2 games out in late August, a team with only one Hall-of-Famer on its roster and he in his rookie season, a team which...but back to Megaglopoulis, where the scramble has engaged the maximum efforts of 25 thoroughbred athletes on each team over a sustained period of six months. But if one could distinguish the relative calibers of these Mutants and Lemon Sox, the measure would be not in inches but in nanometers.

"Today's starting batteries: For the visiting Lemon Sox, Hector "Lave sus Manos" Guadalajara on the hill; he throws to Hector Cajones. For our home team Mutants, the would-be bridegroom, Whizzo Mark Salot IV, going like 60 for 20 wins in his shortened rookie season. Behind the plate with Horst Throttlemeyer out with a fractured phalange, Charley Orange. The Mutants could sorely miss Throttlemeyer's sock. But having the sagaciousness of one of the game's most crafty players behind the plate in perhaps the closing day of his career may prove to be a big plus for our boys. —the Megaglopoulis Mutants, that is. Ah yes, here's the sheets: Charley Orange, lifetime BA .238, has a .310 lifetime percentage in the last three innings, a .299 average with runners in scoring position, and—get this one, folks—a .422 average in game situations that the Society for American Baseball Research defines as "critical;" to wit, the last three innings with runners in scoring position and the tallies two runs or less apart. We'll take that bat, too. —That is, the Megaglopoulis Mutants will. And now, here's one way to get a jump on this year's Christmas shopping..."

O-oh say can you see
By the dawn's early light

Clarence Henry had sung a good many gigs in his life, before a good many people, but never before had he been asked to perform "The Star-Spangled Banner" to a live audience of 100,000 and on national TV, accompanied posthumously on guitar by Jimi Hendrix. When he arrived at the park he realized to his chagrin that he didn't know the words. No problem, Wellington P. Sweetwater told him, nothing that a little rehearsal and a teleprompter couldn't fix.

...And the rocket's red glare
The bombs bursting in air...

The unusual range requirement didn't faze Henry: he could sing like a girl, and he could sing like a frog. A little voice inside wondered if it might not be more appropriate for an Afro-American like himself to sing the national anthem of his own country—whatever that was. No, he thought as he readied his falsetto to reach the high notes, he belonged to the planet. To the stars. To the vast everywheres forevers.

...O'er the la-hand of the free
And the home of the brave.

As already reported, the first seven innings were scoreless.

The Sox pinch-hit for Lave sus Manos Guadalajara in the eighth. Although they failed to score, they brought in their ace closer, Hector Quetzalcoatl. "Quetzalcoatl," Bluster Hyman told his listeners and viewers, "has been the best closer in the big leagues in the second half of this season, saving 27 of 28 opportunities since the All-Star game and winning the other. He has not pitched more than two innings in an appearance all season, but he told Macarena Gonzales Gonzales he could go 10 today if necessary.

"Quetzalcoatl's fastball has been clocked at 102 miles per hour. He once threw a ball through a brick wall. His split-finger drops like names at a Hollywood party. Now his curve, he only spots. It can cross the plate sideways, on those days when it crosses the plate at all.

"Charley Orange leads off for the Mutes. Charley started tonight's contest hitting .199. He's 0 for 2, down to .194. After a terrible start this spring, his average still hovered around the .160 mark as late as August. It has been an uphill struggle for Charley Orange to raise his average in this, his final season, to the .200 plateau, the so-called Mendoza Line. A base hit here, in possibly his final at-bat, will do it.

Charley Orange is a proud man. He wants nothing more for himself than to retire with his final season mark over .200."

Charley, oblivious to any of these numbers, stepped to the plate. Quetzalcoatl's first pitch cracked into the mitt of Hector Cajones before he even saw it. "Did he really throw that ball, or did you set off a firecracker?" he asked Cajones. Strike one.

Another pitch; another crack. This time Charley swung. Strange, he thought: his ball goes faster than the speed of light, but not faster than the speed of sound. Was the ball entering a parallel universe when it left Quetzalcoatl's hand and re-emerging, electron-like, when it crossed the plate? Strike two.

Quetzalcoatl's third offering was a splitter, 10 feet short and 10 feet wide of the plate. Charley swung for strike three. The ball caromed past Cajones and Charley sprinted to first, well ahead of the throw.

"But Charley Orange wants more for the team than for himself!" Bluster shouted over the crowd's roar. "He unselfishly sacrifices his chance for personal gratification to contribute to his team's chance of victory. Unless this game remains tied for a few more innings, he will finish his final season in the majors batting .192. Yet there he is on first base: a heads-up player of the Old School, Charley Orange. Getting on base creates a bunt situation and allows Whizzo Mark Salot IV, who is 9 for 11 in sacrifice attempts in tie or one-run situations this year, to stay in the game. The situation calls for a runner, but the Mutants have no one on the bench who can catch. Charley Orange will run for himself."

While Bluster was still orating, Whizzo moved Charley to second with a perfectly executed dribbler down the first-base line. As Whizzo headed toward the dugout, he stole a glance at Section 12. eminem was being searched for concealed weapons by two park policemen. Don Ho and Ice-T stood arm-in-arm in the aisle, harmonizing.

Whizzo's heart sank. The bridal bower, like a severed link in the chain of humanity surrounding it, was still bare.

Bobaloo Boynton grounded to second, sending Charley to third with two down. Quetzalcoatl blew two freight trains by Joe Revige, then tried to induce him with a curve. It broke like a scared rabbit and scampered through the briarpatch at the far side of the lefty box.

"Cajones dives and knocks it down; it squirts 10 feet away!" shrieked Bluster Hyman. "Here comes Orange! Here comes Quetzalcoatl! Here comes the ball! Three things occupy the same space at the same time, and mix in a cloud of dust. Quetzalcoatl slaps the ball onto Orange's thigh, BUT NOT BEFORE CHARLEY'S FOOT SAILS ACROSS THE BAG! HE'S SAFE! HE'S SAFE! MUTES LEAD!"

"ROAR! ROAR!" roared 54,192 lion-hearted fans inside Mutant Stadium. "HONK! HONK!" blasted the horn section, 17,000 strong, in Parking Lot C. Boomboxes cranked up to full volume. Seats rumbled like thunderstorms. Sound waves careened off the stadium walls and crashed into each other, filling the area with sonic BOOM!s. Beer spilled from upper-deck spectators' cups onto lower-deck spectators' heads. Beach balls, confetti, paper airplanes and a live octopus rained down onto the field.

When the debris was cleared, Onions Malone struck out. The hullabaloo did not subside.

Eight played. Mutants 1, 5 and 0. Lemon Sox 0, 5 and 0.

A helicopter. A gun. An angry man. A woman holding balloons floats through her living room. As a UFO takes out the Water Tower of Hope and torches a city, Mighty Mouse sits in a restaurant eating cheese. (Some superhero!) *Hi! I'm Jody Jenkins and I'm so excited about the great...*Ready to wet its pants with exuberance, the voice was more than a match for Bluster Hyman's.

"What a finale, ladies and gentlemen. In the long and storied annals of the Grand Old Game, has there ever been a contest to match this? For only the sixth time in major-league history, two teams face each other in the season finale tied for the lead. For only the second time, seven innings of scoreless baseball in that game. Then in the bottom of the eighth the amazing Mutants, who in their 34 years in Megaglopoulis have never won a pennant, scratch home the lone tally so far in this cliff-hanging contest. Can the Boy Who Talks to

Baseballs, Whizzo Mark Salot IV, the kid who just three short months and 19 victories ago was pitching high-school ball, maintain the season-long spell he has cast on the best-hitting team in the majors for one inning more?

"In six previous starts against the Lemon Sox this year, all young Salot IV has done is to compile a 6-0 record with six complete games, two shutouts, 55 strikeouts and an earned-run average of 1.00. They're batting .252 against him on his first 45 pitches and just .168 thereafter. He's fanned 10 tonight, bringing the total to 65 in 62 innings. His eight goose eggs tonight reduces the ERA to 0.87. One more scoreless inning will run his record to 7-0. No pitcher in major-league history has ever gone 7-0 against the top-hitting team.

"And as you very well know, ladies and gentlemen, unless you've been lost in some sort of parallel universe, that's not even half the story unfolding here tonight." Although he lived in one, Bluster knew nothing of parallel universes; his use of the term was merely a spontaneous figure of speech (which instantly spawned a nearly infinite number of new universes). But it caused two ears to pick up. Those appendages were located in the appropriate places on the sides of the hirsute head of a hobbitlike man steering a lime-hued Harley-Davidson motorcycle through the open gate of the Meriwether Lewis mansion.

"Who among us," Bluster Hyman continued, "can begin to imagine the personal drama residing inside the breaking heart of young Salot IV? How heavy as an anvil must it weigh, each time his eyes wander over to the nuptial box, all gussied up with a rose-covered trellis, and see the empty space where he hoped his bride-to-be would be seated? Can you remember, Mutant fans, when you were 18 years old and love was the most important thing in the world? In a way, doesn't Whizzo Mark Salot IV bring back the memory of that feeling in us all? And while there are no statistics kept on what percentage of us who lose the love of our life on our wedding day still go out like troopers and pitch eight innings of shutout baseball with the pennant on the line, of this I can assure you...I *assure* you, ladies and gentlemen, that it would be lower than..."

Bluster paused in mid-runon to think of an analogy.

"Charley Orange's batting average!" yelled a nearby fan, loud enough to make the airwaves.

"...lower than the percentage of errors made by Ozzie Smith in his glory years. For that ignoramus in the stands, he must have missed my remarks on the subject of Charley Orange's batting average just moments ago. To continue, there are those who tell me the mouth of Whizzo Mark Salot IV is too big. Let me say to them right here and now, from Yours Truly himself: When it comes to heart, this kid's heart is bigger than all the mouths in baseball, including Yours Truly.

"Last inning he gave the Sox their fifth hit and a free pass. It's been a long season. Can the Boy Wonder's arm be tiring? Foo Foo McGonigle is taking no chances, keeping both Lightnin' Larrabee and Power Brakes O'Toole loose in the bullpen. Now Whizzo addresses some remarks to the ball, holds it to his ear, casts a glance toward the empty seat in Section 12 and tosses his final warmup pitch. He has his work cut out for him as Poo Poo Perez steps to the plate, with Mucho Dinero Quintero on deck and Hector Cajones in the hole. And traffic in Disfunction Junction, Arkansas slows to a crawl.

"Now Charley Orange settles in behind the plate and sizes up the defense. Onions Malone and Twinkletoes Butler hug the lines at first and third, guarding against a ground-ball double. The outfield plays Poo Poo, who has 46 rainbows, deep and shaded to left. He makes his living off fastballs, but Whizzo's Sweet Patooties have been hopping like Mexican jumping beans tonight and he's retired him on them three times."

A breeze stirred, sending a paper plate skipping out to play first base. As Pudge Rummell, the first-base umpire, moved in to play tag with it, Whizzo's head turned first left, then right. He motioned Charley to the mound.

"She's here, Charley. She's here! Ah can smell her!"

Charley glanced at Anloie's vacant seat. "She's not here, Whizzo. Forget it. Focus on the game."

"Oh, Ah'm focused on the game, Charley. Poo Poo's crowdin', we'll slip Choo-Choo Charley over the outsahde corner, let him foul off Uncle Scrooge low and in and whiff him with a change-up. Me and the baseball have been in locked-door conference, but of course you are invahted. Say Charley, are you still prepared to be mah Best Man?"

Roscoe Riordan, the home plate umpire, started out to the mound. Charley headed back. The sequence worked: on a 1-1 count Poo Poo popped the offspeed pitch to third. "Changed him up!" Whizzo bellowed to the blind children in Section 1.

Mucho Dinero Quintero up, a lefty, always dangerous. The defense shifted right and stayed deep. Whizzo paced the mound, sniffing the air and jabbering like a madman to the ball. Charley flipped a sequence; he nodded. Sweet Patootie, high inside corner, setting up Quintero for the curve. The pitch missed: Ball 1. The curve broke early and hung, fortunately a foot wide. Whizzo's curve, Charley noted, was done for the night. Buenaventura had singled off the last one, also a hanger, in the eighth.

Through Maxwell Veribushi's earphones, Bluster Hyman was sowing the seeds of fear. "That's two straight nothing balls from Whizzo, and he seems to be sidetracked, stomping about the mound with his nose in the air and talking a blue streak to the baseball."

Maxwell prayed that this was not yet Sadie's final sleep.

"Now Whizzo sets; here it comes...Riordan calls it low! We'll be sure to take a look at that one on instant replay. 3-0. Quintero a good hitter, but my bet is he's taking here: the Sox need a runner. Here comes...ball four! Oh! What a call! The stands break out in boos as Quintero trots down to first and Charley Orange makes a visit to the mound to calm Whizzo. Quintero has only average speed; will Gonzales Gonzales send in a pinch runner? No, Quintero stays. Gonzales is of the two bops and a bang school, and he has the bops and bangs to do it. Here comes Hector Cajones to the plate, a sixth-place hitter with enough bopbang to start a jazz cathouse."

Even with the slow-footed, power-hitting Cajones, Charley would call bunt in this situation. But the infield was playing back. Charley glanced at Foo Foo: under his hat the manager's face was hidden, and he made no sign. This game could end with a bang, or whimper out with a double play: Charley called for Big Peter, low and away.

Cajones swung for glory and powdered the air six inches above the ball to kingdom come.

As Whizzo went into his stretch for the next pitch, Charley caught a tremor in Cajones' thumbs. "Oh-oh," he thought. "Bunt coming; Butler and Malone both too deep. No time to signal them; no time to change the pitch." He shot his glove up a foot, praying Whizzo would understand and execute.

As Mucho Dinero Quintero broke for second, Choo-Choo Charley came in shoulder-high: good boy, a tough pitch to lay down. Cajones squared; the pitch, for good measure, rose at the plate. Cajones popped it foul onto the screen.

"That big first-strike swing was a decoy," droned Bluster Hyman: "Cajones knew he wouldn't get a dinger pitch off Whizzo. Now he's 0 and 2, with a lifetime on-base percentage against lefties from 0-2 of .081. Now Whizzo jams him high and hard: 1 and 2. Whizzo toes the slab, checks Quintero, not going anywhere, delivers: Cajones pops it to the sky!"

"Sweet Patootie!" Whizzo yelled to Section 1.

"Two down," said Bluster. "I hope you can hear me over this roar. Fifty thousand faithful in Mutant Stadium are on their feet. Fifty thousand more in the parking lot are yelling and honking their horns hoarse. Traffic in Disfunction Junction, Arkansas is stalled in the street as Guacamole Guanabana, representing the last hope of the Lemon Sox, strides to the plate. Guanabana, at 38 past his MVP days but still carrying plenty of sock with 23 rainbows and 77 across in less than full-time duty, and all the savvy of someone who broke into the league the year Whizzo Mark Salot IV was born. Now Gonzales Gonzales, his deke failed, sends in Hector Jalapena, the former college track star, to run for Quintero."

As the tension mounted, Whizzo and Jalapena spent the next five minutes negotiating Jalapena's lead at first, Jalapena inching ever farther off the bag and Whizzo moving him back, first with lobs, then ginger tosses and finally a few snap throws. At last they settled on precisely the same distance that they had agreed to in each of their previous encounters and Whizzo addressed Guacamole Guanabana at the plate.

The hullabaloo was deafening. Charley called Sweet Patootie, low and away. Guanabana swung and cued it foul. Strike one. The din grew louder.

As Whizzo congratulated the ball, Jalapena took this as a sign that their agreement was off, and he and Whizzo re-enacted their contract negotiation, arriving once again at the exact same figures.

Choo-Choo Charley, high and in. Strike two!

Pandemonium. In the bullpen, Larrabee and O'Toole stopped throwing to watch. The police were lined up on the field, ready to assist any spectators who got ahead of the situation back to their seats. The roar was a constant din; in Parking Lot C the carhorns were on key. Whizzo talked to the ball and listened; listened and talked.

Imagine it is the five billionth birthday of the world and you are in a season-deciding situation talking to a baseball. What do you say? Do you share gratitude with the ball that you are both part of the world's epochal processes? Or do you worry that at five billion the gig may be just about up? Do you suggest buying the world a present together? But what could Gaia want—another ocean, another mountain? She has so many now, where will she find room to put yet one more? Perhaps a new species or two? How about just a pledge to help her save a few of the children that she already has? How about a celestial journey through a stream of comets that plunge into her refrigerated poles, replacing her ice cubes and lowering her fevered temperature enough to keep them from melting? Or maybe it's a day to put aside such concerns, to celebrate the breezes in her tropics, moonlit snowstorms in her northern climes, the sound of the frogs singing in her swamps, the finny, cetaceous and cephalopudlian antics beneath her seas, the west winds moaning over her plains, her dragonflies and spiderwebs glistening in the sun like the bright stones in her streams—and, in one corner of her known as Megaglopoulis, the annual return of that hallowed human tradition, the pennant race.

In the mind of Whizzo Mark Salot IV, the urgencies of the immediate situation precluded any such flights of fancy. He asked

the ball a question and held it to his ear: what to throw Guacamole Guanabana, Sweet Patootie or Choo-Choo Charley?

Charley Orange called for Sweet Patootie, high and in. Whizzo shook him off.

Charley called Big Peter, high and in. Whizzo shook him off.

Choo-Choo Charley, high and in. No.

Charley called time and headed for the mound. "What's going on?"

"This here baseball is callin' for a curve ball."

"Curve ball! What's left of your curve ball couldn't get my grandmother out."

"Ah jist been dekin' them gahs. Hit does seem a mahte peculiar to me too, but it hain't mah call. Hit's up to the ball."

Charley looked into the dugout for a sign from Foo Foo McGonigle. Foo Foo was asleep!

There was no point in arguing with Whizzo. He thought the ball was always right. "Curve ball it is," said Charley. "Keep it out of the strike zone so he can't hit it out."

The pitch started off aimed straight at Guacamole Guanabana's head, but spun and arced until it roundhoused itself right over the plate, where Guanabana watched it stop and well up like a big white balloon looking for a ride out of the park. Guanabana couldn't believe his eyes. Starting from his heels, a wave of muscle action rippled though his body like a cobra about to strike. It culminated in an explosive swing and a sickening KONK!

In the universe of baseball, the shortest distance between two points is a line drive. Paradoxically, however, a circular arc carries the ball farther, sometimes popping it through a Schwarzchild Radius and right out of that universe altogether.

"Oh-oh-oh!" cried Bluster Hyman, as the ball soared off in a sky-sweeping rainbow arc toward the centerfield bleachers. "Back, back goes Developed Smith, he of the glove where triples go to die. He's on the track...at the wall..."

And here, dear reader, we must freeze-frame the ball in its merry trajectory toward destiny, to report on a number of unusual occurrences that converged upon this particular vector in spacetime. First, Developed Smith, he wearing the graveyard of triples on his left hand, as he ran, suddenly felt like the earth beneath his feet had turned into one of those old-fashioned carnival funhouse floors and at any step it might open up and swallow him. Everyone in the park was too caught up in frenzy to notice, but Mutant Stadium, which in its 34 years of existence had been subjected to nary so much as a 100-year storm, at that moment hosted the epicenter of a magnitude 3.4 temblor.

At what point was the action on the diamond? Hector Jalapena had just touched third base and was headed home with the tying run. Guacamole Guanabana was steaming toward second with the winner and the flag. Pork Chop Chyczewski, the left-field umpire, and Buster Hyman, on the right-field line, were waddling toward center for the call.

The ball advanced one frame. It landed squarely on Developed Smith's head, caromed off and headed for the bleachers. With a grunt as mighty as a constipated ape, Ladye Hannah Aura, sitting not 20 feet away in those very bleachers, smashed a vial she had smuggled into the park in her handbag, sending a swamplike stench into the surroundings.

Several blocks away, at the Lewis mansion, Sadie Lewis, who had just opened her eyes, scrawled her feeble Jane Henrietta across the paper that that funny little man held before her. At least he had sense enough to wear earmuffs, she thought as she closed her eyes and felt the delicious, seductive mix of oxygen, nitrogen and carbon dioxide rush through her rusty bronchia, filling the shrinking labyrinth of her lungs for the last time.

◆◆◆ ◆◆◆ ◆◆◆

To the baseball cognoscenti, the essence of the game is pitching. The more common taste prefers the home run: the ultimate triumph over the pitcher, with its explosive thrill, its sheer distance, its instant power to reverse fortune: its finality. Walter Johnson, Tom Seaver, Steve Carlton—they did not save baseball, Babe Ruth did. In countless parallel universes scattered all over Creation, Lemon Sox announcers were going wild: "Guanabana went yard!" "A four-bagger!" "He dialed long distance!" "He took Whizzo downtown!" "It's a round-tripper!" "A dinger!" "A rainbow!" "It's in the cheap seats!" "Mabel, open the window, here it comes!" "In plain English, he pasted it over the fence!"

Back here, in the front row of the bleachers, Billy Beanball leaned out, glove in hand, and snagged the ball.

"Home run!" bellowed Pork Chop Chyczewski (who didn't see the glove), pointing his finger toward the bleachers.

"Ground-rule double!" bellowed Buster Hyman (who didn't see the glove either), gesturing toward the infield.

"Holy shit, what are we gonna do?" asked Chyczewski, as half the fans, who saw Hyman, erupted in ecstatic hosannas and the other half, who saw him, screamed boos of outrage. "Flip a coin?"

"Relax, Pork Chop. I have seniority. Pick a number from one to 10."

"Seven."

"Wrong, it was three. It's a double. Now we have to confer with our esteemed colleagues to make it official."

The instinct of self-preservation being as strong in umpires as in bureaucrats and other living things, their esteemed colleagues rubber-stamped Buster Hyman's call. Relief swept like a sorcerer's apprentice through the stands, through Parking Lot C, through the urbs and burbs of Megaglopoulis. The rejoicing that followed shook Mutant Stadium at least as much as the earthquake. (Perhaps that's what the seismic monitor recorded, and Developed Smith just stepped into a parallel universe.) Ecstatic fans shouted themselves hoarse, banged their seats, littered the field and otherwise carried on like adults at an ephemeral event devoid of meaning.

Their disport was, however, as nuns at their vespers compared to that of Lemon Sox manager Macarena Gonzales Gonzales. He charged toward Buster Hyman like a kamikaze pilot, flanked by a squadron of berserk ballplayers. Gonzales Gonzales jumped up and down. He waved his arms. He threw his cap on the ground and jumped up and down some more, mangling it to shreds. He thrust his face as close to Buster's as he could without actually making forbidden contact with Buster's belly and shouted unkind words at him. He kicked up dirt in 320 degrees of a circle, carefully avoiding kicking any on Hyman.

"Why, Buster?" he shouted when he had calmed down to mere apoplexy. "Why you do thees to me? Why you let their fan steal home run by my player and call eet two base? Why you rob my team from thees pennant?"

"Be careful with that dirt, Macarena. It stirs up dust. I spit-polished these shoes for national TV. I know you're upset. It's been a long day for all of us. I'd hate to boot you out of such a critical game, so don't show me up on national TV."

"If home team fan interfere, you can award home run. Why you no do eet?"

"It wasn't going out. There's the Commissioner, sitting in the box by the dugout. Take it up with him."

"Eet no can be because you play for Mutants your career, hey Buster?"

Buster Hyman's placid face grew florid and his body contracted into a motion resembling a called third strike against Dumbo the Elephant. "That's it, Macarena. You're outta here!"

Fit to be tied, Gonzales Gonzales sprinted all the way to the Commissioner's box, followed by 25 pairs of angry Lemon-stockinged legs.

"I can't override them, Macarena," said the Commissioner, "and even if I could, I didn't see it as well as they did. Neither did you. Now calm down. You're on national TV."

As Maxwell Veribushi gunned his bike toward the stadium, almost physically ill from missing the greatest game played in his lifetime but giddily elated at having saved the *Rana onca* from extinction, he heard

Bluster Hyman burst into broadcast tears. "The umpire—Buster Hyman, my brother Buster—has just made the toughest call of his career, and he made the right call. I am so proud of my brother, and I take back all the unkind words I've ever said about him. Here, they're showing the replay now."

The replay showed the ball heading for the top of the wall when the glove came out. Even computer projections of trajectory, spin frequency, drag retardation and Magnus force the following day could not determine whether it would bounce over or back in.

Hector Jalapena returned to third. Guacamole Guanabana was on second with a ground-rule double. It took 10 minutes before order was restored. Thank goodness! Maxwell still had time to prepare the Harley.

Foo Foo McGonigle made his weary way to the mound, carrying a hook. The fans erupted again: not with Foos but boos. Whizzo Mark Salot IV had brought them this far and they wanted him to finish. But no manager in his right mind would have Lightnin' Larrabee and Power Brakes O'Toole ready to fire and leave in a tired, battered starter in this situation. No starter would question the move.

"Foo Foo, Ah'm so sorry Ah scared you, and mah teammates, and even mah own self. Ah don't know who throwed that there pitch, but it twaren't me. Ah don't know whah that baseball called curve or whah that curve ball hung up there lahke some big ol' Japanese lantern. Ah did notice one thang: that there ball talked to me in a different voice from any ball ever before. Normally the ball has itself a nahce, clean, clear, sort of tenor voice. This one was deep and guttural, lahke it had a frog in its throat."

Foo Foo McGonigle's life goal was on the line. "Well now, there's my righty out there, he's converted 43 times in 47, that's a lot of odds to call for if you were me when the situation comes down like this here in front of us. But there it is: he's my righty. Their man in the box, he's goin' southpaw, meaning the odds don't fit unless my righty parks him over there with the first bag open, and that brings us to they got their righty and their lefty spittin' on their hands on the bench waiting to be a hero in the pitcher's place, and who do we want to go, north or south in the box, with the sacks all full and the whole shittin' shebang comin' down to this?"

"Borracho's tailed off in the stretch," said Charley. "I think his knee's still not 100 percent. Better him than Pina Colada."

"What do you figure the chances?" Foo Foo asked Charley, nodding at Whizzo.

"His Sweet Patooties are still hopping like frogs with fleas. His curveball died in the sixth."

"OK young feller, I'm playin' my bungee. No more breakers!"

To a deafening roar of approval, Foo Foo hobbled back.

They gave Quesadilla four wide ones and up came Hector Borracho.

Well, to make a long story even longer, Borracho worked the count to 3-2. Bluster Hyman reverted quickly to form, excoriating Roscoe Riordan on each of the three balls. Borracho fouled off the next six pitches, inducing apoplexy in everyone within 50 miles of Megaglopoulis and traffic in Disfunction Junction, Arkansas.

Whizzo wound and delivered the last pitch of the season: Sweet Patootie, knee-high and a little closer to the center of the plate than he aimed for.

Borracho caught it right on the sweet spot. KONK! "Line drive!" screamed Bluster Hyman. "It's off Twinkletoes' glove! —Wait!— Terwilliger at short leaps for it! —It's off his glove too! Here comes Doodles Osborne streaking in from left field! He dives! Does he have it? HE'S OUT! MUTES WIN THE PENNANT! MUTES WIN THE PENNANT!"

After that Bluster Hyman fell wisely silent, letting the 100,000-note harmony of exultation override his own.

Bedlam.

Fireworks farted and flared. Strangers hugged in the aisles. Men danced with their wives. Martha Stewart and Sinead O'Connor embraced. Evel Knievel cannonballed from the second deck to the dugout roof on a pogo stick. Men who had kept a stiff upper lip when their parents died and stayed dry-eyed when their wives ran off with their girl friends—these grown men (well, physically grown) shared the waters of catharsis in each other's arms. Bluster Hyman fired an hysterical fusillade of game stats and records tied or broken to an audience too giddy to hear a word.

In the parking lot, horns blared out monotone versions of "Take Me Out to the Ballgame." On the freeways of Megaglopoulis, citizens erupted from their cars and threw spontaneous gridlock parties. Looters, wife-beaters and drive-by snipers took the night off to toast the champions. All across town, car alarms set themselves off, dogs howled and police, fire and ambulance sirens wailed backup harmony. Little old ladies who couldn't tell two baseballs from their granddaughters' boob jobs yelled and hooted and dyed their hair purple. Outside the Lewis mansion, Nevermore and the *Rana oncas* belted out the definitive version of the world's oldest non-stridulatory love song, composed 150 million years ago by a poet known only as Ngaio.

Back inside the stadium, phalanxes of guards held back the surging tide of fandom. Whizzo Mark Salot IV was borne aloft by his Mutant teammates. He heard them shout and laugh as Triclops squirted him with seltzer. He cast a final look at Section 12. Jim Carrey stood in the vacant bower, igniting a mini-explosion by holding a lighter to the seat of his pants. Whizzo could stay the tide of fornlornness no longer: he gulped down its bitter brew, all the while wearing a smile as wide as a football: he was an athlete. Did no one notice that the football was deflated, that the delirium filling the Megaglopolitan area was taking a detour around him?

Maxwell Veribushi, watching on the television monitor by the old bullpen under the centerfield bleachers, noticed: Whizzo looked like a little boy who had lost his parents in the crowd. "OK," he shouted. "Let 'er rip!'

The last statistic from the PA system had just died in the arms of its own echo. Suddenly organ music blared forth, accompanying Clarence "Frogman" Henry:

Here comes the bride
Here comes the bride...

Four ushers swung open the bullpen gates and onto the field *vroom! vroomed!* a lime-green Harley-Davidson, trailing balloons and streamers, followed by a lime-green Corvette convertible. Waving from the hood of the Corvette, and dressed in matching lime green, was Clitorea Pearl—the bridesmaid. Standing and waving from the back seat, also lime-bedecked, was Ladye Hannah Aura—the minister.

But where was the bride? All eyes rose as the hot-air balloon slowly descended and settled in shallow centerfield. As Anloie stepped out, to cheers, whistles and shouts of admiration, the train from her wedding gown choo-chooed regally in the breeze halfway back to Chattanooga. Beneath her tiara, under her veil, those hibiscus-adorned blonde tresses, those salmon lips and cobalt eyes played peekaboo with the world, and with Whizzo Mark Salot IV.

Never underestimate the power of pheromones.

That was the lesson Charley Orange learned that day, and the message of this humble tale, if a message is to be found. It's one of those timeless homilies that, no matter how deeply we think we have ingrained it, we can always take in a little deeper—like breath itself. Witness the moment of doubt that clouded the visage even of Whizzo Mark Salot IV.

But clouds pass. Whizzo took one look at the love of his life, leaped from his teammates' arms and cartwheeled toward centerfield. "Mah love! Ah love you! Ah love you! Ah knowed it! Ah knowed you was here! Oh Sweetie Pah! Whah did you give me such a fraght? Ah know: you jist wanted to surprahse me!"

"Silly! I couldn't very well sit there in that box seat for three hours dressed like this now, could I, Whizzo? And with everyone in the world looking at me, too."

Whizzo lifted her out of the basket, faked a stumble and brought them both tumbling down onto the lawn. Anloie's hand brushed against the perpetually semi-erect Mr. Twister, causing him to struggle to attention under Whizzo's cup.

"Oh, Whizzo! You're so—inappropriate!" She pushed him away.

"Less consecrate our love raght here!"

"Let's get married first!"

"Yes ma'am. Ah hate to say it, Sugar Punkin, but what did Ah tell you?"

"You told me so. Yes! My hero."

"Mah sweet angel."

Ladye Hannah Aura stood by home plate, holding an open book that only looked like a Bible. A hundred musicians were escorted to an ad hoc bandstand wheeled into position in centerfield.

Before the ceremony could begin, Whizzo grabbed the microphone. "Hey y'all! Is they anybody else out there wants to git hitched up? Now's your chance to do it free: preacher's on me!" To mammoth encouragement, couples streamed down onto the field *en masse*. The final tally kicked the Rev. Sun Yung Moon right out of the Guinness Book of Records.

The ceremony had barely concluded when, as if to upstage its principals, the full moon made her dramatic entrance, dressed for the occasion in a stunning tinfoil wrap. A helicopter droned over, showering the proceedings with hibiscus, frangipani, anthurium and rose petals.

Once more the gate under the centerfield bleachers banged open and in wheeled a wedding cake 25 feet in diameter and two stories high, surrounded by a crew of 100 with knives to cut 50,000 pieces.

"What about all the extra people from the parking lot who came in after the game?" Lulu whispered to Wellington P. Sweetwater.

A second cake followed the first. "Let them eat cake!" roared Sweetwater.

High above Megaglopoulis, computers in space relayed the joyous tidings to the people of the world, who were hungry for some good news. Butchers and bakers rejoiced; no candlestick makers could be found. Divorce court was closed. The sewer snoids living under urban subway tunnels emerged and went to the beach. Soldiers in each of the 56 wars being fought around the world agreed to cease-fires until the ceremony ended. Looters were seen walking *into* stores with TV sets and coming out empty-handed. In Disfunction Junction, Arkansas, traffic exploded: drivers leaned on their horns and played Bang-'em with real cars. In Australia, aborigines honored the Virgin Bride with a round of boomerang frisbee. (What they didn't know about Anloie wouldn't hurt them.) In Antarctica, a cheer arose that dislodged a small iceberg. On Mt. Kilimanjaro and Mt. Fujiyama, sun broke through the clouds, sending Blakean shafts of light to bounce off trees and streams like balls of India rubber from a parallel universe. (The mountains' counterparts, knowing they would never be rubberized themselves, wiggled their nipples gleefully against the semi-translucent gauze of Anloie's nuptial gown.)

Clarence Henry handed the mike to the Fat Lady, who warbled the Ave Maria to the world. It was over.

Their I and Ah do said, the happy couple cut the cake as Bluster Hyman relayed statistics of its Guinnessian proportions. As Moon Unit Zappa, the leadoff performer, took the mike, Whizzo and Anloie hopped into the balloon basket, unhitched the rope and, to a shower of rice, streamers, firecrackers and huzzahs, floated out of the stadium, forming a silhouette against the tinfoil moon.

Charley Orange found himself standing beside Clitorea Pearl. Actually, he had maneuvered considerably to place himself there.

"Would you like some cake?" he asked.

"Is this a peace offering?"

"I'm sorry. I'm better now. I never was in love with you, was I? I was in need. I did love you, though, and I still do."

"Bless you, Charley. I love you too."

They kissed and performed frottage.

◆◆◆ ◆◆◆ ◆◆◆

BZZZ-ZAP! POW! BLAM! More fireworks. Overhead the stars danced and burned like there was no tomorrow. (For a star, there *is* no tomorrow.) The Andromeda Galaxy spun on its axis like a pinwheel—although, relativistically speaking, it would not receive the news for another two million years. Maybe it was celebrating the birth of Ngaio ^{1,000,000}, back in Pleistocene times. Or may it be that in this universe of parallel universes, love travels faster than light; love is already everywhere forever? Whatever. Any excuse for a party.

Electrons come and go, twinkling like cigarette lighters in and out of here and there through the vast everywheres forevers, as the wormholes turn.

POST-SEASON

The Megaglopoulis Mutants won the World Series, four games to two. The following July, Megaglopoulis experienced a population mini-explosion.

Clarence Pijole was retired, without honors but with a pension slightly less than the gross national product of Botswana.

Billy Beanball sold his baseball card collection for $125. Today it is valued at $32,500.

Bluster Hyman received a scholarship to umpire school anonymously from Wellington P. Sweetwater. He went, and eventually wound up with brother Buster's job.

Buster Hyman wrote a *roman a clef* about a baseball Commissioner and his league presidents. He was re-assigned to Class D Tidewater, resigned, went to broadcasting school and eventually wound up with brother Bluster's job.

His first guest was Whizzo Mark Salot IV. "Whizzo," Buster asked him, "what if, on that fateful day, Anloie hadn't shown up?"

"Ah never thought of that."

Wellington P. Sweetwater gained two more World Series trophies before passing over. He is said to have donated his wooden lingam to the Smithsonian Institute on the condition that it be kept next to John Dillinger's.

Foo Foo McGonigle woke up dead one morning. He'd had cancer all year but didn't let anyone know. A memorial tribute to him filled Mutant Stadium.

His tombstone read:

He died with bugs inside but a smile on top of it.

Ladye Hannah Aura proved her dictum that "the future is as predictable as the past," winning $10,000 by betting all the money she could borrow on Whizzo Mark Salot IV winning the season finale, 1-0. Saying she got a tip from a parallel universe, she used the money to set up a desktop publishing venture. She passes out leaflets at all Mutant home games.

Professor Maxwell Veribushi gave up his island retreat and moved to Megaglopoulis to found the Meriwether Lewis Frog Farm, where he breeds rare and endangered species. He releases the offspring into wetlands around the world. Emily keeps the curious away by making faces at them through the gate, dressed in her slip. To Maxwell's consternation, Sage took up with Billy Beanball.

Heqt, her wrath assuaged, forgave and forgot.

Whizzo Mark Salot and Anloie honeymooned at Mt. Fujiyama and then made a passel of babies. Whizzo won 224 games by the age of 29, at which time Big Peter torqued his left bicep into pudding. He taught Anloie the motion he used to throw Choo-Choo Charley and she applied it to the Whammo to create a new form, the Flapdoodle, of which she became the first world champion.

Anloie studied wicca with Ladye Hannah Aura and erotic massage with Clitorea Pearl, and she and Whizzo lead a magical, lubricious life in Hawaii, where they both wear hibiscus flowers in their hair.

Clitorea Pearl has her finger in various pies. She sits on the Megaglopoulis City Council, where she has introduced the Free Sex Act.

When Charley Orange retired, the mayor of Megaglopoulis honored him with the key to the city. Charley bought Maxwell Veribushi's interest in his research laboratory, where he met a polyamorous tantrika parallel universalist physicist. They are happily unmarried.

A man named Charles Darwin discovered that the universe in which our story is set was created by a gaseous being of astronomical heft at 9 a.m. October 23 in the year 4004 B.C.

In a number of universes Anloie didn't show up for the wedding. This book had an unhappy ending and couldn't get published.

The winter rains caused flooding, and in the spring, in Veribushi Pond (Freeways and skyscraper complexes get named after master criminals; exo-salientologists get swamps), which rose to the level of Meriwether Lewis' grave, Ngaio XV^{14} +34 (never Nevermore, really; that was just a *rib'et!* imposition) spotted a sweet lovely with onyx eyes who bulged where she should and didn't where she shouldn't. He crooned like Clarence Henry; he barked like a dog; he scratched like a flea on a washboard; he woofed like a tweeter and ate many a skeeter. The Fountain of Youth, he mused, gushes not for one frog but through him down through the race. He's got the ladies hopping: Love's Imperative movin' on down the line. SKRIEEK-EK-EK! SKRIEEK-EK-EK! SKRIEEK-EK-EK!

If you enjoyed this book, please post a review
to your favorite online bookstore today.

About the Author

Don Strachan has been playing baseball since age 5, catching frogs since he was 7 and chasing girls since before he could count birthdays.

In between, he was writing. In the Sixties he was Managing Editor for the *Los Angeles Free Press* (the granddaddy of the underground press) and an Associate Editor at *Coast* magazine.

At *Coast*, he discovered the ecological crisis. He created *Save the World*, the cooperative environmental board game, and wrote an environmental column for *Whole Life Times*.

His articles have appeared in numerous national and regional magazines, including *Rolling Stone*, *Crawdaddy* and *California*. For two years he wrote a book review column for the *Los Angeles Times*. He sold his only screenplay and ghost-wrote two Ph.D.'s.

His fiction has appeared in *Knight, Adam, Elite* and the *Los Angeles Star*. He wrote serious articles for *Chic* (the uptown version of *Hustler*) and submitted erotic vegetables to *Oui*.

He served as Press Secretary to Marty, the Marijuana-Munching Mouse, and was a founding editor of *St. John's Bread Wednesday Messenger* (later *Light Times*), about which Abbie Hoffman said, "It's hard to read, man. Get a new mimeo."

Don resides at a clothing-optional hot springs and teaches Wassage, a healing form of warm-water massage. He also serves as an Intern for workshops in "Love, Intimacy and Sexuality."